RUSSIAN AND ROYALLY COMPLICATED

THE CROWNED HEARTS SERIES
BOOK 2

GWYN MCNAMEE
CHRISTY ANDERSON

Russian and Royally Complicated
© 2023 Gwyn McNamee & Christy Anderson

Cover Design: Michelle Johnson at Blue Sky Design

Cover Photography: Wander Aguiar

Cover Model: Jose

Editing: Stephie Walls

To those who have allowed themselves to see past initial impressions to the core of what makes someone who they are.

ACKNOWLEDGMENTS

Russian and Royally Complicated would not have happened without our amazing team. A huge thanks to our beta readers, to our incredible editor, and proofreading team.

1

DAPHNE

GODDAMN, why does that man have to look so fucking good in uniform?

The way his tattoos creep up his neck, playing peekaboo above the starched white collar, make my fingers itch to rip off the perfect crisp, black, impeccably knotted tie to touch them and my mouth waters to run my tongue over every colorful swirl of ink across his tanned skin.

I swallow back a moan and tighten my grip on the bouquet, so I'm not tempted to leap across the altar and fulfill the fantasies I've had since the moment I caught sight of him at the back of the cathedral.

It's so damn wrong—all *kinds* of wrong—but Lev Orlov is nothing short of the epitome of a walking sexual fantasy...

And, unfortunately, my worst fucking nightmare, all rolled into one muscular, inked, stoic, grumpy, assholey package.

Of all the people Fyn could choose to be his best friend—and best man at this wedding—it *has* to be the one person in all of Lovolia who hates my guts almost as much as I hate his.

Actually, he probably hates me more, given the way he's glared at me every time our paths have crossed since Bridget moved here and I began visiting—like I'm the loud, brash, uncouth American blonde ditz men like him view as gum stuck to the bottom of their thousand-dollar loafers.

Even now, while we watch our best friends tie the royal knot, the love in their gazes so damn cloyingly sweet it makes my stomach hurt, his russet eyes practically boil with rage, staring at me across the dais.

My skin heats with a strange mix of *I should probably run before he dismembers me with his bare hands* and *good God...I want those strong, capable hands all over me.*

Such a strange dichotomy—to be attracted to someone physically but want nothing more than to throttle them when they open their mouth to speak. I can't say I remember feeling this way about *anyone* in my entire life, but from the moment I walked off the plane on my first trip here, Lev has been nothing but a giant, handsome pain in my ass.

Who is *impossible* to avoid.

With him attached to Fyn at the hip, and when the prince can't bear to be away from Bridget for long, we all end up spending far too much time together.

And now that our besties are—*almost*—officially attached for life, it means *we* will be, too, through them. Which makes my homicidal feelings toward the man a bit...problematic.

And my sexual ones even more so.

Especially since we're standing in a damn church and I'm imagining what it would feel like to have those big, powerful, tattooed hands all over me right here on the altar. That big cock of his I've seen pressing against his pants more times than I can count powering into me while I'm laid across these stairs that Bridget's veil cascades down. Those perfect lips capable of spewing such hateful things to me against mine, swallowing every scream and moan—

"I, Bridget, take you, Fynix, to be my husband, to have and to hold, from this day forward; for better, for worse, for richer, for poorer, in sickness and in health, to love and to cherish, till death us do part; according to God's holy law. In the presence of God, I make this vow."

Oh, shit.

I almost missed the best part in my distraction with the infuriating man at Fyn's side. Lev steps forward and flips open a box with the ring.

Fyn takes it with a nod to his best friend and turns back to Bridget, slipping it on her finger with trembling hands. "With this ring, I thee wed; with my body I thee honor; and all my worldly goods with thee I share: in the name of the Father, and of the Son, and of the Holy Ghost."

Bridget turns to me, tears shimmering in her eyes.

Crap.

Get it together, Daphne. You're on!

I dig into the hidden pocket of my dress and pass her the simple gold band for Fyn. She smiles at me and swipes away a tear before turning back to the man who holds her heart and slipping the ring on his finger.

"With this ring, I thee wed; with my body I thee honor; and all my worldly goods with thee I share: in the name of the Father, and of the Son, and of the Holy Ghost."

The officiant raises his hands to the congregation, but my gaze drifts from him to the rogue standing next to Fyn. "Those whom God hath joined together, let no man put asunder."

It's a lovely sentiment, but one I've never really believed in. Love has always seemed like some sort of fairytale. Something I never witnessed in real life. Certainly not with Mom bouncing from boyfriend to boyfriend.

I saw lust, pure and simple, and *lust* I can believe in.

That primal pull between two people, even if it's a horrible idea...

It's very real.

Staring at Lev now, taking in his thick, unruly dark hair and neatly trimmed beard, the hard lines of his perfect cheekbones and strong jaw, his large, tattooed hands held in front of him respectfully, dark eyes locked on his best friend...I can almost see how Mom fell into that trap—over and over and over and over again—with the wrong men.

Being constantly soaked in booze didn't help her decision-making skills, either, but she gave in to her most base needs and never apologized for it to anyone.

Is there really anything wrong with that—sex without love?

It brought Fyn and Bridget together and developed into *this* —an epic tale so sweet and fairytale-esque it almost makes me gag. Lust *can* become love. They've proven it, but something tells me it's the exception to the rule.

Shit. That's the end of the ceremony.

I jerk my gaze away from Lev, trying to pretend I didn't zone out again.

That bastard and his smug sexiness just made me miss the most important part of my best friend's wedding...

Fynix leans in and stops just short of kissing her, whispering something that makes her smile and lean closer as she replies. He crushes his lips to hers, clearly ignoring the demands for a decorum he hasn't stuck to since meeting Bridget. The way he kisses her so thoroughly leaves little to the imagination about what they'll be doing later.

I can't count the times I've stumbled in on them doing something horny in one of the palace rooms definitely not intended for sex. Fyn just doesn't care, and Bridget seems more than willing to enjoy the ride.

Why wouldn't she?

He's the smoking-hot heir to the Lovolian throne, and the man worships the ground she walks on. Now that he has her locked down legally, I can only assume his sexual antics will continue in full force until he knocks her up and gets his own little prince or princess.

They turn on the dais to face the congregation, and Fyn surreptitiously slips his hand down the back of her dress and grabs her ass. I fight a smirk at Bridget's cheeks flaming red with the completely inappropriate—and oh, so Fyn—act done in the holiest place on the island. She gives him a reproachful look filled with love and slips her arm through Fyn's so they can make their way slowly down the steps.

The recessional song begins, and I hand her the bouquet and fan out her train to ensure it's picture-perfect for her walk back down the aisle. The white lace flows gracefully behind her, making her look every bit the princess she now is.

A princess...

This really is a fairytale for her.

I stand again and glance toward Lev. His hard, dark eyes lock on me, and a muscle in his clenched jaw tics. Only his ingrained manners prevent him from walking off the dais and hustling after them without me, but he knows everyone is watching, waiting for the best friends of the groom and bride to follow their retreat.

He takes a slow step toward me, then another, pausing at the center, where Bridget and Fyn just exchanged their vows. His right elbow extends to me stiffly, like he has to force himself to make the gentlemanly gesture.

I slap on a saccharine-sweet smile and slip my arm through his. He dips his head slightly toward me. That heavenly scent of leather and sea air always hanging on him envelops me.

Why does he have to smell so damn fantastic?

Even his warm breath tickling my cheek holds a peppermint quality. "I'm shocked you didn't shout some obscene American cheer when they announced them as married. What is it you say over there? *Yee-haw?*"

His mock Texas accent might as well be fingernails on a

chalkboard. I glare at him and jab the point of my elbow straight into his ribcage with as much force as I can muster.

"I'm shocked you didn't lock Fynix in a closet somewhere today so he couldn't get hitched and leave you behind to die lonely and alone."

Lev scowls at me but moves toward the steps leading us down to the main aisle. Perhaps my comment *was* a low blow since he's clearly a bit bothered by losing his bestie to mine, but he started it with his "yee-haw" comment.

The man knows I'm from Colorado, not Texas, and only said that to rankle me. So, he deserved what he got with my jab at his friendship with the prince.

Eat it, asswipe.

He pauses before the first step. His long, exhaled sigh flutters the hair on my neck as he brings his lips closer to my ear, further drowning me in his manly musk. "Careful on the steps, *Yankee.* Those heels are a lot different than the *thongs* you prefer."

I dig my nails into the Yates family Lovolian crest tattooed on the top of his hand as hard as I can, hoping to draw blood.

Of course, he'd bring up my favorite footwear while I barely manage to balance in four-inch stilettos.

And use the term for them that has a double meaning just to get under my skin.

I'd much rather be comfortable in a pair of my signature flip-flops, but Bridget—and Jaqueline, the obsessive royal wedding planner—insisted on these monstrosities currently pinching my feet.

Their only redeeming quality is the way they bring me closer to Lev's towering six-foot-five height, making it easier to whisper snide remarks and witty comebacks at him while we slowly descend toward the aisle.

"I know how obsessed with my *thongs* you are, Lev, but I

wasn't about to wear them to a wedding—on my feet or to cover my pussy."

His head whips toward mine, and I grin at him and mouth, "*commando*" as we reach the first set of pews and clapping dignitaries.

Thick black lashes surrounding brown eyes that hold flecks of bourbon blink rapidly as he processes my words. He presses his lips together in a firm line and returns his focus forward, his entire body stiffening.

Yee-haw, jerk.

My chest swells with pride at being able to unnerve the man, but my heel snags on the corner of an old stone tile at the side of the aisle runner, and I stumble, my free hand flailing wildly in the air. Every moment of my life up to now flashes before my eyes: living in the trailer with Mom, her endless string of boyfriends, cleaning up after her when she went on binges, finally breaking away for college, meeting Bridget, getting what I *thought* was my dream job, coming to Lovolia with for her non-honeymoon...

Just when I think this grumphole will let me fall, he shifts toward me and wraps both arms around my body, keeping me upright, his large palms splayed across the exposed skin on my back.

Electric sparks shoot through me from that focal point where our bodies touch. His thumb strokes across my shoulder blade and goosebumps pebble over my skin. A tiny gasp escapes my lips, and he seems to remember where we are and who he has in his arms, stilling his hand.

He leans farther into my personal space, far too close for what the typical royal etiquette he follows so closely should allow. "You're like Bambi taking his first steps."

I dig my nails into his arm—partly to steady myself and also to inflict some pain—but the thick material of his Royal Guard uniform protects him from my assault.

Lucky break.

But if he makes one more comment on our way out of this church, I can't be held responsible for my actions.

One of the royal party planners stands at the end of the aisle, waving her hands in a *come-on* motion, urging us to move it along.

Wouldn't want to cause a spectacle.

Even though I despise the man currently holding me in his arms, I won't ruin Bridget's big day with our bickering. Everyone seated waits on our exit so they can begin to file out, and I want to get away from Lev as quickly as possible.

Not without a parting shot.

"Why are you such an ass?" Forcing a fake smile at him, I lean in slightly to ensure none of the celebrating dignitaries only feet from us can hear. "Small penis? I'd be mad, too, if I were built like you and was only packing a Cheeto-sized cock."

His eyes slide to mine, and a murderous rage darkens them to an almost black. "Don't tempt me to ram it down your throat to show you that nothing about me can be described as 'Cheeto-sized.' I wouldn't want you to choke, *Yankee.*"

My entire body heats with his threat, but the moment shatters when he releases me and turns us to face the massive double doors at the back of the abbey.

What the hell was that?

We take the final few steps to reach the end of our torturous walk and approach the open double doors leading from the church. Crisp, fresh air blows in from outside and hits me, and I close my eyes and inhale deeply, trying to rid my lungs of Lev's intoxicating scent.

A few more hours...

I only have to play nice with him for a few more hours until I can retreat to my room alone and crash. Hopefully, a few glasses of very expensive champagne at the reception will help me forget whatever momentary insanity has caused me to be attracted to Lev Orlov.

LEV

WHAT THE BLOODY *hell is wrong with me today?*

Ty soshel s uma.

Snapping off a comment like that to Daphne in the middle of the abbey certainly doesn't fall under proper "best mate" behavior. Neither does picturing her on her knees in front of the altar with my cock down her throat to shut her up and prove I don't have a "Cheeto dick."

On top of that idiotic slip, Gran—not to mention the king and queen—would frown on me drowning myself in vodka while I stand in the shadows of this reception, brooding and avoiding any and all contact with the other guests.

Especially Daphne.

It should be one of the happiest days of my life, seeing Fynix tie the knot with the love of his. But instead, I've spent the entire time on edge, feeling like I'm barely clinging to the precipice of something life-altering—and not in a good way.

Maybe it's the atmosphere.

Weddings tend to make people deeply examine their own lives.

Gran would say I could use some of that self-reflection, especially now that Fyn is married and sure to produce an heir sooner rather than later. I'd be surprised if Bridget doesn't return from their honeymoon with a bun in the oven...

If that doesn't make you reevaluate your entire miserable existence, nothing will.

I'm now officially the third wheel—a wheel that broke and allowed Fyn to be dragged into a life-and-death situation—and fuck does that hit me square in the chest harder than any blow I've ever taken in training or action.

I bring the vodka to my lips and take a long pull, watching Bridget and Daphne on the dance floor at the center of the palace ballroom. My gaze travels over the bane-of-my-existence blonde—her perfect curves...her gorgeous ass.

That fucking dress.

No matter how much I may disapprove of Daphne Jennings, no one can deny how phenomenal she looks tonight. The blush-colored silk clings to her perfectly, just like the road hugs the coast on the way out to Elysium, meandering easily over every damn dip and bend and swell of her body as she moves, with delicate lace sleeves on a woman who's anything but.

Always so loud.

So brazen.

So *vulgar.*

I should look away.

I *should*...but...

Damn...that dress.

Bridget must have known what she was doing, putting her best friend in a gown like that for the big day. Likely trying to help her catch the eye of someone, like that bloody guard I overheard Daphne joking with Bridget about marrying when they were in the garden the other day.

Even if it was said in jest, my hand tightens on the tumbler I wish wasn't empty. The mere thought of her with one of the guards heats my blood enough to make me want to smash the glass all over the expensive parquet floor.

Pochemu, Lev?

You don't even like her!

Something I have had to keep reminding myself of a lot today.

It's impossible to deny her beauty—and I wouldn't mind getting lost in her curves—but that damn mouth of hers and the total lack of etiquette in the palace make any pleasant feelings for her evaporate as quickly as my drink disappeared.

Who the hell hugs the palace staff when they're working?

Daphne—that's who.

Always chatting.

Always skipping down the halls like she's twelve and not thirty.

Always so kind to everyone, like they're old friends.

Except me.

The woman never seems to miss an opportunity to lash out at me with choice words from that wicked tongue of hers.

Cheeto dick.

I snort and shake my head at the audacity.

Maybe I shouldn't feel bad about what I said at the church. After all, she gives as good as she gets—and sometimes more. Hardened military operators who have seen the worst of the worst don't dare speak to me the way she does without even thinking about it.

She's fire and ice rolled into one and doesn't take my shit.

Refreshing and sexy and infuriating all at the same time.

But I don't have time to deal with the distraction of her constant ribbing and antagonization. After the prince's kidnapping and the changeover to the new government structure, everyone has teetered on a perilous edge, waiting for something to go wrong again. Keeping things locked down and Fyn and his parents safe has become even more essential.

Which is what finally forces me to drag my focus away from Daphne to scan the rest of the ballroom and the people in it for any potential issues.

It doesn't matter that I'm technically "off duty."

This isn't something I can turn off.

Dignitaries from almost every country in the world fill the space, mingling with the higher echelon of Lovolian citizens. The full orchestra plays from the stage on the right, and the center dance floor vibrates with everyone enjoying themselves at one of the most important events in Lovolian history.

Their prince has married a commoner.

An *American* commoner.

And he couldn't be happier.

Fyn approaches Bridget from behind and wraps his arm around her waist, twirling her to face him so he can whisper something in her ear. She giggles and glances around conspiratorially, then drapes her arms over his shoulders to start the waltz the orchestra just struck up.

I continue surveilling the room as I return to the bar. The bartender inclines his head toward me and pulls out the bottle of vodka, but I slide the empty glass across the wood to him and hold out my hand. His gaze darts between the bottle and me, and I motion for him to hand it over without explanation. He scans the area around us for witnesses before sliding it into my hand and slinking away, hoping no one noticed.

Very mature, Lev.

Drink away your problems.

I return to my spot in the shadows and catch a glimpse of Gran talking excitedly with someone on the other side of the room.

Who the hell is that?

Dancing couples block my view, but eventually, the man shifts more into the light—the ambassador from Russia. He surreptitiously checks around them, then rests his hand on Gran's arm in a familiar gesture I wouldn't have expected from the man who has always seemed so aloof in our previous meetings.

Gran rests her hand over his and leans in to say something else, her shoulders tense, face twisted in concern, then slips away into the vibrant crowd.

What the hell was that about?

I start to push off the wall to go after her and ensure she's all right, but Manuel approaches, and his gaze automatically darts down to the bottle dangling from my fingertips.

He raises a heavy, white brow. "Do I need to have someone fired for giving you that?"

I bring the vodka to my lips and down what's left. "I'm not the one you should be worried about."

Immediately, his body stiffens, and his observant gaze sweeps over the crowd. The Captain of the Royal Guard is *always* on duty, *always* vigilant, which means I can have a drink and "enjoy" my best friend's wedding.

"Did you see something?"

Shaking my head, I step away from my shadowy hiding space. "Just the Russian ambassador hitting on Gran."

Manuel's lips twitch as he fights a grin. "Overprotective much?"

"Shouldn't I be?" I take another swig and hiss at the sharp bite of the alcohol. "She's my only family, and she's too old to have men chasing her skirt."

He barks out a laugh and slaps me on the back. "I think you need to cut back on the vodka and get some fresh air, Lev."

It isn't an order. Manuel knows better than to give me one, even if he *technically* is my boss. But he's also known me my entire life, and if he thinks I'm losing my shit, it might be obvious to someone else I don't want seeing it—like Fyn.

Fresh air might do me good.

I brush past him and make my way down the hallway toward the doors that lead out to the garden maze and the one spot I *know* I can be alone.

For as many people as are milling about the reception, the halls back here remain almost eerily quiet. I turn the corner, drawing to a stop at the cracked door to the Reading Room.

What the hell is this doing open?

No one should be back here, in the private residence portion of the palace, except the staff, who would never leave a door ajar. I tighten my grip on the bottle, the only weapon available to me, and slowly ease the door open a little more so I can slip inside.

Darkness envelops the room, only faint hints of moonlight filtering in from the high windows falling in even intervals on the marble floor. I pause and listen, but the *whoosh, whoosh, whoosh* of my blood rushing in my ears overpowers anything else.

You're overreacting.

On edge.

Manuel was wrong—I need more of this vodka.

I scan the Reading Room one more time before I turn back toward the door, taking a swig from the bottle. A rustle behind me makes me whip around so fast the alcohol splashes onto the floor.

"Looking for something, Lev?"

Goddammit.

Daphne's sultry voice floats over me, stirring places in me I'd rather ignore indefinitely.

I steel myself against what will surely be an oncoming verbal assault. "What the hell are you doing in here?"

She saunters forward into one of the streams of moonlight, which only further highlights the way the dress clings to every bloody inch of her lush body. "Likely the same thing you are." She takes one step toward me, then another, the sound of the flip-flops she changed into after the ceremony slapping against the floor, making me cringe. "Trying to escape *that.*" She motions backward absently, in the direction of the ballroom, and her shrewd blue gaze darts down to the bottle in my hand, then back up at me. "But you were smart and brought booze."

"Did you just call me *smart?*" I cross my arms over my chest, letting the bottle dangle from my fingertips. "That might be the only compliment you've given me in all this time we've been acquainted."

Two more steps bring her within inches of me, and she reaches out and takes the vodka, letting her fingers linger on mine a second too long. "Don't let it go to your head, buddy."

It's certainly going to one of them...

Daphne slowly raises the bottle to her lips, and I can't help but focus on the way they wrap seductively around the top or how her throat moves with her swallow. She winces, pressing the back of her hand over her mouth. "Gosh, that's potent shit."

"So is the malarkey that spews out of that foul mouth of yours."

Her eyes widen as she takes another drink. "You have no idea how foul my mouth can be."

Bloody hell.

I shouldn't be doing this, but I take a step closer until the heat of her body radiates against mine and peek down at her perfect breasts tumbling out of the top of the devil dress. "You talk a big game, Yankee." I tug the bottle from her and take a massive glug from it before crowding her even more. "But you don't have the guts to play it."

She locks her gaze with mine, defiance flaming in it, along with lust. Her pink tongue darts out to trace along her red-painted plump bottom lip. "Try me."

Two words.

A challenge I can't ignore.

Perhaps I could resist her if I weren't three sheets to the wind, if my heart and gut hadn't been mangled today by the guilt that's eaten away at me over the last two years for almost getting Fyn killed and the realization that everything has changed since then.

Definitely not as it stands now.

I clutch her loosely by the nape of her neck and hover my mouth a mere hairsbreadth from hers. Her sunshine and lemon scent wraps around me, spiraling in my lungs with each inhale and seizing my ability to maintain control. I feather my lips over hers—not a kiss. Barely a whisper. "Tell me to stop, Yankee."

Please give me a reason to.

Because all the ones I have don't seem to matter at this moment.

I cling to that last bit of sanity like a lifeline. If she grasps it, I'll walk away and forget this day of absolute, sheer madness.

Her eyes lock onto mine, and this woman assesses me as if she has all the time in the world, as if every second my lips aren't on hers isn't absolute fucking agony. Her vodka-laced breath comes out in small, soft puffs. Each one like a finger wrapping around my stiff cock and trying to draw me closer. "Okay."

"Okay, what, Yankee? You want me to stop?"

She shakes her head, and the blond tendrils not gathered away from her face swing around it, almost glowing in the moonlight.

I place the bottle on the table beside us to free my other hand, then capture her cheek in my palm. "Okay, Lev, kiss me? Or okay, Lev, make me come so hard that I go blind? Which one sounds good, Yankee?"

My vote is for all the above and more.

"Don't call me that."

Fuck, if my cock doesn't swell even more at her imprudence.

"I guess I'll choose for you, then." I tighten my grip on her neck, angling her face even more toward me. "Would you like that?"

A tiny mewl slips from her throat as her only answer, and I don't give her any room to make any more cheeky comebacks. I close my eyes and press my lips to hers, gliding my tongue across the seam, requesting access. She obliges, opening for me. Our tongues twirl and war for dominance the same we always do with words, while I palm her neck in one hand and hike up the long skirt of her dress with the other.

My fingers trail up her bare thigh the higher I lift the garment, her butter-soft skin breaking out in goosebumps beneath my touch. I work my caress toward her center and brush against her bare, wet skin. My fingers glide easily over her soaked pussy, my thumb brushing the moisture on her inner thighs.

I drag my lips from hers, and she whimpers, her fingers tightening on my shirt. My cock twitches at that little sound, and I shift my lips to her ear, teasing them against the sensitive spot just behind it.

"You didn't wear knickers to the royal wedding?" I smile against her heated flesh. "I thought you were just fucking with me back at the church with your *commando* comment. Such a naughty girl."

"You have no idea."

2

DAPHNE

LEV'S fingers brush against my core, and I buck my hips to force the connection. He must feel how wet I am, how my arousal practically drips now that he's kissing me, touching me, twining his tongue with mine in heated desperation. He has to know what he's doing to me.

He spreads my sensitive flesh, and a needy whimper tumbles from my lips to his. It's all too much and not enough at the same time. Wanting to push him away but needing him closer.

His other hand firmly latches onto a handful of hair at my nape, and he uses his grip masterfully to bend me to his will. To move me exactly how and where he wants me, shifting us backward until my ass hits the old wooden table.

The bottle of vodka rattles, and I reach back to catch it before it falls and shatters. Lev tears his mouth from mine and glances at it, watching me bring it up to take a sip. Before I can swallow, he smashes his lips to mine again, sucking the harsh liquor from my mouth into his in the most erotic expression of pure lust I may have ever experienced.

Sweet mother of God...

I shouldn't need this. Shouldn't need *him* like this. Not here. Not now. Not after everything that happened—back home and with him since I arrived. But I can't say no. I can't stop this train from barreling down the track any more than I could stop the sun from rising in the morning.

Whatever this tension between us is, we need to rid ourselves of it before it tears us apart. A razor-thin tightrope we already walk. As it stands now, my entire body vibrates, hovering on the edge of madness if this doesn't happen in the next damn minute.

Almost as if he can read my thoughts, he easily slips two fingers into me and flicks his thumb across my clit.

"Oh, fuck!"

I jerk in his hold, picturing his tattooed hand thrusting between my legs, wishing I could *see* it instead of just imagining how fucking hot it must look. Those long, deft inked fingers move in and out of me, coated in the arousal he caused, toying with me, driving me to buck my hips against his hand.

He shifts his hold so he can grind the meaty part of his palm against my clit while he pumps into me, still devouring my mouth with a passion I didn't know existed.

No.

This isn't passion. This is pure, animalistic *need*. We need to fuck. We need the release. And then, we need to move on from whatever this animosity has been between us. For our sake as well as Bridget and Fyn's.

Lev starts to pull back, but I chase his mouth, nipping his bottom lip and briefly capturing it between my teeth before letting go. Something feral flashes in his darkening gaze, and he presses his body against mine tighter, pinning me against the table and holding me immobile.

His scent wraps around me like a cocoon, invading every breath as the long, hard length of his cock presses into my stomach. He stills his hand even as his mouth works me into delirium.

Christ, the man can kiss.

He pulls back again and nips my lips. "Watch it, Yankee."

The hand he has tangled in my hair finally releases its death grip, and he slides it around and cradles my face in his palm. His gaze bores into me. I couldn't turn away if I tried. Not that I want to, but with one hand on my core and one holding my face, those mahogany eyes assess me so deeply it sends a shiver through my spine.

"You're biting off more than you can chew, Daph."

Oh, hell no, I'm not.

People always underestimate me. They see my blond hair and my bubbly personality and automatically assume weakness. This man is only one in a *long* line of people I've had to prove myself to, and I'm more than ready to do it.

I push up onto my toes in my flip-flops, eager as hell to have his lips back on mine, but first, I have to defend myself against his words. "You don't scare me, Lev. Not even a little. I can take whatever you dish out."

He closes the minuscule distance between us, and his lips crash on mine in a dominant display intended to make a statement. His grip on my face and between my legs holds me steady while his tongue twirls in soft strokes against mine. A true seduction that makes me clench around the fingers that have stilled inside me.

Lev grins against my lips, then pulls back.

Good God.

His usual scowl has vanished, replaced with a smile that would melt off my panties if I were wearing any. "Oh, Yankee, you just made my night."

I'm glad something did. The way he was skulking around

the edges of the party, looking grim as ever despite his best friend's nuptials, made it clear he needs this release as badly as I do.

His hand slides off my face, but I don't have time to miss it, not when it travels leisurely down my body, leaving goose-bumps in its wake. Fire and ice war across my skin the lower he moves until his fingers slip inside the scoop neck of my dress, past my bra, and capture my nipple. The sharp bite of pressure zings straight to my core, and he resumes his assault on my cunt, too, curling his fingers and probing my G-spot as he grinds his palm to my clit.

"Fuck." I moan wantonly, sounding every bit the needy, lustful, greedy woman I feel like at this moment.

He slides away from my mouth, but before I can complain about the loss, he's kissing across my cheek to the column of my neck. I sigh and tilt my head, offering him access. His trimmed beard tickles the sensitive flesh and shoots electric currents throughout my body.

With my free hand, I grip his wavy, thick hair, refusing to let him leave this spot until he can't help but ram his cock into me.

He chuckles and smiles against my skin. "Getting demanding now, are we, Yankee?"

I groan in response, clasping around his fingers, trying to pull them deeper inside me to that spot that aches for him.

"You're very wet, Daphne." His voice lowers an octave, and he practically growls my name. "Is this for me?"

He moves his head away from my neck, looks down to where he plays with my pussy, and raises a brow while biting his bottom lip. It's there in his eyes. This smug fucker knows it's for him and what he's doing all too well.

Driving me absolutely insane.

I need to get us back on common ground and force him to act instead of just toying with me. We're used to arguing, and the snark and sass spur him on in most situations. "You waiting on an invitation, Lev?"

"Such a smart mouth." His deep chuckle rolls over me like the waves lapping at the Lovolian shore, holding a promise of something sensual and wrong. "Maybe I should put something in it to help you be quiet. Would you like that, Yankee?"

Hell yes!

But not now.

I need his cock somewhere else.

Lev pulls his hand from between my legs, picks me up as if I weigh nothing, and sits my ass fully on the wooden table. I wrap my legs around his waist, drawing his hard, uniform-covered cock against my center.

"Dammit, Daphne."

Lev growls low, and I rub my pussy up and down his hard length while I fumble with his belt, trying to get my hands on what's encased inside.

Frustrated by my lack of progress, he undoes his belt and frees his cock.

Sweet holy hell.

I don't bother trying to bite back the gasp.

"No Cheeto dick here, Yankee." Lev grins proudly.

And he should be proud.

It might as well be a goddamn third leg...

That I can't seem to stop staring at. My pussy clenches involuntarily, and I try to press my thighs together to dull the throb of my clit, but Lev's wide body keeps them spread.

Lev squats slightly and puts his face in my line of sight to regain my attention. "My eyes are up here, Yankee."

He points at his face, and a frantic laugh bursts from my lips. Heat creeps up my neck and across my cheeks. The flush spreads over my entire body the longer I stare him down, knowing *he* knows I was ogling his cock.

Fuck, that's embarrassing.

But that gorgeous smile flashes for a second before he captures my face with one hand again. My breath stalls. The years of push and pull between us sparks like a live wire, sizzling across my already-heated skin. We couldn't stop this from happening now, even if the palace burned down around us.

♕

LEV

THE HOT-PINK BLUSH rushing over her pale flesh stirs something deep in my chest, something I'm not prepared to examine. I shouldn't care how she reacts to me, shouldn't feel swelling pride knowing my cock pleases her. None of it should matter when it's just a shag to get it out of our systems.

I should shove into her and just get to it. Give us both what we need. But still, my mouth waters, craving one thing I never thought I could want from this woman.

Blame it on the dress. Blame it on the vodka. Blame it on how bloody messed up things have been in my head. It's true all the same.

"Need to taste you."

That's all the warning I offer her before I slide my hands under her thighs, throw her legs over my shoulders, and lift her cunt to my lips.

"Oh, fuck!" Daphne drops her head back, arching her pussy to my face.

Hell fucking yes.

I glide my tongue through her arousal, the sweet taste coating it and making my dick ache to be inside her. She pushes her fingers into my hair, gripping it roughly, and grinds against my mouth, trying to take charge of her orgasm.

Oh, hell no.

This is mine.

Daphne will *not* take control of *this.*

Every gasp. Every moan. Every twitch of her body belongs to *me* until she comes down my throat and I empty myself inside her.

And fuck does she taste good.

She could suffocate me between these lush thighs and I'd die happy, probing my tongue deep into her cunt and drowning in her wet heat while eating at her like a man starved.

Because I am.

Starved for *this.*

A connection.

To anyone.

Anything.

Daphne's aggressive jerk on my hair prevents me from falling down that depressing rabbit hole, and I redouble my efforts, sucking her clit between my lips while I flick it with my tongue. That earns me another sharp gasp from the infuriating Yankee, and I slide my left hand down to grasp my cock, stroking it to relieve some of the ache that builds the longer I eat her out.

"Oh, shit." She arches into me even more, her legs stiffening over my shoulders and pushing down so she can thrust her pussy against my mouth even harder. "*Lev...*"

The way she moans my name makes my cock jump in my hand.

How can the woman who enjoys busting my balls so much now be the one about to make them blow?

That reality sends a strange rush of anger mixed with ravenous need coursing through every fiber of my being.

I lightly bite her sensitive bundle of nerves, and her strangled cry echoes around the old room as her orgasm slams into her so powerfully she almost twists my damn head off with the thrashing of her powerful thighs.

By the time her orgasm subsides, my cock practically *screams* to be buried deep inside her. I release my tight grip on it to help lower Daphne's arse back to the table.

She props herself up on her elbows, flashing a satisfied grin. "That was…"

I thump my hard shaft against the apex of her thighs—a reminder that we aren't finished—and a gasp falls from her lips. She wriggles around on the table, spreading her legs further to welcome me in. Her glistening cunt draws my gaze like a moth to a flame, and I pinch her clit between my fingers.

Her body jerks, and I rub the tip of my cock up and down her slit, aligning myself perfectly. "Tell me I don't need a damn condom."

She shakes her head. "No. Birth control and—"

I shove inside in one harsh thrust that rocks her back on the table slightly. *"Blyat!"*

A moan climbs up my throat, and I fight the low tingle in my balls that threatens to end this before it even starts.

So damn tight.

Gritting my teeth, I shift my hips back slightly, and Daphne whimpers.

I pause a moment to let her adjust. "You all right, Yankee?"

Her azure eyes lock with mine, hunger simmering in their depths. "I will be. Just *move*."

She kicks off those damn flip-flops, wraps her legs around me, and digs her heels into my lower back, urging me to drive into her again. Any thoughts about moving slowly. Of making sure this lasts. Of worrying she won't be able to take all of me… all disappear with another thrust of my hips.

The head of my cock drags against her G-spot on my withdrawal, and she digs her fingers into my wrists, where I grip her body to keep it in place. That little bite of pain makes my cock twitch inside her, and I pick up my pace, my hips pounding steadily against hers. Staccato grunts and labored breaths fill the silence around us, the erotic sounds spurring me on.

"Fuck me harder, Lev." Daphne moans out her command, then rolls her head to the side, her lip pulled between her teeth, like she's fighting back a scream that would surely bring unwanted visitors into the Reading Room.

As much as I'd love to toy with her, to revel in watching her quiver and thrash and beg, I don't have it in me to hold back. Not when it feels like I have been for almost two bloody years.

I grip her thighs tighter, mesmerized by the red marks my hands leave on her pale flesh, and shift her slightly, altering the angle in a way that draws a strangled gasp from the woman unraveling me.

My thrusts become erratic.

Each deep plunge allows me to grind my pelvis against her clit.

Her eyes roll up into her head, and her clasp tightens almost painfully on my arms. She moves with me, her hips bowing to meet mine, squeezing my cock with her tight cunt on each withdrawal.

That's all it takes for the tingling at the base of my spine to surge through my body. A wave of ecstasy instigated by the woman who usually causes so much frustration. She stiffens and gasps, her body convulsing and cunt clutching at me like a vise with her orgasm.

I slowly push inside Daphne a few more times, releasing all my tension in hot spurts deep in her cunt before I sag on top of her, burying my face against her sweat-dampened throat.

Fuck!

A few moments pass with our heaving chests pressed together, our heavy breaths coming in a shared rhythm, her warm, soft body aligned with mine, her cunt still cocooning my semi-hard cock.

She shifts under me slightly, releasing a heavy, almost resigned sigh. "Well, that was...something."

Something?

I lift my head to examine her, and any hints of softness I had caught in her gaze during our rendezvous have vanished, replaced with the hard wall of sass and sarcasm she always puts up. "*Something?*"

Her brows rise. "Did you expect applause?"

Fucking hell.

"No, but maybe you could lose the attitude while I'm still inside you, Yankee." I pull out of her and tuck my wet cock back into my pants. "You are unbelievable. Has anyone ever told you that?"

She nods slowly, pulling her legs back together and sitting up on the edge of the table. Her gaze never leaves mine as she slides off it and slips her feet back into those obnoxious pink flip-flops. "Once or twice."

Sumasshedshaya!

This woman is insane!

Daphne hustles to the door and pauses. "*Thank you*, Lev, for giving me the 'royal treatment.' I'm glad you don't have a Cheeto dick."

She tugs open the door, and Bridget stumbles backward, Fynix's arms around her the only thing keeping her from tumbling into the Reading Room.

Fuck.

Daphne stands with her hand on the doorknob, eyes wide, staring at them. "Shit. I'm sorry." She quickly runs her hands over her disheveled blond hair. "I didn't know anyone was there. Are you all right?"

Fyn releases a sigh and pulls his mouth away from Bridget's. "Just fine, love. What are you doing in here?"

She quickly glances over her shoulder at where I stand in the darkness and adjusts one of the long lace sleeves of her gown. "Just needed a little break from the madness." She plasters on a smile. "Diplomats and royalty"—she rolls her eyes—"you know what I mean, but I'm good now." Daphne points at them as she brushes past them into the hallway. "You two good?"

From my vantage point, I lose sight of Daphne and watch Bridget and Fyn step toward her, away from the door.

The only exit.

And I have to get the fuck out of here.

I scrub my hands over my face and instantly regret it when the scent of her cunt on my fingers fills my nose.

Fyn brings Bridget toward the door. "What do you suppose—"

My cue to leave.

I stalk toward them, still concealed in the darkness. "That woman is a lunatic!"

They jerk their heads toward me as I adjust my tie and slide a hand over my now-wrinkled shirt.

Fyn's blue eyes bore into mine. "Lev, what's going on?"

I clench my jaw. "Nothing you need to be concerned about."

Bridget opens her mouth. "But—"

I cut her a look that silences her immediately and stalk past them, my body even more tense than I was all day. Getting shagged did nothing to relieve any of it.

All fucking Daphne did was royally piss me off.

3

DAPHNE

UNSHED TEARS STING MY EYES, but I rapidly blink them away before Bridget catches them. If she sees me lose my shit, she'll only feel guilty about leaving. And I can't let her head off on her romantic three-week honeymoon to Italy with her real-life prince husband worrying about me.

She cares too much, which is precisely why I've kept everything from her. If she knew the truth of what's been happening in Colorado since she moved here, the shitstorm my life has become, and what I'm planning to do tomorrow, she wouldn't set foot on that beautiful private jet.

And all I want for her is to go and enjoy her time with Fyn —completely unencumbered by my bullshit problems. I need to find a resolution myself, without relying on Bridget to come up with the answer for me.

Bridget turns from her conversation with Fyn and narrows her eyes on me. "Are you okay?"

Shit.

Busted.

I force the brightest smile I can. Hopefully, she'll be too distracted with excitement to leave that she won't see what I'm hiding. I pretend to focus on the limo, SUVs, and the members of the Royal Guard standing around them, as if I haven't seen them a hundred times during my various visits. "I'm fine. Just so happy to see you happy."

Not a lie.

If anyone deserves this, it's Bridget. After everything she and Fynix have been through—the time apart, the palace drama, the attacks in Lovolia, the kidnapping, the general complications that seem to chase them to try to break down the bond they share—I would never stand in her way, for *any* reason.

Her lips twist down, and she crosses her arms over her chest. She taps her foot rapidly, like she always does when she's about ready to throw down verbally. "Nope. There's more. Spill it before I have to get in that limo."

Crap.

I should have known she would see right through my façade and call me out. After over a decade of friendship, there isn't much we can hide from each other—though being thousands of miles away helped. From Colorado, I could convince her I was okay, that my life and job were perfect. Doing it while looking her in the eye is another matter entirely.

The truth weighs heavily on my chest, threatening to come out in a rush of words. Images of the night before I flew here flash through my head, threatening to make me sob. I desperately struggle to swallow it back, to find something else to say to get her off the topic and into the sleek limousine set to whisk them off to the royal jet.

I have to lighten the mood, make her think this is just my being clingy and needy because if she gets even a *hint* that something is really wrong, Fyn couldn't get her in that limo for anything.

Twisting my hands in front of myself, I put on a pout. "It's just that...it's only been four days since the wedding, and I'm already losing you."

Bridget releases a heavy sigh, rolling her eyes, about to call me out on my dramatic bullshit. Like always. "How are you *losing* me, Daph?"

In a way, I lost her the day she met Prince Fynix Michael Elander Yates.

Even during the year they were apart, her heart was always here with him. She wasn't fully present in Colorado while she was physically there. This was always meant to be. Deep down, I *knew* she'd eventually end up here; I just didn't want to admit it to myself.

Now, she's moved across the world and sleeps in a palace. A far cry from our dumpy apartments in Denver and the trouble I've managed to get myself in there since she's been gone.

Lovolia is a Mediterranean paradise, and Bridget just *fits* here. While I fit nowhere and have no one but her. My entire life, I relied on myself. I didn't have a choice, but Bridget showed me true friendship, true, unconditional love, the kind of ride-or-die connection we'll never lose.

The one that makes me *want* to tell her everything and ask her for advice.

I *can't* do that, though.

Better to sound shallow and self-centered with some lame, flakey excuse for my behavior than vomit the painful truth.

"You're sleeping in bed with your husband—the *prince*—at night instead of crashing out with me after too many wine coolers." Or the high-end wine we've been drinking since I arrived to prep for the wedding. "Who will I gossip with about the *Real Housewives* since you've abandoned me?"

She scowls. "Daph, you know I don't like reality TV."

Which is exactly why I chose it.

If she thinks I'm being melodramatic, she won't have any qualms about leaving.

"I know, but you at least tolerate my bitching about it. Now, who will listen? You're going away for weeks, and I'll have no one to rant to about that or..."

I barely manage to stop myself from mentioning the *other* thing I usually complain about because if I think about it now, I might break down and tell her what's really going on.

Giving a mock pout, I try to add some humor to my very real almost-breakdown. Before the wedding, Bridget being here in Lovolia never seemed *real*. Once she officially moved here, we talked every day, and it almost felt like we were still together at times, even with half the world separating us. It felt *temporary* even when I knew she and Fyn were anything but.

Now, she's officially a princess married to the only heir to the Lovolian throne, and while I *can* tell her everything, spill my guts and tear out my heart to come clean, I won't. That would be a really selfish, dick move since this Italy trip is likely their last chance to bask in their newlywed status before returning to Lovolia and all the responsibilities their positions hold.

They'll be flung back into the deep end of royal protocol, like that stuffy state dinner the other night that prevented them from leaving on the honeymoon immediately after the wedding. Plus, Bridget's new position means endless charity events and photo ops—which she will undoubtedly handle gracefully and throw herself into fully, since she has the biggest heart of anyone I know. But their schedule post-honeymoon won't leave any room for the new princess to slum it with her trashy American best friend or help her with the stupid position she's found herself in.

I have to figure this out on my own...

"Aww, Daph." She wraps her arm around me and hugs me to her. "Maybe I can come to Colorado for a visit in a few months, once things settle down here, and we can do a marathon."

It isn't lost on me how she doesn't refer to Colorado as *home* anymore. That's the reality—she lives in Lovolia now. *This* is her home; this is her country. She has a whole new life ahead of her—one I can't be much of a part of from thousands of miles away, especially when my life is a mess.

I force another smile. "That'd be great, Bridg. I'd love to spend more time with you."

Not the whole truth but not a lie.

I can't tell her how lost I feel or how screwed up my life has become since she moved away. It's not her responsibility to ensure my happiness. And I certainly won't burden her with everything that's been going on since she moved to Lovolia right before she drives away for her honeymoon.

She squeezes me again before sliding her hand into Fyn's outstretched one. He brings it to his mouth and brushes his lips across her knuckles, leaning in to whisper something in her ear that makes a blush spread over her cheeks.

Damn, that man is romantic.

I can only imagine how they'll spend their honeymoon—likely naked and tangled together twenty-four-seven.

Something I do not want to think about.

Instead, I avert my gaze from the happy couple, only to meet Lev's hard one. His dark eyes bore into me the way they did that night and every time our paths have crossed since then, despite my best efforts to avoid him. A wave of contempt with an undercurrent of lust hit me so hard my legs wobble. Heat spreads from my core, and visions of our sexcapades in the Reading Room assault me—*not* for the first time since then.

His touch haunts me.

His calloused fingers caressing my thigh as he lifted the skirt of my dress.

The press of his hot flesh to mine.

His soft lips against my neck.

Warm breath in my ear.

Those little grunts and moans that vibrated in his chest.

Shit.

I press my thighs together and squeeze my eyes closed, unable and unwilling to relive it again.

It was a mistake. A one-time release of tension. Definitely not anything we ever need to repeat.

A hand falls on my shoulder. "Is everything okay, Daph?"

I open my eyes and stare into the face of a very concerned Bridget. "I'm fine. Just feeling a little light-headed. Not used to this heat."

The cool ocean breeze picks this moment to kick up and swirl around us, and I release a little relieved sigh and fan my face.

Bridget squeezes my shoulder. "You're sure you're okay? Do we need to call the doctor in to come to see you? He can be here in no time."

"No." I shake my head a little too aggressively. "That won't be necessary. I'm okay. Promise."

Her brunette brows draw together. "I don't want to leave my best friend if she needs me. We can postpone the honeymoon until you're feeling better."

"No." I reach up and grab Bridget's hand, tugging it down by my side and tightening my grip. "I'm fine, thank you. Now let's get you loaded up in this fancy-ass limo and on your way. You have a new husband and Italy to enjoy."

Though I doubt they'll even leave Fyn's grandmother's villa, given how he's been devouring her with his gaze the entire time we've been saying our goodbyes.

"You're sure you're okay?" Bridget pulls her hand from mine and sticks out her tiny finger. "Pinky promise?"

Those damn tears return to my eyes with the simple, childish gesture. In almost fourteen years of friendship, I have never lied to Bridget on a pinky promise. My stomach churns, knowing I'm about to. I swallow back the truth threatening to spill out, grip her pinky with mine, and squeeze. "I promise."

The lie tastes like ash on my tongue, but somehow, I manage to keep myself together.

By the time she returns, I should have some of my life sorted. Things will be fine. So...technically not a lie, just a delayed truth.

She squeezes her pinky around mine tightly. "Good, because you know that if you need me, I'm here for you."

"Trust me, Bridget, I know. I love that about you."

It's the entire reason I can't tell her what's been happening the last few months...what happened the night before I flew to Lovolia. Why I won't tell her my plan once she leaves.

I'll be okay.

Nothing a few days of sun and time to think won't cure.

I'll have a chance to clear my head and figure out my next move. As long as I can get away from the ever-vigilant watch of the man standing next to Fyn. But every time his gaze hits me, my skin crackles, heating like a flame crawls across it.

I shouldn't have said what I did the other night after we fucked, shouldn't have quipped and slipped right back into the way we've always been. It was harsh, even for me. But anything else would have been unthinkable.

Lev and I can't be friends.

We can't be anything.

It's better that way.

And one great hour together doesn't change that.

It can't.

LEV

37

Bridget pulls Daphne in for another hug, and those blue eyes that have haunted my dreams since the wedding lock with mine over the new princess' shoulder.

I force myself to look away and back to Fynix. "You're good then, mate?"

He watches the girls together and releases a chuckle. "They're acting like they'll never see each other again." His gaze flicks to me. "Drama queens."

A grin spreads across his face, and he elbows me playfully.

I keep my arms folded over my chest, back straight. "Yeah. Drama queens."

"Oh, come on. Lighten up. That was *funny*." He spreads his hands toward the limo and Royal Guard vehicles lined up in front of the palace, ready to carry them off to the airport and their honeymoon. "You're on holiday now. You're allowed to laugh."

"*Ha*. Fucking. *Ha*."

He mutters something about being a stick-in-the-mud even when I'm off duty and turns to talk to Manuel.

I might be offended by his remark if it weren't true. No one who knows me would consider humor one of my primary traits. And it's hard to act carefree when Fyn and his bride are jetting off to Italy without me.

He calls it a "holiday" away from my guard duties, but it seems more like a punishment for how I failed him during the Lovolian Liberation Movement uprising. Letting my best friend and charge get kidnapped won't be at the top of my curriculum vitae. While he insists it wasn't my fault and that no one's harboring any bad feelings over the fiasco, the fact that he's insisting I stay behind while other guards travel with them feels like the ultimate brush-off from the person closest to me—and who is the only other "family" I have besides Gran.

Things are changing.

Hell, things have been changing since the night Bridget showed up on the beach.

Fyn changed.

The country changed.

My relationship with him changed forever.

So maybe I can sympathize with Daphne clinging to Bridget tightly, as if she might never see her again. It feels like that with Fynix, too.

Things have shifted, and I'd wager they will continue to.

Gone are the days Fyn and I would take off to Elysium for a week or head to Crown Point—the private royal beach—to surf for hours. He has a wife, a woman who complements him and completes him in a way I can't even describe, and she's his family now, his top priority.

It's the way it should be.

Doesn't mean it doesn't bloody hurt.

As his personal guard, *I* should be the one discussing the trip plans with Fynix, but instead, I'm relegated to standing here among the exit party, to wave and smile and pretend everything isn't all fucked up.

Needing a distraction from my current thoughts, I turn my head, and of course, my eyes land immediately on Daphne. I can't look at that woman without thinking about the sound she made when she came in my mouth and on my cock in the Reading Room. Or the sharp bite of her nails raking against the back of my neck. Or the way lust simmered in her eyes for a brief moment instead of the hatred and anger that's usually there.

But it was gone just as fast, replaced with a facetious comment before she dismissed me.

It was a one-time thing. Like she would say in what Americans consider English—*one and done.* It can never happen again, and Bridget and Fyn can never find out.

A casual dalliance with his wife's best friend could get

messy and cause a strain on their marriage and our friend-ship, not to mention our working relationship. Even more than the already tense situation between us—pre-hot sex—did. That's the last thing I want. Besides, Fyn knows I have no interest in a romantic entanglement, and I don't need the distraction, especially not after what happened to Fyn right under my nose.

An unforgiveable failure.

Bol'shoy proval.

It doesn't matter that things turned out all right or that Lovolia is moving forward in a much better direction. Those few days of not knowing where he was or if he was dead or alive took decades off my life and will always weigh on my soul.

But even with all the turmoil swirling through my head watching them prepare to leave, I still can't stop following Daphne's every move.

Another pair of God-awful flip-flops adorn her feet, leading up perfectly toned calves to thick thighs my fingers have dug into that are barely contained in cut-off short green jean shorts.

Does she even know how inappropriately she's dressed?

Apparently, she can't be bothered by the fact that we're standing in front of the royal palace and there are standards and protocols in place for a reason.

She couldn't care less.

Made even more apparent by the too-tight, baby-blue crop top shirt that reads *ADD TO TBR.*

What does that even mean?

Too Bloody Reckless?

Or perhaps it has something to do with the way her long blond locks sit in a tangled mess on top of her head.

Can't even be bothered to brush her hair today.

I can't help but snicker and shake my head at the absurdity and audacity of this woman being in the presence of the prince and princess dressed like a hung-over university student on her way to the corner café for an all-day fry to sop up the booze in her uneasy stomach.

Daphne's eyes dart over to mine. I stare her down, doing my best to convey my displeasure at her impudence in dress, while hiding the fact that her showing so much skin brings very vivid reminders of our night together and how she was far too covered up.

Fynix steps up next to me, nudging me with his shoulder. "What in the bloody hell are these looks you two are giving each other? It's like you're shooting daggers. Did you two have it out after the wedding? You never did tell me what happened in the Reading Room."

I turn back to face him and release a sigh. While I didn't intend to lie to him today, I damn sure can't tell him that I was a sad wanker after his wedding and feeling sorry for myself, so I shagged his bride's best friend. It isn't the kind of confession you want to make to your boss, and that's what he is—my employer.

"Nothing happened. You know we are like oil and water. We don't mix. I'm just happy she's going back to the States."

Fynix clucks his tongue. "I don't understand your animosity toward her. You've had it out for her since she first stepped off the plane on her initial visit here."

"You mean when she tripped in her flip-flops, and I had to catch her to keep her from going arse over tit onto the tarmac in the low-cut top and high-cut shorts?"

He smirks. "Maybe if you found some common ground before she returned home..." He glances at the girls again. "I think it would make my wife happier if our best friends didn't despise each other. Getting together in the future could be awkward otherwise."

Even more awkward, since she rode my cock in the Reading Room...

And further discussing mine and Daphne's relationship—

or non-relationship as it may be—with Fynix will only lead down the path of more required lies I don't feel like telling.

I motion toward the limo and the guards milling around the vehicles. "Since Manuel can't travel with you, and you *insist* I don't, I'm sending three trusted Royal Guard members with you. The Italian Special Forces will also provide a protection detail once you land, but you will never see them. You will be safe."

A slight grin pulls at his lips. "I know we will. I've never doubted you for a moment. What will you do? It's been years since you've had time off. Why not travel?"

I considered it, but in the end, thinking about being away from the island, where I might not be reachable if something were to happen to Fyn and Bridget in Italy, not to mention Gran, ultimately stopped that thought before it got off the ground.

"Just heading to Elysium. Hoping for some good waves there in the morning and at Crown Point in the afternoon."

"Well, you know you are welcome in the main house. Enjoy yourself for a change. Rest and recharge your batteries. This is a good break for all of us. I assume once we return, there will be a lot of adjustments that will need to be made since Bridget's schedule will change radically."

"I'm already working on it. I won't let anything happen to Bridget, or you...*again.*"

Fynix swipes his hand through his hair, his go-to motion when he's on edge. "I've told you countless times, Lev, you weren't at fault for what happened to me. Please believe that."

He reaches out and claps my shoulder, but I can't bear to look at him.

I let him get fucking kidnapped.

How can he trust me so implicitly again after that?

I can't even trust myself.

Daphne laughs, and the light sound floats across the small space between us and heads straight to my cock.

Case in point.

I glance over to find them embracing again, like one is going off to war. The villa is more like paradise. I roll my eyes, and Daphne must catch it because she flips me the bird with the hand behind Bridget's back.

The woman doesn't give a single fuck.

Fyn approaches them and pries Bridget out of Daphne's grip. I descend the steps and open the back door of the limousine. The happy couple walks down, arm in arm, with the irritating blonde hot on their heels, but instead of sliding in, Bridget flings her arms around me.

"Bye, Lev. Please be nice to Daphne. She's only here another day."

I embrace her and chuckle, already starting the countdown clock until that woman is gone from my life for a while. "I can't make any promises, Princess."

Bridget pulls back and looks up at me, shielding her eyes from the sun with one hand while pointing a stern finger into my chest. "Be nice. And enjoy your downtime."

She climbs into the limo with one final wave at Daphne, and Fynix approaches next.

"Take care, mate. See you soon."

We shake hands, and he lumbers into the seat beside a giggling Bridget. Those two won't make it out of this car without shagging.

Daphne steps up beside me and waves again. "Later, losers."

I don't even acknowledge her, just shut the door and tap the roof to let the driver know to go. The big, armored limo pulls away smoothly, two SUVs in front and two behind it.

Something tightens in my chest, that same nagging worry that I should be going with them that's plagued me since Fynix first told me he wanted me to take their honeymoon off for a little holiday of my own. One he *insists* I need after the stress of the LLM attacks, the kidnapping, the elections, the political turnover, and the wedding.

Maybe he's right.

I must be out of sorts to have let Daphne get me in that position the other night.

After the last SUV pulls out of the open gate, the guards close the entrance. I turn back toward the palace, but not before I catch a glimpse of Daphne standing motionless, her usually happy face devoid of any emotion I can place.

Her empty gaze flickers away from where our best friends just disappeared, and we stare at each other for what feels like an eternity.

Finally, I turn away from her and stalk up the steps, into the palace, away from the one person who could ruin my enforced holiday before it starts.

4

LEV

"You're sure you don't want to come to stay with me at Elysium?"

Grandmother barely glances up from her knitting and shakes her head. "No, *dorogoy moy*." Her old blue eyes cut to mine. "*Spasibo*. You won't see this old lady cramping your style. Besides, you haven't had any significant time off in ages, and it will do you some good to unwind."

Releasing a heavy sigh, I lean back on her silk settee, scanning her suite in the palace, even though I know exactly what I'll find in every inch of it. The same things that have decorated it my entire life—trinkets and mementos from Mother Russia. All brought by Gran's family or Grandfather and Mother when they arrived in Lovolia. The items fill every shelf and wall. Even though, as far as I know, Gran has never even set foot there, the pride she feels for her heritage still lives in her blood, just as it did in Mother and Father, too.

Though I was only eight when they died in the car accident, vivid memories of them still live in my head.

Mother teaching me songs in Russian that her mother sang to her while growing up there...

Father showing me books of photographs, introducing me to the history of the country Grandmother's family left long ago...

What would they say if they were still alive?

If they knew what happened to Fyn on my watch?

The guilt gnaws at my stomach again, and I grab a Matryoshka nesting doll from the table beside me and twirl it between my fingers, taking in the beautiful craftsmanship of the iconic piece of art.

A strange mix of longing and annoyance simmers in my blood. Gran loves a country she's never seen. Stuck between her loyalty to her home of Lovolia and a deep-seated love for the place her family came from generations ago after they fled when it wasn't safe for them anymore.

Supposedly, old ties put the family at risk then, made it necessary for them to leave. And though she doesn't talk about it, the fact that neither she nor Grandfather or Mother and Father ever went back makes it clear that threat might never disappear.

It certainly hadn't by the time I had to go—against Grandmother's wishes. My time there, pretending to be someone else, doing what I had to in my role in the Royal Guard in order to protect the Yates family, terrified Gran and left a bitter taste in my mouth, one I haven't been able to eradicate even after all these years.

I *had* to do certain things to protect Fynix and his parents, but no matter how many times I tell myself that, no matter how much I *know* it to be true, my actions haunt me the same way my recently botched job does. And seeing all these reminders of Russia only makes those memories stronger.

A "holiday" with nothing else to do but look back on my

successes and failures will only make me relive things I'd rather forget.

"Yes, that's what everyone says, Gran, that I need a *otpusk,* but I don't do well with idle time."

"*Yerunda.*" She releases her knitting needles long enough to wave a dismissive, wrinkled hand my way. "You're just not used to it. You can surf, exercise, and read. Whatever you don't have time for when Fynix is here." Her gaze darts up to meet mine, seeing far too much. "I know this adjustment must be hard on you."

"Adjustment?"

The woman who raised me and knows me better than anyone on this planet narrows her old blue eyes on me. "I'm talking about adjusting to your best friend getting married. You two are thick as thieves, always have been, but now, Fyn has a wife."

Nu, pizdets. She picked right up on that, didn't she?

"*Vse normalno. I'm* okay. I'm happy for Fyn and Bridget. It's just..."

The right words just won't come to express my feelings adequately. I set down the doll and scrub a hand over my short beard, trying to process my thoughts that have been so jumbled since the night Fynix was taken.

Gran reaches over and pats my knee. "I understand, *dorogoy moy.* He's your family as much as I am. You two are brothers in every way that matters. I am thankful for that and everything the Yates family has done for us and the Orlov family over the years. But when your best friend gets married, things will naturally change about your friendship. He has a wife; she will come before you or your friendship with Fynix. It's okay to be upset about that. The dynamics will change, but at the end of the day, he's still your best friend." A sly grin spreads across her lips. "And hopefully, one day soon, you will have a wife of your own."

"Doubtful..."

Gran hit the damn nail on the head.

Things will change for Fyn and me, and I have to accept it and move past this feeling. And I love Bridget, so it's like I'm gaining a sister. That's how I need to look at this. I'm not losing Fyn; I'm gaining her.

But I'm also gaining her fit, but incredibly annoying best friend.

There will be no escaping her for the rest of our lives, and our constant bickering has already strained the happy couple, if Fynix's words before he left are any indication.

I don't want to make life harder for him or Bridget, which means putting as much distance between the feisty American blonde and me as possible.

Thank God she's leaving today...

Maybe by the time she visits again, the tension between us will have subsided to a manageable level, where we aren't barking at each other constantly.

Gran returns to her knitting, the familiar sound of the clicking needles soothing some of my distress. "One day, a woman will come along and knock you off your feet, *dorogoy moy.* Just wait and see."

I want to deny it, want to argue that I have no intention of ever allowing a woman to wrap me around her finger the way Bridget has Fynix. But she looks so content—her silvered hair pulled back in the ever-present bun and her frameless glasses resting on the edge of her wrinkled nose—and it hits me.

My days with this amazing woman are numbered.

The thought slices like a knife through my heart, and I rub at the spot absently, thinking about all she's done for me throughout my life. My only remaining family...

How would I ever make it without her?

I push up from the settee and stride over to where she sits perched on her favorite wingback chair, a bag of yarn beside it. She glances up at my abrupt movement, and I swoop in and hug her to me, crushing her knitting between us and not even caring about the sharp bite of the needle digging into my chest.

"Lev...what is it, *dorogoy moy*?"

I squeeze her even harder. "*Nichego*, Gran. I appreciate everything you do and have done for me, and I want to ensure you know that."

"Lev, I certainly do..." She pauses and pulls back slightly, her brow furrowing. Her humor disappears almost instantly. "When that time does come, and you meet the right woman, there's so much you need to know—"

The seriousness in her voice gives me pause, but my phone chimes with a message, and I release her to dig it out of my pocket.

MANUEL

I'm taking Daphne to the airport. You'll likely be gone before I return. Enjoy your holiday.

Glad she's Manuel's problem and not mine.

Although Bridget no doubt ensured it wasn't up to me to take her since she knows how we feel about each other.

LEV

Thank you. You know how to reach me if anything happens at the palace or with the prince and princess.

I shove my phone back into my pocket, the mention of Daphne returning the tension to my shoulders.

It's time for me to get away for a while.

A little time alone is starting to sound better and better. There are too many reminders here at the palace, too many places she's been. Every time I walk past the Reading Room, I have to steel myself against my body's reactions to the memories.

"I'm going to head out, Gran." I lean in and kiss her wrinkled cheek. "If you need me, call."

She pats my arm. "*Bud ostorozhen*, Lev. When you're back, we need to chat about a few things."

"Sounds good, Gran. *Uvidimsya skoro*."

I toss a wave on my way out the door and release a little sigh. Gran's perspective on my place in Fyn's life has given me a lot to think about during my compulsory holiday, but I'll likely spend most of my time worrying about their safety in Italy.

It isn't something I can turn off.

From the day I came kicking and screaming into this world, I've been trained to protect Fynix at any cost. My mental and physical well-being means nothing when it comes to keeping the prince safe. Now, it's in someone else's hands.

That will lead to many sleepless nights at Elysium...as will the vivid, heated dreams I keep having about Daphne.

The American haunts me as much as my failure in Fyn's kidnapping. I push all of it to the back of my mind as I hustle down the private stairwell to the rear entrance of the private residences and the car park where my restored 1966 Fiat Spider awaits.

With the sun shining down and the light breeze blowing in off the water, it's the perfect day to take her for a drive to Elysium. I fire her up and head out the gate. The pea gravel crunches under the tires before giving way to road, and the moment it does, I slam on the accelerator and eat up the asphalt.

This classic beauty purrs, hugging the corners like she's on rails. The Mediterranean sun beams down, warming my exposed skin and helping melt away a bit of the tension.

Buildings damaged by the Lovolian Liberation Movement stand fully reconstructed or very nearly complete. We've put the angry mobs, the rallies, and the terror that swept the nation in our rearview, the same way I am trying to with any negative lingering feelings over my forced time off.

I hit the coast road and cruise along the shoreline, past the cove where the Battle of Lovolia took place—the very reason our country exists and a member of the Yates family sits on the throne.

What would it have been like to be part of that rebellion?

Back then, it was all about escaping a crown they found oppressive, but my family has spent our entire lives serving one that strives to do the best for their people—even if it means stepping down from political control of the country.

The move may have cured the unrest, but it hasn't alleviated any of the danger Fynix and his parents still face from those who see them as a threat to the new government structure.

Which is why I doubt I'll sleep soundly for the next few weeks...

I take the final curve as fast as the Spider can handle. The speed causes adrenaline to course through my veins like a drug. I slow to turn onto the secluded drive tucked behind a hedge. Gravel crunches under the tires, and the sea air fills my lungs with every breath.

Even though the ocean surrounds us on the small island, the air here at Elysium always holds something special that instantly calms any turmoil I might be feeling when I arrive.

The iron gates block my path, and I push a button on my phone to open them. Driving through, I check my rearview mirror to ensure they shut behind me, then continue toward the house.

Three weeks effectively cut off from the rest of the world.

Why was I dreading this?

I continue slowly down the long drive and round the last curve—Elysium comes into view.

God, how I've missed this place.

With all the drama surrounding the attacks, Fyn's kidnapping, the elections, and the wedding, it seems like forever since I last set foot inside this space that Fyn and I rely on so much for an escape.

I open the garage, park the Spider, grab my bag, and climb the steps to the carriage house over it. Fyn may not be using the main house, but that's still *his* domain, and this is mine.

The small space feels as much like home as my private suite at the palace, but here, I'm unencumbered by the expectations and demands put on me there.

I toss my bag onto the bed in the open concept one-room space and grab a beer from the fridge. The first taste of the hoppy liquid hitting my lips draws a relieved sigh from deep in my chest.

Fyn was right.

It kills me to admit that, but I needed some time away, to decompress, to relax, to think about what I did wrong and how to ensure it will never happen again. We've all been going non-stop for so long that I've almost forgotten how it feels to have *nothing* planned for weeks on end.

Even with the windows closed up here, the ocean waves lapping at the beach below Elysium call to me—a siren song audible through the glass. It lulls me to sleep at night, but right now, I need to see the water, need to watch the sun set over the perfect glass-like surface.

I make my way down the steps, across the breezeway, and to the main house. My fingers fly across the keypad to unlock the door. The lock pops, and I open it and beeline straight through to the kitchen and folding doors that make up the entire back wall.

Opening them lets in the last light of the setting sun and the salty sea air I so desperately need. I inhale deeply and release a contented sigh.

Nothing could disturb this peaceful feeling that washes over me.

Nothing.

👑

DAPHNE

MANUEL OPENS my door and extends a hand to assist me, offering me a kind smile that fills his soft-brown eyes.

I slip my palm into his and climb from the car, scanning the drop-off area for anyone else who might know me besides the head of the Royal Guard, who insisted on personally escorting me to the airport. Tugging my big-brimmed hat down over my face, I turn away from a group of chattering tourists—just the type to have watched the royal wedding on TV and who might see the new princess' best friend and keep an eye on me the whole time I'm here.

If anyone recognizes me, this could go very wrong.

Acid churns in my stomach, and I press a hand against it. I am not cut out for lying and sneaking around.

Manuel returns from the back of the vehicle with my suitcase and inclines his head. "Until next time, Ms. Jennings."

It may be sooner than you think.

I force a smile I absolutely do not feel. Just like saying goodbye to Mira this morning—the sweet old woman who somehow managed to raise a true grump like Lev—lying to anyone here about what I'm doing leaves a sour taste in my mouth. Everyone connected with Fynix has always been so accommodating and willing to help with anything I need.

But what about when I don't have a fucking clue what that is?

"Thank you, Manuel."

Please don't walk me in.

Please don't walk me in.

Please don't walk me in.

His shrewd gaze follows me inside the main building. With

53

my overnight bag hanging over my shoulder and my suitcase rolling behind me, I peek back to make sure he's left.

He stands at the driver's side of the car, still watching. Still waiting to ensure I've made it safely. Doing the job he's so damn good at. I offer him a wave that seems to placate him, and he slips into the black vehicle and pulls away from the curb.

The breath I've been holding since the moment I walked in rushes out in a loud whoosh of relief, and I take a look around at the people bustling through the tiny airport.

This is it.

My last chance to back out of this plan that seemed to make so much more sense when I boarded the plane *here* than it does standing in the airport, about to ditch my return flight.

You had to lie.

If I had told Bridget what was happening, she would never have left. I can deal with the fallout of my fib when she gets back and I have to face her and reveal all. And hopefully, by then, I'll know what the hell I'm doing with my life.

That starts with hightailing it out of here before anyone recognizes me. I step back out and grab a cab parked at the curb, giving the driver directions to the only place I can think of where I might be able to lie low for a bit while I sort out my situation.

The beautiful Lovolian scenery passes by—hundreds of years of history in stunning brick and stucco, happy residents, and tourists wandering along the narrow streets seemingly without a care in the world.

We reach the coast quickly since the island isn't any bigger than Monaco, where the crystal Mediterranean waters lap at the shore of perfect beaches like the one where Bridget met her prince.

Which never would have happened if I hadn't pissed her off and sent her scurrying away angrily with a bottle of tequila.

Fate—the only word that can possibly describe how her

future was determined, and now I'm here, trying to figure out my *own* future without a fucking clue which direction to go. Though the water seems to call to me in a way I've never experienced, each incoming wave pushing a sense of calm over me.

It's no wonder Bridget loves it so much here. It's a far cry from the cold winters of Colorado and having to deal with PR nightmares athletes and celebrities get into. Now she's royalty, on the arm of one of the sexiest men on the planet, and the people of this island will look to her the same way I do—as a pillar of strength in a life that has nothing else solid to cling to.

We turn a bend in the road, and the driver slows and pulls over to the side, narrowing his eyes at the barely visible gap between the hedges.

He glances over his shoulder at me. "I think this is it, ma'am. Houses on this end of the island tend to be pretty isolated and tucked away from the main road. You want me to try to go down there?"

"No." I pull some money from my wallet and shove it at him. "That won't be necessary."

The last thing I need is to accidentally expose Prince Fynix's hidden, private sanctuary.

Elysium...

Where better to lie low?

The way Bridget described this place, it sounds like absolute...utopia. And since they aren't using it while they're in Italy, I plan on taking advantage of the remoteness and solitude.

I climb from the cab and meet him at the back to get my suitcase. His kind gray eyes dart down to my flip-flops, over my exposed legs, to my jean shorts, and then to the gravel drive.

"You're sure you don't want me to take you down?"

I'm not sure of anything anymore.

I suck in a heavy breath and start down the rocky path that will lead me to my own little private retreat. "I'm sure. I'm tougher than I look."

His door closing echoes behind me, and I slowly make my way through tall trees that block out almost all the sun. The wheels of my roller bag get stuck in the gravel every few feet, and I curse and jerk on it, pulling myself off balance and backward. My flip-flop edge catches, and I wind up on my ass in the rocks.

Fuck.

Groaning, I push myself to my feet and brush off the shards embedded in my thighs, then continue on the long stroll toward the house on the water. I scan for the gate Bridget described, and it comes into view, far higher and more imposing than I expected.

The code is his birthday...

Thank God she told me that little tidbit offhandedly one day, or I'd never get in. This gate was designed to keep people out—for good reason. Fynix doesn't have anywhere he can escape who he is or the stresses and expectations placed on his shoulders...except here at Elysium. If it were easy to find or easy to get to, it would defeat the purpose.

I don't want to invade his sanctuary, but lately, I've had to make choices I never imagined I would ever face. Options were limited, and this was the best one with what little time and money I had to plan this.

Hopefully, Fyn will be as understanding as I hope Bridget will be when I tell her everything.

I trudge the rest of the way to the keypad and punch in Fyn's birthday in six-digit format. Nothing. I enter it again, this time adding the "19" in front of the year. Still nothing.

Shit. Did they change the code?

I check the entire surrounding area, but the only things out here are gravel, trees, and insanely high hedges on either side of the gates, running as far as the eye can see.

Now what?

The tall iron topped with metal spikes stands between me

and the house. Over or back—neither is a particularly appealing option.

"I can totally do this!"

Maybe if I say it out loud, it will make it true.

All the hours on the treadmill and Stairmaster will pay off if I can climb this sucker. I grab my duffel and toss it with all my strength toward the top of the gate, watching it thunk to the ground on the other side with a wince.

It will be a miracle if nothing is broken.

The suitcase will be harder to get lofted that high. I pull off my leather belt, wrap it around the handle, and throw the makeshift strap over my shoulder so I can drag it up on my back.

Here goes nothing.

I place my foot on the bottom rung of the gate, and the flip-flops with little yellow emoji faces and heart eyes stare up at me mockingly. Although cute, they might not be practical for trespassing.

That proves true when I pull myself up to the next bar of the gate and try to move up my foot. The wide plastic sole gets stuck between the bars, and the bag jostles on my back, threatening to pull me over.

Somehow, I manage to right myself and keep climbing, but the closer I get to the top of the gate, the more my arms shake.

Reminder: do more upper-body strength workouts.

I reach the top, my feet wedged between iron rods, my legs quaking so badly, they almost give out from under me to send me careening backward. Forward doesn't look much better.

Damn. How high is this thing?

My head swims and I squeeze my eyes closed instead of continuing to stare down at the ground far, far below me.

First things first—I pull the belt holding the bag free from my shoulder and grip the gate with one hand while I push it over the top and watch it plummet to the gravel drive below to join my duffel.

Of all the hard things I've had to do in my life, this actually seems manageable at the moment. It may be false confidence, but it's all I have to cling to right now.

I hoist my leg over, my poor footwear choice made even more apparent when the flip-flop strap gets hung on one of the metal spikes.

"Shit!" My scream echoes through the silent woods, and the more I tug and try to yank myself free, the louder my unlady-like grunts and curses become. "Fucking hell! Come on!"

I give it one final hard tug, the strap on my flip-flop snaps, and those heart-eye emojis laugh maliciously as I plunge toward my fate. I barely have enough time to cover my face with my arms before I crash into the rocks below.

All the air whooshes out of my lungs with the impact, and I gasp for breath, rolling over to push myself up to a seated position and physically assess my condition.

Dammit all to shit.

Tiny cuts cover my hands from the gravel, but overall, I survived relatively unscathed. I unzip the big pocket on the back of the suitcase and grab my Chucks to replace the broken flip-flop with better footwear.

Well, at least I made it over the fence.

For my first crime, I seem to have come away successful. I climb to my now-shoed feet, toss my duffel over my shoulder, and return to dragging my suitcase down the rest of the drive. I make it around the curve, and the massive, modern, Mediterranean-style home appears. But even the master criminal that I am, I wouldn't dare invade Fyn's private space. I approach the side door on the garage that Bridget said has a carriage house above it.

Please let the code be Fyn's birthday...

I repeat the same numbers I attempted at the gate.

Nothing.

Of course.

The longer code earns me the same results.

There has to be another way in.

How many times did I have to break into the trailer when Mom got drunk and locked me out?

Those memories, while painful, give me the confidence not to give up. I dig around in the flowerpots and the landscaping around the carriage house entry for a hidden key, even checking under the mat.

Oh, my God.

You're a moron, Daph.

The Prince of Lovolia isn't going to have a damn hide-a-key…

But I've already come this far, and I don't give up. If I were going to, there were plenty of times in my life when I would have already. This locked door won't break me.

Besides, what's breaking and entering on top of trespassing?

I look around for a rock or something to bust the window, but I can't find anything heavy enough to do any damage.

Shit.

That leaves one option. I unzip the duffel, grab a T-shirt, and wrap it around my fist. This will work; it has to. People do this all the time in movies and typically come out unscathed.

I muster up all I've learned about throwing a punch in kick-boxing class and fire my fist through the windowpane inset in the door. A shard of glass slices my arm, and blood pours from it, unimpeded by the wrap I tried to use to protect it.

"Dammit! Fuck, that hurts!"

I am not cut out for the criminal life.

It doesn't appear to have sliced any arteries, but it bleeds like a son of a bitch, and I am no nurse. All I do for Doctor Douchebag is answer the phones and schedule appointments, so for all I know, it could be worse than I think.

I wrap the T-shirt around it as tightly as I can. If I don't get this bleeding to stop soon, I may pass the fuck out right here on the doorstep of the carriage house.

That would be the cherry on top of the shit-cake life has served me lately.

I slide my good arm through the broken window, twist the lock, and open the door.

No alarms blare.

No warnings sound.

It seems Fyn thinks his codes and the semi-remote location of Elysium keep it safe enough.

Except from criminal masterminds like me.

I leave my bags outside for now and dodge the broken glass scattered across the floor at the base of the stairs. Ascending slowly, I try not to look down at the blood soaking my shirt, where I hold my injured arm to my chest.

Maybe I should have paid more attention to what the nurses do back at the office. Then I might have a better idea of how bad this is. It would be just my luck to die at Fynix's secret house and remain undiscovered for weeks until he finally comes back and brings Bridget here for a little getaway.

A low grunt and a creak cut through my thoughts, and I freeze mid-step.

What the hell? Is someone here?

I could turn around and hightail it out of here, but I'm potentially bleeding to death and have nowhere else to go. Doesn't offer me many options. I move quietly and cautiously up the few final steps. Given that the owner of this house and his new bride are already in Italy, it can't be them. It'd be just my damn luck to walk in on a burglary...

Another low grunt.

Definitely a man.

I crest the top of the stairs, where a large potted plant partially conceals the open bedroom to the left and stop in my tracks.

"Fuck!" Lev growls where he lies naked, stroking his absolutely not Cheeto dick in his large, clenched hand. Eyes closed, his head thrashing against the pillow, a flush spread across his cheeks. "Daphne!"

Holy shit!

A gasp of surprise escapes my lips, and Lev's eyes pop open and lock squarely with mine.

5

LEV

WHAT THE BLOODY hell is Daphne doing here?

Her presence ought to give me pause. It should make me still my hand immediately, but I'm too far gone, too damn close to the edge to stop. I should look away from the woman who always manages to get under my skin and set me on edge before I lose control and blow my load.

But I don't...

I lock my gaze on her—the cascade of blond hair floating around her face and down over her shoulders, piercing blue eyes the color of the water outside focusing directly on me and heating with a dangerous flame, pale pink lips that tasted so good under mine opening slightly. Her tongue darts out and licks her bottom one, and that does it.

"*Fuck.*"

I growl like a caged animal being released, and ribbons of cum shoot across my stomach and rain down around my fingers and onto my abs. Twisting my palm against the head of my cock, I flex my arse and raise it slightly, fucking my hand, letting the warmth flood my body as my release continues until I'm biting my lip to keep myself from crying out this woman's name again.

Flashes of us together in the Reading Room dominate my mind.

Her mouth all over me.

Fingers tangling in my hair and scoring down my neck.

The way she moaned my name echoing in my ears.

I keep my stare locked on Daphne, and a low, long breath slips from her lips while she keeps wide eyes on me.

Keep watching, dorogaya.

It's the last time you're going to see it.

I pump my cock until I'm spent. My body wants nothing more than to collapse onto the mattress so I can drift into a relaxed, peaceful sleep—the entire reason I even ended up in this position. But I can't. Not when *she's* here.

Shifting onto my elbow, I narrow my eyes on her. "What the hell are you doing here, Yankee? And how the fuck did you get into my house?"

She moves around the potted plant, finally allowing me to see her fully.

Chto za chertovshchIna?

Blood soaks the front of her shirt and drips down her left arm that's cradled to her chest and onto the wooden floor.

Bolting upright, I take stock of her injuries as much as I can from across the room while I scramble to grab my boxers and wipe the cum off myself. "What happened?"

I climb from the bed and make my approach, trying to get a better view of the wound on her forearm.

Her eyes widen, and she retreats a half-step. "What are you doing? You're naked!"

And you're fucking bleeding!

I scoff and toss the cum-soaked boxers onto the floor. "Are

you suddenly shy now? You sure as fuck weren't at the wedding."

Daphne's lips twist into a scowl. "Asshole."

Any other time, I might take her insult as an invitation for some verbal sparring, but by the looks of her, she's already had a run-in with something or someone else.

A large gash bisects her left forearm, the blood flowing freely and far too fast for my liking, even with what appears to be a T-shirt wrapped around it.

"What happened to you?" I take a step closer and reach for her. "Let me see your arm."

She jerks back, pressing her right hand over the cut. "It's fine, Lev."

"I'll be the judge of that." I grab her arm, tug her toward me, and pull her other hand off so I can examine it. "You'll need stitches." *Fuck.* "I'll put clothes on and take you to the hospital."

Panic dances in her eyes. "No, I'm fine." She tugs her arm from my grip and presses her hand over it again, blood oozing between her stained fingers. "Give me a first aid kit, and I'll take care of myself."

This woman is a stubborn as a mule.

"You need to go to the hospital and get stitches."

I'm not about to let the new princess' best friend bleed to death here at Elysium when she's supposed to be safely tucked away on a plane back to the States.

I storm away from her, grab a clean pair of boxers from the top drawer, and jerk them on with my back to her, tucking my semi-hard cock into the fabric. She doesn't need to see how my body *continues* to react to her presence even despite the dire circumstances.

"What are you doing here, anyway, Daphne?"

This is the *last* place she—or anyone else, for that matter—should be.

I glance over my shoulder at her when she doesn't answer

immediately, and she sways unsteadily on her feet, squeezing her eyes shut.

Shit, maybe she's one of those people who can't stand the sight of blood.

It would be the only weakness the feisty American has exhibited since I met her. Even with all her clumsiness and inability to maintain any sense of decorum around the palace, she never backed down or showed an ounce of insecurity about suddenly being thrust into the royal mess that Bridget somehow landed squarely in the middle of.

If she looks this bad, then something is *definitely* up.

I tug on jeans and don't even bother with the zipper or button before I stalk back over to her. Her eyes flutter open slowly and struggle to focus on me. I lower my shoulder and scoop her up easily, settling her small frame against my bare chest.

She struggles against my firm hold, twisting her shoulders to try to move away. "You don't have to carry me, Lev."

I drop my head closer to hers and growl in her ear. "Apparently, I fucking do since it looks like you're about to pass out. I'm not letting you do those stairs, or you'll end up tumbling down. Then, I'd have to call Fynix and Bridget to let them know you broke your fucking neck when you were supposed to be thirty thousand feet in the air by now."

She winces, and I descend the stairs, sliding to a halt at the glass scattered around the bottom of them near the door.

"You *broke into* my fucking house?"

Anger and defiance flash in her glare. "It isn't *your* house. It's Fyn's."

"In name fucking only!"

And technically, it's owned by a shell company no one can ever trace to him. This is the only place he and I have where we can get away from everything, and now, the last person I wanted to see somehow ended up here—bleeding like a damn stuck pig and with enough attitude to make me want to leave her to fend for herself.

Just my fucking luck.

"And how is breaking into the Crown Prince of Lovolia's house any better than breaking into *mine*?" I snarl as I carefully maneuver around the shattered glass, through the door Daphne left wide open, and out into the breezeway that connects the garage to the main house. "I'm quite confident the Crown Court would frown upon that intrusion against Fynix."

Daphne has the balls to look incredulous. "I didn't think anyone would be here..."

"Which makes breaking in justified?"

I shift her weight slightly so I can enter the code on the main house door with my right hand and twist the knob to get us in.

"You *did* change the code!"

"What?"

"The code. Bridget said it was Fyn's birthday, but I tried that, and it didn't work."

Despite the seriousness of her condition, her failure makes me chuckle as I step inside. "We didn't change the code, Yankee. You just entered it the American way with the month first instead of the day."

"Goddammit! Why didn't I think of that?"

Her warm breath flutters against my cheek, and the scent of lemons and sunshine, which always seems to follow her, invades every breath I take.

Of all the fucking places she had to go, why did it have to be here?

There goes any chance of relaxing tonight.

I stalk inside to the kitchen, kick one of the chairs out from under the table, and set her on it. "Stay."

Her well-practiced glower shoots right at me. "I'm not a fucking dog."

But you are a bitch.

I bite back the retort and raise a brow at her. "Maybe not, but you don't follow directions very well. *Ostan'sya.*"

Stay.

She scowls but doesn't respond, just watches me rummage under the sink for the medical kit. I pull out the large plastic bin and set it on the table next to her.

"You want to tell me what you're doing here instead of on your way back to Colorado?"

Those perfect lips press together before she pulls the bottom one under her teeth, shaking her head. "No."

"Well, you're going to because Fyn and Bridget are going to have a lot of fucking questions."

That same panic I saw up in the carriage house darkens her gaze again. "You can't tell them."

"Excuse me?"

"You"—she shakes her head, sending her pale locks swinging wildly around her face—"you can't tell them I'm here."

"Why the hell not?" I manage to find the suture kit, gauze, and a bottle of rubbing alcohol, but there isn't anything else in here that will be useful in this situation. "This is going to fucking hurt."

Under different circumstances, I might revel in that when it comes to Daphne, but her panic and weak state prevent me from being able to take any pleasure in this.

"Not as much as if Bridget finds out I'm not on my way back home."

I spread her knees and kneel between them, trying to block out the memory of the last time I was in this position. "You're *going* to tell me why you're here, Daphne."

She watches me with her brow furrowed for a moment before resolve settles in her gaze. "How about you stop asking me why I'm here, and I won't mention the fact that I just walked in on you jerking off?"

Hell...

There's that smart mouth.

I grit my jaw and glare at her but don't verbally answer as I pour the rubbing alcohol over the wound.

"Motherfucker!"

She lurches on the chair, trying to jerk her arm from my grip, but I hold it steady, tightening my fingers on her wrist.

"We need to get this cleaned out. If you had gone to the hospital like I fucking told you to, they could have numbed the area first."

She clenches her teeth, and all the color drains from her face. "I'll tough it out."

"Mm-hmm." I grab the suture kit and examine the wound, wiping away the blood that continues to flow from it with the gauze. "You did a real number on yourself here."

"But you can stitch it?"

I snort and glower at her. "I can do just about anything, Daphne. My only job in the world is to protect the prince's life, which means I have to know how to save it if necessary. I've trained with our special forces medics and seen a hell of a lot worse than this."

👑

DAPHNE

SOMETHING DARKENS LEV'S chestnut eyes to an almost black.

I can't even imagine what he might have seen over the years. Despite the relative safety of Lovolia since it gained its independence, their special forces often help countries they're allied with. If they were trying to ensure Lev was trained well, they would've sent him to the front lines as often as possible.

GWYN MCNAMEE & CHRISTY ANDERSON

He's deadly. I knew that much the moment I met him, and he's always given off that dangerous, "stay the fuck away from me" kind of vibe.

Probably what drew me to him in the first place. It would be just like me to be attracted to the worst possible man for me—just like Mom always was. Our insanity seems to be genetic, but I refuse to give into it the way she always did.

He jabs the needle into my skin without warning, and pain slices through me, making me twist on the chair to try to get free of his hold.

"Fuck!"

His strong grip around my wrist keeps me from jerking my arm away. "You need to stay still, or it's going to hurt even more."

I grit my teeth again and clutch the edge of the table with my other hand, still covered in blood, trying to stop from lashing out and smacking him each time he digs the needle into my skin.

Only I could be clumsy enough to slice my own fucking arm.

While trying to break into the Prince of Lovolia's super secret house...

Jesus, Daphne, way to go.

I squeeze my eyes and try not to think about the pain radiating through my arm as Lev puts the stitches in place. The bastard is probably reveling in my agony, getting off—again—on being the one who inflicts it.

The needle pricks pause for a moment, and Lev shifts slightly between my knees. "You need to breathe, Daphne. You're going to pass out."

"What?"

Was I holding my breath?

"Breathe. Deep breath in. Deep breath out."

I release a long rush of air from my lungs, then suck in one that's heavy with his manly scent and blow it out steadily. It helps release a little of the tension and push away some of the fog encroaching on the edges of my vision.

"Good girl. Keep going."

Fuck.

My entire body clenches at his words as memories of our little rendezvous flash against my closed lids. Heat creeps up my neck and over my cheeks.

God, that was such a mistake.

What the hell was I thinking, sleeping with him?

You thought it would get it out of your system and eliminate the tension between you two.

A lot of good that did, but at least he's dropped questioning me about why I'm not on that plane. I'm not ready to answer that. At least, not to him. Not until I can trust he won't call Fyn and Bridget on their honeymoon and reveal everything. Or maybe I won't ever be ready. It isn't something I want to tell Lev Orlov.

"Done."

I snap my eyes open and stare down at his handiwork.

Lev rips open a package and grabs what looks like a pen with a purple liquid in it. He presses on it firmly, releasing whatever it is into what must be an applicator, then holds it over the wound. "I'm putting Dermabond over this to ensure you don't get it infected." He slowly applies the liquid over the wound. "Keep it dry for twenty-four hours, then you can shower, but no submerging in water for a week. The stitches can come out around then. Hopefully, you won't get an infection or scar."

Hell, I hadn't even thought about that.

I was too distracted by all the blood and his big cock in his hand to consider the possibility of having a permanent reminder of my idiocy. Though, looking at Lev now, something tells me he won't ever let me forget, even if this wound heals well.

His jaw tight, Lev pushes to his feet, steps back, and leans his ass against the edge of the kitchen island, crossing his arms over his chest. "Now, it's time to tell me what you're doing here, and then...go."

"No." I try to jump up from the chair, but the room spins slightly, and I drop back down and press my palm against my forehead. "I can't go back to the palace."

"Then I'll drop you off at the airport. You can catch the next flight off the island and get a connecting flight to Colorado from wherever you land."

Can't get rid of me fast enough.

I shake my head. "I came to Elysium because I didn't think anyone would *be* here. I need to stay for a little while—"

"Absofuckinglutely not."

"Please, Lev..."

The words burn, leaving my mouth. I can't think of anything I hate more than asking this man for anything, but I can't go back to Colorado. Not when everything is so...complicated. Just the mere thought of returning and having to face what's waiting for me there makes my stomach clench more than the slash on my arm.

"This is a big place, right? The guest house, the main house. We wouldn't even have to see each other."

He scowls at me, his perfect lips surrounded by the trimmed beard twisting down. "No."

"Lev, please. I won't be in your way. In fact, I'll stay as far away from you as I can, but I *have to* stay, just for a little while. And you can't tell Bridget or Fyn."

His dark brows fly up. "You don't think they're going to work it out?"

"I think they're going to be too wrapped up in their honeymoon to give a shit, and they won't know where I am if she calls unless *you* say something."

"I won't lie to Fyn."

72

Dammit.

Lev's undying loyalty to his best friend only makes this harder, even as it's another endearing quality to mark in the "reasons I should stay far away from him" column.

"Don't lie...just...don't offer any information." I do my best pleading with my eyes. "Please, just...I need a little time."

That muscle in his jaw tics, and he stares at me as if I'm some sort of mystery he can't wrap his head around. "You can stay *one* night. *One.* Tomorrow, I'm taking you to the airport, or you can figure out something else on your own."

Fuck.

He pushes off the counter and moves around it toward the fridge. "Right now, you need to eat."

"What?"

"You need to eat." He pulls out a loaf of bread and tosses it onto the counter, along with a brick of what looks to be cheese, and butter. "You lost blood, and it looks like you were about to pass the fuck out. You're probably starting to go into shock. You need some food."

Have I even eaten today?

In all the rush and excitement of planning my escape from Manuel and sneaking away from the airport, shoveling something in my face seems to have slipped through the cracks.

My stomach rumbles loudly, but I can't admit Lev's right. He's already arrogant enough. He certainly doesn't need his ego stroked.

The corner of his mouth quirks. "I heard that. I'm making you a toasted cheese sandwich."

"A grilled cheese? What am I—five?"

He slams the refrigerator door. "You most certainly are not, but I don't fucking cook, especially when I'm here. I can make exactly three things, and this is one of them." He motions to the ingredients. "Now stop bitching and accept that I'm doing something nice for you."

He is...

For *one* day.

But then, he's going to kick me to the curb, even though I have nowhere to go.

That's not entirely true...I could go back to the palace. The king and queen would welcome me with open arms, but they would also have a lot of questions I'm not ready to answer—the same ones I'm not prepared to discuss with the annoyed, tense man on the other side of the kitchen.

The *shirtless* man...

Now that I'm done bleeding and my head has started to clear, I watch Lev move around, opening cabinets to grab plates and silverware, slathering butter on the bread with a knife.

The muscles of his massive chest and arms bunch and flex with each movement, making the colorful tattoos spread across the skin dance beautifully.

I let my gaze rake over them, soaking in every vibrant image I haven't had the chance to see before since he stays buttoned up around the palace.

Other than the tats on the back of his hands and the ones that crawl up the sides of his neck, he keeps the rest well covered. And something tells me it's not just because of his job as Prince Fynix's personal guard.

These ink art pieces hold personal meaning to him. Some I recognize vaguely as Cyrillic words I'll never be able to decipher, which make sense given his Russian background, but others only offer more mystery. Dark and somewhat violent, they seem to fit the man making me a child's sandwich.

My fingers itch to trail over them, to explore every inch of skin and demand he explain why he has each one permanently etched onto his perfect body, but that can't happen again.

One time.

That's all it was.

A mistake brought on by too much champagne and vodka

and all the emotions of seeing our best friends get hitched brought up in both of us.

Once he kicks me out tomorrow, we'll put what happened in the rearview and move on with our lives.

If only I knew which direction I was heading...

I thought I'd have time to figure it out here, that I could sit alone in the pool or beach below Elysium, staring out at the Mediterranean, and the answer would just *come* to me easily. That I would just *know* what I am supposed to do now. Instead, I found an angry man who wants nothing to do with me.

And I can't say I blame him.

We've done nothing but bicker and pick at each other since we met almost two years ago. Aside from the flash of insanity that brought us together at the reception, we can't even stand to be in the same room.

So why would he want me here? Why would he want me invading what is clearly his personal time in his private space?

"I'm sorry, Lev, that I just showed up...and broke your window."

He looks up from his prep and quickly glances back down. "I'll get it fixed tomorrow. They can come while I'm taking you to the airport."

I wince and cradle my bandaged arm in my good one. He turns his back to me and drops the sandwich into a pan on the stove. The sharp sizzle breaks the awkward silence between us, and I swallow thickly and climb from the chair to approach the island.

The smell of browning butter and melting cheese hits my nose, and I bite back the groan threatening to fall from my lips. Lev's broad, muscular shoulders ripple as he flips my dinner, the huge image of St. Basil's Cathedral spread across the skin almost appearing to come alive with his movements.

"Thank you, Lev."

His entire body stiffens, and a long moment passes before

he finally turns his head slightly to look at me with his hard, dark eyes. "Don't thank me for anything. I'm not doing it because I want to. I'm doing it because Fyn would never stand for anything bad happening to his new wife's best friend."

Ouch.

That hurt more than the glass slicing my arm open.

6

DAPHNE

FAT MELTING off the bacon sizzles and pops in the frying pan, and the rich, familiar smell wafts through the kitchen. My stomach growls angrily, and my mouth waters.

Hopefully, it'll do the same for Lev.

"They" always say the way to a man's heart is through his stomach. Maybe that's the *only* way to reach that iced-over organ in Lev's chest. It certainly wasn't enough to let him ram his magnificent cock into me in the Reading Room. If his reaction yesterday was any indication, he might actually hate me *more* now than he did prior to our drunken hook-up.

Buttering him up is the top priority now, or I'm going to find myself out on my ass in that gravel again. Cooking like this always worked to keep Mom in a decent mood when she was battling a wicked hangover in the morning, and something tells me I'll need every weapon in my arsenal to battle him today.

I scan the counter, from the tray piled high with buttermilk pancakes, over the plate of freshly sliced fruit, to the stack of bacon I'm about to add to it. All that's left are the eggs. Then, I've covered all my bases.

If there isn't, at minimum, one thing that infuriating man likes, then I can say I at least tried everything before I failed miserably at getting him to lighten up enough to let me stay at Elysium while I try to figure out what to do with my life.

I grab the last pieces of crispy bacon from the frying pan and add them to the pile, then crack six eggs and drop them into the sizzling fat.

If he doesn't want me to stay after this *epic smorgasbord, the man is more than a royal grump; he's downright insane.*

Or maybe I am for thinking coming here was a good idea at all.

Maybe I made a mistake *not* getting on that plane and returning to face what awaits me at home. Running from your problems never works. It would simply be another in a long list of mistakes recently—two of which involve the dark, mysterious Lev Orlov.

Almost as if thinking about him led him straight to me, I feel his heated gaze sweep over me from the kitchen entryway. I hadn't even heard him enter the main house, but with his badass royal bodyguard skills, he could likely sneak up on anyone and put a bullet in their head before they knew he was within a mile.

He wouldn't do that to me, would he?

I freeze at the stove and slowly look over my shoulder at him, the same way he did me last night when he was begrudgingly making me the sandwich I don't want to admit was—actually—decent.

His hard, dark eyes move across me slowly, from my *thongs* over my bare legs to the tiny shorts I slept in that barely cover my ass. They sweep across my breasts pushing up out of my camisole until his gaze finally meets mine. His brows draw low. "What are you doing?"

I move the eggs around in the pan to ensure they cook

evenly and release a sigh at his stupid question. "Playing golf." I glance at him again. "What does it look like I'm doing? Cooking breakfast."

He snorts. "It looks like you're feeding a goddamn army."

Okay, maybe I overdid it a tiny bit...

But Lev is a *very* big man—*everywhere*—and I didn't want him to be hungry when I try to sway him into allowing me to crash here for a while.

I offer a shrug and focus on the pan, even though I can hear him moving around the kitchen behind me and don't like giving him my back. "I figured you might be hungry."

"Are you trying to butter me up?"

Shit.

I dump the eggs onto a plate next to the stove, take it in hand, and turn to face him at the counter. He slides onto one of the stools and eyes me suspiciously.

Instead of admitting his comment is spot-on, I do my best to look innocent—something that certainly doesn't come naturally to me. "What makes you say that?"

One of his brows rises, and he spreads his hands wide over all the food. "Because I don't think you are going to eat all this yourself."

I slide the eggs across to him. "Wasn't planning on it, no. But I wasn't trying to butter you up. Just trying to thank you for your help last night."

He grimaces and averts his gaze. "I already told you not to thank me."

About as tactfully as a sledgehammer...

I wave a hand at him. "Yeah. Yeah, because you would've left me to die if I weren't the best friend of your best friend's new wife."

His nostrils flare. "I never said I would've left you to die."

Snorting in an incredibly unladylike way, I shake my head, my building annoyance tightening my hands into fists at my sides. "You didn't have to. You made that abundantly clear with how badly you want me out of here."

Lev crosses his massive arms over his just as muscular chest, the tattoos on his forearms rippling with the movement. "This is my personal space, Daphne. The *only* place I can come to get away and find some peace and fucking quiet. I can't do that if you're here."

I twist my lips together and contemplate how to approach this. Despite running it over in my head a thousand times last night while I tried to fall asleep in the incredibly comfortable bed in the guest room, in the main house, all I ended up thinking about was what I saw when I walked in on Lev yesterday in his little apartment above the garage. Which leaves me at a loss now, staring at the man who currently holds my life in his hands.

He eyes the food, and I slide him an empty plate.

"Dig in before it gets cold."

He narrows that mahogany gaze on me again, mistrust written all over his face. "I know what you're doing."

"I'm not doing anything but eating breakfast."

I pick up a piece of bacon to prove my point and take a bite, but as soon as I chew it, my stomach roils slightly—likely the result of all the excitement yesterday.

Lev freezes. "You all right?"

"Yeah." I swallow the bite and try not to show how much it feels like lead going down. "Why?"

"You just went really pale."

I force a smile. "I'm fine."

The way he presses his lips together into a firm line suggests he doesn't believe me, but he doesn't force the subject. He just starts piling food onto his plate. "How's your arm?"

That *would* be the obvious reason for not feeling great, but I had almost forgotten about the gruesome injury.

I glance down at his expert work from last night. "Fine. It doesn't even really hurt anymore."

Unlike my pride...

"Good." He says it almost absently before pouring syrup, cutting into his pancakes, and shoveling a bite into his mouth.

Silence lingers between us as he chews, the only sound that of the Mediterranean Sea lapping at the shore beneath the house. It floats through the folding glass wall of doors I opened when I came into the kitchen this morning constantly like the ticking of a clock.

I drum my nails on the counter as he digs in.

His eyes dart to them immediately, and his hand pauses with a pile of eggs halfway to his lips. "Do you always have to make so much bloody noise?"

I still my hand at his reproach. "No. Is that why you hate me so much?"

He scowls, takes his bite, and chews violently, his jaw gnashing far harder than necessary. "I don't hate you."

The laugh that slips from my lips echoes off all the expensive marble and stainless steel, and I shake my head. "Bullshit, you don't. You haven't given me a single look that hasn't been filled with disdain, or said a kind word to me, since the first time we met."

Excluding our little late-night rendezvous in the Reading Room.

He scowls again and takes a few bites of pancakes. His tongue darts out across his lips to wipe away a drop of syrup there.

Christ, why is that so hot?

It shouldn't be, not when the man who's doing it obviously can't stand to have me around.

Lev sets down his fork and knife and locks his gaze with mine. "I don't hate you, Daphne. I..." He considers his words for a moment. "I have some trouble with your brash American attitude."

GWYN MCNAMEE & CHRISTY ANDERSON

I raise a brow at him. "My 'brash American attitude?' You've got to be fucking kidding me." I spread my hands wide. "Please enlighten me on how awful I am."

He jabs his fork into a pancake and shoves it into his mouth, the brief second of potential reprieve from his grumpiness long gone. "I never said you were awful."

"It was implied."

A long sigh slips between his lips. "Look around you, Daphne. If you paid any attention to what went on in the palace when you've visited over the last couple of years, you would know that a certain level of decorum is expected."

"Oh, you mean all that uptight, stuffy, formal shit?"

He rolls his eyes. "Yes. That uptight, stuffy, formal shit. It's there for a reason, Yankee. There are expectations within those walls, ways people should and shouldn't act. You running around in your flip-flops, shouting down the halls, and fraternizing with the staff are not things the royal family can tolerate."

Fraternizing with the staff?

Like having a cup of coffee with their full-time chef after he makes it for me is such a sin...

My aggravation at his comment prevents me from being able to bite back the words I know I shouldn't say about the *thing* I shouldn't point out. "Aren't *you* the staff?"

His jaw locks so hard I'm surprised his teeth don't crack as his hand tightens around the fork enough to whiten his knuckles. "That's different."

"How so? You're a guard. Your grandmother was Fyn's nanny. Yet, you two seem to have a very close, *not* professional, relationship."

Anger darkens his eyes, and his shoulders tense. "Prince Fynix and I are like brothers, and my father's family has worked for them for generations. It's the only reason I get any leeway. But you"—he points the fork at me—"you aren't anyone to them. They barely accepted Bridget as it is, and she adjusted very quickly to palace life and expectations. And then, *you* show up, talking a mile a fucking minute, no filter, no volume control, with your goddamn flip-flops smacking on the floors."

"What's wrong with flip-flops? I wear them everywhere in America."

"Well, we aren't *in* America. That's the entire point, Daphne. We're *in* Lovolia. And the fact that you don't seem to give a fuck about that is what rankles my nerves. So, I don't *hate* you, Daphne. I just don't know that having you around is good for my blood pressure."

Well, this conversation certainly isn't going the way I hoped.

Here, I thought the big breakfast spread might soften him up enough to let me stay, but instead, we've descended into the "bashing Daphne" portion of the day when the sun has barely come up.

There isn't any reason to put it off any longer. I highly doubt Lev's mood will improve if I wait to broach the subject.

"I have a proposal for you."

He takes another bite and chews slowly, watching me suspiciously. "Oh, really? Do tell."

I drum my nails on the counter but manage to stop myself as soon as I realize I'm doing it. "I need a little bit of time here... to sit on the beach, to sit by the pool, just to...think."

His brow furrows deeply. "You can't do that at home?"

I'm not about to explain my predicament to him. It's none of his business, and I don't know what I *would* say even if I *wanted* to.

"I came here for the same reason you did, because I thought it would be somewhere I could come and be alone. So, let me stay, please. I don't have anywhere else to go."

He opens his mouth to argue, but I hold up a hand.

"You said you can only cook three things. Well, I"—I spread my hands wide—"can cook a hell of a lot more than that—and better. My mother wasn't very maternal, and I had to take care of myself, so I learned my way around the kitchen very young. I may not be a chef, but I know a thing or two. I'll cook all your meals and, otherwise, stay completely out of your way."

Leaning back slightly, he motions behind him. "I intend to spend most of my time on the beach or in the pool."

"A schedule, perhaps, so we can ensure we avoid each other? I wouldn't want to *annoy* you with all my *annoying* American habits."

He scowls and crosses his arms over his chest, staring at me with a mix of anger and distrust. "Christ, I can't believe I'm going to say this, but *if*"—he holds up a finger—"and that is a big *if,* I do let you stay, there'll have to be rules."

♛

LEV

I CAN'T BELIEVE I'm fucking considering this, even *thinking* about *potentially* allowing this woman who drives me up a fucking wall to invade my personal space for God knows how long...but there's something in the way she looked at me last night when she asked if she could stay and begged me not to tell Bridget and Fynix.

Something about the way she's looking at me now.

The pain in her blue eyes.

A pleading...

A desperation...

A sense of need that won't let me look away—just like I couldn't at the wedding.

Whatever's going on with her, whatever reason she has for not getting on that plane yesterday and heading back to the States, I can sympathize with her search for somewhere quiet to decompress.

That's why I'm here—even though my presence was forced by Fyn's hand while hers seems to be quite voluntary.

And no matter how annoying and obnoxiously brash she might be, she's still a human being going through something that's left her uncharacteristically humble.

As much as I may try to deny it, seeing her this distressed claws at something in my chest. That constant need to protect people, to try to fix things, ingrained in me since I was old enough to speak, won't let me turn my back on her. Although, the thought of having her here at Elysium while I'm trying to work through my issues makes my skin tighten uncomfortably.

This might not be something I can mend, but if giving her a few days here could help ease whatever is causing the panic swimming in her gaze, maybe I can suck it up long enough to give that to her.

From arm's length...

She already caught me in a moment of weakness when I used the recent memory of her hot cunt squeezing around my cock to make myself come. We don't need a repeat of that awkwardness.

If she's staying, she's doing so on *my* terms.

As soon as she crosses the line, I'll send her away without an ounce of guilt. She will know exactly what she's getting into before she agrees, and I *will* hold her to it.

I spread my hands out on the counter, squaring my shoulders to ensure this feisty spitfire of a woman understands I'm serious. "I'm not kidding, Daphne. These are the bloody rules, and you are going to stick to them, or you are getting the fuck out of here."

She threads her arms over her chest defiantly, and the motion shifts her breasts even higher out of her low-cut, thin tank. Then she seems to reconsider and offers a resigned sigh, holding up three fingers on her right hand. "Scout's honor."

I snort and shake my head. "I don't think they allow girls, so that doesn't offer much credibility to your words."

She scowls at me, her perfectly pink bow lips twisting, and crosses her arms over her chest again, right back into fight mode. "Actually, they *do* allow girls now."

"Really? And were *you* a member?"

Somehow, I can't see this woman—who can't be more than five-foot-one, weighs less than sixty kilos, and wears nothing but flip-flops on her dainty feet—traipsing around the woods with rope and kindling. And after watching the surveillance video of her climbing over the gate last night, it's evident she doesn't do many activities requiring physical strength.

Except for fuck like a bloody champion.

She twists her lips. "No, that whole 'outdoorsy building fires' bullshit isn't for me."

"I'm shocked."

Her glare sweeps over to me. "You could cut down on the sarcasm."

"You could cut down on being so argumentative, especially since you're the one trying to convince me to let you stay."

It seems like she might continue her combative stance for a moment, but the longer we stay in this staredown, the softer her gaze becomes. Finally, she shakes her head and sucks in a deep breath. "Fine. What are your rules?"

I hold up a finger. "Number one, you are *never* to set foot in the carriage house as long as you're on the property."

She winces, undoubtedly thinking about walking in last night and not wanting a repeat of that incident any more than I do. Not that I plan on jerking off again with thoughts of this woman in my head. It was only because she was my most recent escapade. That night was still fresh in my mind, and once I bury my cock in another willing cunt, I'll be able to get her luscious, tight, perfect one out of my fucking dreams.

Hell...

My cock stirs to life as I think about locking eyes with her while I came.

So don't...

"Got it?"

Daphne nods slowly. "I can agree to that."

"Brilliant. Two"—I hold up another finger—"you will cook every meal while you're here at the times I like to eat. But ensure you do it when I'm not in the main house and have it ready and waiting. I don't want to accidentally run into you while I'm in here."

She purses her lips, obviously annoyed with my demand, but she doesn't voice it. "Fine. What else?"

I lean back and point out the open glass doors toward the pool. "Three—I intend to spend a lot of time out there and on the beach, and I don't want it interrupted. I will take the mornings on the beach since that's the only time there are any decent waves over here. You can have mornings at the pool and the afternoons on the beach. I'll likely either relax here after lunch or go elsewhere to surf, where the waves are better later in the day."

The corner of her mouth quirks. "The beach where Fyn met Bridget?"

"Yes, the one where Fyn met Bridget."

The best waves hit that side of the island in the afternoon before sunset. By then, I'll likely need to get away from Elysium and this woman more than I need oxygen.

"Okay." Daphne nods. "I can agree to that."

She won't agree so easily to the next one.

"Rule number four"—I lock my eyes with hers—"no noise at all...of any kind."

Her eyebrows shoot up to her hairline, and her mouth opens so wide I can't help picturing what it would look like with my cock rammed in it. "So what? I'm supposed to be a mute while I'm here?"

I grin at her. "Can you? Is that an option?"

"Asshole." She shakes her head. "That's insane—"

"There's no reason for us to be talking. If there's anything you need brought in food-wise, I can have it delivered. Just make a list and leave it on the counter for me. But I don't want to hear you blaring music. I don't want to hear you chit-chatting on the phone with anyone—"

"Who the hell am I going to call? Bridget's on her honeymoon."

"I don't care who you call. Your family, your boyfriend..." That one makes something unpleasant tighten in my chest. "Just make sure I don't hear it. I want it to be as if you're not even here."

And if I could go back to the wedding and stop myself from stumbling into the Reading Room and running into this woman, I would.

All it's caused me is problems.

Daphne taps her flip-flop-clad foot on the tiles, the constant thwapping of cheap plastic echoing slightly and proving my point completely. "So, you just want me to be the cook? *Got* it." Her sharp words try to cut me, but I don't let them. "Is that all?"

I stare at her for a long moment, trying to remember how we ended up in the dark with my dick embedded inside her because when she's like this, defiant and hostile, it makes it hard to imagine we ever got there.

"And rule number five, you will leave me the fuck *alone*." I motion toward her bandaged arm. "Unless you're bleeding out again, I don't want to hear a peep out of you."

"No *peeping*. *Got* it."

Our eyes lock, and a flush spreads across her pale cheeks.

Did she hear me saying her name while I stroked my cock yesterday?

Does she know I imagined how good it felt to drive into her relentlessly?

Can she possibly understand how hard it is to forget the sound of her gasps of pleasure that still echo in my head?

She leans forward slightly across the counter, almost as if she can sense what I'm thinking. "I can abide by those rules, Lev. Can you?"

What the fuck is that supposed to mean?

I push up from the stool and lean toward her. "You have no idea the level of restraint I'm capable of."

I've been fighting my desire to gag and fuck the attitude out of her since the moment she set foot in the palace almost two years ago. The night of the wedding was a fluke. A rare crack in the otherwise rock-solid control that makes me so good at my job.

A mistake.

Her blue eyes spark with interest at my words, and her tongue darts across her lips. "It didn't look like you had much yesterday..."

Bloody hell.

I issue a low warning growl. "I like breakfast around this time. Lunch around noon. Dinner at six."

"Yes, sir." She slowly lifts a brow. "Would you like anything else, *sir*?"

My body stiffens, and my cock jumps to attention. Despite the clear sarcasm and animosity in her tone, her words set my body aflame. Heat licks across my skin, a burn that goes straight to my balls and threatens to make me erupt in a way that would be very bad for both of us.

"Yeah, the silence starts *now*. I'm going down to the beach, so the pool is all yours until I return."

I surreptitiously adjust my cock in the hope she won't see it threatening to punch through my swim trunks and shove away from the counter.

The cool Mediterranean waters on this side of the island should help put it down quickly.

If I'm lucky...

I move toward the open doors, then pause and look over my shoulder at her. "And Daphne?"

"What?"

"Make sure you clean up after yourself. The only thing I hate more than unnecessary noise is unnecessary mess. The glass company will be here in three hours to replace the pane you broke. I'll be back up for that."

"I'll pay for that, you know."

I glower at her.

Why does it feel like I'm the one paying for it?

My sanctuary has been invaded by this woman who seems intent on driving me bloody mad. The only thing that will keep me from completely losing my shit are these rules—although, I'm not sure Daphne has it in her to abide by them.

She likes nothing more than to rebel against anything anyone tells her to do, and I've just laid out a laundry list of demands.

Even now, as she stares at me, her hands clenched tightly at her sides, her anger at my words heating her cheeks again, I can see her ready to snap.

This won't last more than a day or two before I have to force her out of here. Hopefully, I'll survive until then, and if she's lucky, she might, too.

7

LEV

THE FINAL LATE-MORNING wave crests toward the wet sand, and I ride it into shore, sliding off my board to stand in the waist-high water. I stare at the high sun shimmering on the seemingly endless crystal blue expanse of water, just like I have the last few mornings since arriving at Elysium.

It was the perfect early surf...that I may have let go for too long.

I wouldn't usually spend this long out on the waves in one session, but today...it was necessary. Lying around on the beach wasn't going to work. I needed the challenge.

Letting all my tension wash away with each cut across a barrel and dip into the ocean. The familiarity, the muscle memory taking over, so I don't have to think, just *do*. Exactly what I needed. But after hours of stress on my body, my back, and legs ache with the exertion. And my stomach keeps reminding me that it's time to eat.

Which means it's also my turn to relax poolside.

Not that it will happen with how Daphne's presence still

lingers there even after she's returned to hide in her room in the afternoons.

After you chase *her back...*

Blyat!

I wipe my hands over my wet face and shove them through my soaked hair to shake off the excess water, thinking back over the last few days we've "shared" Elysium.

How did we think it was going to be a good idea?

Splitting time around the property...

Pretending the other isn't here...

Kak budto my mozhem eto sdelat.

My jaw tightens, thinking about how her summery scent invades every breath I take as soon as I walk into the damn house. I can't even escape it in the carriage house. The few minutes she was in there when she first arrived were enough to leave the evidence of her presence hanging in the air. Even outside by the pool, little reminders of her being here taunt me.

The beach coverup she constantly leaves dangling across the back of one of the chaise longues...

The empty coffee cup, resting on the table beside it...

The flip-flops haphazardly kicked under the chair and left when retreating inside to prepare my lunch before I come up from the beach...

Everything about her permeates the space, even though she's long gone when I return to the house at mid-day.

Dva dnya...

It's only been *two bloody days*, and already, the sheer insanity of the situation screams for me to end it. I never thought she'd make it this long with the *rules* intact and assumed she would have given me a reason to kick her out for violating them.

But somehow, she's managed to stay quiet, cook delicious meals, and avoid crossing paths with me.

Even though I might find myself *wanting* to see her every time I head to the main house.

Pizdets!

What is it about this American that drives me so batty?

I climb from the water and up onto the dry sand. The high sun beats down on my shoulders and back, warming my skin and drying most of the water almost instantly. I slide my board into the small storage shed at the base of the cliff before I climb the wooden steps back to Elysium.

My shoulders tighten with each tread up I take, anticipating what I may find when I finally reach the house. It's almost like she's leaving me the little reminders on purpose. Poking at me. Toying with me to see how far she can push before I finally snap.

She won't like it when I do.

I freeze at the top of the steps, my vision filled with the vast expanse of flawless skin, now slightly tanned after several days here. Barely biting back a groan, I glance down at my wrist before remembering I forgot my watch this morning. But given the sight of Daphne in a tiny bikini sprawled out poolside, I must be early.

Intentionally?

Hell no.

The last thing I want is another run-in with her. Even subconsciously, I want to avoid it at all costs, so I refuse to consider that I might have come up before noon to catch a glimpse of her. We've managed to avoid seeing each other since we parted ways after breakfast two days ago, and it would be best for both parties involved if I turned and descended back to the beach for a while.

But now that I'm up here...

I glance back at the beach fifty feet below me down the cliff. All those steps. My exhausted body screams at me to stay, and the hot tub on the far side of the pool—which requires me to walk directly past Daphne—calls my name.

Bloody hell. Maybe if she realizes I'm back, she'll go inside.

I snort at the absurdity of my thought.

Yeah, right.

As if Daphne will ever back down on anything.

It's one of her most frustrating traits—and one of the reasons I hold a modicum of respect for her. In most circumstances, holding your ground is a good quality. Something I look for in members of my guard teams. But when it's *this* woman, sometimes, all I want is for her to concede and let things go.

I step onto the wooden decking surrounding the pool area, and even with her sunglasses covering her face, I know her eyes are on me. My skin heats at the same time goosebumps rise on the damp surface.

Don't react to her.

You didn't go through all that brutal military training only to crumble under the scrutinizing gaze of this interloper.

I inhale deeply, and chlorine from the pool water mixed with salty ocean air fills my lungs.

Thank God I can't smell her from over here.

On top of that ever-present lemon and sunshine fragrance she carries with her everywhere, the sweet smell of her cunt still lingers in my brain even more than a week after our little rendezvous at the wedding—and I don't think I could take much more of the reminder. Given how little she's wearing, getting close to her might expose my weakness.

"What are you doing here?" She grabs her phone from the table beside her and glances at it. "I still have half an hour of pool time."

I scowl and stalk past her, avoiding looking at her again because if I do, my eyes will linger on her full breasts, barely contained in the itty-bitty bikini top. Her toned, flat stomach.

The swell of her shapely hips with the minuscule triangle of material covering her pussy.

Bloody hell.

"I need a beer."

Or six.

"It's 11:30."

"What's your fucking point?" I stalk past her to the small fridge tucked into the cooking island near the wood fire oven, tug out a beer, pop off the cap, and drain half of it before I turn toward her.

That was a mistake.

She pushes herself up on her elbows, thrusting her chest higher, giving me an even better view of her glistening expanse of perfect skin. "Are you going back to the beach?"

I slowly take a sip as I examine her. "Wasn't planning on it."

Daphne scowls and lets herself fall back onto the chaise with a huff. "Well, I still get half an hour, and I plan on soaking up as much sun as I can in that time."

"Is this all you've been doing for the last two days? Lying out here in the sun?" I narrow my gaze on her arm and the wound I closed only days ago. "I hope you're not swimming."

Her head turns to the side so slowly it's like waiting for a laser beam to slice through me. She glares at me from behind her reflective sunglasses as if she were cutting me in half. "First, I'm not a moron, Lev. I've kept it out of the water other than a quick dive in to cool off. No long-term submersion. Second, why do you care how I spend my time?"

I chuckle. "I don't give a fuck what you do, Daphne. I'm just making sure you don't ruin my handiwork, and I'm curious why you're here."

Still.

She stiffens at my question the same way she did when I asked the day she crash-landed at Elysium.

Why didn't she return to the States like she was supposed to?

Fyn and Bridget will be gone for another few weeks, and she's already been in Lovolia over two weeks, helping her best friend prepare for the wedding and now here.

What kind of job would give her that much time off? What about her family?

Nichego iz etogo ne imeyet smysla.

"I don't have to answer to you, Lev."

I approach her slowly and lower myself onto the lounger beside her, taking another sip of my beer. "You're at my house —uninvited, I might add. I think I have a right to know why."

She presses her lips together in a firm line like she's contemplating how to respond and fighting the desire to hurl her usual attitude at me.

"Don't you have a job?" I raise a brow. "A family? Someone *else* waiting for you in Colorado?"

A pink blush spreads across her cheeks, and she averts her gaze. "Nothing that can't wait."

"Wait for what? I'm starting to get a little suspicious here, Daphne. Is there a reason you don't want to go home? Something you're hiding?" A sick feeling twists my gut, churning the beer that was so refreshing only a moment ago. Something I didn't even consider until this moment because I was trying so hard *not* to think about Daphne Jennings. "Are you...afraid of someone back home? Did someone hurt you?"

My hand tightens around the glass bottle until my knuckles whiten, and fury roars through my blood, just asking the question.

I swear to Christ, if anyone touched her, I'll—

"No, nothing like that." She shakes her head, and her blond hair floats around her like a halo on a temptress rather than an angel. But her answer comes too fast to believe her fully. "It's just..." She sucks in a long, deep breath, and releases it slowly. "Fuck, I can't believe I'm going to tell you this." She pushes herself up until she's sitting but doesn't turn to face me—

another sign she's not about to tell me the whole truth. "You know Bridget's my best friend."

I nod slowly. "Yeah, I know. You are two peas in a fucking pod."

"Well, it's been...hard, being there without her. The thought of going back and knowing she's here permanently now..."

I freeze with the bottle halfway to my lips.

Daphne—strong, independent, fierce Daphne—feels the same way I do. Like she's alone in the world now that her *person* has found someone else.

Who the fuck would've thought we had that in common?

DAPHNE

LEV WATCHES me with his dark, hooded eyes, beer bottle poised halfway to his mouth. He lowers it slowly, disbelief in his gaze, like he's seeing me for the first time even though we've known each other for years. "Believe it or not, Daphne, I do under-stand exactly what you're saying."

Well, I'll be damned.

The last thing I expected were those words from Lev's luscious lips. It's the closest thing to an admission of weakness I've ever heard him make. He isn't one to open up about anything, which makes the intent of the statement even more unclear.

Did he say that, hoping I'll tell him everything now?

Or was it a genuine comment he made without thought?

Given our history, it's easy to believe the worst—that he's using some interrogation technique on me to get what he wants by making me lower my guard. But he seemed sincere—as much as possible for the man who rarely shows any emotion.

Which leaves me with two choices.

Either come clean and tell him what's *really* going on, or close my mouth, tell him to fuck off, and continue to harp at each other until he finally throws me out on my ass to walk up the long drive and down the road in my flip-flops back to the palace.

Neither sounds particularly appealing at the moment.

Instead, I stare at the crystal-blue water in the pool and try to let the sound of the waves crashing on the beach below drown out the turmoil in my head.

Only all it does is paint vivid images of Lev cutting through the water effortlessly, his muscled, tanned, tattooed body twisting and curling, like he's one with the board and meant to be there. One with the waves.

Not that I've been watching him every morning since I got here...

I barely managed to retreat from the top of the steps before he saw me today, and embarrassment at having ogled him while he tried to find some solace surfing makes my face heat again.

Thank God for these sunglasses hiding it.

Lev lifts his beer to his lips and takes a long, slow drink, staring at the pool as an uncomfortable silence draws out between us. I wrap my hands around my feet and stretch them, trying to give myself something to do rather than have this discussion with Lev. It's been awkward enough the last few days, knowing we're under the same roof but avoiding each other.

Cooking his breakfast and leaving it, then hiding out until he goes to the beach and I can spend some time out here.

Cooking him lunch and leaving it, making sure I'm back in my room before he reappears to take over the pool area or lounge in the house if he doesn't do more surfing on the other side of the island.

Cooking him dinner and leaving it while he's showering so we don't have to see each other at all.

I feel like the goddamn hired help, but I guess I can't complain since I *am* here uninvited—as he loves to remind me. It's only fair I earn my keep somehow. And his unexpected statement of camaraderie plays over and over in my head.

While I don't particularly want to discuss my abandonment issues, it's better than telling him what happened the night before I left Colorado. His statement opened the door for me to delve into the topic, and perhaps it will offer him enough to get him to stop asking me questions.

I run my hands through my hair, tangled by the Mediterranean breeze, and peek his way. He reaches out with his free hand and catches my left wrist, pulling it toward him to examine the wound through the invisible barrier.

His thumb softly brushes across my wrist, sending a flutter between my legs. "This appears to be healing nicely. Continue to keep it as dry as you can, but diving in for a moment is fine. It would be a shame if you couldn't utilize the pool."

He lifts his focus from my arm across my chest and slowly up to meet my gaze.

"Yes, a shame..."

Mesmerized by the flecks of amber in his usually brown eyes, I stare a little too long, until the heat simmering between us matches that of the sun beating down from directly above.

I swallow thickly, trying to think of any way to break this trance I'm somehow in. This—these types of moments—is what got us in trouble in the Reading Room that night.

Lapses in judgment we can't afford if we're forced to share this space for the foreseeable future.

The longer it goes on, the hotter the fire rages through me, out from between my thighs and through my limbs.

Stop.

You have to stop this, Daphne.

Any way I can—like bringing us back to the pain we're both feeling.

I grasp onto his earlier admission. "Do you think things will change between you and Fyn now that he's married to Bridget?"

Lev blinks rapidly and drops my arm, breaking the spell. He rubs the back of his neck before draining the beer. "It already has."

The pain in his words makes me turn slightly toward him to respond, but he holds up a hand to stop me from interrupting.

"But he's my best mate, and I'm happy he finally found the love of his life. I'm not about to interfere with that because I've lost my drinking buddy."

I offer him a half-smile. Those two have been attached at the hip since birth, and nothing could ever come between them —even a damn kidnapping. "He's far more than a drinking buddy. He relies on you for everything. You're his safety net as much as Bridget is mine."

Family by choice—the only one that matters. Mom may have brought me into this world, but any hope I had of maintaining a relationship with her disappeared long ago. Lev and Fyn are family by choice, too, and I hope my acknowledgement of that makes up for my insult from the other night about him being the *staff*—even though I technically *wasn't* wrong.

When it comes down to it, Fyn is the crown prince, and even though the monarchy may not be in control of the country anymore, he's still the public face of Lovolia. For the next fifty-plus years, he will define what it means to be a king while Lev stands in the background, ready to protect him as his bodyguard—and his best friend and closest confidant.

Only instead of my words further softening his hostility toward me, Lev's lips tighten, and he goes stock still. His hand clenches tightly around the empty bottle. "If you're hanging around here because you need your 'safety net' and think Bridget is going to miss you enough to leave her honeymoon early, then I'm sorry to break it to you, but you need to get over yourself."

Whoa!

Where the hell did that *come from?*

I freeze and whip my head toward him. "Are you fucking kidding me? You think that's why I'm still here?"

Somehow, we've gone from finding common ground to being back at each other's throats in a damn instant.

He shrugs, but there's nothing nonchalant in the movement. His entire body practically vibrates with barely contained anger. "I don't know. It certainly seems that way. I can't think of any other reason you'd be so insistent on staying here when there's no reason for you to be in Lovolia."

Wow.

Just wow.

"Fuck you, Lev." I swallow through the emotion clogging my throat. He actually believes his own bullshit. "You really think I'm that selfish?"

"All you Americans are the same—"

"Oh, we're back to this."

"Yeah, we are. You all think the world revolves around you." He points a finger at me. "You never stop talking because you think everything you have to say is so important. Well, Bridget has something more important now. She's a bloody princess. She's married to the man who will be the king, leaving you as what? Her old friend from her old life...and maybe you can't handle that."

"Holy shit." I gape at his tirade—so unlike the calm, cool, collected Lev he usually is. "You really are a dick, Lev. Don't project your bullshit on me. Do you talk to your grandmother like that?"

He freezes, his entire body stiffening menacingly. His hand tightens on the bottle so hard it looks like it might shatter. But it can't stop me now that the floodgates have opened.

GWYN MCNAMEE & CHRISTY ANDERSON

"I bet you do. If you talk to me like this, after your dick has been inside me, you probably don't show your grandmother an ounce of respect." I shove up from the chaise, grab my towel and phone, and step in front of him. I'm far closer than I should be, but I lean down to get even closer. "Knowing your grandmother as I do, I would've thought she had taught you some fucking manners."

He bolts up from the chair and gets in my face, his massive chest making me stagger back a step. "Don't talk about my fucking family!" He pushes a finger into my bare chest, and the place where we touch instantly heats. "You don't know anything. And you don't know me."

I scowl at him. "I guess only in the Biblical sense."

"Yeah, well"—he issues a low growl—"that's never fucking happening again."

He storms away, tossing the bottle into the garbage can on the deck. The glass shatters inside it, and I wince at the sound. A reminder of my imbecilic behavior the other day that left me with this gash on my arm.

Apparently, I hit a nerve with my comments, but so did he.

Who the fuck does he think he is, judging me and making assumptions about why I'm here?

Well, you didn't give him the real reason, did you?

I clamp my eyes closed against the voice in my head. Lev doesn't want to know. Lev *wants* to make his assumptions about who and what I am and live in a world where the only thing that matters is himself.

Let him.

8

DAPHNE

M<small>Y FEET BARELY MAKE A SOUND</small>, padding across the cold tile through the dark house, but I pull on the refrigerator door and wince at the creak. Even though Lev is in the carriage house, I can't help the reaction whenever I make the tiniest noise.

Rule number four—no noise at all...of any kind.

His gravelly voice rings in my ears, repeating that damn rule over and over each time I breathe too loudly.

Asshole.

An asshole who makes *me* feel like the jerk for being a human being. It's physically impossible not to make a *single* sound the entire time I'm here. He's asking for unattainable perfection, and he knows it. He set me up to fail with rule number four. Probably looking for a reason to kick me out when he can't handle having me around any longer.

But still, he's right.

This is his place—or at least, it's Fyn's, and he lets Lev use it. And I don't want to do anything that might wake him up in the middle of the damn night and have to deal with the same grumpy beast he became this afternoon.

Is he sleeping, though?

The image of what I walked in on only a few short days ago flashes through my head, and my entire body heats.

Again.

That memory is what woke me in the first place...with my hand between my legs, moving and reaching for the same release he gave me in the Reading Room. But then I remembered what a *dick* he was earlier and abruptly stopped myself.

Which means, I desperately need a cooldown now, and the chilly air from the open fridge isn't cutting it.

I need a drink.

The beer stocked on the shelf looks tempting, but my eyes drift over to the special wine storage area to the left that keeps the bottles at the perfect temperature.

It can't be bad if Crown Prince Fynix Michael Elander Yates stocks it.

I scan the options and pull out a bottle of Bordeaux from a vineyard I've never heard of that the Yates probably own. Some people might covet Bridget's new lavish lifestyle, but I'm happy to sip shitty wine coolers if it means avoiding the weight of expectations that come with the good stuff.

May as well enjoy it while I'm here, though.

After what went down with Lev today, chances are I'll be out on my ass tomorrow. I pop the cork with another wince at the noise and pour myself a generous amount into a wine glass with the Yates family crest etched into the side. Then I add a little more.

I deserve it after my confrontation with Mr. Tall, Dark, and Cranky...and my dream.

How can one man light up my rage and set my body on fire?

He pushes my buttons in ways I didn't know were possible

and seems almost gleeful about doing it. That knowing tilt of his lips when he says something dickish that will set me off...

Smug bastard.

What set him off?

I thought my comment about his relationship with Fyn made the solid and deep nature of their friendship clear and made up for my "*staff*" dig the other day, but it was like a switch flipped as soon as I said it.

And I haven't been able to shake the unease of seeing him like that or the anger of his accusations the rest of the day. Letting him fend for himself for dinner was probably a passive-aggressive response, but the man can't expect me to cook after what he said.

Actually, he probably did.

Another reason he'll throw me on my ass in the gravel tomorrow.

I sip the chilled red wine, but it only heats my blood further and warms my exposed skin. The pool water sparkles outside the sliding glass doors, the single underwater light left on at night providing an almost ethereal glow.

And God knows I could use a cool down.

It's too inviting to ignore, and I peek at the clock.

3:00 AM.

I have at least two and a half hours before Lev will be down here expecting breakfast.

Expecting.

I snort and drink my wine, letting the sharp bite of the tannins coat my tongue, matching the bitterness filling me at this entire situation with Lev.

Who the hell have you become, Daphne, that you're at this man's beck and call like a servant?

That's all he wants from me while I'm here, and maybe that's for the best. The one time we tried to have a personal conversation, he proved he was happy to think the worst about me.

So good riddance to that man.

All I have to do is survive the next few days, until I can wrap my head around my current predicament. Either I'll come up with a solution and have to make a choice, or Lev will kick me out, and I'll be forced to.

Neither sound appealing.

What does is the wine. I grab my glass and meander to the door, slide it open, and step out onto the teak deck. The cool wood beneath my feet sends a slight shiver through me as I meander toward the water.

I set down my glass at the edge, grab the hem of my tank top, and pull it off with one smooth motion, letting it fall next to me. Cool night air hits my skin, instantly pebbling my nipples, and I release a little sigh as I shimmy out of my sleep shorts and glance up.

A million stars sparkle overhead, a canopy of wonder I can't stop staring at. The sky looks so different here than back in Colorado. The vast expanse above the mountains seemed daunting there, but here, it feels more like endless possibilities laid out for me.

That's exactly the problem, though. No clear direction... except I know I can't go to Denver. Not after what happened. Not after what he did. I've survived too much to end up back in a position like that, so I can't go back.

Only forward...to somewhere.

I shake my head to clear it of anything that might further sour my mood, turn my attention back to the glowing pool, and dive in. The slightly cool water engulfs me, sending goosebumps skittering across my skin. I swim toward the other end, closest to the cliff's edge, and burst out of the water when my lungs can't take it anymore.

"I suppose we never talked about who gets the pool after midnight."

Fuck!

I jerk away from Lev's voice, then whirl toward the dark corner of the pool, the one spot the light under the water doesn't reach.

Of course, that's where he'd be lurking.

"Jesus, you scared the shit out of me. What the hell are you doing out here?"

I can barely make out the outline of his head and shoulders above the water and his arms outstretched across the pool's edge. He lifts something, and the moonlight glints off it.

A beer bottle.

Guess we had the same idea.

I tread water, slowly moving my arms and legs to keep me afloat while he continues to analyze me, taking a long, slow pull from his drink.

He sets it down and keeps his gaze locked on me. "Looks like we both needed to cool off tonight."

You could say that again.

Lev inclines his head toward me. "You're lucky we don't have any neighbors out here."

It takes a second for his comment to register.

Shit.

The man just watched me strip and dive into the pool, naked. I might be embarrassed if he hadn't been between my legs already. But still, knowing his gaze raked over me as I undressed and dove in, sends another round of goosebumps across my skin.

I try to ignore his statement and stick to a less embarrassing topic. "How long have you been out here?"

The sound of movement hits my ears, and he glides across the deep end toward me. "Long enough to finish two beers and have time to think."

Shit.

Lev thinking usually doesn't bode well for me.

I continue to tread water lightly, keeping my hands and legs under the surface. The closer he comes, the more the light from the pool reveals his dark eyes shimmering, his skin practically glowing.

Instinctively, I retreat slightly, making my way toward where I left my drink, both to get my arm out of the water and to give myself some distance from Lev. But the farther I move away from him, the easier it is to see that he decided to swim nude, too. "What were you thinking about?"

Lev pauses for a minute, stopping a few feet away from me. Well over six feet, he can easily touch here, while I'm left hanging and feeling very exposed without footing. "What you said earlier."

"Shit. I'm sorry if I hit a nerve. I didn't mean to insult your relationship with Fyn or your grandmother."

He presses his lips together, his jaw hardening. "I know you didn't, but that's the thing about you, Daphne. You always say whatever's on your mind before you think about what will come out of that damn mouth of yours."

He isn't wrong.

It's always been my problem, what's gotten me into trouble since I was young.

Why should it be any different because I'm currently shacked up with a member of the Royal Guard who happens to be the prince's best friend?

I offer a slight shrug. "I am who and what I am. No filter."

His head bobs slowly. "I know, but perhaps I was being unfair, too, with what I said."

What?

I hang my mouth open in mock astonishment. "Was that an apology I just heard come from the lips of Lev Orlov?"

He smirks, and if my body weren't already soaked, it would be between my legs.

Goddamn. Why does he have to be such an ass?

Such a beautiful, strong, domineering man with a magnificent cock is far too tempting. All the reasons I promised myself I would never touch Lev again seem to float away the closer he shifts toward me in the water.

His eyes glow with a hunger that makes my clit throb. "I don't know what you're doing here, Daphne, but your presence has fucked up all my plans."

"Yeah?" The word comes out breathy, almost a whisper. "What were those?" I retreat quickly toward where I left my wine, needing to get away from the intensity of the way he looks at me. "Spend a week with your dick in your hand?"

Shit. Did I just say that out loud?

Almost immediately, I open my mouth to apologize, but before I can, he's on me and has me pinned against the edge of the pool, his hard, muscular, nude body blocking me from moving.

"How long were you standing there the other night, Yankee?"

I swallow thickly. With him this close, the scent of hoppy beer on his breath, mingling with the sea air, and that scent that's all Lev, hit me with every attempt to fill my lungs.

"*How. Long*?"

He rests his hands on either side of me, caging me in like an animal. The way he's devouring me with his heated gaze, like a predator stalking his prey and already imagining how he'll tear it apart, sends a shiver down my spine.

My tongue darts out across my suddenly dry lips. "Long enough."

That's all I have to say for him to know what I heard. His eyes darken even more, to an almost obsidian, and he leans in until his lips hover over mine.

"You heard me say your name while I stroked my cock?"

Gulp. I nod. "Yes."

His gaze zeroes in on my mouth. "Have you touched yourself since we've been together?"

Jesus.

The way he says it...

I close my eyes against the assault of the memory of his cock driving into me, of the orgasm that waylaid me and knocked me over sideways, of the dreams I've had every night since, of having him in my bed and inside me.

"Open your eyes and look at me, Yankee."

They flicker open slowly, my fear of what I'll see in his trying to keep them closed.

"Answer the question." Lev doesn't give me any room to move, any ability to deny him a response. "*Answer.*"

I swallow thickly. "Yes."

He nods slowly, drawing his head back but keeping me caged between his thick, muscled arms, with the hard edge of the pool digging into my upper back. "I think it's time we renegotiate the rules for your stay."

LEV

I KEEP my eyes locked on her uneasy ones and reach behind her to the glass of wine set on the pool deck. Swirling the thick red liquid, I bring it to my lips and take a drink. The heavy Bordeaux coats my tongue, the bouquet of flavors filling my senses—smoke, earth, graphite, a hint of something flowery. "Did you open one of Fyn's bottles?"

Her focus darts over to the glass. "I'm not sure what it is."

Of course, she doesn't.

Despite my best efforts, I can't hold in my laugh. "You

opened a bottle of wine that costs three thousand American dollars and didn't even know what it was?"

Her eyes widen. "Shit, I'm sorry."

I chuckle and set it back on the ledge, and her smaller body quivers against the side, held in place by my much bigger one. "He won't even notice. But I have noticed *you* here, despite my best efforts to ignore your invasion of my sanctuary. And that's why I think it's time for a change."

Her soft brow furrows. "Are you kicking me out?"

The fear in her voice makes me want to question her again about her reason for being here, but every time I do, we end up fighting. What went down today left me more shaken than I care to admit. The connection we made and how easily her words cut straight to the heart of my guilt over failing Fyn.

I shake my head. "Not unless you want to leave, but I thought a new rule might make things easier."

"Oh, yeah." Her eyebrows rise slightly. "What's that?"

I skim my fingertips across her cheek, and she shivers again.

"We both came here to relax, to unwind, to escape whatever stressors we have in our lives."

"Yes."

To hide from things we can't or don't want to face.

I drag my thumb across her lips. "What better way to relieve stress than to fuck it out?"

Just saying the words makes my already semi-hard cock stand at full attention, and I shift my body even closer, ensuring she'll feel my entire rigid length against her belly.

She issues a tiny little groan and squeezes her eyes closed again. "Do you really think"—she releases a heavy breath —"that's a good idea? You hate me, Lev."

Her words still my hand, and I cradle her cheek in my palm.

"Look at me, Daphne."

She does as I command, locking those crystal-blue orbs with mine.

"I told you before; I don't hate you. Sometimes I just wish…"
I slide my thumb across her bottom lip again and push it inside
her mouth. "I just wish I could shove something in your mouth
to shut you the fuck up."

Lust flares in her eyes, and instead of biting down on me
like she would have every right to, given what I just said, she
sucks my thumb between her lips as hard as she can, and the
feeling goes straight to my cock.

She swirls her tongue around the pad and lightly bites
down as her hand circles my shaft and squeezes tightly. I
release a low groan, and she drags her head back, releasing my
thumb with a popping noise.

Her eyes glow with heated intent. "Is this what you're
talking about?"

She strokes my length slowly, and a deep growl rumbles in
my chest.

Daphne is starting a dangerous game, one I hope she
intends to give her all. I hate playing against someone whose
heart isn't in it, who doesn't pose a challenge, but staring at this
woman, there isn't a doubt she's ready for battle.

My eyes immediately dart to her mouth, imagining what it
would feel like wrapped around my cock instead of her hand.
"Yes."

"You want to fuck me again?"

What harm could it do?

At least, that's what I tell myself.

It's hard to believe that lie when I know it isn't true. Daphne
has rankled me since she stepped foot off that plane during her
first visit to Lovolia.

Her inappropriate comments and questions. Her loud voice
booming through the palace halls. Her bloody flip-flops slapping on the marble floors like she's at a bloody children's pool
rather than the home of the royal family.

All of it built to the crescendo we reached the night of the wedding, and I was stupid to believe fucking her one time would be enough. Still, I have to look at this for what it is—a hate fuck.

Enemies with benefits.

Two people who can't stand each other but who happen to have sexual chemistry.

A biological connection that has nothing to do with feelings or expectations.

I feather my lips across her cheek to her ear. "We're just roommates, right? Having sex to relieve the tension? And whenever this is over, you'll go back to the States, and I'll go back to the palace. We'll pretend none of it ever happened. Just like we would if we had only fucked at the wedding."

She considers me for a moment, languidly stroking me almost absent-mindedly as I fist my hand on the pool's edge to keep from lifting her into position and driving up inside of her before she can give me her answer.

This vicious woman is toying with me, and she's taking far too much pleasure in it if the tilt of her lips is any indication.

She shifts closer to me, wrapping her free arm around my neck to play with the hair at my nape. Slowly, she leans forward and brushes her lips across my ear, her warm breath fluttering over the sensitive skin. Her tongue snakes out along the lobe, and she sucks it into her wet mouth. "If you fuck me, do I still have to stay quiet?"

Fucking smart-aleck.

I growl a low warning to her, the only one she gets before I wrap her hair around my hand and tug her head back so I can smash my lips to hers. She releases a little moan into my mouth, and I glide my tongue across her lips, demanding entrance she eagerly grants me. Her hand tightens on my neck, her nails digging into the flesh with a sharp bite that makes my cock twitch in her grip. I slip my free hand between her legs, using my entire body to pin her to the side of the pool.

Sweet bloody hell.

My fingers easily slide through the arousal between her thighs. Even submerged in the water, she's fucking dripping for me.

Apparently, I'm not the only one turned on by our constant bickering.

I tug on her hair, jerking her face back from mine as I roll my finger over her clit and watch her mouth fall open and her eyes flare. "There's no one out here to hear you but me, Yankee. And you screaming while I pound my cock into your cunt is a sound I want ringing in my ears."

She groans her approval, wraps her hips around my waist, and aligns my cock with her slick core, dragging the head through it. "Just sex, right?"

"Just sex." I pull back my hips and drive inside her so hard it lifts her from the water a few inches. "*Fuck!*"

A gasp falls from her open lips as her warm, welcoming heat clasps around me greedily.

Blyat!

I drop my head and sink my teeth into her collarbone as I roll my hips back and slam into her again. Her nails score my neck, and her hips rock against mine urgently, trying to take me deeper, make me move harder.

She forces her heels into my lower back and leans forward slightly, searching for the angle she needs, and the head of my cock catches that perfect spot inside of her.

"Oh, God, Lev."

Though I hate that she has no filter, that she's constantly yammering and driving me up a fucking wall, hearing those words from her almost makes me blow my load immediately.

I grit my teeth and pound into her, tightening my grip on her hair and hip to angle her exactly where I want to grind my pelvis against her clit and get my lips on her neck.

Kissing. Licking. Sucking.

Devouring that beautiful column of pristine flesh.

I suction my lips over her rapid pulse, and she bucks on me, mewling and clenching her cunt around my cock almost violently. It only spurs me on more, and I take her mouth, capturing her tiny gasps of pleasure as I roll my hips and thrust up into her.

Daphne groans as our tongues war, the same way our wills have since the moment we met. She clings to me, clutching on for dear fucking life, like I'm the only thing keeping her from flying off into the sky with the millions of stars above us.

The water sloshes around us, and I know what I want more than anything, more than this even...and it isn't that fucking blowjob she suggested. I pull my head back and drag my cock from inside, the loss of the heat and contact instantly sending a pang of regret through me.

Her eyes fly open with a surprised gasp. "What are you—"

"I'm fucking hungry"—I lift her from the water easily, setting her on the ledge next to the wine and spreading her legs open under the moonlight—"for this."

I've been craving the magnificent taste of her cunt since the night of the wedding, and I plan to drive her as mad as she's always driven me. Maybe it's a sadistic need to watch her beg for mercy; the part of me trained to make people suffer if they threaten the crown makes me want to do the same to her. Because she's a threat to *me*.

No doubt about that.

A blond-haired, five-three, foul-mouthed, no-filtered, perfect-breasted threat whose pussy glistens with her need directly in front of my face...

I drop my head and plunge my tongue into her without preamble. Her mouth falls open in a silent gasp, and she buries her fingers in my hair, adjusting my position and clamping her thighs against my head. The taste of her arousal coats my tongue, and I groan my approval at the sweet tang I've dreamed about.

It's better than any expensive wine I've ever had.

And I can't get enough of it.

I probe into her, licking and sucking her most sensitive flesh, trying to get deeper into the woman who has somehow burrowed her way under my skin. Her fingers tangle in my locks, and she tugs. The sharp sting across my scalp makes my cock spasm in the water and throb to be back inside her.

But I'm enjoying this too much to give into my base needs. The unwavering control I live by won't disappear in a moment of weakness.

I lave relentlessly at her clit, flicking the tip of my tongue across it rapidly and reveling in how her body vibrates, her thighs shaking violently the harder I push her toward release.

Water churns against the edge, splashing up and onto the deck, and I reach for the glass of wine beside her and pull my head back. Her eyes fly open and look down at me again, begging me to continue, but I pour the wine across her taut stomach and watch it trickle down between her legs.

The tangy, red liquid coats her cunt, and I dive back in. The sharp tannins mix with the flavor that's all Daphne, making my cock ache so badly that I drop a hand and stroke myself while I continue to devour her.

Her body starts to shake, and I know she's close. But so am I, and I want to come inside her again. Want to feel her cunt wrapping around me and dragging out my orgasm.

I suck her clit between my teeth and suction around it, shoving two fingers inside her grasping walls, and she blasts off like the fucking fireworks that danced across the sky during the wedding. Her cry echoes across the water as she practically twists off my head with her thrashing and clenching thighs.

Unwilling to yield for even a second, I keep sucking until she finally tries to shove my face away, then I stop and drag her limp body back into the water to drive my cock inside her again.

She groans and clenches around me, wrapping her arms around my neck as I brace my forearms against the edge of the pool and plunge home one final time, emptying myself inside her.

Just sex.

9

LEV

THE SCALDING-HOT WATER beating down on my shoulders slowly helps wake me from the semi-asleep state I can't seem to get out of this morning. Even fucking Daphne before the sun fully came up couldn't help me shake this bone-deep exhaustion that has hit me hard.

Maybe it's because you haven't stopped fucking Daphne every time you've seen her over the last three days.

Between *that* and all the surfing, my few hours of relaxation beside the pool—alone—each afternoon have become even more essential. It gives me time to think and consider how I could have done things differently during the LLM uprising to ensure Fyn's safety and prevent him from ever being taken. But constantly going over it a million times in my head may not be a good thing. If Gran were here, she'd tell me to stop obsessing over things I can't change and look to the future instead of the past.

It's better than the alternative—obsessing over the woman I can't seem to keep my hands off even while we attempt to stick to our "pretend the other isn't here" rules. Only spending time together when I seek her out to repeat what happened in the pool the other night...

Gran would have a field day with that one.

I've managed to keep her appeased with my texts that I'm "enjoying" my holiday, but it's a lie. This "break" has gotten more complicated the longer I'm here.

So uncomplicate it.

Keep your bloody hands off Daphne.

Annoyed with my thoughts, I crank off the water, step out, and pull a towel from the rack, wrapping it around my waist where my semi-hard cock seems intent on focusing on the thing I probably *shouldn't* keep doing with my unlikely housemate.

The shrill ring of my phone from the bedroom cuts through the quiet of the carriage house.

Shit.

That can't be good.

Of the few people who have my number, even fewer would be calling me when they know I'm on holiday—unless it's urgent. And urgent at this early hour usually means bad when you're in charge of security for a prince.

If I didn't trust the Italian security detail implicitly and Fyn hadn't insisted on me staying, I'd be at his grandmother's estate with him—the third wheel on his "romantic" honeymoon. As it stands, the multiple-times-a-day text updates from the head of the team there have been the only thing preventing me from catching the next plane out, even if I need this break.

The phone rings again, and I grab another towel and hustle into the bedroom, water still beaded on my chest and arms. Gran's picture flashes across the screen, and my gut tightens.

It's easy to convince her everything's fine when all I have to do is type a few words to her every day, but as soon as I answer, she'll hear it in my voice. I lower myself to the bed and take a deep breath to remove any evidence of my distress before I answer.

"*Alloh*, Gran. You all right?"

"Oh, Lev, *dorogoy moy*. You sound out of breath. Did I interrupt something?"

No, but if you'd called a few hours ago, you would have.

Images of me bending Daphne over the kitchen counter and railing into her after we had breakfast assault my brain, but I try to shake those memories free.

"Uh, no, I was in the shower."

Thinking about pinning her to the shower wall and slamming into her again when I was just trying to wash away the memory before going for my morning surf.

"Oh, I'm sorry to interrupt—"

"No, no, I'm done." I run a hand over my damp beard. "Is everything all right?"

Her somewhat strange behavior at the reception and her insistence we needed to talk when I got back rush to the front of my mind.

"Um, yes." Her response isn't convincing, the unsteadiness in her voice apparent even through the phone line. "I just wanted to check in and see how you were doing. This is the longest we've gone without talking in quite a while..."

Since I was working in Russia...

The hardest time of my life prior to Fyn's kidnapping. Being away from him, from the palace, from Gran almost killed me as surely as what I was doing there could have.

I rub the towel over my head to dry my hair, trying to assess her uneasiness to determine if it's something I should be worried about. Gran has always been very direct and open, demanding the same from me, but she's holding something back.

"I'm doing all right, Gran."

Gran *tsks* softly. "That doesn't sound too convincing, *dorogoy moy.*"

Her use of the nickname calms a bit of the distress filling my mind, just like it has my entire life. I release a heavy sigh and drop back onto the bed, staring up at the high ceiling. "Things feel different now..."

And it isn't only because Fyn's gone off on his honeymoon with Bridget and forced me to take this holiday; it's because of that damn woman in the main house and my inability to stay away from her despite *rules* I've initiated to do just that.

It almost slips out, but Daphne's terror at the thought of anyone finding out she's still here makes me bite back discussing her unexpected appearance with Gran.

"I know it's hard to see Fyn find such happiness, but you will, too, *kogda-nibud*. I'm confident the right woman will come along soon."

I let out a sardonic laugh, trying to picture myself standing at the altar with someone the same way my best mate did, slipping a ring on someone's finger and promising to love, honor, and obey for the rest of my life. But I just can't see it. I have yet to come close to meeting anyone who would ever make me *consider* settling down, let alone *want* to.

This life isn't conducive to having a girlfriend or wife. My job requires me to be wherever Fyn is—at all times. That means traveling the world when he makes required trips, sometimes with little notice. That wouldn't be fair to any woman left waiting at home for me.

Something Gran knows only too well.

"I'm not so sure about that, Gran." I don't want to further discuss my life, or my feelings about Fyn and Bridget's marriage, with the woman who knows me far too well. She sees and knows far too much. We said what we needed to say on that topic before I came out to Elysium. I'm more interested in why she sounds so off. "How are you doing? Is everything quiet there?"

"Oh, yes, dear. With the king and queen off on their own little European tour, things are very quiet here."

"Then why do I hear so much tension in your voice?" If I didn't know *her* so well, I might have missed it, but the typical light airiness is gone. I let it slide when I left the palace to come here, since she said we could talk when I came back. But now, I can't ignore that something is off with the woman who raised me. "Gran, tell me what's going on."

A low sigh floats through the line, full of frustration and perhaps a hint of annoyance that I haven't dropped it. "Nothing you need to concern yourself with."

Something twists in my stomach, and I sit up, my hand tightening on the phone. "That doesn't instill a lot of confidence that things are all right, Gran. Tell me what's going on, or I'll get in the car right now and drive back to the palace to ask you personally where you can't put me off. *Skazhi mne seychas.* Talk."

She's silent for a moment, like she's contemplating whether she's going to answer or make me uphold my threat. "Don't leave Elysium, *dorogoy moy.* There's no need for anything so rash. It's just...some...trouble...with some family back in Russia."

"Family back in Russia?" I scrub a hand over my face and pinch the bridge of my nose against the growing ache forming in my head. "I thought we didn't have anyone left there."

"Distant cousins." Her answer comes fast and definitive, like she doesn't want me to pry any further. "No one you would have heard anything about."

Why the hell not?

I wish I were sitting in the room with her right now because I'd be able to read her like a book. She's holding something back, but I can't tell what or why. Which means I have to tread lightly. Gran isn't a suspect to interrogate. If I want her to come clean, I need to finesse her a bit.

Start with an easy question.

"I have cousins in Russia you never told me about?"

It doesn't make any sense.

If we have family there, why wouldn't we be in touch with them?

"Like I said, dear, distant relatives. But you know what's been going on there, how tense and dangerous things have been. They've run afoul of some people very high up in the government, and a few of them have been rounded up and taken into custody."

My spine stiffens. This no longer feels like a light conversation about very remote relatives. "Why don't I know anything about these people, Gran?"

A flicker of a memory from the wedding reception flashes through my head. I had too much to drink, but I can still vividly remember Gran's heated conversation with the Russian ambassador. At the time, I thought it was merely him making a pass at her, but given what Gran just said, it appears something more may be going on that I've been kept in the dark about.

"It's better if you don't get involved, Lev."

"Don't get involved?" The headache grows with her evasive responses. "I lived in Russia for two years, and you never told me we had family there—"

"I'm sorry, Lev, I have to go." She jostles the phone slightly, like she's trying to move locations. "I just wanted to check in. How long are you planning on staying at Elysium?"

Nice change of subject, Gran.

"I don't know, another week maybe, since there's no reason for me to rush back. Fyn and Bridget don't return for another two weeks, but I don't know that I can handle that long a holiday."

Especially if Daphne stays that long.

"It's better if you remain at Elysium, Lev. Stay as long as you need to."

"Well, that's cryptic, Gran." I run my hand over my beard again. "I really wish you would tell me what's going on..."

"I swear, nothing you need to worry about, *dorogoy moy*. Just try to relax. We'll talk later."

She ends the call abruptly, and I set my phone on the bed beside me, staring out the window at the ocean. The waves continue to churn, just like the turmoil now raging inside me.

That was the strangest phone call I've ever had with the woman.

Distant relatives in Russia she never told me about?

The family histories on both sides have always been a bit of a mystery to me, but I was always led to believe we didn't have any relatives left there.

That conversation has left me more confused than ever. Throw in what's going on with Daphne, and all of this is a tangled web I'm not sure I'm going to be able to extricate myself from.

I can't stay here any longer.

With Gran being so evasive and Daphne being...*Daphne*...it's better if I just head back to the palace early. Even if my cock doesn't like that plan.

I grab my phone again and fire off a text to Gran.

LEV

I don't know what's going on, but you need to fill me in. I'm coming home to talk.

The three little bubbles pop up almost immediately, and her response appears.

GRAN

Just stay at Elysium. Please. I'll keep you apprised of anything important.

GWYN MCNAMEE & CHRISTY ANDERSON

Definitely cryptic. But if Gran were really in trouble, if there was something she needed me to do, she would tell me.

Wouldn't she?

I push off the bed, finish drying off, and tug on a pair of swim trunks to go out and hit the surf. I've already spent too much time today worrying about other things instead of relaxing and clearing my mind like I'm supposed to, and that conversation with Gran has made it worse.

👑

DAPHNE

THE COOL WATER slides easily down my throat, and I chug the entire bottle and toss the empty into the trash.

Who would have thought I could get so dehydrated sitting outside in the sun by the pool this early in the morning?

But that's not all you've been doing...

All the sex might have something to do with feeling so tired and wrung out.

When Lev suggested the new "rule" and rocked my world in the pool the other night, I had no idea it would lead to us banging like bunny rabbits every time we saw each other. Yet, that's exactly what's happened.

We cross paths in the kitchen at breakfast...his dick ends up inside me.

He comes up from the beach at lunchtime...and his swimsuit and mine hit the damn ground before he drives into me on the chaise.

I cook him dinner...and he bends me over the counter for dessert.

Banging away the tension in order to truly relax sounded like a great idea, but all it's done is increase this weird vibe that hangs between us when we're not coupled in the Biblical sense.

Almost as if on cue, the door to the breezeway clicks open, and I freeze.

Shit.

Why am I nervous, knowing I'm about to see Lev?

The man was literally inside me two hours ago, at the crack of dawn, when I got up to make us breakfast. For some reason, my stomach roils, and I glance toward the hallway back to my room.

Do I have time to sneak down there before he comes to the kitchen?

His heavy footsteps approach. This isn't stealthy Lev, who usually sneaks up on me. He doesn't care if I hear him coming this time.

And now, I've waited too long to make my escape. My indecisiveness is going to cost me in the form of another awkward run-in with the enigmatic man who sets my body aflame as much as he makes me want to smack him in his smartass mouth.

He appears around the corner and jerks to a stop when he sees me, then runs a hand through his damp hair and glances away. "Oh, I didn't know you were in here."

"I'm sorry."

Why are you apologizing?

He's supposed to be at the beach in the mornings, not in the house. By this time, he's usually already out on the waves.

You've done nothing wrong.

But it still feels like I'm not supposed to be here, like I'm invading his domain each time I'm caught out of my room.

He doesn't want to be reminded that you're here.

Unless his dick is in you...

I clench my thighs together against the sudden throb. "I was just getting a drink and was going back out by the pool. I assumed you were surfing..."

My babbled excuse trails off when I notice the tension in

his shoulders and his hands clenching and unclenching at his sides. He lifts one and rubs at the back of his neck, staring out at the pool.

Something's wrong.

Acid and the bottle of water I just guzzled down churn violently in my gut. "Is...everything okay? Fyn and Bridget?"

His gaze snaps up to meet mine. "No, they're fine. At least, I assume they are. I haven't heard from them or the guards in Italy otherwise, so that should mean there's nothing to be concerned about."

"Then why do you look like you just sucked on a lemon?"

He presses his lips together in a firm line and considers me for a moment.

You shouldn't pry...

This is exactly the behavior he despises so much about you.

I hold up my hands in apology at his continued glare. "Sorry, I shouldn't have asked."

Be silent.

Pretend you're not even here.

I turn to head back outside and leave him to whatever he's doing.

"I'm worried about Gran."

A lump lodges in my throat, and I spin back to face him. "Is she okay?"

The sweet old woman, *everyone's* stand-in grandmother at the palace, welcomed Bridget and me with open arms. Just the thought that something might have happened to her makes me nauseous.

Lev sighs and moves to stand on the opposite side of the counter from me, putting the giant slab of marble between us —which is probably safer considering what tends to happen when we're close.

Fire spreads through my body at the memory of this morning when he appeared in the kitchen. I was about to head back to my room after making us breakfast when he slid up behind me, pressing his lips to the back of my neck and his hard cock between my ass cheeks.

Fuck! Stop it, Daphne. We're talking about his grandmother.

He slides his phone onto the counter, a faraway look in his dark eyes. "I'm not sure. She's been acting...*off.*"

"Off how?"

"Distracted...like she had something she wanted to say but wouldn't spit it out."

That doesn't sound like Gran at all. The woman never holds back if she has something to say—even if it might not be her place. She and I share that trait, which is probably why I've gravitated toward her when I've been here on visits.

"That's certainly odd for her."

"Yeah"—he nods slowly, like he's going through their conversation in his head again—"and so is the fact that she brought up family I didn't even know existed."

"What?"

He drums his fingers on the counter. I'm tempted to make a comment and call him out on it the way he did with me for doing the same thing. I somehow manage to bite it back when I see the tension building in the man who usually remains so calm and stoic.

His gaze flicks up to meet mine. "She said some of my cousins back in Russia were having some problem with the current government."

I narrow my eyes on him. "I knew you were Russian, but I didn't know you had relatives there. I thought your family had lived in Lovolia for generations."

He nods slowly and runs a hand over the stubbled jaw that's left the inside of my thighs so red. "That's what I thought, too. My father was born here, so was Gran."

"And before that?"

He shrugs almost nonchalantly. "I was always told my great-grandmother Irina fled Russia in the 1930s or 1940s because of some old political ties that put her at risk. She sought asylum here and got a job at the palace."

"Where your family has worked since then."

Lev offers another slow nod. "But I was always led to believe she didn't have any other family, nowhere else to go."

"Could these mysterious family members be from one of the other sides? Weren't your grandfather and mother both born there? Maybe one of their families?"

He shakes his head. "Not that I know of. My mother was an only child, as was my grandfather. They both said their parents were, too, which meant we shouldn't have anyone still there who Gran would know." He drums his fingers again. "And the really strange part is Gran never mentioned any sort of family left, even when I was *in* Russia."

"When were you in Russia? I thought you grew up here."

Goes to show how little I know about the man I let get all up inside me. Given our uncanny ability to bicker every time we're in a room together, we've mostly avoided each other whenever possible during my several visits to Lovolia since Bridget moved here. So, it's not like we've been spilling our guts and swapping family stories.

No, you just let him spill his cum in you and pretend you don't exist afterward.

I inwardly cringe and watch his eyes harden slightly.

"I did, but while Fyn was off at boarding school in the UK and the States, I was neck-deep in my training and then put to work for the Royal Guard."

"And that included going to Russia?"

He tenses and glances out the door toward the pool, probably wishing I was out there instead of in here yammering and asking him questions he doesn't want to answer.

His fingers continue to drum on the marble, the constant

sound the only thing hanging in the air between us besides the tension.

"You know I trained with the Lovolian military."

I nod. As the crown prince's personal bodyguard, Lev is responsible for his safety, at all times. And given what Bridget told me about the things he's done to protect his best friend, I had to assume he had training similar to that of our SEALs or Delta Force operators.

"Well, part of our job is protecting against foreign and domestic threats. One of those was the Russian bratva."

"Here? In Lovolia?"

He glances at me and nods. "I know it doesn't seem like it would be somewhere they're interested in because Lovolia is so small and a relatively peaceful country, but we also have a tremendous tourism business, and of course, they wanted to get in on it."

"How do *you* factor into that?"

He runs a hand through his hair and leans back against the fridge. "When I was in my early twenties, things got a little tense with one of the bratva groups. We knew they were running girls here, some of whom were trafficked out of Eastern Europe."

"Oh, my God."

His hands fist at his sides, like the mere thought of what was happening is enough to make him want to hit something. "Our local police force tried to stop them, but then threats were made against the royal family."

"Which made it a Royal Guard issue…"

He nods. "I was the only one who spoke fluent Russian, the only one who 'fit the part' and could potentially infiltrate the group."

"You infiltrated the Russian mafia?"

His hard eyes meet mine, heavy with anger, regret, and something else unplaceable. "I did. I moved to St. Petersburg, where the leadership for this particular group was located, and I did what I had to in order to prove my loyalty..."

Jesus.

Proving his loyalty to a bratva.

I can't even imagine what that might entail. Given what I do know about how vicious and violent they can be, it definitely isn't anything I want to spend any time thinking about.

Almost instantly, my gaze darts to the tattoos visible on his arms, hands, and neck, and I visualize the ones on his chest and back currently covered by the T-shirt.

"Is that why you have some of those tattoos? I wondered because a few of them are..."

There's no way to say it without it sounding insulting. One in particular flashes into my head. Over his right pec—a skull wearing a communist military insignia on its hat. I always found it a little odd, given that they went to work for the monarchy here.

He snorts and shakes his head. "Yeah, I had to look and act the part, or they would have seen right through me. I've had a few of them covered up since then, but not all—yet."

Constant reminders of what he had to do to protect his friend...

"So, you became a Russian mobster."

The corner of his mouth twitches. "I wouldn't go that far. They trusted me because I did a bit of their dirty work, and it got me access to their *pakhan*, who I needed to get to in order to put an end to the group there and here in Lovolia."

Put an end to?

His words send a chill down my spine. "Did you kill him?"

He doesn't answer me, but he doesn't have to. I see it in his eyes. The cold, calculating man he is when required. A formidable bodyguard, he's committed to doing anything he has to in order to protect Fyn.

I just didn't realize it went this far.

Infiltrating the damn bratva and killing the leader?

"Anyway"—he releases a dismissive sigh, like he didn't just admit to murdering someone—"I was in Russia for two years, and Grandmother never mentioned *once* that I might have family there."

"It was probably to protect you *and* them, given the reason you were there."

He nods slowly, considering my suggestion. "Probably, but still. Something more is going on."

No one knows Mira better than Lev, so if he's uneasy about the situation, it's likely for good reason.

"Why don't you call the Lovolian consulate in Russia and see if they know anything?"

His lips twist into a frown, his brow furrowing deeply as he begins pacing. "I might."

I haven't spent the amount of time with Lev that Bridget has, but from what I have seen, he doesn't spook easily. "You're worried about her."

"How can I not be? She's in her eighties and keeping secrets."

"We all keep secrets, don't we?"

He narrows his eyes on me. "I guess we do."

An awkward silence hangs between us. I need to change the subject before it devolves into another question-and-answer session about why I'm still at Elysium. I swallow thickly and motion to the refrigerator he's leaning against. "I was thinking about doing a seafood stew for dinner. Does that sound good?"

He bobs his head slowly, his attention elsewhere, staring out at the water. "Sure. Whatever you want."

What I want is for you to talk to me, to do more than just put your hands and cock on me and then walk away and not look back. We just had our first real conversation that didn't include hurling any insults or snide comments, so it *is* possible, but something tells me it won't happen much.

I won't hold my breath.

10

DAPHNE

My stomach roiling finally wakes me from what was already a restless sleep, just like it's been every night since I arrived in Lovolia for the wedding. A cold, clammy sheen covers my skin, and I throw back the covers and clamp my hand over my mouth in my rush to the bathroom.

The darkness of the room and my semi-awake state disorient me, and I slam my toe against the doorjamb before I hit the cool tile.

Fuck!

Pain slices through my foot, but I manage to hobble across the bathroom. The second I pull my hand away from my mouth and drop to my knees, my stomach empties itself violently into the toilet.

I retch and heave, and new sweat breaks out across my skin.

Oh, God.

My stomach revolts so violently that it feels like the whole thing might come up my raw throat.

Try to breathe.

In and out.

I take a deep inhalation, then exhale, but it only brings on another round of fierce spasms. Praying to the porcelain god has never been particularly high on my to-do list, and it's been a long fucking time since I got so drunk that I made myself sick.

You only had two glasses of wine with dinner last night.

You weren't drunk.

I wasn't, which means it must have been the seafood. Something in the stew I made must have gone bad. And now, I'm paying the price.

So much for my incredible culinary skills.

Though, maybe I should count myself lucky this is the first time it's happened. In almost thirty years of cooking for myself and others, as far as I know, I haven't poisoned anyone. Until today.

Brutal quakes vibrate through my entire body. Sweat trickles down the sides of my temples, and I heave again and again.

The last time I was this sick, Bridget held my hair back, got me a cool, damp towel, and sat with me on the floor all night. That time, tequila was to blame.

What I wouldn't give to have her here now, when it feels like my life is crumbling and my body betrays me.

Braced over the toilet, I wait for the next round of brutal assault. Everything I've done wrong in the last few weeks comes rushing back to me, almost like my current state was brought on by my shit decisions.

You should have told Bridget what happened the moment you landed in Lovolia...

You never should have been in that position in the first place...

Memories of that night hit me from all sides, and I heave again, tears streaming down my face.

Then you came here and fucked Lev...

Of all the damn men in Lovolia...

The attack on my stomach and my decisions finally stops. At least, temporarily.

Holy shit.

I fall back onto my ass on the cold tile and drop my forehead into my shaking hand, trying to suck in a deep breath of cleansing air. My stomach gurgles wildly, and that clammy feeling settles over my skin.

Did Lev get sick, too?

I wince just thinking about it.

No doubt he'll blame me if he does...and probably accuse me of trying to poison him. It's pure insanity how the man can go from so hot to so cold in such a short amount of time. After he told me more about himself yesterday morning than I've learned the last two years, he shut down and disappeared to the beach until the sun went down.

He went right back to pretending nothing happened.

But I guess I can't judge him for it, considering that my feelings toward him tend to waver between absolute hatred and a vicious, burning lust I can't fight as soon as he puts his hands on me.

Hopefully, he's okay and isn't suffering like this. I'm not sure I could bite back my response if he came at me now with his usual attitude. Any leeway and slack I've given him because of his situation with Fyn and concern over his grandmother just got flushed along with the contents of my stomach.

I struggle to my feet, my legs like Jell-O as I grasp the counter to keep myself upright. My death grip on the edge of the marble starts to slip, and I switch my hold on it to keep from ending up on my ass on the floor again. I'm not sure I could get up a second time.

Squeezing my eyes closed, I wait for the room to stop spinning, clinging to the counter like a lifeline. Finally, I ease open one eye. Then the other. When my stomach doesn't revolt, I crank on the water to ice-cold and splash some on my face.

It helps cool me down, but when I glance in the mirror, I cringe.

Holy shit, do I look like crap...

Pale, splotchy skin.

Red-rimmed, bloodshot eyes.

A vacant look I can feel deep in my soul...

I grab my toothbrush, slather on a giant dollop of toothpaste, and violently try to brush away the flavor of my vomit. That stew sure tasted better going down than it did coming up. Even thinking about that makes me gag again, and I drop back to my knees over the toilet.

But there's nothing left in my stomach.

Dry heaves rock my body, and I squeeze my eyes together, willing it all to end.

This must be what death feels like.

I manage to crawl back into bed and slip under the covers, but the shaking takes a while to subside. Vacillating between freezing and too hot. Throwing off the covers and tugging them back up. I drift in and out of consciousness, tossing and turning, unable to get comfortable before the sun finally begins to filter through the windows.

Shit.

Lev will want breakfast, and that *was* our deal. I cook for him, and he doesn't toss my ass out onto the street. The last thing I need is to give him a reason to do just that when he already seems so on edge about everything.

As far as I know, Fyn hasn't called him from Italy yet, but if and when he does, Lev will be put in an impossible situation. Either he'll have to lie to Fyn—or fail to volunteer information —or he'll come clean and out me. Which means I would receive an immediate call from Bridget, filled with far too many questions I won't answer over the phone.

Her few text check-ins were easy enough to reply to. Keep it light. Keep it breezy. Pretend everything back in Colorado is as boring as ever. But once she gets me on the phone, it will be a different story.

How have I managed to keep it from her this long?

Only sheer will to ensure she had the perfect wedding and honeymoon—and hopefully, Lev doesn't ruin it by mentioning I'm here.

The best way to ensure that is to keep him happy.

That starts with breakfast...even if I do feel like death warmed over.

I shove back the covers and sit up. The room spins slightly. I rest my elbows on my knees for a minute before I push myself up to standing. Somehow, I manage to trudge to the dresser, pull out a clean pair of shorts and a tank top, and slip out of the ones I wore while I lost my stomach this morning.

Throwing my hair back into a messy ponytail, I wander down the hall to the kitchen, relieved my stomach seems to have settled enough for me to get vertical without puking again.

Lev sits at the counter, reading a newspaper that gets delivered every morning. "Sleeping in today, huh? You know I like to eat before I go surfing. I'd appreciate it if—" He looks up, and his eyes widen, then narrow. "Wow, you look like shit."

"Gee, thanks." I rub my eyes and head for the refrigerator. "I appreciate your brilliant observation."

"Are you all right?"

"I think I got food poisoning or something from the stew last night." I glance over at him and scowl. No worse for the wear. In fact, he looks absolutely delicious in nothing but board shorts—his muscled torso on full display this morning. "Are you feeling okay?"

He raises a dark brow. "I'm perfectly fine."

"Damn, I guess I'm just the lucky one then. Probably a bad piece of shellfish or something."

He winces. "Yeah, that'll do it." His gaze lowers to my arm. "Unless you have an infection. How does your arm feel?"

I hold it up for him. "It's fine. No redness. It doesn't even hurt anymore."

"Then it's probably something you ate."

"What do you want for breakfast, eggs?"

The paper rustles behind me. "You don't have to do that, Daphne. You're sick."

I wave him off without turning around and pull out the carton of eggs. "I *do*. It's one of the *rules*, remember?"

A hard wall of heat hits my back. He grabs the carton and leans around me to take out the cheese and milk. "I said you don't have to do that. You're sick. Go back to bed. I can make my own breakfast."

I spin to face him as he sets everything on the counter. "But that's breaking one of the rules."

He tosses me an annoyed look. "Amendment to rule number two. You will cook for me *unless* you have food poisoning." He raises an eyebrow. "Better?"

Wow, is Lev being nice?

An awkward silence fills the space between us, and I slowly nod. "Okay, thanks."

I start to move back down the hallway, but his voice stops me. "Take several bottles of water with you. You need to stay hydrated."

A snarky comeback calling him "Daddy" sits on the tip of my tongue, but that might just turn him on. I swallow it down and turn back, but he's busying himself with making eggs.

Why the hell is he being so nice?

Don't let it go to your head, Daphne. He just wants you healthy so you can go back to servicing him stomach and his cock.

I make my way back to the fridge to grab two bottles of water. He doesn't even bother looking at me as I trudge down the hallway toward my room. But I can't care. All I want to do is climb into bed and go back to sleep for the rest of the fucking day.

♔

LEV

THE ABSOLUTE SILENCE of the main house should be peaceful.

Only hearing the ocean waves lapping at the shore *should* make me issue a sigh of relief.

It's exactly what I wanted when I came out to Elysium.

I *should* be thrilled.

Instead, a hard knot forms in the pit of my stomach, and I make my way to the kitchen, knowing what I'll find.

Nothing.

No breakfast lined up on the counter.

No note saying it's in the fridge.

No Daphne.

My gaze automatically drifts to the hallway leading back to the bedrooms. She hasn't reappeared since she went back there after breakfast yesterday. I assumed she was sleeping and recovering from the food poisoning and would be fine today, but the fact that she isn't here waiting for me with some snarky comment or witty comeback makes acid crawl up my throat.

Go and check on her.

If it were anyone else, I would already be back there doing just that, but Daphne has never wanted my help. She almost seems to see it as an insult when it's offered.

Though that could be because it's usually accompanied by a sarcastic comment from me.

Still, if I don't check on her and Fyn and Bridget—or Heaven forbid, Gran—ever find out, it will make me look like a massive prick more than how I act around Daphne already does.

I skirt the counter and amble down the hall toward her room, then listen at the closed door for any signs of life from inside. Silence greets me. Unease coils around my spine, tightening as I rap my fingers on the wood and again, get no response.

Shit.

"Daph?" I wait for a reply but get none, then turn the handle and ease open the door slowly. "Daphne, I'm coming in..."

No barked order to leave her alone.

No mumbled joke about "coming" too soon.

Not even a groaned resistance to being woken this early.

And the rumpled bed sits empty, the covers tossed aside and falling halfway to the floor.

"Daphne?"

A low moan comes from the open bathroom door to my left.

"Shit..."

I hustle across the room and step through. Daphne lies on the tile, her cheek pressed to it, hands held protectively over her stomach.

Bloody hell.

"Daph..." I approach her and squat next to her prone body. "Daph, can you hear me?"

She groans slightly and turns her face away from me even more.

"Yankee, you need to get up off this floor." I nudge her shoulder, forcing her to roll onto her back with a moan. "Come on."

Squeezing her eyes even more tightly closed, she shakes her head. "No. Staying here. Easier for the next time my stomach revolts."

Always has to argue...

"You are *not* staying on the floor."

And that's the end of that.

I scoop her up easily, and the woman is too weak to even protest it like I know she wants to and would be if she weren't trembling uncontrollably. Her small body clutched to my chest shakes the same way my knees did the first time I touched her —a feeling I am not at all ready to explore.

Blyat. She's really sick.

Her cheek presses to my neck. Soft breaths hit my skin and send a rush of goosebumps over it. One of her hands lands on my chest, and she clings to my T-shirt, crumpling the fabric in her fingers with what little strength she has left.

I take the few steps back to the bed and gently slide her back into it before I tug the covers up over her. "You need a doctor. You should be fine by now."

"No!" She tries to push herself up on one elbow but collapses again almost immediately. Her eyes, which were closed only a moment ago now stare back at me in a silent plea. "Don't call a doctor. I'm sure I'll be fine tomorrow. Whatever this is just needs to work its way out of my system."

"I'm calling Doctor Hatzis. He's the treating physician for the entire royal family."

"No!" Daphne somehow finds the strength to bolt up, wavering slightly, and grabs my arm. "Please, Lev. Don't. He'll tell Manuel, or Mira, or the king and queen, and it will get back to Fynix and Bridget that I'm still in Lovolia when I'm supposed to be long gone and back in Colorado. Bridget will worry and rush back here, no matter what I say." She tightens her grip on me, digging her nails into my skin the same way she does when I'm inside her. "Please. I don't want to ruin their honeymoon because I ate some bad shellfish."

Whatever the hell Daphne is running from, she doesn't want her best friend to know about it.

Can I really blame her for that when I'm doing the same thing?

This may be a forced holiday, but I needed to work through

my feelings about Fyn's kidnapping and my role in it, as well as how his marriage to Bridget is going to affect the relationship that's become the most important in my life. Whatever she's working through, she needs more time.

I consider her for a moment. Her pale, mottled skin. Quivering lips.

The heat of her palm wrapped around my forearm sears the skin there as if an actual flame licks at it.

And her damn eyes.

They beg. Plead. The desperation there is the same as I've felt. Her distress tugs at something in my chest I'm not in any place to feel.

"Fine, but if you're not better in a day or two, I'm calling the bloody doctor. There isn't any reason for you to suffer if there's something he can do to help you."

She releases a relieved sigh and uncurls her fingers from my arm, then slowly drops back onto the mattress. Her eyes drift closed, and I reach out and brush a strand of her blond hair back from her damp forehead. She leans into my hand slightly and issues a little sound in her throat that makes my cock twitch.

Fuck.

I jerk my hand back and push to my feet. "I'm going to bring you more water. Let me know if you need anything else."

Daphne doesn't respond, the soft, even breaths of sleep already raising and lowering her chest. I shove my hand back through my hair and stalk from the room, pulling the door closed behind me softly so I don't wake her.

The utter silence of the house surrounds me again, and I drop my forehead to the wood and fight the urge to pull out my phone and call Doctor Hatzis over Daphne's protests.

Tomorrow.

If she's not better tomorrow, make the call.

But that doesn't mean there might not be something else I

can do for her in the meantime. Pulling out my phone, I head back toward the kitchen, dialing the one person who always knew exactly what to do when I was sick as a child.

"Lev?" Panic laces Gran's usually calm voice. "What's wrong?"

I stop in the kitchen and lean back against the counter. "Nothing, Gran. I'm fine. But..."

How do I ask this without outing Daphne?

"But what?"

"I have a...*friend*...at Elysium with me who isn't feeling well. Probably food poisoning, but it may be a bug of some sort. I was hoping you had some super-secret grandmother recipe for something that might settle the stomach."

Silence lingers on the line.

"Gran?"

"Yes, sorry, Lev. I was just surprised you aren't alone."

Me fucking too...

"The visit was...unexpected."

Gran *hmms*. "I see...well, I have something that should be excellent for your friend's condition. I'll text you the recipe. Even with your lack of domestic skills, I think even *you* can make it easily."

I chuckle. "Thanks for the vote of confidence, Gran."

Her odd behavior the last time we spoke niggles at the back of my mind. "Gran, I need to ask you something about what you told me regarding family back in Russia."

"What?" Voices chatter in the background. "Oh, Lev. I have to go. Manuel just came to talk to me about something."

"Gran, wait. *Pozhaluysta!*"

"Sorry, *dorogoy moy*. I hope your friend feels better."

She ends the call before I can get out another word.

Gran has never been cagey. She's never been mysterious or withheld anything from me before. At least, not that I know of. But that's the nature of secrets, isn't it? You don't know you aren't privy to one until it's revealed. And she has one she has no intention of telling me anytime soon.

My phone buzzes with an incoming text, and I open it to find the recipe Gran mentioned. I quickly scroll through the ingredient list for the simple cabbage soup and send a text to the grocery delivery service that keeps Elysium well-stocked, then glance at the clock.

Prime time to hit the waves and work out some of the frustrations tensing up every muscle in my body right now, but instead, my gaze darts back toward Daphne's room. I push off the counter, tug open the fridge, and grab two bottles of water.

As much as I don't want to disturb her, she needs to stay hydrated if she's been this sick for twenty-four hours, and it's not like there's anyone else here to take care of her.

I carry the bottles back to her room and ease open the door again. She remains exactly where I left her, burrowed under the comforter, her chest rising and falling slowly, lips slightly parted, eyes moving rapidly behind closed lids.

It's the way I've always wanted her—silent.

She looks so peaceful like this, like whatever drew her to Elysium in the first place has finally stopped plaguing her. But looks can be deceiving, and knowing the reason she's not snarking back at me and making my blood boil with her cheeky comebacks is because she's sick means I can't enjoy this one bit.

I reach out to brush some sweat-soaked hair from her forehead, and she shifts slightly, leaning into my touch, her cheek against my palm.

Fuck.

I've never wanted to wring someone's neck so badly while simultaneously slamming my cock into them. This woman is more dangerous than anything I've ever had to protect Fynix from, and I need to get her out of here.

Fast.

146

11

DAPHNE

THE BEDROOM DOOR creaking open stirs me from a near-death sleep. I groan and turn away, unwilling to let anyone or anything disturb a surprisingly good dream about a man who doesn't always elicit pleasant thoughts.

All I want is to allow the sweet darkness to envelop me again, but a heavenly rich scent that reminds me of chicken soup hits my nose. My stomach growls.

Oh no, not again.

While I've managed to stay out of the bathroom since Lev picked me up off the goddamn floor and tucked me into bed like a damn child, the smell of food might be too much for me to handle.

"Daphne?" His deep velvet voice floats over me, that hint of command in his tone only making me more annoyed by his intrusion.

I groan again and bury myself even deeper into the covers. It was embarrassing enough that he had to physically move me off the tile. I don't need him seeing what I look like after I've been passed out in bed all day.

At least, I think it's been all day.

I've lost all sense of time since I've been here at Elysium. Having no responsibilities—or at least ignoring them completely—tends to do that.

I crack open an eye, but no sunlight streams in the window, so it must be late.

"I let you sleep as long as I could." Lev lowers himself to the mattress, and the bed dips. A large hand tugs back the covers, exposing me. "But you need to get up and try to eat something."

"I'm not hungry."

"Bullshit. You puked all day yesterday and this morning. I've been checking on you every hour or so. I know you haven't been retching the rest of the day today, which means whatever made you so sick is probably out of your system. Now, it's time to fill your stomach with something that will make you feel better and help you regain your energy."

My stomach gurgles again, and I press my hand over it. "I'm not sure I can."

It does smell good, though.

Not that I'd ever admit that to this man.

Lev already has a big enough ego; the last thing he needs is me stroking it and making it grow any more.

"You said you couldn't cook, so what did you have delivered?"

He chuckles and absently rubs his hand on my back. A slow and gentle stroke of his large palm against my spine. "I called Gran, and she gave me an old family soup recipe that she swears will make you feel better."

I cringe and glance at him over my shoulder. "I love your grandmother, Lev, but I've seen some of the things she cooks... and the 'old family recipes' don't really mesh with my American palate."

He chuckles again, low and deep, and leans in, brushing his lips against my ear. A shudder rolls through me as the leather and sea scent that always lingers around him invades my lungs. "If you don't get out of this bed, I'll simply pick you up and throw you over my shoulder."

I gape at him, mouth hanging open. "You wouldn't."

A slow grin spreads across his lips, and he climbs from the bed to his full height. "Oh, yes, I would, Yankee. Come on."

He tugs at my shoulder until I finally relent and roll onto my back, staring up at him looming over me. With the lights off, the moon streaming in through the window hits the right side of his face, half illuminating him, while the other half remains in shadow.

It's the perfect view of the enigmatic man.

Even when he's around Fyn, he doesn't say much. He just watches everyone with that assessing gaze that seems to see right through any metaphorical walls.

Maybe it's the way he grew up, always knowing he would be a member of the Royal Guard and that the prince's safety would ultimately be in his hands.

It made him hard.

It made him cold.

It made him calculating.

It made him far too serious for his own good, which is precisely why I must annoy him so much, because God knows, I haven't taken anything seriously in a long time. And I should have.

Something I was vividly reminded of the night before I left Denver and as I watched Bridget walk down the aisle to her future when mine is a murky, cluttered mess of instant gratification, temporary happiness, and long-term nothingness.

Drowning myself in vodka probably wasn't the best way to handle the whole situation. Nor was running off to Elysium instead of going home to face what waits for me there. But I can't regret coming here when the man who usually glares at me with so much hate is now looking at me with genuine concern.

It's exactly what I needed.

Not the arguing or the rules, but simply being somewhere I can *think* without any pressure to put on a performance...or have to deal with the fallout of my idiocy back in Colorado.

It is inevitable. I won't be able to hide forever, but this little break from reality has already helped me get my head around what I need to do. I just need to muster up enough courage to actually do it.

He holds out a hand, waiting for me to accept it. Those perfect, soft lips surrounded by a rough beard twitch slightly, as if he's prepared for me to say no again so he *can* throw me over his shoulder like a caveman.

I won't give him that satisfaction.

No matter how badly I want to stay in bed, *not* giving Lev Orlov the fight he wants takes precedence. I slide my palm into his and allow him to tug me up until I'm sitting. The room spins slightly, and I press a hand to my temple.

His warm touch settles on my shoulder. "You all right?"

"Yeah, just a little dizzy after being horizontal all day."

His light chuckle fills the space between us, but he doesn't say anything.

"Come on, Lev. I know you have *something* to say about that comment."

He pulls me to my feet, settling his hands on my upper arms to steady me. "Well, if you must know, a quip about being *horizontal* in other ways *did* cross my mind."

I glare up at him. "I'm shocked."

"No, you're not."

"You're right. I'm not."

That same electric charge that builds whenever we're in the same room—whether we're fighting or fucking—crackles across my skin. He jerks his hands away like my skin is on fire and steps back. I wobble slightly on my feet, making my way to the bathroom and pressing my hand against the wall as a guide.

Lev follows beside me, his concerned gaze locked on my every move. "Where are you going?"

"To use the bathroom and take a shower. I feel disgusting."

"But—"

I hold up a hand to silence him. "Then, I promise I'll try your gran's soup. Okay?"

His eyes narrow as I grip the doorjamb to keep myself upright. "I don't think you should be getting in a shower like that. You're too unsteady on your feet. You could fall."

I grit my teeth. "I'm fine, Lev."

"Bullshit, Yankee. While I appreciate the American can-do attitude, sometimes, you have to accept help from people when they offer it."

"Oh, yeah"—I snort—"you're real charitable." The snide comment slips out before I can bite it back, making him recoil slightly. "Shit. I'm sorry. Force of habit with you. I really do appreciate you helping me today."

He approaches me slowly. "Don't say that like I'm done and am going to leave you to do something stupid."

Do something stupid?

"What the hell does that mean?"

Lev reaches around me and flips on the light in the bathroom. "You're going to take a shower, and I'm going to make sure you don't fall and crack open that pretty little blond head of yours."

"*What?*"

I can't have heard that right.

He pushes past me into the bathroom with a firm hand at my lower back, cranks on the water in the shower, and raises a dark eyebrow. "You coming?"

Jesus.

It isn't the first time the man's asked me that question, but the last time, he had his dick jammed so deeply inside me I could feel it in my fucking chest.

"Do I have a choice?"

He shakes his head and crosses his arms over his barrel chest, his shoulders set and unwavering. "The way I see it, you either get in there voluntarily with my help, or I'll stop you from getting in there at all, and you can lie in your own filth for another twenty-four hours—after you've had some soup."

Control freak asshole.

I glower at him and take a step farther into the bathroom, my knees wobbling enough to clutch the counter to keep myself upright.

Hell...

I don't want to admit he's right about me not being in the shower alone, but the water sounds so good. The steam filling the room promises to help relax some of the kinked-up muscles from sleeping so long on the tile floor.

Pick your battles, Daphne.

Easy to tell myself that, not so easy to execute when staring down the most aggravating member of the male sex I've ever met.

I release a heavy, resigned sigh. "Fine," I grit through my teeth. "I'll let you help me, but"—I hold up a hand and lock eyes with him—"no funny business."

That damn smirk he loves to pull out when he knows he's won a verbal sparring session with me hits his lips. "I wouldn't dream of it, Yankee."

He might not dream of it, but I sure as hell do—and have many times since our hook-up at the wedding.

Him pinning me to a slick tile wall while he pounds into me. Dropping to his knees on the shower floor and burying his face between my legs. Our screams and gasps echoing around the small, enclosed space.

A shiver rolls through me, and he narrows his eyes.

"Are you going to be sick again?"

I shake my head. "No, I'm okay."

Although there must be something wrong with me mentally to have allowed myself to continue to have sex with him and think it wouldn't fuck with my head more than that one drunken night already did.

Once can be explained away.

We were both drunk.

We were questioning things about our lives after seeing our best friends get married.

We were both horny as hell.

We were both willing to overlook the animosity between us in favor of relieving the sexual tension.

But this continued...whatever it is...is far, far more complicated.

I take the final few steps separating us and stop in front of him.

Lev stares me down, dark brows slowly moving upward toward his unruly dark hair. "You waiting for something, Yankee?"

"Yeah. You." I poke him in the chest. "To close your eyes or turn around or something."

He snorts and leans in slightly until his warm breath, carrying a hint of something sweet—bourbon maybe—hits me. "I hate to break this to you, but I've seen you naked—several times."

I scowl at him. "That's different."

His brows wing up. "Do enlighten me."

"If you don't see the difference, I'm not wasting my time explaining it to you."

Swear to God, this man was put on the earth to drive me fucking bonkers.

I nudge him out of the way, and he steps to the side with an exaggerated eye roll while I reach down and grab the hem of my shirt. A glance over my shoulder assures me he won't see anything, and I tug it up over my head, letting it fall unceremoniously to the floor before shoving down my yoga pants and kicking them off my feet in front of the shower.

If he insists on babysitting me while I get clean, at least he'll be far away, on the other side of the bathroom, not staring at every flaw my body contains under these bright bathroom lights.

I slide open the glass door to step in, and Lev's warm hands settle on my shoulders before the hot press of his bare chest and everything else, going all the way down, meets the rest of my body.

"What the fuck? Why are you naked, Lev?"

His lips tickle my ear. "You didn't think I was letting you get in there by yourself, did you? What is it you thought me assisting meant?"

"I sure as hell didn't think you'd be climbing in the goddamn shower with me, that's for sure. I would've said no."

"And I would've made you do it, anyway."

👑

LEV

OR AT LEAST DIE TRYING.

Given her current condition, I'm not sure I would have thrown her over my shoulder like I threatened, but it would have been bloody close because there was no *way* she was getting in this goddamn shower by herself.

I've seen too many people do daft things in weakened states when they were too stupid to know better or too defiant and tried to prove a point. Daphne definitely falls under the latter.

She would rather collapse in the shower and potentially

drown than accept my help—typical Daphne. The spitfire didn't even want me helping when she sliced open her damn arm.

I lift her left arm and examine the wound there. "This has healed nicely. I can remove the stitches before we get in."

Daphne turns her head slightly to peek at me over her shoulder. "Really? I won't need to keep it covered anymore?"

"No, you won't." I reluctantly pull my body back from hers and turn to the counter where I left the medical supplies in case we needed them again.

She stays facing the shower, unwilling to let me see her nude from the front. I slide back into my place behind her and gently use my nail to peel up the edge of the Dermabond. She winces slightly, and I lower my mouth to her ear.

"Don't be so melodramatic. This doesn't hurt."

Her lips twist in a scowl, and I keep pulling, removing the barrier from over the stitches. She remains still, and I grab scissors and carefully cut and pull out the stitches, one by one.

I brush my thumb across the marred skin, now bright pink but closed, and she shudders against me, stirring my cock to life where it's pressed between us.

Bloody hell.

I jerk my hand and body away from hers and push on her lower back, urging her to move into the shower. She steps under the spray without a glance back at me. It hits her chest, and she releases a tiny sigh that makes my entire body tingle.

Daphne twists slightly under the water, letting it hit her face and neck and slide down her smooth skin. "I can't even be mad at you for being so demanding when this feels so good."

My cock twitches.

Down, boy.

This isn't the time to be thinking like that, not when she's sick and vulnerable. But watching the water cascade over her naked body, her lush arse swaying slightly as she tilts her face toward the spray, it's impossible to get control of that particular part of my anatomy.

I set the scissors back on the counter, follow behind her, and slide the glass door closed, sealing us in for what will undoubtedly be a very uncomfortable and not remotely relaxing shower for me.

Stepping closer, I stop short of pressing my chest against her back and shoving my hard cock between her cheeks like I want to so badly. Her beautiful arse calls to me like a damn siren, drawing me in when I should be keeping this shower *strictly* platonic.

"You let me know if you're getting dizzy."

Khorosho. Remind yourself why you're in here.

"I don't want you falling."

Daphne glances over her shoulder at me, her wet lashes thick and black, but the annoyance that filled her eyes a moment ago seems to have passed. "I will. I know you don't want to have to explain any injuries I might suffer to Bridget and Fyn."

How are you going to explain why you're still here?

I want to ask the question, but every time I bring it up, she gets cagey, if not outright angry, to the point that it makes me want to tie her to the bed until she reveals everything.

What does she expect to do? Hang out here until they return and then try to explain away that she's been here the whole time, and I knew about it and didn't tell them?

Fat fucking chance.

I can't get away with that, and neither can she, so the shit is going to hit the fan long before that. Until then, I'll bide my time, wondering why she's hiding out and lying to her best friend.

She leans forward to grab a bottle of shampoo, and her bum brushes against my crotch.

Shit.

I bite back a growl that threatens to slip from my lips at that slight touch, and she peeks back at me under her arm.

"Don't worry about it, Daphne. I'm not going to ravage you when you're in this condition."

"Gee, thanks."

Not that I wouldn't if she were up for it.

Christ, she's a beautiful woman.

As annoying as she is stunning.

Her blond hair darkened in the water.

Lightly tanned, freckled skin pinkened by the heat.

Wide flared hips and an beautiful arse that goes on for days that I want to plunge into.

But that's not what this is about. It's about ensuring she doesn't hurt herself, even if it is agony for me.

I reach around her and grab the bottle from her hands, squeezing some shampoo into my palm. "Let me do that."

She turns toward me, her brow drawn low. "Do what?"

"Wash your hair." Before she can object or find a reason to argue with me, I slide my hands through the silky wet strands and lather. "Don't fight me on this."

Daphne's eyes roll to the top of her head, and she issues a little moan I've only ever heard when my cock is inside her. I give her a low warning growl and still my fingers against her scalp.

"If you keep making that noise, this shower is going to become very un-platonic."

Her lids open slowly, and she stares up at me with wide blue eyes, drops of water hanging from the thick black lashes surrounding them. She stares at me for a moment, like she's contemplating her options, then swallows thickly before fighting a grin. "Sorry, I'll behave."

I snort and continue shampooing her hair. "I've never known you to be the type to behave. How did you and Bridget ever end up friends?"

They're so different that it's hard to imagine how they became best friends. Bridget can be poised and appropriate when the situation requires it. She's the type of woman who can be on the arm of a prince. But this spitfire blonde in front of me seems to relish causing chaos and flouting rules.

"We met in college, and our differences are exactly *why* we ended up friends. Opposites attract and all that..."

I pull my hands away from her and raise a brow. "Rinse."

"Yes, *sir*."

Fuck.

My cock twitches between us, and she glances down at it before a smirk crosses her lips. She tips her head back and runs her hands through her hair, thrusting her breasts toward my face as the water cascades in rivulets down the front of her body.

Over her heavy tits.

Her perfect nipples.

The flat expanse of her stomach.

Flared hips that beg to be gripped.

The little vixen is doing it intentionally. I know it, and she knows that I know it. But I'm not giving her the satisfaction of acknowledging it, not when she seems to be enjoying this game she's playing.

She must be feeling better if she's up for doing this to me, even if she's not going to follow through. This woman *lives* to get under my skin—any damn way she can—and she's already wormed her way there permanently.

Even after all this is over and she's back in Colorado, it would be impossible for me ever to forget Daphne Jennings.

She tilts her head back up and opens her eyes to meet mine, a challenge dancing in them.

Game on.

Reaching around her, I let my hand brush across her stomach and over her hip before I grab the conditioner from behind her. She sucks in a sharp breath, and her body stiffens. I pull back, squeeze a dollop into my palm, and slide my hands back into her hair.

I slowly massage it into her scalp, relishing her heavy breaths and each little twitch of her body against mine. She pulls her bottom lip underneath her top teeth, fighting that little noise she knows drives me mad.

Why, when she seems to enjoy torturing me?

Perhaps this is too much and my concern about the heat of the shower when she's weak and unsteady was warranted. "How are you feeling?"

She peeks one eye open. "Okay. Most of the dizziness is gone. My stomach feels"—she rocks her hand side to side —"okay-ish."

"Gran swears this soup will put you right as rain."

She giggles.

"What? What's so funny?"

"'Right as rain' coming from *that* mouth."

I pull my hands away from her. "What's that supposed to mean?"

She stares up at me, her head quirked to the side. "Just not something I'd expect to come out of your filthy mouth."

"You think I have a filthy mouth?"

If anything, she does.

I've never met a woman who talks like her, so unencumbered by concern about what anyone might think of what she says. That mouth is nothing but trouble. So is the woman attached to it.

Daphne shakes her head and turns away from me to face the water. "Oh, I *know* you do. Like what you threatened in the *church.* You're a real contradiction. You know that, Lev?" She peeks back at me, not bothering to hide how her gaze traces approvingly over every inch of my body. "All muscle, tattoos, swagger, and grumpiness when you're on the job, but then..."

I slide my hand around her, across her breasts, and tug her against me so she can feel my erection pressed between her ass-cheeks. "But then what?"

She releases a little sigh. "But then, every once in a while, you let people see that you're actually human."

Hell.

That wasn't what I was expecting her to say at all.

Her words rip me open, leaving me exposed, like she can see inside to something I do my damnedest not to show.

"Or maybe people just see what they want to see." I release her and step back, putting some much-needed distance between us. "If you're sure you're all right, I'll leave you to finish your shower in peace."

She glances back at me and opens her mouth like she's about to say something. Instead, she bites it back and lets me slide open the glass door and step out onto the mat.

Water drips from me and my still-hard cock. I grab one of the towels off the rack and wrap it around my waist before I snatch my clothes from the floor and stalk out of the room.

Bloody hell.

Why'd you do that, Lev? Why'd you get in the bloody shower with that woman?

I release a heavy breath as I stalk down the hallway toward the kitchen. Gran's soup simmers on the stove over a low heat, and I pause long enough to stir it and inhale the pleasant scent. It's not something I remember having as a child, but something about the smell is almost calming.

I'll let Daphne find her own way out here to feed herself.

My job is done.

I put the lid back on and head through the breezeway to the guest house, slamming the door behind me, then wincing. The last thing I need to do is break the new glass after replacing it. Daphne would have a fucking field day, letting me have it if I did manage to undo the fix so quickly with my frustration.

Why do I want to hear what she would have to say about that? Why do I fucking care what kind of smart-aleck remark she would have?

That maddening woman means nothing to me.

When whatever she's running from finally comes to a head, she'll leave and go back to the States, and I'll only have to see her a few times a year when she comes to visit Bridget.

We just need to be able to be in the same room when we're forced together without arguing or going at it like rabbits.

That seems like a tall fucking order right now.

But it will happen.

Eventually, whatever this heat is will fizzle out, and we'll be something resembling friends—for Bridget and Fyn's sake. Because ultimately, that's all that matters.

They're the most important people in our lives, and we can't continue to let our animosity create tense situations for the royal family.

We need to act like adults and get along without ending up with my hands around her neck or my dick inside her, which would be far easier if she weren't so damn tempting...

12

LEV

FLAMES dance in the outdoor fireplace before me. Their warmth reaches the chair where I recline and lazily sip my bourbon, soaking up the few minutes of silence and the cooling night air.

I tip my head back and stare up at the thousands of stars visible above Elysium, a cosmic expanse of twinkling lights that make me feel even smaller than I have been lately—which I wasn't even sure was possible before this moment.

So small and unimportant compared to the vastness of the universe.

That whole situation with Daphne in the shower earlier didn't help the turmoil brewing inside me since Fyn's kidnapping.

Bad decisions breed bad consequences.

I lowered my guard and let Fyn go after Bridget alone that night...

It got him kidnapped and almost killed.

I let my guilt and distress over it weaken my control the night of the wedding...

It ended up with my dick inside the one woman who can draw me off my game and make me lose my cool.

And now...

I let her pain convince me to allow her to stay here...

Which is creating a whole different set of problems.

At least I managed to avoid her after our shower by staying in the carriage house and pretending she wasn't only yards away.

I should have stayed there, locked away, but I needed the fire tonight, something to distract me from all the random thoughts racing around my head.

A deck board creaks behind me, and I wince.

Daphne...

Rather than look her way, I keep my head tipped back, trying to maintain the relaxed posture and clear mind I *had* managed to attain for a few brief moments, even as her nearness seems to tense every muscle in my body again.

Finally, I bring the glass to my lips and sip the warm, fiery liquor, letting it burn down my throat. "Are you just going to stand there and stare at me, Yankee?"

I catch her flinch out of the corner of my eye, and she steps forward, rubbing her bare arms against the goosebumps pebbling her skin in the chilly sea breeze.

"I didn't want to interrupt you."

Too fucking late for that.

Any semblance of calm I may have achieved disappeared with that single creaking board.

I glance over my shoulder at her, fully taking her in for the first time since our naked bodies were pressed together in the shower earlier. Compared to her appearance this morning, she looks incredible, like nothing ever happened. Blond locks floating around her face in the light wind, skin glowing and healthy instead of the deadly pallor of the last few days. Pink lips plump and moist, as if she's just run her tongue over them.

Blyat!

"You're not interrupting anything." It's a lie, but it comes easily before I take another sip of my drink. "You feeling better?"

"Yeah, surprisingly." A half-smile curls those lips I can't stop staring at. "Whatever Gran put in that soup works miracles."

I smirk and offer a shrug as she approaches me slowly. "She said it was the cure-all for stomach issues."

"Well, it worked because I feel great." Daphne motions over her shoulder toward the hallway. "And now that I've changed the sheets on the bed, my room doesn't feel so hospital-y sick anymore."

I narrow my eyes on her. "Is that what you were doing in there?"

I've been trying *not* to imagine what Daphne has been up to most of the evening while I did everything to avoid her. Changing the sheets on the bed is the last thing I expected.

She nods. "Just got done."

"I could have called the housekeeper to come and do it. That's what she gets paid for."

"I know." She gives me a half-shrug. "But I don't want anyone to have extra work or go out of their way for me."

Just like she never lets anyone around the palace do their job and insists on getting in their way to do it herself.

"I would've helped you."

Her eyes soften slightly, and she tightens her arms around herself. "I think you've done enough for me."

The sincerity of her words causes another kind of warmth to bloom in my belly. One I don't want to explore further. I take another long drink to wash it away and drag my gaze from hers to stare at the stars again.

She moves closer, the soft rustling of her clothes and scrape of her bare feet on the deck making me stiffen. "Really...thanks again."

I focus on the vast sky above us, trying not to think about how close she is and how the heat from her body warms my right arm more than the fire. "For what?"

"For taking care of me the last couple of days, for letting me stay."

My entire body tenses, and I tighten my hand on the tumbler and bring it to my mouth to take a sip. "You know I'm uncomfortable with lying to Fynix and Bridget."

Whatever she's hiding from, she should come clean with her best friend—just like I should with Fyn about how I've been feeling since the kidnapping.

Easier said than done.

She releases a little frustrated sigh. "I know."

"And it would be much easier if *I* knew why you weren't returning to the States." I glance over at her, and that hint of a crack in her usually strong armor flashes in her gaze. "I've never known you to run from anything. You certainly don't back down from me."

A slow, satisfied grin spreads across her lips. "That almost sounds like a compliment, even though I know it's not meant that way."

I watch her over the glass rim as I take another sip. "Most women don't do that."

"Don't do what?"

I let a shoulder rise and fall. "Stand up to me, openly defy me, come back at me hard, and get under my—"

Bloody hell.

It almost slipped out—that truth I refuse to acknowledge about the woman standing in front of me.

Her mouth falls open, eyes widening. "Wow. Are you actually admitting I get under your skin?"

I flash her a grin and shake my head. "Never."

"What do most women do, Lev?" She shifts closer, until her bare feet almost touch mine where I sit. "Fall on their knees in front of you?"

I smirk.

"Oh, hell, they do." She throws up her hands. "Don't they?"

I raise my free hand, palm up, and shrug.

"I guess I shouldn't be surprised." She waves a hand up and down my body. "Given the way you look."

My eyes drift down my simple gray T-shirt and black board shorts, then back up to her. "Like a grungy surfer?"

She scowls at me. "That's not what I mean. And you *know* it."

"No, I don't *know* it, Daphne." I take another drink, trying to figure out how to ask this question and unsure if I really want the answer. "Tell me, what is it you see when you look at me?"

The blue of her eyes darkens as she assesses me, her lips twisting. "That's a loaded question, Lev, and it doesn't have a single answer." She wraps her arms around herself protectively, like what she's about to say might hurt *her* and not me. "I see Fynix's best friend. I see the person responsible for the safety of the prince who is the future of this country. I see a man who lets that fact weigh heavily on his shoulders. I see someone used to keeping people out, both because it's his job and because he's been hurt by something deeply in the past. I see one of the strongest human beings I've ever met who doesn't want to admit any weakness or acknowledge he's hurting because his best friend found the love of his life, and it feels like he's abandoned you when you're already feeling guilty about what happened to him on your watch."

I flinch at the truth in her words and how easily she sees right through me.

She steps closer, nudging my legs open to stand between my spread knees. "I see a man who's too handsome for his own good, whose dark eyes are practically molten right now with the fire-light dancing across them. A man who has somehow managed to surprise me in ways I didn't think he ever could."

Definitely wasn't expecting that.

The sheer vulnerability makes goosebumps spread across my skin, and I slowly lift the glass to my lips and down it, then set it on the teak table between the chairs.

I push to my bare feet, and with her this close, my body molds to hers. "How did I surprise you?"

"At the wedding. You and I"—she motions between us—"we've never gotten along. We've always bickered and intentionally said things to get under each other's skin. So, I wasn't expecting—"

"You weren't expecting to end up with my dick inside you?"

She releases a heavy, warm breath that flutters over me. "Yeah, *that*."

"I wasn't expecting that, either. And I sure as hell wasn't expecting you to walk in on me here at Elysium."

Daphne winces. "Yeah. Still sorry about that, *Yanky*."

Her play-on-words jab about what I was doing when she arrived and the nickname I always call her makes my lips twitch. "Are you?" I raise a brow. "It's given you fodder for any number of jokes, something I'm sure you'll never let me live down."

She doesn't bother to hide her grin. "Well, you're not wrong there. I do have a reputation to uphold as a stone-cold bitch where you're concerned."

I lift my hand to brush my fingers across her lips. "It doesn't always have to be that way between us, does it?"

"I don't know." Her blond brows rise. "You tell me."

As if it's that bloody simple...

"I don't know about any of that, Daphne." I feather my fingers over her cheek, brushing her hair from her face. "What I do know is that my cock hasn't been hard since the wedding without thinking about you."

She stares up at me from under her thick lashes, her lips parted, breathing heavy.

I glide my hand down to grasp her chin, tilting her face up to mine even more. "No witty retort or smart comeback, Yankee? Have I finally managed to render you speechless?"

"Oh, I have plenty to say."

With one quick motion, I slide my free hand around her back and drag her up against me fully, pressing my hard cock into her belly. "I promised you I was going to figure out a way to shut you up, didn't I?"

A whole-body shudder rolls through her, and I drag my thumb across her lower lip and slip it inside her mouth.

She sucks on it gently, sending a jolt straight to my dick, then lets it slip from her warm mouth. "I think it's time you tested out your method."

👑

DAPHNE

My mouth waters at the thought of finally having his cock in my mouth. The dozen or so times we've been together over the last week, it's always been so rushed, so frantic. So hard and fast. I've never had the chance to taste him, to drive him absolutely insane the way he has when he's gone down on me.

He narrows his eyes on me. "I don't think that's a good idea given—"

"I'm fine." I wrap my palm around the bulge against his board shorts and squeeze. "I *feel* fine. I *very much* have my appetite back, and there's only one thing I'm craving."

I drop to my knees on the decking and tug his shorts down as I go, freeing his length, heavy, hard, and jutting out in front of me, just waiting for me to devour it.

His fingers slide into my hair. "Fuck, Daphne."

My warm breath flutters over his cock, and he shudders, his jaw hardening before I've even touched him. I swirl my thumb against the bulging head, spreading the bead of pre-cum against the hyper-sensitive flesh, and he burrows his grip deeper into my hair, tightening it.

It would be so easy to suck him down, to swallow inch after inch, to take him to the back of my throat in one gulp, but I love riling up Lev too much to make this quick and have every intention of driving the man insane before I finally taste his cum.

It's only fair...

I lean forward and ever-so-softly glide my tongue across where my thumb just wet the head. His entire body jerks, and he tugs on my hair, shifting his stance slightly. The heat of the flames in the fireplace licks at my back, and the warmth of his body blocks my front, cocooning me from the cool breeze that had chilled me before.

Or maybe it's the fire of arousal coursing through me while I twist my palm around him, loving how his shaft twitches with the motion, how his body rocks forward, wanting more. The throb between my legs matches the rhythm of his thrusts, but still, I toy with him, sliding my left hand up to cup his balls, earning me a low, deep groan in his chest. I lift his length and slide my tongue from the root all the way back up around the head and down the side, slowly kissing, licking, and sucking but never fully taking him into my mouth.

He mutters something in Russian that makes me grin against his flesh, and I slowly take the tip between my lips and suck as hard as I can. His entire body bows until he's on his tiptoes, and he wrenches my hair hard enough to make my scalp sting.

Fuck.

I love that I can do this to him. Love that I can watch him start to lose control with one simple action. Love that when we're like this, he *isn't* the one calling the shots like he always insists on doing everywhere else.

It won't last long.

He won't allow it.

And that means I have to make use of the time I *do* have.

I let his cock slip from my lips, then slowly work my mouth over him again and suck him to the back of my throat. The warm flesh sits heavy on my tongue, the scent that's all Lev— leather and sea—permeating every breath I take. I swallow and suction hard enough to make him cry out.

"Fuck, Daphne. Fuck, fuck, fuck."

He thrusts his hips forward, driving himself slightly farther down my throat, and I swallow again, the head sliding so deep that my lips press to his pelvis. Lev groans, then jerks himself free of my mouth and slides his arms under mine to drag me to my feet before I can process what's happening.

I grip his biceps tightly, trying to catch my breath. "Wh-why'd you do that?"

Lev captures my face between his palms roughly. "Because I'm going to be inside your fucking cunt when I cum, not down your throat. We'll save that for later."

My pussy clenches at his words, eager for them to come to fruition. The feral need in his gravelly voice promises all the delicious things he always gives me when we're together, and I'm helpless to resist.

He kicks off his board shorts from his feet and lifts me to wrap my legs around his hips. His cock pressed between us aligns perfectly with my core, and I rub against it. He turns and stalks back into the house, down the hallway, into my room, heading straight for the bed, his lust-darkened gaze locked with mine the entire time.

Another first for us—an actual bed to have sex in.

Somehow, it feels more intimate. More personal. One more step toward what we've been running from.

He lowers me to the mattress and retreats to lift his shirt over his head. Lev stands above me in all his naked glory, every muscle and vibrant tattoo shimmering in the moonlight filtering through the window.

His shirt falls from his fingers to the floor as his heated gaze scans over me appreciatively. "You have far too many clothes on, Yankee."

Deft, calloused fingers skim the waistband of my pants, and he pulls them and my panties down and off my legs, exposing my wet cunt to him. His eyes zero between my legs, and his tongue darts across his lips. "Fuck, Daphne."

"I thought that's what we were doing."

His gaze cuts to mine, and the corner of his mouth quirks into a grin. "Always such a smart fucking mouth."

Can't deny that...

It's gotten me into a lot of trouble, and not only with him. It's the reason I'm even *here*.

If I hadn't been such a smartass...

If I had just held my tongue...

If I hadn't put myself in that position...

None of it would have happened, and I wouldn't have to hide out here with this man who drives me wild.

Lev prowls across the bed toward me on his knees, grasps the hem of my shirt and tugs it off, tossing it onto the floor with the rest of our clothes. One strong hand reaches above me to grip the headboard while the other clutches my chin to drag my face up to meet his. "You thought you were cute back there, didn't you, Yankee?"

He brushes his lips over mine, the taste of the bourbon he was drinking sweet and spicy on my lips, toying with me, teasing me, trying to unravel me.

A lie sits on my tongue, ready to slip out, but staring into his russet eyes that darken the longer he eye-fucks me, it melts away. "I was trying to make you come. I wanted to see you lose control."

He grins, and for the first time, I *really* see it—the man who went undercover to take out the head of the Russian bratva, who's capable of unspeakable violence with the hands he also uses to bring me pleasure. "Well, you're going to pay for that, Yankee." His head dips until his warm breath flutters over my ear. "I'm going to make you *beg*."

"For what?"

His teeth sink into the lobe, making my entire body jerk against him. "For me to let you come."

"But...I was going to let you come!"

He pulls back and smirks, shaking his head. "Somehow, I don't trust that's true."

Even now, the man doesn't trust me. Even after all the times we've been together, he still knows I'm holding back, keeping things from him the same way I am Bridget.

Trust can't exist between us, not when we keep so much withheld and contained.

He releases my face, reaches between us to stroke his cock, and aligns the head with my slick opening. One hard thrust drives him into me, rocking me back and creaking the headboard.

"Fucking Christ, Daphne, your cunt is a vicious vise."

Vise or vice?

Either seems appropriate at the moment. I squeeze around him to make even more of a point, and he issues a low growl that rumbles from his chest to mine. He lifts my hips with his free hand, leveraging himself with the headboard to push his cock even deeper.

A low, strangled groan falls from my mouth, and I drop my head back, arching into him, trying to find the friction my clit pulses for so badly. He grinds his pelvis down, and a flash of pleasure shoots through my limbs, tingling my fingers and making lights flash against my eyelids.

"Yes, God. That. More."

He stills, instantly stopping the ecstasy.

"Why'd you..." I open my eyes to meet cold, hard, almost black ones, and the rest of the words vanish from my lust-fogged brain.

The intensity lingering in his gaze sends a shudder through me. A slow grin pulls at his lips, and he lowers them to mine, feathering them across, then darting out his tongue to lick at the seam, remaining buried inside me, unmoving.

Fuck.

I squeeze around him and try to shift to get him to move, to get some friction, to get *anything,* but his answering groan and deep chuckle confirm he has no intention of going on easy on me or giving me what I need.

Smug asshole.

He releases his grip on the headboard and shifts back, grasping my hips hard enough to likely leave marks on the sensitive skin. Something gleams in his eyes before he slowly draws back, leaving just the head of his cock inside me, then slowly plunges back in deep, stilling again.

Our gazes locked, he repeats the motion.

Agonizingly slow.

Long.

Punctuated strokes.

Designed to drive me to the brink of insanity.

I claw at his forearms, digging my nails into his inked skin, trying to roll my hips to meet his, but his firm hands hold me down to the mattress, pinning me in place so he can work me over any way he wants.

He took back control.

Even though I knew it was coming, *knew* it was inevitable, I hadn't expected him to go *this* far.

I hate it.

I love.

I despise it.

I need it.

I want him to stop and go harder at the same time.

I *despise* what I'm about to do, that I'm going to give him exactly what he's searching for, that I'll have to watch that smug, satisfied grin spread across his lips when he wins.

But I can't stop it.

"Pl-please, Lev!"

He drives into me again. A smooth roll and retreat. Him clearly ignoring my plea, making me thrash my head.

"*Please!*"

"*Please!*"

"*Please!*"

"*Look* at me when you beg, Yankee."

Hell.

His demand makes me squeeze my eyes closed tighter, my body tensing even more until I'm quaking under his expert torture.

He glides his tongue across my lips as slowly as he does his cock into me, then stills again. "I know you don't want to, Daphne. You don't want to give me that satisfaction." He grinds his hips against my clit, drawing a soundless gasp from me. "But it's the only way I let you have what you want."

Jesus Christ...

He's brutal.

And I'm too far gone to keep fighting it.

I let my eyes flutter open to meet his. "Please, fuck me, Lev. Hard. Fast."

He doesn't waste a second, plunging into me instantly and rocking me back an inch on the bed.

God, yes!

The punishing rhythm he sets places pressure in all the

right spots. Hips driving. Pelvis rolling. The head of his cock dragging inside me.

He already has me so primed that it only takes a few moments before a surge of heat bursts from deep inside me, spreading out through my limbs, seeping into my blood—pure, unadulterated pleasure filling every fiber of my being.

My pussy clenches around him, and he grits his jaw and rams into me harder, reaching up to grip the headboard again with one hand to give himself leverage to find the angle he needs to find his release.

He comes on a low groan, spilling himself into me before he collapses to the side, heavy breaths fluttering against my cheek.

I bask in the peaceful silence for a moment, loving the sound of his labored breathing mixing with mine.

How am I going to pretend this didn't happen when Bridget and Fyn get back?

I shouldn't ask, but I can't bite the question back. "When are they coming back from Italy?"

Somehow, I've completely lost all sense of time since coming to Elysium.

Lev stirs beside me but doesn't look up. "Another two weeks."

"Wait"—I try to clear the lust still fogging my brain activity to do the math—"how long have I been in Lovolia?"

He finally lifts his head, his brow furrowed. "Three weeks. Why?"

Shit.

The sweat covering my body cools instantly, and I shiver, mentally counting backward to before I left Colorado.

My stomach roils.

I lurch out of bed and race to the bathroom, dropping in front of the toilet just in time to puke up everything I ate today that had made me feel so much better.

Lev comes to the door and leans a hand against the jamb. "Are you all right?"

Fuck. Fuck. Fuck.

Shaking my head, I pull it back and stare into the bowl rather than look at him when I say this... "No. You need to go get me a pregnancy test to take in the morning."

13

DAPHNE

I DRAG my head back from the toilet, flop onto my ass, and flush. That familiar sound fills my ears, and I wince, pressing my hand over my stomach.

Is this really happening?

It all feels like some wild, erotic, traumatic bad dream.

I scrub my hands over my face, then pull them back and stare down at the healing wound on my arm—evidence of the stark reality of the situation..

It fucking is.

Heavy footsteps down the hallway make me lift my head as Lev appears in the doorway, white paper bag in his hand, his jaw locked as tight as it was a few hours ago when I told him I might be pregnant.

He didn't say a fucking word then, just turned from the bathroom, grabbed his clothes, and hightailed it back to the carriage house. But now that the pharmacies are finally open for the morning, it appears he went and got me what we need.

Lev doesn't bother asking if I'm okay because we both know

what's likely causing my stomach issues. He steps in, squats in front of me, and holds out the bag. "The pharmacist told me to use this one."

I take the bag from him, yank it open, and glance at the box. "Yeah, this should work."

He pushes to his feet and shoves a hand back through his unruly dark hair, the bags under his eyes dark and giving away that he didn't sleep a wink after we parted ways. "Isn't it too early to test for this?"

I shake my head as I stumble to my feet. "No, it's been two weeks. Some women's bodies react strongly to the hormones and develop morning sickness right away. If I'm pregnant enough to have morning sickness, I'm pregnant enough to get a positive on this test for the hormones."

Which means any hope this will be negative is a false one.

He leans against the counter and scrubs his hands over his face before cutting an uneasy look at me. "Could it be someone else's?"

A vise tightens around my chest, the pain so real, it forces all the air from my lungs. I swallow back the newest wave of nausea and glare at him, trying to take a breath through the agony. "Fuck you, Lev."

He pushes off the counter and throws up his hands. "Well, I have to fucking ask, Daphne. The first time we fucked was only two weeks ago, and suddenly you're up the duff? Seems a lot more likely you fucked someone before you came here for the wedding. Maybe whoever you're running from and why you don't want to go back to Denver..."

I squeeze my eyes closed and take a deep breath before I lash out at him.

It's insulting as *hell* and shows how little he *really* thinks about me and my integrity.

But it's a fair question.

Given what little I've told him about why I've stayed in

Lovolia and how secretive I've been about why I won't go back home, it isn't an extreme leap to make that I might be running from someone who could be the father.

Still, the thought that he would believe I would lie about being pregnant with his kid…

I shake my head. "There isn't anyone in Denver and hasn't been for a long fucking time."

He opens his mouth, and I throw up a hand.

"And before you ask, there wasn't anyone else *here* either, during the week leading up to the wedding. Like I had any fucking time to go out and get laid by some rando with all the wedding prep."

A scowl turns his lips, and he crosses his arms over his chest. "Take the damn test."

"I will." I grip the toilet and use it to leverage myself from the floor. "Now get the fuck out of here."

I grab the door and push him toward it with the other hand on his chest, forcing him to step back until he's in the bedroom. The latch clicks into place, and I flip the lock, tear open the box, and set the test on the counter. I rest my hands on the granite and stare at it for what feels like an eternity.

Is this really happening?

Jesus Christ.

Please be a mistake. Please be a mistake. Please be a mistake.

Maybe it's a stomach flu, not food poisoning.

That's why it's not going away.

And maybe my period is late because of all the stress I've been under because I'm trying to make an epic life decision without my best friend here to talk to about it.

Yeah, maybe that's why. Keep telling yourself that as you pee on the goddamn stick.

I inhale a long, shaky breath, tear open the package, and piss on the little piece of plastic that's going to determine my entire future.

Fuck, fuck, fuck.

When I'm done, I set it on top of the empty box to wait for what will undoubtedly be the longest five minutes of my fucking life.

I lean against the counter, refusing to stare at it as it processes.

What if you're pregnant with Lev's baby?

The thought turns my stomach again, and I fall to my knees to dry heave over the porcelain throne. It goes on for what feels like an eternity before I can finally swallow and take a breath. The effort strains my sore muscles from the hour I've spent on the floor already this morning. I press my hand against the ache and drop onto my ass to lean against the glass shower door.

Was it only yesterday he was in there with me?

So sweet and gentle in the way he tried to take care of me when I was sick. The man cooked for me.

Dammit.

The man who is *useless* in the kitchen cooked for me, and now, he's looking at me like he doesn't trust me and thinks I would lie to him about this being his baby, if there is one.

Because remember, it could just be the flu and stress. Flu and stress, flu and stress.

Maybe if I say it a million times, it'll make it true.

I drop my head back and sigh, the sound echoing off the tile and glass in the space.

At least Lev can have a drink while he waits for his future to be decided.

I bark out a sardonic laugh.

Goddammit, Bridget's going to have a field day with this. And Fyn, God, what is he going to think?

His new wife's best friend came over and banged his best friend and got pregnant immediately.

What the fuck does that make me besides a whore?

A gold-digging whore, apparently, because even though Lev might be "the *staff*," he certainly isn't hurting for money, if this place is any indication.

I glance at my watch.

How long has it been?

My knee bounces up and down, the nerves starting to make my body shake violently.

Something vibrates in my pocket.

Shit.

I grab my phone and glance at the name of the caller.

Jesus, of all the times to call...it had to be now?

My finger hovers over decline, but if I do that, she'll only call back a thousand times until I answer. I hit accept. "Hey, Bridg. I didn't expect to hear from you..."

"Wow. That's a nice greeting from someone who was so upset I was leaving..."

"Sorry." I pinch the bridge of my nose and sigh. "I didn't mean it like that. I just figured you'd be too busy boning Fyn to call to chat."

She barks out a light laugh that brings warmth to a very cold moment. "Well, there has certainly been a lot of that, but I would have called sooner. I only didn't because I remembered you said you had a big project at work the week you got back, and I figured you'd be swamped."

Shit. Shit. Shit.

I *did* have to do inventory and reconciliation reports for mid-year...

"Oh..." I clear my throat. "No problem. I've been busy."

"But things are good?"

"Yep."

Fucking peachy.

"Then why do you sound so weird?"

"Weird? Um...maybe it's just a bad connection. I'm good. „. Tell me about the honeymoon."

She chuckles slightly. "It's been great. Lots of sex. Fyn cooked me pizza in this incredible wood-fire oven at his grand-mother's villa—"

"Oh, like the one at Elysium?"

A brief silence controls the line. "How did you know there's a wood-fire oven at Elysium?"

Oh, fucking hell.

"Because you told me Fyn made you pizza here, remember? Something about an argument over the monstrosity that is Hawaiian pizza?"

"Oh!" She laughs, and Fyn calls out something to her in the background. "Right. Yeah, hey, Fyn is calling. We are heading out on the boat. I'll call again. I promise. I love you."

"I love you, too."

I end the call and slide my phone back into my pocket. The lie I told her about everything being okay turns my stomach again.

Shit. Just look, Daphne. Go determine your fate.

I climb to my feet and walk to the counter but stare at myself in the mirror first. With my disheveled hair pulled back in a messy bun and my pallid skin, I might as well look homeless.

That's what you are, aren't you?

No real place to call home anymore.

What does that mean for this baby, if there is one?

I close my eyes one final time before I force them open and make myself look at the tiny little plus sign staring back at me.

♔

LEV

CHRIST, I really am a bloody wanker.

I shouldn't have fled from Daphne and driven to Crown Point when she showed me the plus sign.

I should have stayed and talked to her.

I shouldn't have said, "You've got to be bloody kidding me," and stormed out like I was ready to go on a rampage.

I shouldn't have ignored that terrified look in her eyes when she showed it to me.

All I did was confirm the very reason she was so afraid.

Bloody hell.

Coupled with the fact that I basically accused her of being a big fucking slut and I'm having a banner day when it comes to Daphne.

I suck in a deep breath filled with the salty tang of the ocean, waiting for the perfect set, the one I'll be able to ride long and hard.

Like you did, Daphne.

Over and over and over again.

Fuck. What the hell was I thinking sleeping with her? What the hell was I thinking, doing it repeatedly without a condom?

She said she was on birth control, and I had no reason not to believe her, but now, I can't get the lingering doubt out of my head.

Was this all some sort of plan? Staying in Lovolia after the wedding to shag and trap the prince's best friend? Thinking she could get what from me? Money? Connections?

Fuck.

Anger heats my blood as my wave finally comes in—at myself for even *considering* it and at her because it *could* be true.

I throw my pent-up wrath into paddling and wait for it to hit, then pop up on the board and ride it out. A massive tunnel of water builds behind and over me, cocooning me in a rush of something so clean and pure. But rather than continue on my path, coasting along the front of it, taking it as far as it can bring me away from the beach where Fyn and Bridget met, away from Elysium, away from Lovolia, away from Daphne, I turn into the wall, letting it crash over me and drag me under.

The rushing cascade pushes me deeper. My board billows above me on the surface attached to my ankle, bobbing and jerking wildly against the incredible force of nature.

But I don't come up for air even when my lungs start burning.

I'm not prepared to face what's waiting up there for me.

If she's telling the truth and that baby is mine, what the fuck does that mean?

My entire life will change more than it already has since Bridget walked into Fyn's life.

Why does this have to be happening now when Fyn's gone? The one person I could talk to about this?

Though, he would probably tell me I was a fucking idiot for ever hooking up with her. The woman I can't do anything but argue with ends up with my cock—and apparently baby —in her.

Bloody hell, what am I going to tell Gran?

The damn near saint of a woman raised me *not* to be the guy who impregnates a woman and leaves her crying in the damn bathroom alone when the reality of our actions stares us in the face.

But lately, it's impossible to tell who I am or where I'm supposed to be.

Fynix may say what happened wasn't my fault, but this forced holiday suggests otherwise. He thinks I need a break and can't handle the job anymore.

Maybe he's right.

My decision-making has been suspect lately.

Case in point—staying under so long. The burning of my lungs intensifies until I finally have to kick toward the surface before I'm forced to swallow the sea.

I thrust up and out of the water, gasping, and another wave

crashes over me and pushes me back under. After almost a full day of surfing and emotionally shredding myself, I don't have the energy to fight it. I let it roll over me, dragging me toward the beach in a frantic rush that mirrors how I've felt since I saw that plus sign.

It finally stops a few yards from shore, and I swim in until I hit the wet sand and collapse onto my back. My board floats at the water's edge, bumping into the bottom of my foot occasionally as I stare up at the crystal-blue sky—a perfect morning that's turned into a perfect afternoon as I've tried to hide from my problems on a board.

The waves will only get better here as the sun starts to set, but no matter how many hours I've spent cursing myself and thinking about all the things I did wrong, I can't come to any sort of resolution that doesn't hurt.

You have to talk to her, idiot.

I do, but I can't bring myself to get back in that car and drive to Elysium. I can't bring myself to look her in the eye, knowing she's pregnant with what could very well be my baby.

She told you she wasn't with anyone else.

Why don't you believe her?

I fist my hands at my sides in the sand and slam them down, then push myself up into a sitting position, running my fingers through my hair to get rid of the excess water.

A huge part of me wants to believe that she isn't the type of person to flagrantly have random, unprotected sex with people, let alone while she isn't on birth control.

What would that say about what I am to her?

At the same time, if she *did*, if there were a *possibility* this was someone else's baby, it might make things a lot easier for me.

I pound my fists into the sand again before reaching down to unstrap my board, dragging it up as I climb to my feet. The tightening in my chest only intensifies walking from the water onto the dry part of the beach, where my bag and towel sit against a tree.

This pristine white sand started it all.

The fateful place Bridget and Fyn met the night she got into an argument with Daphne.

Tequila led her to this beach and Fyn. Vodka and that wedding brought Daphne and me together.

Now, there's going to be a baby...

Your baby.

Deep down, I know that it is. I knew it the second she told me I needed to get her a pregnancy test. And I fucking ran away.

You've never run away from anything in your life.

Yet, the thought of being responsible for a tiny human being *and* being tied to Daphne for the rest of my life made me tuck tail and run.

What the fuck does that say about me?

That I'm a real piece of shit.

I shuck my swim trunks, pull on my clothes, grab my board, and trudge up through the sand and down the hidden path to where I parked my car. On this side of the island, with all the tourists a few hundred yards down the beach on either side, it's easy to be seen and recognized, so I load my gear as quickly as I can and tear out of here.

Two choices—the road back to Daphne and uncertainty or the one that will take me around the island the long way.

The one away from Elysium calls my name. I floor the accelerator and speed off toward the hotels and casinos, looping around the shoreline that will give me an hour to think while I drive.

I need to feel the wind in my face and hair, the illusion of freedom.

There's nowhere to go, nowhere to hide here on this tiny

island. Nowhere I can escape the reality of what's waiting for me back at Elysium.

You're going to be a father.

I swallow back the bile rising in my throat that instantly reminds me of how sick Daphne's been.

Blin!

She feels like hell and is scared, and all you're doing is being a fucking wanker to her.

I clench my fists on the wheel, tightening them around the hard leather as I shift gears and tear around the corner that'll take me along the coast. Maybe if I drive long enough, the answers will come to me.

Keep telling yourself that, even though you know it isn't true.

My phone ringing cuts my thoughts short, and I grab it from my pocket and quickly glance at the screen. "You have to be fucking kidding me..."

When your prince calls, you fucking answer.

I bring it to my ear. "Hey, how's the honeymoon?"

He chuckles. "As you'd expect. Fucking blissful, mate. How is your holiday? Sounds like you're on the road."

"Just got finished surfing at Crown Point."

"This time of day? You usually hit Elysium now and then go to the point."

Bloody hell.

"Yeah, I was out for a drive and decided to stop for a few sets."

"But things are going well? You've managed to keep yourself entertained in my absence?"

I manage a laugh that I hope sounds genuine. "I'm trying. Lots of surfing, sleep, reading, time to reflect..."

Fyn releases a sigh. "I hope 'reflect' isn't code for 'dwelling on what happened' because that's precisely what I *didn't* want you doing during this time."

The man knows me too well.

"Dwelling isn't the right word." I take a turn in the road, passing the hotel Bridget and Daphne stayed at during their first visit. "You can't expect me to forget it happened or ignore what my failure caused."

"Bloody hell, mate. You need to get off this and move on, Lev. You didn't fail. No one did. No one could have predicted what happened. No one could have stopped it."

"I wish I believed that. Enjoy the rest of your honeymoon."

I end the call and toss my phone onto the passenger seat.

And here I thought my day couldn't get any worse.

14

DAPHNE

THE PEACEFUL WAVES lapping at the beach below the cliff should calm and lull me into a sense of well-being like a lullaby singing me to sleep. But I never had a mother who did that. I put myself to bed—after I cooked myself dinner and cleaned up the house because she trashed it in a drunken rage and vomited everywhere. Instead of relaxing, my gut tightens more and more with each coil of water that rolls in.

For the first time in the almost two weeks I've stood here, watching Lev surf in the mornings, trying to remain inconspicuous about ogling him, guilt settles over me, tightening my skin until I want to crawl out of it.

I press my hand against my still-flat belly and look down at it, the pink scar on my arm next to the thing that will change my life.

I'm having Lev's baby.

The reality doesn't compute in my head, and no matter how often I keep telling myself—over and over again *ad nauseum*—that it's happening, my mind can't accept that in nine months,

I'll have a little screaming, kicking version of the man who seems to be doing the same thing.

He ran away.

One look at the test...and he fucking *ran*.

He left. Just like everyone else in my life who was supposed to stay.

That isn't the Lev I know, the one who would run into a burning building to save someone. The man who risked his life by going undercover in a tremendously dangerous situation to protect his best friend and prince.

I'd give anything to be able to talk to Bridget about this, but she doesn't even know I'm still in Lovolia.

Or that I slept with Lev.

Or about *why* I didn't go back.

I've lied to her about so much, especially over the last year, and I'm not sure there's a way back from it. There isn't a potential end to all of this where she doesn't feel betrayed and hurt.

Rightfully so.

If I found out Bridget was keeping things like this from me, I wouldn't be happy, but I can't just call her and come clean now. Not when she's blissfully happy with Fyn and enjoying their brief break from reality.

So, what do I do?

This is when having a mother who isn't totally useless would be beneficial. But if I call her, all she'll do is ask me what he's worth and assume I did it to get to his money—and act proud about it.

It's what *she* would have done had she been given the opportunity to be with a man who has the type of money and resources available to Lev. She would have trapped him any way she could.

But she and I couldn't be more different.

I would never do that to him, and I was *on* birth control, so this should never have happened...

Fuck.

I scrub my hands down my face and rest my elbows against the banister, staring at the water. The rocking of a boat out on the water brings a fresh memory.

Of the boat ride we went on that week before the wedding...

Of puking over the side due to my damn motion sickness...

Only half an hour after I took my pill in the morning...

Shit.

Could it be that simple? Missing ONE pill?

If I don't talk to someone, I might physically explode. Only one person comes to mind who's always been there, helpful, wise, willing to assist anyone with anything and welcome them into a warm embrace.

I pull out my phone and dial her number, letting the fresh sea air roll over me and pulling it into my lungs in long, deep breaths to try to calm myself before she answers. It rings three times.

"Hello?"

Her familiar voice almost makes me end the call, but I swallow back my fear and try to put a smile into my words. "Hi, Mira. It's Daphne."

"Oh, Daphne, dear. How are you? Was your return flight pleasant?"

Shit, my return flight.

She thinks I'm back in the States, assumes I went home like everyone else. I swallow the truth. "It was good, but, um..."

"Are you all right, dear?"

The genuine concern lacing her words stabs at my heart. Lev is so damn lucky to have a grandmother like her. Maybe if mine had been alive, I would have had somewhere else to go, someone else to turn to when I needed an adult to *adult* so I didn't have to before I even hit double-digit age.

I fight back the tears, inhaling deeply through my nose and out through my mouth. "Yes and no."

"Oh, *miliyah*, what's going on?"

Watch your words, Daphne.

"Anything I tell you stays between us, right?"

"Of course, you needn't even ask." Her answer, without a second of hesitation, releases some of my unease.

"I can't talk to Bridget." I tighten my free hand on the wood railing. "I don't want to interrupt the honeymoon, but..."

"Oh dear, this sounds serious."

"Life changing." I inhale a deep breath of ocean air. "I'm pregnant."

Mira is silent for a few moments before she clears her throat. "I would say that's wonderful news, but from the sound of your voice, I sense perhaps you're not feeling that way about it."

"I...I don't really know what to feel, to be honest. Things are...complicated with the father, to say the least."

They haven't *invented* a word to describe whatever this is between Lev and me.

Hatred.

Lust.

Annoyance.

Attraction.

None of them seem right.

"Does he not want to be involved?"

I push the hair blowing in my face behind my ear. "I don't know. It doesn't seem like it. At least, initially, when he found out."

She hums lightly, a soothing sound that settles over me like a warm blanket. "And do you *want* him involved?"

A good question I hadn't even begun to consider.

"If he doesn't want this baby, then no. I wouldn't force him to be a father to a child he cares nothing about."

Even saying those words makes me gag again, and I lower my head over the banister in case something comes back up.

Dry heaves rack my body violently, and I can't bite back the groan when they finally stop.

"I know that sound. How far along are you?"

"Not far."

"Given the way you're talking, I assume you plan on having the baby."

My eyes fly open. "Yes, of course, I am. I may not be ready for this, but I've always wanted kids. I just didn't expect it to happen this way."

"Oh, honey, I know how hard it is raising a child by yourself. My husband died when our son was quite young, and then the car accident took my boy and Lev's mother when he was only eight, so I raised him, as well. But I had everyone at the palace, an entire village, to help with him. You can have that, too. You can do it."

"Not in Colorado. There's nothing for me there anymore. But I could never stay here, either, not when..."

"Not when what, dear?" She pauses a moment. "Is the father..." She trails off. "Someone in Lovolia?"

I bite my lip to keep the truth from slipping out inadvertently. "It's just...always a bit tense when I'm at the palace. I don't fit in there. I'm not meant to be around royals."

Mira barks out a laugh that instantly warms my heart. "Oh, child. No one is 'meant to be around' the royals. They're just people, the way you and I are. My family has worked for the Yates family for generations, and I can tell you that they eat, sleep, and shit the same way you and I do."

My mouth drops open. "Mira, you can't talk about the king and queen that way."

She chuckles. "I can talk about them any way I so choose. Though, maybe not in front of them."

I grin even though she can't see it. Pressing my palm to my forehead, I close my eyes. "I'm not sure what to do."

"You'll figure it out, dear. And I'm always here if you need help or need to talk."

"I could use some more recipes like the one for the soup. This morning sickness is killing me and is more like all-day sickness."

Silence lingers on the line, drawing out second by second until I finally snap my eyes open.

Oh, shit.

My mistake slams into me word by word.

"My soup, dear? How would you..."

I can almost *see* the wheels turning in her head. The truth registering in her wise old eyes that often see too much.

"Daphne, you referred to Colorado as 'there' and Lovolia as 'here' just now. Are you at Elysium?"

I wince. *Fuck.* "Um..."

"Daphne, listen to me very carefully." Mira's entire tone changes, an edge of tension and perhaps fear lacing her words. "I need you to tell me if you're at Elysium. It's important."

There isn't any point in denying it—I fucked up. "Yes, I am."

"I need to talk to Lev."

Panic seizes my chest, making it impossible to draw in a breath. "No, you can't say anything to him. He can't know that I told you. He—"

"Where are you right now?

I glance around me with unfocused vision. "Standing outside on the deck near the top of the stairs down to the beach, looking at the ocean."

"Where's my grandson?"

"I don't know. He left this morning, and I haven't heard from or seen him since."

Since he ran from me like I had the plague.

Mira jostles her phone like she's moving around quickly. "I'll find him. Go inside and stay there."

What the hell?

"Mira, what's going on?"

Lev's words from earlier about the strange way his grandmother was acting come rushing back.

"Don't worry, dear. Just please go and lie down. You have enough to think about right now. You need rest. I'll find Lev."

♔

LEV

ALLOWING my damp towel to slide to the floor in my closet, I tip my head side to side, trying to release the tension by getting it to crack. It finally does, and I huff in relief before grabbing my jeans and tugging them on.

I pull a white button-down from a hanger and slide the final button into place when the continued beeping near the bed pulls me from the closet.

All right, all right, I hear you.

I needed that shower to get all the salt and seawater off my body, but knowing Daphne was so close in the main house returned the tension immediately when I stepped out from under the hot, soothing spray. Now the incessant noise from my phone ratchets it up tenfold.

What now?

Fyn knows better than to try to call me back so soon. He will understand my need for space. But it could be someone from the security team calling with a problem.

Bloody hell.

I hustle to my nightstand, grab it, and check the screen.

Four missed calls from Gran.

Her weird behavior during our last call rushes to the forefront of my mind. The old woman is keeping something from me and has no intention of revealing her secrets until she's damn well ready. Which she's made abundantly clear isn't now.

That means her call could be a problem at the palace that Manuel hasn't reached out to me about yet.

I call her back as I return to the bathroom and run my hand through my hair, trying to tame the wild curls.

"Lev, thank God—"

"I saw you called a few times. What's wrong, Gran?"

She pants slightly, as if she's out of breath. "You need to come back to the palace."

"What?" I freeze with my hand buried in my unruly strands. "Are you all right?"

"I am. I'm fine. Truly. But we need to talk. Privately. Just you and me."

I groan, press my hands against the counter, and let my head drop low, stretching out my neck. "Can it wait, Gran? I have some other things going on."

"I know."

Two words cause ice to flood my veins, and I stiffen, unable to move or breathe until I confirm what I know in my gut. "What do you mean? You know *what*?"

She releases an almost annoyed sigh. "I talked to Daphne, Lev. I know she's pregnant, and I know it's your baby."

Bloody hell.

Why the fuck did she tell Gran?

"And don't you be angry at that poor girl. She didn't mean to let it slip. You have no idea what happens to your body and brain when those hormones start kicking in."

I don't want to know.

Daphne is already a handful enough. More like two handfuls. Her luscious backside. Her breasts. Her flared hips. Her thighs that have the perfect jiggle to them when she walks.

Fuck.

"Get back here now, Lev." It isn't a request from the woman who raised me. It's an order, something she doesn't often do. "It's urgent we speak."

The word *urgent* rings in my ears.

What could possibly be so urgent all of a sudden when she was avoiding me like the bloody plague only days ago?

"Gran, just tell me what the fuck is going on."

"Lev Alexander Orlov, you do not speak to me like that."

I wince, her reproach more than warranted. "Sorry, Gran. I'm a little out of sorts at the moment."

"I can imagine. But I need to see you. There are things you need to see and things I need to tell you." She sounds out of breath again, the strain in her voice thickening. "And it can't wait any longer. *Priyezzhay srazu.* Get back here as fast as you can."

I release a heavy sigh. As much as I wanted to crawl into bed and drink away my problems for one more night before initiating a very uncomfortable talk with Daphne, this gives me a good excuse to take a bit more time to prepare.

No one says no when Gran commands their presence.

"Fine. I'll be there in forty-five minutes."

"Meet me in my suite where we can talk privately."

Talk privately?

We've never had any issues openly discussing anything anywhere in the palace. We're surrounded by friends, people who have become more like one large family. There shouldn't be anything we can't say in front of anyone within those austere walls.

Instantly, my chest tightens. "Gran, are you sure *you're* all right?"

"I'm quite all right, *dorogoy moy*. But—"

"Yeah, I know. You need to talk to me."

"Lose the attitude."

I snort. "How long have you known me, Gran? The attitude comes with the package."

"I know, *dorogoy moy*, but that attitude is going to get you in a whole lot of trouble."

"It already has. I'll see you soon."

I end the call and stare at myself in the mirror, seeing every bit of the stress I've been under during this forced holiday in the bags under my eyes. If I can't pull myself together and control my emotions and life, things will only deteriorate.

This break was supposed to help me clear my head and move past the kidnapping, but it's only complicated things even more.

The constant bickering with Daphne is what led to all of this. If I'd stayed away and left the tension between us to fizzle out on its own, none of this would be happening.

Why couldn't you leave well enough alone?

Because you're weak, and that weakness has caused everything that's fucked up in your life right now.

"Fuck..."

There isn't any time to linger and consider what a royal mess I've created.

I quickly finish my hair, brush my teeth, and throw my stuff into the duffel bag I brought, then hustle down the steps, through the repaired door, and open the garage.

The quicker I can get out of here, the better.

Perhaps this forced chat with Gran will give me the perspective on the situation I desperately need.

The door to the main house opens behind me, and the slight creak in the hinges Fyn and I never bothered to get fixed fills my ears like a grenade going off. Even keeping my back to her, I can *feel* her gaze raking over me, examining me with an intensity that might as well set me on fire.

"Are you leaving?"

Her usually strong voice reaches me, vulnerable this time. Full of questions I can't answer at the moment.

I rub the base of my skull and scowl over my shoulder at her. "Are you my keeper now?"

She recoils slightly. "No, I just wanted to tell—"

"Tell me that my grandmother knows. Yeah, I fucking got that. Thanks."

Her mouth falls open. "I didn't mean to say anything. I wasn't thinking. I just—"

"You just told my grandmother that you're pregnant with my baby before I got a chance to figure out what the fuck any of this means."

"I'm sorry, Lev—"

I hold up a hand to stop her from continuing. "I don't want to hear your apologies. I need to go to the palace to see Gran."

"Is she mad?"

That isn't the right word.

"I don't know what the hell she is, but she wants me to come home to talk. So that's what I'm doing."

"Rather than stay here and talk to me?"

I keep my back to her, standing at the door. "You can stay here until Bridget and Fyn get back. Then you're going to have to figure something else out."

"You aren't coming back?"

I peer at her over my shoulder, trying not to focus on the red rimming her eyes or the puffiness of her cheeks from crying. "I don't know. You know where I'll be."

She takes a single step forward, her arms wrapped around herself protectively. "We're really not going to talk about this?"

Shaking my head, I stalk toward the open garage. "Not right now. Not until I find out what the hell is going on with my grandmother."

That was another dick move.

Yet it doesn't stop me from throwing my bag onto the passenger seat and sliding into the car.

Whatever has Gran so riled up put me right back on the edge I was teetering on all day. If I stay, I may fall off it and say or do something I regret later.

It's better I go. Take some time away from Daphne and the

pressure of making decisions I'm not ready for. That way, when we do talk, I can do it with a clear head and heart.

Neither of which I currently possess.

I start the car, throw it into reverse, and back out of the garage, intentionally avoiding looking at Daphne where she stands near the front door.

If I look back, I might stop. That wouldn't be good for either of us right now. Not when I'm like this. First, I need to find out why Gran has been so shady lately. Once that's resolved, I can concentrate on *other* matters.

But I know she'll want to discuss something else the moment I walk through her door.

Daphne told her she's pregnant, which means I'm about to get a patented Gran lecture.

Probably one for the ages.

15

LEV

A HEAVINESS SETTLES over me pulling out of the driveway from Elysium—just like it *always* does. Only this time, the weight crushes my chest, making it harder and harder to breathe despite the crisp, fresh air floating around me.

I'm not in the headspace to process the current situation, nor am I inclined to hash this out with Daphne or my Gran today. Although, one of those women isn't so easily put off. I can drive away from Daphne and Elysium, but I can't say no when *Gran* demands my presence.

Fuck...

Daphne...

I scrub a hand over my beard, and that look she gave me from the front of the house as I drove away, her arms wrapped protectively around herself, flashes before my eyes and shreds my soul.

You've been a dick.

She doesn't deserve any of this. She doesn't deserve to be

tied to and have to deal with a wanker like me for the rest of her life.

Selfish. Hard-headed. Set in my ways. Stubborn as the day is long...

Not my best qualities.

Plus, being the personal guard to the Crown Prince of Lovolia and in charge of his and his new wife's safety isn't exactly conducive to siring children and being home to tuck them into bed every night.

I have responsibilities that will always be top priority.

Even over the woman having your baby?

"*Blyat!*" I slam my hand against the steering wheel before raking it through my hair. The sea air swirls around me but does nothing to help blow away any of my frustration. "You're a real fuck up."

I can't seem to do anything right. First, I failed Fyn. Then I made the bloody ridiculous decision to hook-up with Daphne. And now, I'm acting like a total wanker when it comes to dealing with the consequences.

How in the bloody hell am I supposed to be a father?

I don't have time to consider the answer to that question. Tires squeal behind me, and a cacophony of horns blares. An engine revs.

What the fuck?

My eyes dart to the rearview mirror in time to catch a blacked-out SUV veering around a car a few hundred yards behind me. It barrels into oncoming traffic before jerking back into the proper lane and accelerating toward me.

"Shit!"

The driver must be under the influence.

Their erratic driving will cause a crash. Only the light traffic on the coastal road has prevented one from happening already. As soon as I can pull over, I'll alert the police to ensure they stop the driver before any damage is done. The closer we get to the city, the more threat they'll pose to residents and tourists.

I step on the accelerator, pressing it to the floor, trying to find somewhere to get off the road and out of their path. The engine purrs, and I take the next turn along the coast, passing the cove.

The SUV roars around the corner after me. It eats up the distance between us, like the driver is on a mission. This is no mere tourist who's had too many drinks on the beach. Whoever's driving that SUV has the skills of the a professional, otherwise they would have flipped or slammed into another vehicle by now.

Bloody hell.

I shift gears and skate around another corner, casting a quick glance to my side mirror to see the SUV careening after me.

This isn't random.

They're chasing me...

Dropping the car into second gear, I take the next right turn off the main road to confirm my suspicion. I know this island like the back of my hand, including multiple routes in and around the city. As Fyn's personal guard, it's imperative I have multiple escape plans in place. My mind and body go on autopilot. Muscle memory takes over to enact one of those plans to extract myself from what could be a deadly situation.

If someone's after me, are Fynix and Bridget safe?

That question tightens my gut and my hands on the wheel.

I should have gone with them.

I should have forced the issue.

The SUV continues its chase, following me down the side street no tourist would have reason to be on—unless they were following me. It confirms my suspicion and allows me to lead them away from the most populated areas we were quickly approaching on the coastal road.

A loud crack sounds at the same instant my driver's side window shatters, sending glass shards flying against the side of my body.

Bloody hell!

Those fuckers are shooting at me.

Another crack sounds, and a sharp bite of pain lances my left arm.

Fuck.

Crimson blood saturates my shirt sleeve at my bicep and spreads, dripping down my elbow and onto the leather seats.

"Fucking hell!"

I pound the steering wheel, my frustration growing with each passing second. Blood seeps from the wound, but the adrenaline and anger coursing through my veins block the pain enough for me to grip the wheel with my left hand while I pull my gun from the holster at my back.

Sirens wail in the distance, growing closer. Someone probably called the police about the erratic driving, but it may be too late.

They close in on me, the SUV's revving engine roaring in my ears.

I brace the wheel against my knees, grasp the gun with both hands, and rack the slide before returning one hand to steer and resting my weapon on my lap.

These fuckers aren't going to stop until I'm dead.

Not today.

I clutch in, throw the Spider into second gear, and throw the wheel to the left, spinning with squealing tires to face the oncoming SUV.

The abrupt move leaves only a few hundred yards between us, the distance disappearing quickly as we barrel toward each other. I grip my pistol, lean to the left, and fire.

Someone leans out the passenger side of the SUV and

returns the volley. Bullets slam into the Spider, tearing easily through the metal and shattering the windshield.

Several of my shots hit their mark, leaving spiderwebbing on their windshield, but with an empty clip, I'm a sitting duck.

I can't risk taking more gunfire or putting innocent people in harm's way. Our game of chicken brings us within a few yards. At the last second, I jerk the wheel to the right and barrel around the next corner with a sharp turn the SUV can't make in time.

They'll have to double back to track me, which buys me time to put some distance between us. But the incessant wail of sirens grows louder. They won't chase me now. Not if they're as smart as I think they are. They'll haul arse out of town to regroup rather than make another attempt with the police so close.

As much as I want to chase after them and determine who these fuckers are, I need to get to the palace. To safety. Ensure Fynix, Bridget, and the king and queen are all secured.

I wince, gripping the wheel with my injured arm, and shift gears, racing toward home. Gritting my teeth against the burn in my arm, I dig into my pocket for my phone and call Manuel.

Had I been paying better attention instead of having my head shoved up my arse, I might have noticed my tail sooner.

This is why I shouldn't be a father or have a relationship with anyone.

What if Daphne had been in the car?

Rage surges through my veins, invading every fiber of my being and instantly replacing the pain.

They followed me.

She's at Elysium alone...

"Aren't you supposed to be on holiday?" Manuel greets with a chuckle.

"I bloody thought so. I've been attacked and shot at along the coastal highway between Elysium and the palace. I led them away from downtown and managed to escape. Get Doc dispatched to my suite, and I need you to get Daphne from Elysium immediately. She may be in danger."

Fuck, she better be safe.

"Damn..." His phone jostles, and he yells out orders to someone with him. "I'm coordinating as we speak. I will personally pick up Ms. Jennings. I am leaving now with a few other guards. Do you know why they were after you? Retaliation from the LLM for what you did saving the prince, possibly?"

"The thought crossed my mind."

It could be the start of another uprising, perhaps relatives and comrades of the LLM members who were killed seeking to cause further unrest despite the new government structure firmly in place for over a year now.

God help them if it is.

What happened to Fyn will never occur on my watch again.

Not to anyone I care about. I won't fail that way—I can't.

"Thank you, Manuel."

I disconnect the call and race through the streets, a heavy rock of dread settling into the pit of my stomach.

It will take Manuel at least half an hour to reach Elysium—leaving Daphne exposed for far too long.

I tap my phone where it lies on the console and punch in my code to pull up the camera feed at Elysium, quickly returning my attention to the road. Weaving my way through the city along the main drag, each moment I can, I glance at the screen.

Daphne sits tucked in on the couch watching TV, completely oblivious to the danger she may be in. If these assholes followed me from Elysium, they could double back *there*.

Not on my fucking watch.

I have to keep her—them—safe.

The agony in my arm intensifies, blood pooling on my seat the more I have to use it, but at least knowing Elysium is locked down gives me a modicum of comfort. Once Manuel and the guard arrive, only he knows the code to enter the gate that will allow them to pass through.

I speed through the last turn leading me to the private entrance of the palace. On my approach, the gate swings open. Members of the Royal Guard stand ready outside and inside the metal barrier—prepared to do battle with whatever enemy we may be facing.

They part to allow me through, and I speed across the grounds, my tires eating up the pebble stone drive. I pass the pond, the maze, and the gardens and stop at the palace's rear private entrance.

With far more effort than it should take, I grit my teeth and climb from the car, grabbing my phone and gun before I ascend the steps. The guards open the palace doors for me, but I pause at the top of the steps, looking back at what was once a beautifully restored classic—now riddled with bullet holes and broken windows.

Bloody fucking wankers.

Entering the palace, I stride down the hall toward the servants' staircase—the quickest route to my suite. I take the old narrow stairs two at a time and hustle down the hall.

The adrenaline high ebbs, and the pain of my wound starts to seep into my vision. Dark spots dance in front of me, but I can still make out Doc standing by my door, ready to treat me.

Thank fuck.

I've lost a lot of blood and don't have any time to be laid up while the entire royal family and Daphne may be in danger.

"I hear you managed to end up with a bullet in you." Doctor Hatzis waves a hand at the door. "Let's take a look."

I grunt my annoyance before turning the handle and

pushing my way inside. The familiar smell of leather and gun oil greets me.

Home sweet home.

But the usual sense of relief I get from entering the rooms that have been mine since the day I turned eighteen doesn't come.

It can't.

Not when so much is at stake.

I'll find whoever is responsible for this and mount their heads on my fucking wall.

Doc follows me, still as patient and unassuming as he's been our entire lives—always patching up Fynix and me, from falls and scrapes as youngsters to minor injuries with surfboards from us trying to do too much.

I lay my phone and pistol on the kitchen counter, unbutton my shirt, and peel the blood-soaked garment from my body with a hiss. The stab of pain makes the room spin, and I grit my jaw and toss the ruined shirt into the sink to deal with later.

Right now, I need my arm sewn up, Daphne safely brought to the palace, and revenge—precisely in that order.

"All right, son. Have a seat. Let's see what we're working with."

I round the kitchen island and sit on one of the stools while Doc places his black medical bag on the counter. He pulls out a pair of medical gloves and tugs them on with practiced ease.

"A good grazing, at least." I glance down at my seeping arm. "I think my car took the brunt."

Poor old girl.

Doc pokes around the wound. "Not a graze. Through and through. But it doesn't appear to have struck any arteries. Some stitches should take care of it. Let me get my things together, and we'll get this cleaned up."

I nod, but before I can answer, a light knock at the door has me whirling toward it. "Come in."

The door swings open cautiously, and Gran steps in, concern etched on her already-lined face.

She's safe.

Now, if only Daphne and the baby would arrive, this ache in my chest might ease.

I rub my fist against the spot to release the tension.

"I heard you've been shot. *Ty v poryadke*?" She approaches us slowly, her age suddenly so obvious, where it wasn't only a few years ago. "What happened?"

"Lev, this might sting a bit, but I'll be quick." Doc swipes something over my skin to cleanse it, then pushes the needle through the marred flesh. He glances up at me. "Are you doing all right?"

I manage a nod through the agony and try to focus on answering Gran's question. "I was ambushed on the drive here from Elysium. They shot me before I was able to escape." I tighten my hand into a fist on my thigh. "I don't know anything else."

A fact that pisses me off more with each passing second.

"All finished." Doc pulls back from the work he's been doing on me and returns his tools to his bag before slipping off the gloves. "You know how to keep it clean."

I glance at my arm.

That will be sore tomorrow.

But I'm still alive.

My phone buzzes on the counter, and I slide off the stool to grab it.

Gran's hand presses to my chest, pushing me back to my seat. "Lev, we need to talk."

A severe look replaces her usually calm demeanor, and the worry I heard in her voice the last few times we spoke laces her words.

"We will, Gran. But I need to figure out what's happening first."

I reach across the counter, grab my phone, and find a message.

MANUEL

I am arriving at Elysium now.

Thank God.

The vise around my lungs seems to release slightly, and I inhale a deep breath and let it out slowly. "Manuel has Daphne..."

"Oh, thank God." Gran releases a heavy sigh and opens her mouth but quickly snaps it shut when she meets Doc's gaze.

Doc offers her a kind smile and finishes cleaning up after himself. "All right, Lev, I'll have some medications sent up to you shortly. Follow the instructions, and you should be just grand; a little sore for a few days, but no permanent damage."

Gran wrings her hands in front of her, pacing slightly while Doc retreats from the suite to the hallway. The door closes behind him with an ominous click, and I turn my attention to the most important woman in my life.

"What's wrong, Gran? You're as pale as a sheet." I rub my hand along her arm. "*Ne volnuysya.* I'm all right."

Her failing health and struggles over the last year or two come rushing to the forefront of my mind, quickly replacing my worry over Daphne.

"We should have had this talk a long time ago. After today, I'm positive of that..." She fidgets with the necklace she always wears, rubbing her fingertips over it almost reverently. "I'm sorry that I didn't, but there is so much to discuss. It's time you knew the truth, Lev."

Knew the truth?

What the bloody hell does that mean?

"You're scaring me, Gran." This isn't the woman I've known my whole life. Looking at her now, she's morphed from a strong, vibrant matriarch into a frail, worried old lady, who apparently has a secret that's been weighing on her. "What do I need to know?"

She lifts her eyes to meet mine, an apology and pure terror deep in them. "Everything you think you know about your life is a lie."

♛

DAPHNE

I PACE the pristine wooden floors of Elysium for at least the hundredth time since Lev drove away from me without even a backward glance.

Back and forth...

Back and forth...

Back and forth...

My bare feet make soft slapping noises that explode through my head like damn grenades going off with each step.

Boom. Boom. Boom.

The deathly silence of the house makes it feel like more of a tomb than the luxurious, peaceful retreat it has been for Fynix and Lev. And it's all my fault.

Fuck—I did this.

I drove Lev from the *only* place he can come to relax and unwind when he so badly needs that. Fyn knows him better than anyone. If *he* insisted Lev needed a break, then the cracks in the bodyguard's armor had already begun to show to those closest to him.

My presence has only aggravated an already tenuous situation, and this isn't something that will just go away or get better with time. The longer Lev is gone, the worse my anxiety gets.

Back and forth...

Back and forth...

Back and forth...

Constantly in motion physically because my mind won't stop whirling and spinning no matter how hard I try to concentrate on something—*anything*—else.

Even my go-to mindless television drama hasn't been able to hold my attention since Lev fled like his ass was on fire. If *The Real Housewives* and their first-world problems can't distract me from this clusterfuck of my real-world problems, *nothing* will.

Cue endless pacing.

And thinking about all the ways I've fucked up so badly.

Going back weeks, every decision I've made has resulted in dire consequences. First, my smartass mouth got me in trouble in Denver. Then, the string of stupid actions since I got here. Trespassing on the prince's property. Breaking a window. And now, I'm going to have to pay to have these floors refinished because I'm wearing a damn groove into the beautiful wood with my neurotic movement.

Best houseguest ever.

Though, I guess I never was a *guest*. Far from it. I was—*am*—an intruder.

Unwanted.

Unneeded.

An interloper not fit to be spending time with the new princess.

The only reason I was even allowed to cross the threshold into the palace was because of Bridget. Otherwise, I wouldn't have gotten anywhere near the damn gates. They would have taken one look at me and tossed my ass back on the tourist beaches faster than I could snap a photo of the opulent exterior.

And now, my only tie to Lovolia, the only person I can rely on, is off enjoying married life with her new husband while my life is crumbling around me.

Everything in me says to call Bridget and unload it all. Get her feedback on my predicament with Lev and what happened back home. But no matter how many times I've brought up her name on my phone, I can't make myself hit "call."

I can't bring her into this when I don't even know what *this* is right now. Lev and I need to talk first, so I can have some indication of what he's thinking or feeling besides the obvious.

Angry.

He was so *damn* angry. And it devolved into yet *another* argument.

Typical.

Unless we're fucking, we're arguing. Two very different ends of a wide spectrum. One I never thought I'd find myself on with Lev Orlov—or anyone else, for that matter.

The push and pull. Hot and cold. Pleasure and pain. Hate and...lust. It all threatens to overwhelm me like one of the massive waves rolling onto the beach below Elysium during a Mediterranean storm.

I'm one hell of a swimmer and have battled against many things that have tried to drown me over the years, and I've never given up, never backed down, never worried about coming out on top.

Until now...because it isn't just *me* anymore. I'm responsible for another human being. Not for the first time...

Though caring for Mom when she went on benders was a far cry from what being a mother myself will require. I thought I'd have time to prepare, that it would happen with someone I loved, who I was in a committed relationship with. I definitely never expected *this* with a man who can barely stand to be in the same room unless his dick is inside me.

How can I have a baby with Lev?

How can we possibly co-parent?

He won't even stay here long enough to *talk* to me, but we're supposed to plan our lives, our child's life together. It seems impossible given what's already happened. Not when we can't sit down together and try to work things out like calm, rational people.

Not that I would know what to say.

Sorry my birth control failed, and now you're tied to me for life?

Sorry I ruined your bachelor lifestyle by saddling you with an unwanted kid?

Sorry I royally fucked up your life?

None of it seems right. None of it seems like it's *enough*. And he ran away before I could say any of it, anyway. We can't even have an adult conversation about the life we created *together*, but we're supposed to be adult enough to raise this child.

How did you get in this position, Daphne?

The answer is simple—by letting Lev get me into *another* position in the Reading Room during the reception.

It should never have happened. I wasn't in any place mentally to be making that decision. To be making *any* decisions. Things had just been so...complicated. I wanted to lose myself in something that felt good. And avoiding my mess of a life back home only led to a bigger one here.

Christ, what am I going to do?

The thought of calling Bridget flickers through my head again, but I quickly bat it away. She'll be back soon. That gives me time to figure out things with Lev and decide what I'm doing about Denver.

You can make it, Daph.

As long as I can get Lev to actually discuss this with me.

I keep pacing along the wall of folding glass doors lining the back of Elysium, peering out at the ocean and truly feeling its vastness. Here on Lovolia, I'm surrounded by the seemingly endless crystal blue in all directions. But the longer I stare at it, the more it morphs into dark brown specked with amber...

It's impossible to separate Lev from the sea. His love for it and spending time on the waves so inherent to his nature. The way he moves naturally and fluidly on the water, as if he's part of it.

Because he is.

He loves this country, this island, and the people on it. The citizens of Lovolia are his life as much as protecting Fynix is. He's committed himself, his *life* to the royal family.

Where does that leave room for a baby and me?

Fuck.

Nowhere. That's what he was telling me with his actions earlier—that I will never be his priority. This baby won't be. We *can't* be.

I press my palms flat to the glass and lower my forehead to it. Tears burn my eyes and threaten to fall again. A low sob tries to climb up my throat, but I swallow it, desperate to regain control when everything else seems so out of it.

Will he come back?

I place a protective hand over my stomach and release a long, heavy breath. This little nugget might be a heap of trouble, but I want this baby; that's the only thing I'm entirely sure of. I don't have to figure out everything else today, but it would be nice if Lev and I could at least *talk* about what's coming.

Our lives are changing, whether we want them to or not. Whether we're *ready* or not. We have nine months to prepare for this. To prepare for *him* or *her*.

Our baby.

Those two words alone bring a million and one thoughts rushing through my mind all at once—along with another wave of nausea.

"Oh, hell."

I race to the nearest bathroom and fall to my knees, pulling my hair back with one hand and bracing the other on the edge of the toilet as I retch. The heaving continues until there's nothing left in my stomach, and I can finally take a shaky breath.

Jesus, this is rough.

Pregnancy hormones are a real bitch, and it seems like Lev thinks I am, too. Maybe with good reason. He needs time to process this. I shouldn't have pushed. I should've let him come to me when he was ready.

But what if that's never?

I push myself to my feet, crank on the faucet, and wash my hands, staring at the reflection I barely recognize.

This is not *me.*

Disheveled hair. Puffy red bags under my eyes. Streaks of mascara down my cheeks. I look like I'm on the edge of a break-down...because I am. My life is about to completely change. It already has. It did before I ever set foot in Lovolia this time. And I have no idea what to do about it.

The tears start again, and I splash cool water on my face to stop them. Pre-baby me would have made a massive margarita and drowned myself in tequila, like I have been with any alcohol available to me since I got here from Colorado.

Not smart, Daph.

Given Mom's history with booze and utter lack of control when it came to her drinking, I shouldn't have been using it to cope with anything. Liquor took my mother from me, and now, getting drunk and fucking Lev is making *me* one.

"Ugh."

Talk about irony.

Thinking about how much I drank at the wedding makes my stomach churn again. I press my hand against the still-flat surface and suck in a cleansing breath.

I'll be sticking to saltines, water, and Gran's special soup for the foreseeable future. Now that she knows she's going to be a great-grandmother, maybe she'll share more secret recipes with me to get me through this pregnancy without spending the next nine months on the bathroom floor.

My back certainly hopes so...

I make my way out of the bathroom and toward the couch to try to watch something again. Perhaps now that I've literally spilled my guts and had a good cry, I can concentrate enough to understand what's happening on the screen.

A knock at the front door makes me jump and freeze before I reach the living room.

Who the hell could that be?

Lev wouldn't knock before coming into the main house. Even with the weirdness between us, this is *his* place. He doesn't need to ask *permission* to come in. That would be a sign of weakness, of backing down to me, and that's the last thing he would do right now.

So, who the hell is it?

And how did they get past the damn gate I had to climb over?

Goosebumps break out over my skin, and I suddenly wish Lev were here despite all the tension. Whoever stands on the other side of that door only showed up after Lev left me alone. My stomach churns at the possibility that it was intentional.

I slowly approach the door, as if whoever is waiting will somehow change. I pause in front of the door and check the wall camera display that shows what's outside.

Manuel stares into the camera, two other members of the Royal Guard directly behind him, armed to the teeth with rifles and stern looks.

What the hell is going on?

Horrific possibilities flicker through my head.

Bridget and Fyn...

The king and queen...

Lev...

His grandmother...

My concern over what might have happened overpowers my reluctance to face Manuel after I flat-out lied to him and pretended to get on that damn plane.

I quickly unlock the door with shaky hands and yank it open. "What's wrong? Bridget? Fyn?"

My heart thunders against my ribs, blood rushing loudly in my ears. Since the kidnapping, I've been waiting for the other shoe to drop, for something else to go wrong in the country's changeover to the new government system.

Marrying Prince Fynix has put Bridget in the crosshairs of any number of groups who might want to harm the crown... and they're in a foreign country without Lev...

Manuel quickly holds up a hand. "Everyone is all right, Ms. Jennings. May I come in? I'm afraid I do have some news to share that would best be discussed inside."

Air rushes from my lungs in a massive sigh of relief. "Oh, thank God." I rub my hand over the ache in the center of my chest, trying to ease it away. "Please, come in."

I step to the side and push open the door farther so he can enter. He walks past me, leaving the two guards outside, on alert, scanning the compound like they're expecting something to come through the woods and over that gate.

Something isn't right...

That unease that had started to dissipate returns, tightening around my spine and making it difficult to swallow. I close the door on the other guards and follow Manuel into the great room.

He stops next to the kitchen counter and motions to one of the stools. "Ms. Jennings, would you like to sit?" One of his brows rises. "You appear quite pale."

"No." I shake my head, trying to focus on something *other* than all the possible reasons Manuel is here to calm my anxiety. "I'll stand."

The oranges and pinks of the sun setting on the ocean...

The way the waves roll in so smoothly...

The sand darkening on their retreat...

The crisp sea air coming in the cracked windows...

That smells so much like Lev...

No one can deny the beauty of this house, this country— one that isn't mine. Lovolia isn't my home, and Lev would never leave.

Where does that leave this baby?

Or me?

"Daphne? Are you all right?" Manuel approaches and gently takes my elbow in his hand. His kind eyes narrow on me. "You're shaking?"

I blink rapidly, trying to clear the unshed tears. Manuel stares back at me, worry making the craggy lines on his face and brow even deeper.

Join the club, buddy.

"I'm fine. Please tell me why you're here."

He releases my arm and takes a half-step back, suddenly uneasy in a way I've never seen before. His lips press together in a firm line, and he crosses his arms behind him, taking a military stance, fully in "Head of the Royal Guard" mode.

"Ms. Jennings...it's Lev."

Oh, hell, this can't be good.

Lev ran out of here and peeled away from Elysium like a bat out of hell. He could have come back and spoken with me, but instead, he sent *Manuel* to do his dirty work.

He's kicking me out of Elysium...

Maybe out of Lovolia altogether...

"Are you...here to..."—I swallow through the emotion threatening to choke me—"escort me back to the airport?"

I'm not ready to go. Not only is there a very tiny—and insanely huge—new complication, but I'm nowhere near ready to deal with what awaits me when I step off that plane in Denver.

The thought of doing it makes my knees wobble, and I grasp the counter's edge to keep myself upright. I take a deep breath and exhale slowly before taking one more inhale.

Manuel straightens his shoulders, preparing to give me the bad news. "There was an attempt on Lev's life tonight."

Blackness starts to creep in around the edges of my vision. "Wh-what?"

An attempt?

What does that even mean?

"Lev was shot."

Lev...

Was...

Shot...

The words register slowly, like my brain is enveloped by a fog I can't hear through. A dull roar fills my ears. My heart races. Taking a breath feels like trying to draw air in through the eye of a needle.

"Shot?"

A vise tightens around my chest, and I release the counter to rub at it. I stagger a step, and Manuel grasps my arm again a second before everything around me fades to black.

16

DAPHNE

THE WORLD around me comes back slowly. A soft light at the edges, breaking through the dark fog enveloping me. Sounds—movement, far away whispers. Soft sheets against my exposed skin. Sinking into a comfortable mattress.

Then...pain.

It slices at my temples, banging against my skull, like a hammer trying to shatter it.

Wincing, I groan and try to swallow, but my throat is so dry it's nearly impossible. A huge part of me wants to roll over and fall back into the abyss—where all the things that have gone wrong in so many ways can't haunt me.

It was peaceful there.

No bad decisions.

No threats.

No uncertainty.

It would be so easy to slip back into the void, to let myself drift off again to the welcoming arms of the darkness.

But three words sound in my head through the haze.

Lev.

Was.

Shot.

A familiar voice saying them...concern heavy in each syllable...

There's more. Something else with the words. But I can't quite grasp it.

A nightmare?

A memory?

My temple throbs, stopping me from searching the recesses of my mind for the answer. I shift, releasing a little groan, and blink open my eyes. The light on the table beside the bed blinds me and makes me snap my eyes closed again.

Fuck. That's bright...

White dots dance across my lids, and I turn my head away from the offending light and rapidly blink to clear them and get my bearings.

"Thank God, Yankee. You're awake."

Lev?

I swallow through a desert-dry throat again and reach out a hand toward the sound of his voice. "Water."

My request comes out more like a rasp, barely slipping through my parched lips. If he weren't so close that I could feel him on the bed beside me, he likely wouldn't have even heard me.

"Hold on, Yankee..."

His familiar ocean and leather scent fills each breath I take, and his warm hand slips under my neck, helping support me. I clench my eyes closed and inhale sharply at the buzz the simple contact of his calloused fingertips against my heated skin sends through my body.

"Sip."

Another command in that authoritative tone he loves to use with me. The man always has to be in control. It's no wonder finding out I'm pregnant would make him feel like he's spiraling if it's doing that to *me*, someone who always seems to be teetering on the edge of complete chaos.

Smooth glass touches my lips, and cold water follows. I drink it greedily, swallowing more quickly than I should and sputtering slightly to get it down.

Lev's hand tightens at my nape. "Easy there, Yankee."

He pulls away the glass, and I open my eyes slowly, the final haze dissipating to reveal our surroundings. Thick curtains cover wide windows. Elegant golden wallpaper lines every wall. A tiered ceiling hangs over the bed...

This isn't Elysium.

We're in the palace. And the man staring back at me isn't the same Lev who stormed away from me.

A new emotion darkens his eyes and tightens his beard-covered jaw. He sets the glass on the table beside the bed and cups my cheek in his palm. His thumb slowly brushes across my skin as he examines me. His gaze softens, like he's suddenly seeing me in a completely different way—not as an enemy.

Well, that's new.

The fingers at my nape tighten slightly as we hold each other's gazes, and I finally have to force myself to look away from the intensity in his.

Christ, why is it always like this with him?

I shift my hands to the mattress to push myself up to a seated position, and Lev slides his to my upper back to assist, adjusting the pillows behind me before I lean against the headboard.

My head throbs—that mallet slamming into my right temple relentlessly. I wince and rub at it.

Why is he looking at me like this? As if he's waiting for me to break or fall apart?

"What's happening, Lev? Why are we at the palace?"

Someone shuffles on the far side of the room, and I peek

around Lev to find a man putting items into what appears to be a medical bag.

How did I get here?

The last clear memory I can summon is praying to the porcelain god in the bathroom at Elysium and wondering what will happen now that I'm knocked up.

Oh, God, the baby...

My eyes cut to Lev's, and my hand springs to my stomach, flattening protectively over it.

Lev's gaze softens again, and he squeezes my other hand. "You're both fine. You passed out on Manuel at Elysium, and he rushed you to the palace, where Doctor Hatzis and I were waiting for your arrival. I told him you were pregnant so he could check you."

Oh, thank God.

A relieved breath rushes out, and I relax against the pillows when the memory slams into me like a freight train.

Someone at the door.

Manuel and guards.

Something he needed to tell me.

Manuel's voice reverberates through my brain.

Lev was shot...

His hand still rests on mine, and I jerk forward and cling to his forearm. "Oh, my God. You were shot! Are you all right?"

It seems like a dumb question since he's sitting here, and he appears perfectly fine, but worry claws at my chest.

"I'm all right." He pats my hand where it has a death grip on him. "The bullet went through my arm, and I needed some stitches." He glances at a bandage on his upper arm, peeking out from the sleeve of the T-shirt molded to his muscular frame. "I'm fine."

He shrugs nonchalantly, as if he's just told me what the weather will be like tomorrow in Lovolia and being shot isn't a big fucking deal.

Maybe it isn't to him.

This is his world—danger, guns, assassination attempts, kidnappings, going undercover with the damn bratva, and killing anyone who poses a threat to Fynix or the crown.

It isn't the kind of life to drag a baby into...

A moment of panic seizes my chest, but before I can fall down that rabbit hole, Lev squeezes his palm over mine again.

"I'm more worried about you." He rakes his free hand over his trimmed beard and winces at the movement of his injured arm. "Well, *both* of you."

He glances over his shoulder toward the doctor, who turns back to us and offers me a kind smile.

"Ms. Jennings, you *are* pregnant." His eyes dart to Lev before returning to me. "I took a blood sample at the behest of Mr. Orlov to confirm the home test."

"You took my blood while I was unconscious?"

Something about that feels weirdly like a violation, and I tug my hand out from under Lev's. The doctor flashes a look at Lev, then grabs his bag and moves toward the door.

"I've left some prenatal vitamins and some anti-nausea medication for you, Ms. Jennings." He inclines his head toward me with a tight smile. "You were dehydrated, so we want to control your nausea. I gave you IV fluids, which should help with any headaches and other side effects. We can touch base later on any future care." His gaze darts to the partially healed wound on my arm. "And Lev did an excellent job on that nasty cut. You shouldn't have any further issues with that healing."

He slips out of the room, apparently unwilling to get in the middle of this, and I can't say I blame him. Every time Lev and I are in the same room, it makes it uncomfortable for everyone around us.

Even *I* wouldn't want to be stuck in an enclosed space when the two of us are going at it—physically or verbally. Too much shrapnel flying around. Someone is bound to get hurt by it the same way I have been.

The door clicks closed, and Lev offers something I've never seen from him—an apologetic look. "I couldn't ask for your permission to do the blood test, and for that, I'm sorry, but I won't apologize for being concerned for your well-being and that of our..."

His eyes dart to my belly and then back to my face, but he doesn't say the word—like saying it makes this more real than the two tests already have.

"*Baby*, Lev." I fight back my desire to scream the word at him. "Our *baby*. You might as well get used to the idea."

It comes out harsher than I intended, but after the way he left Elysium and *us* behind so easily earlier today, I can't bite back the anger that's filled me since he drove away.

A muscle in his clenched jaw tics, and he shifts uncomfortably on the edge of the bed and looks away, rubbing the back of his neck. The air thickens between us, that same tension returning almost instantly with my words.

How will this ever work?

How can we raise a child when we can't even be civil?

Mom couldn't do it. She ran my sperm donor off with her drinking and volatile temper, and sometimes, I have far too much of her in me. My hot-headedness and inability to filter my words will only make things worse in this situation with Lev —just like it got me in hot water back home. On top of this surprise growing inside me, the man was just *shot*. That's a lot to deal with, so I need to cut him some slack, even if it feels like I'm spinning off into space untethered to anything.

I muster up the strength to say the two words I know I have to. "I'm sorry."

His eyes dart to mine, and his brow furrows. "What do you have to be sorry for, Daphne?"

Sighing, I point at my belly. "This. All of this." I wave my hand around. "I was on birth control, but I got seasick when we went out on the boat the week before the wedding. I didn't even think about the fact that I puked up my birth control I took just before we went out and it might affect it."

Coupled with the fact that I forgot to take it the night before I left Denver...

Lev scrubs his hands over his face and issues a sigh. "I could have used a condom to be safe, and I didn't have to fuck you that night. I could have left you in the Reading Room and gone out to the maze like I intended. It's just as much my fault as yours."

Fire burns in his gaze, almost like he's still thinking about that night and how even though it was wrong...it just wasn't.

But whatever warmth was there disappears quickly. His gaze returns to the hard one I'm so used to seeing.

I blink away the burn of threatening tears. "I can see you don't want this."

Lev can't even look at me now. He lowers his head and grips the back of his neck, the tendons bulging under the pressure he applies. His fingers dig into the skin, whitening in his firm grip.

A man at war with himself since Fyn was taken on his watch. Lev carries so much on his shoulders, and this tiny surprise is only adding to that crushing weight.

Part of me wants to reach out, to rest a hand on his shoulder and ease the pain he's struggling with, but I force myself to stay back against the headboard. Giving him *and* me space to work through the impossible situation we've found ourselves in.

👑

LEV

Bloody hell...

All the adrenaline and stress of the day make it impossible

to sit any longer. I push off the bed and beeline for the small bar by the window. A thousand different responses to her statement sit on the tip of my tongue. So many things I want to say, yet none of them feel right, considering everything that's happened.

But there's one thing I need her to understand before we have any further discussion.

"It's not that I don't want this, Daphne."

How the hell do I explain this to her?

I stare at the various decanters, my vision blurring from the sheer exhaustion of the day's events and revelations.

What does one drink after an attempt on their life? And then learning something that completely changes everything?

I grab the bourbon and a glass with a shaking hand and pour myself a drink. Bringing it to my lips, I down the whole thing. The smooth warmth filling my belly somehow acts as a balm to my frayed nerves, helping still the vibrations rolling through me after the car chase.

What a fucked-up day.

The revelations just kept coming.

Each more stunning than the last.

Who would have thought being shot would be the least *shocking thing that happened today?*

Every time I think about the words coming from Gran's mouth, the truth she's been keeping from me my entire life, anger floods my veins—just like it's doing now.

I can understand her desire to protect me, why, as a child, she would hide something so huge. That same imperative to protect what's mine thumps at my chest as I glance at Daphne on the bed. I've been *shit* at that lately.

First, putting Fyn at risk, and now, I abandoned the mother of my child and left her hurting and exposed at Elysium to pass out due to the bloody stress.

My hand starts shaking again, and I grab the decanter and pour myself another drink.

Not bloody good.

This child isn't even born yet, and I'm already ruining his or her life and hurting their mother with my asinine behavior.

A sigh slips past my lips, and I down my second drink, wishing I were out on the waves. The only place that ever calms my nerves and quiets my mind.

It's so bloody easy to lose myself when it's just me, the ocean, and my board. My problems seem smaller when the vast expanse of blue surrounds me, but there's no time for that indulgence.

Daphne releases a heavy, annoyed sigh. "Must be nice."

Pulling from my thoughts of azure skies and perfect swells, I turn back toward Daphne. At least she looks better than she did when they brought her in. So pale. So still.

My chest had tightened until I couldn't breathe, and I snapped at the guards who assisted Manuel, to stop manhandling her when they put her on the bed.

That possessive, raw desire to press my lips to hers or kiss her cheek as reassurance that she was safe and *here* with me overwhelmed me at that moment. But now that she's awake and staring at me with so much pain in her blue eyes, I can't continue to hold her gaze.

Not with the weight of the truth resting firmly on my soul.

If anyone had broken into Elysium and harmed her or our baby...

Ignoring that thought, I try to process her question. "What must be nice?"

"To have alcohol."

I glance back at her, and she offers a half-smile.

"I'd kill for a margarita." All the color drains from her face, and she brings her hand to her mouth. "Nope. Never mind. That sounds disgusting."

Oh, hell. She's going to be sick again.

I abandon the bar and rush to reclaim my position next to Daphne. "Can I help?"

She offers an incredulous look, pulling her hand from her face. "No, Lev. You don't strike me as the hold-my-hair-while-I-puke kind of guy."

Ouch.

The comment stings far more than I'd like to admit. That's what she thinks—that I don't care and wouldn't look after her. Maybe I've given her reason *to* believe that.

I grab the glass of water from the bedside table and offer it to her. She raises a blond eyebrow.

"I could be a hold-your-hair-while-you-puked kind of guy."

Maybe, for her.

It certainly doesn't come naturally to me, but she's carrying my child. No matter how much tension and animosity there may be between us, we're going to be tied together forever through it all—the good and the bad.

And there is so much bad that has nothing to do with her.

Daphne has no idea what she's in the middle of now, how dangerous it is for her. How easily I could have lost her today...

She smiles and accepts the glass. "You could be. *Maybe.*"

"Maybe." I don't fight the smile tugging at my lips. "A work in progress."

Why can't it be like this all the time? Why can't our exchanges be easy and not full of enmity?

That's asking too much.

Daphne sips the water, and her color starts to return. I take the glass from her and place it on the nightstand. Knowing that simple act helped her feel better makes that same protectiveness swell inside me again.

She's completely alone. From what Bridget has told me, Daphne doesn't have any family back in the States besides her useless mother, and she can't even talk to Bridget about what's happening because she doesn't want to interrupt the honeymoon.

Neither do I.

That's why I made Manuel promise not to alert Fyn to the shooting. If there is any potential threat to him or his parents, staying in Italy is the safest place for him and Bridget right now —with double the original security. The placement of the villa on the cliffs makes it easily defensible, and I don't want them traveling with so many unknowns. Plus, if they get wind of what's happening, they may try to come back and only make things more tenuous—for me and Daphne.

Whatever else she's been keeping from Bridget, like why she stayed here in the first place, it won't remain a secret for long.

It seems nothing can stay hidden forever...

Elysium might not be safe anymore. It's exposed if whoever shot at me followed me from there. And despite the security measures in place, there's no way I can let Daphne go back.

There's too much at stake. Too many complications I never knew existed. Too many risks I can't take with her or our baby's life.

Not now that I know the truth.

Daphne's gaze moves to my arm. "Who shot you?"

I rub a hand across my beard and release a frustrated sigh. "We don't know. A dark SUV followed me along the coastal road, likely from Elysium. They began shooting, and I had to lead them away from the city to avoid any innocent citizens being hit. I managed to avoid a wreck or major damage, but the vehicle sped away when the police sirens grew too close to our location."

Her eyes widen, her mouth falling open slightly. "Oh, my God. Do you know *why* they were chasing you? Were they after Fynix and believed he was with you? Could it have been the LLM again?"

All good questions.

"I don't bloody *know*."

And that frustration boils over to make my words clipped and annoyed. Not at all how I want them to sound.

But there are so many unanswered questions.

She recoils slightly and shifts uneasily against the pillows, paling again, like she's truly processing the danger for the first time. "Someone could have gotten into Elysium...is that why you sent Manuel?"

I should have been there with her. I never should have left. I should have protected her and this baby...

Anger over my failure tightens my fists at my sides. "Elysium isn't safe until we confirm whether this threat knows about it. You can stay here at the palace, where dozens of Royal Guards can ensure your security, or you can return to your home in America."

It might be the safest place for her, far away from the reality I'm now facing. Where she won't be drawn into a political shitstorm. She can go back to her normal American life without the pressures and expectations laid on her here. But the thought of her getting on that plane makes my stomach roil.

Daphne scoffs, pressing her lips into a thin, hard line.

I seem to have an uncanny ability to piss her off without knowing why. "What's wrong?"

"Really?" She crosses her arms over her chest. "Do you need me to tell you?"

"Apparently, yes." *Because I'm bloody clueless.* "I'd like that very much, actually."

Things never seem clear where this frustrating Yankee is concerned, and now is no exception.

Daphne throws up her hands. "You can't even *say* the word 'baby.' You haven't said it *once* since I told you." A heavy sigh slips from her lips. "I'm sorry that this happened. I'm sorry we got caught up in the moment, and there are consequences. I'm sorry your whole world is going to have to change."

She has no idea...

Anger drips from her every word—at me.

For getting her pregnant?

For being such a wanker when I found out?

For just being me?

All seem likely.

And if that isn't a blow to my ego and my heart.

She might be safer returning to Colorado and leaving me completely out of this baby's life, but something deep inside me screams that it isn't even an option—that they're *mine* to protect.

But maybe sending her home is *the way to protect them.*

"Maybe you should stay here...or maybe you should go. Whatever's best for both of you." I hold up a hand to silence the retort sitting on the tip of her wicked tongue. "And for the record, I can say the word 'baby.'"

Her lips twist as she considers me. "You think I should stay here? Okay...let me ask you, how's this supposed to work between us when we can barely talk without it turning into an argument or a pregnancy? And when I can tell you're keeping something from me..."

Bloody hell, this woman is too perceptive.

The truth I'm barely managing to keep contained will change everything, and I'm still trying to digest it myself. If Fyn were here, I'd have a sounding board, someone I can trust implicitly to discuss the revelation Gran thrust upon me only a short time ago. But I won't worry him now. He doesn't need to know about the attack until we understand more about what happened.

"It's complicated, Daphne."

I stand and let my eyes rake over her. Even like this, recovering and angry, her stunning beauty steals my breath. A woman like this shouldn't be stuck with a grumpy asshole like me.

If things were different, if *I* were different, maybe I'd try to make things work between us, but that would only endanger her. I need to figure out my own life before I make any attempts to discuss the life of this unborn child.

At least with Daphne here and protected, I can concentrate on unraveling what happened today and what the hell I'm going to do to keep everyone in my life safe. I can't bring more danger to the Yates family, not after failing them once already, and I certainly won't let anything happen to Daphne or the baby.

I walk to the door and open it before I stop and turn back to Daphne.

With her arms crossed over her chest, aggravation radiating from her, she raises a brow. "Complicated? That's all you're going to say?"

It's all I can say.

Even if she hates me, I'll do everything I can to keep them safe—even if it means lying about my life crumbling.

"Yeah, I'd say it's royally damn complicated."

17

DAPHNE

THE SINGLE T-SHIRT and pair of jeans I was wearing when Manuel saved me from face-planting at Elysium yesterday look so lonely in the small overnight bag I snagged from Bridget's suite when I borrowed some fresh clothes. But with the rest of my things still at Elysium, there isn't anything else for me to pack.

Lev will have someone grab my suitcase and bring it back to the palace eventually, and by then, Bridget will be here and can ship it to me. Or I can get that stuff the next time I visit.

Or drop off my kid for shared visitation?

I drop my face into my hands and release a groan.

Jeez, how did I get myself into this situation?

By being a horny dumbass, that's how.

But that answer is far too simple for the complicated mess that has become my life.

I'd say it's royally damn complicated.

The truth of Lev's last words before he walked out on me last night still ring in my ears.

It sure as hell is.

He's committed to keeping the royal family safe, and there's been another attack that could very well have been meant for Fynix. The last thing he needs is another complication distracting him from his important role here at the palace.

So, I'll uncomplicate it for him.

It's for the best.

There isn't anything left to say. He summed it up when he turned his back on us and walked away—again—before we could come to a resolution on how we deal with this little nugget growing inside me.

Returning to Denver might provide some much-needed clarity, even if it means facing what I left behind. Running from the consequences of one bad decision only to have to deal with those of another.

Christ, I've really messed things up.

But I can't hide my head in the sand anymore. I can't pretend things aren't happening and wait for them to sort themselves out somehow. I have to embrace what I *do* have control over—starting right now with getting on a plane and away from the man whose indecision will only make this worse.

It will all work out. Maybe not today. Or this week. Or even this month. But it will work out, *eventually*. It has to; there's no other choice. We'll both calm down. We'll meet. We'll hash out the nitty gritty details of how we're going to do this whole "parent" thing, and in a decade or two, I'll look back at this time in my life with fondness.

That's what *they* say, and I want to believe it. But I'm not sure *they* know what they're talking about.

Right now, it feels *hopeless*.

But at least the anti-nausea meds seem to be helping today. I haven't spent any time on the bathroom floor with my head in the toilet. I'll take that as a sign that things are looking up and I'm doing the right thing.

I grab my bag and step out of my suite into the main hallway containing the private residences. My flip-flops echo off the marble floors. If I were trying to make a sneaky escape, this isn't the right footwear, but I'm not trying to sneak around the way I did when I went to Elysium.

The only thing I'm hiding now is what's growing inside me, and by the time anyone can alert Bridget that I'm here, I'll be long gone and over the Atlantic on my way back to Denver.

"Ms. Jennings, may I assist you with your bag?"

I jerk my head to the left to find Manuel approaching, his eyes narrowed on me suspiciously. "Thank you. I have it, but I could use a ride."

Manuel offers a kind smile. "I can do that, but I must take your bag. I insist."

He holds out his hand, and I allow him to take the duffle. There was a time I would have argued that I could handle it and didn't need assistance, but it's that behavior that drives Lev crazy.

You have to let the staff do their jobs.

It's easier to go along with it than to get into a pissing match with Manuel.

"Where are we off to, Ms. Jennings?"

Considering what I did last time he drove me anywhere, I can understand his suspicion. Guilt makes me offer him a smile.

"Going back home, Manuel. For real. It's time to get back to reality."

His lips quirk into a half-grin. "Does Lev know you're leaving?"

I stumble a step, but his firm hand on my arm keeps me upright.

"Uh, yes. I spoke with Lev last night. He's aware I'm heading home."

Sadness fills his wise gaze. "Hopefully, you'll return soon."

Does he know I'm pregnant?

I don't know what Lev told anyone—or if he even *did* tell anyone.

"Thank you. I hope so."

What's left to say?

Even if Manuel is aware of my predicament, I'm not about to discuss baby daddy drama with the man in charge of the Royal Guard and security for the Yates family. That's a sure-fire way to create more drama than there already is.

A true professional, he doesn't push the issue. He leads me down the stairs and through the grand hall. The people who make the palace run scurry in every direction, trying to accomplish their tasks, completely ignoring us as they're trained to do.

The same sadness that always comes when I leave the palace fills me now. Leaving Bridget behind each time feels like leaving a piece of me, and knowing I'm fleeing with this giant secret only makes it worse this time.

She's going to lose her mind when she finds out...

One of the guards stationed at the private entrance to the palace sees us approaching and opens the door. We step out to another perfect day, the sunshine glinting off a shiny black sedan that awaits me.

Manuel reaches it first and opens the back door for me. "Here we are."

I slide in across plush leather, and he shuts the door behind me—the sound so final, it makes me wince.

I'm not the same Daphne who landed in Lovolia. I can't be the woman who runs from one problem just to create another. I need to deal with what's waiting in Colorado, then I can figure out how I'm going to be a mother.

I came here hoping for a change in my life, and damn, I got it.

Be careful what you wish for.

Everything has changed, and it's only the beginning of more massive changes to come. It isn't just about me anymore or protecting myself. This baby and what's best for him or her has to take priority. That means getting away from the father who can't even be in the same room with me without bickering, the father who clearly doesn't want to be involved.

The uncertainty and tension can't be good for this little one —or me.

Manuel places my bag in the trunk, slides into the driver's seat, and starts the car. I take a final glance at the palace, though I have no idea what I'm looking for.

Not Lev.

He won't come running out to stop me. I already know where he stands with our baby and me.

Far, far away.

He told me to go home, to do what's right for both of us, and he's right. The *Yankee* belongs there, not in this lavish palace with rules and protocols I could never follow. I can't be a constant embarrassment to the Yates family by inserting myself into their lives permanently. And given how Lev's been acting, he's likely to sign over full custody to me, making this far easier for both of us.

Manuel pulls away from the palace with zero fanfare.

I settle into the comfy European leather seat and stare out the window as we pass through the gates and turn onto the road beyond the estate. We travel through the city, the buildings passing by in a blur. I'm too caught up in my thoughts to pay much attention, even though the beauty of this place usually draws me in.

All I can see now is this rich history my baby won't be a part of. My chest tightens, and that familiar fuzzy feeling fills my head—the one right before I lose my stomach again.

So much for the anti-nausea meds.

I crack the window, and the familiar ocean breeze wafts into the car. The clean, crisp scent has always been so comforting, but now, all I can see is Lev riding the waves, bringing the smell of the sea with him whenever he touches me.

Shit.

Don't think about it.

Dwelling on what happened between us will only make getting on the plane home harder.

Home.

Somehow, it doesn't feel like the right word anymore, but it's the only place I have left to go.

My phone dings, and I rummage around in my purse until I find it.

A photo of Bridget and Fyn on a boat, hugging and smiling and looking adorably in love, pops up on the screen.

BRIDGET
Miss you!

I shoot off a reply of a heart emoji and a smiley face, then tuck my phone away. It would be so much easier if I could tell Bridget everything and rely on her wise advice instead of hiding it from her. But just like Lev didn't want to interrupt their honeymoon until he knew more about the potential threat, I can't call her and come clean until they're back in Lovolia.

As soon as she finds out I'm pregnant, she's likely to fly to Colorado, but she can't stay. She has responsibilities here that won't allow her to stay to help me with this baby. I'm unprepared and will most likely *not* be the mother of the year, but I'll figure it out.

Okay-est mom ever?

It's better than nothing—which is all I ever had.

I place my hand over my tummy, an action I'm doing more and more.

Am I comforting this baby, or is the baby comforting me?

Either way, it's a *huge* positive in this clusterfuck I've created —soon, I'll have a family of my own—even if it is just the two of us.

LEV

"You catch that match on Saturday?"

The question from my left pulls me from my thoughts. I pause in the hallway and glance at Greggory where he stands at his post near the private entrance.

"No, mate. I was otherwise engaged. Looked like a real nail-biter, though."

Otherwise engaged...

With my dick buried to the hilt inside the feisty blonde I haven't been able to stop obsessing over since I left her last night.

Stop thinking about that. Your dick has already caused enough damage.

Greggory inclines his head. "Aye, maybe you'll join us to watch the next match?"

"Yeah, for sure."

Under normal circumstances, I would look forward to getting together with some of the guards to unwind with a few pints and a good football match, but it's impossible to think about that when everything is spiraling so out of control in my life and with Daphne.

I wanted to come clean last night with what Gran revealed, to tell Daphne the well-kept secret that's changed everything.

GWYN MCNAMEE & CHRISTY ANDERSON

But she wasn't in any shape for that kind of revelation—nor was I.

The attempt on my life shook me far more than I'd ever let anyone see, and I need a clear head to have that conversation. Coupled with what I now know, there isn't any other choice but to tell her the truth. She has to know everything—including how dangerous it has become. It's the only way I will ever be able to convince her to stay.

Hopefully, she feels better now, and we can have a civil talk about the future, which is far more complicated than she could ever imagine or I could ever put into words.

I take the stairs two at a time and continue down the hall toward Daphne's guest suite, the rooms I've avoided for almost two years because *she* was here. Like an absolute idiot, I spent her visits dreading spending time in the same room with her, hearing the slap of her flip-flops on the tile, her raucous laughter at precisely the wrong times, and her quips and jibes that I pretended never affected me.

Now, I can't imagine her ever *not* being here.

Did you seriously tell her to go home last night?

It would be safest for her, to get *far* away from me before anyone can connect us or discover she's carrying my child, but the more I thought about it, the clearer it became that I need to protect her by keeping her and our baby close, or I'll never be able to stop worrying about what danger they may face—even across the pond.

I tap on the door before I push it open and scan the room, expecting to find a feisty blonde full of renewed energy and ready to battle this morning.

My eyes land on the empty bed. "Daphne?"

The continued silence makes the hair on my arms stand on end.

Where the hell is she?

A low humming comes from the bathroom, but as I

approach the cracked door, a male voice says something indis-tinguishable.

What the fuck?

Blood rushes in my ears as I draw my piece and head toward the ensuite. I pause outside, listening for other sounds, but only that low, male hum carries out to me.

I turn the corner, weapon ready—

"Whoa!" David raises his hands, his eyes wide. "Lev…"

Shit. I almost shot the bloody cleaning crew.

I quickly return my gun to my waistband and motion for him to lower his hands. "My apologies, David. I was expecting Ms. Jennings."

And Grandmother's news has pushed me closer to that edge I've been teetering on since Fyn's kidnapping. I'm jumpy and off balance—something Fyn saw when he insisted on my forced holiday. And since he's left, things have only become worse.

Enemies have breached the palace grounds before, and after the attack yesterday, the thought that it had happened again almost caused a deadly mistake.

David relaxes and releases a relieved sigh, swiping a hand across his brow. "You scared the bloody hell out of me, Lev."

"I'm so sorry." I hide my shaking hand behind my back. "Have you seen Daphne?"

"She was here earlier." One of his dark brows rises. "Per-haps she went to see your grandmother?"

Of course.

Gran is the only person who knows she's pregnant, except for Doctor Hatzis. That makes Gran the first person she would seek out here at the palace if she needed someone to talk to.

The old woman better not be revealing all our secrets to Daphne…

This is something the mother of my child needs to hear from *me*.

Along with an apology for how I acted last night. It wasn't the right time to tell her everything, not when there were still so many unknowns. But now I've had a chance to review all the footage of the car chase we were able to collect from various cameras along the roadway. It's clear the attack had nothing to do with my connection to Fyn, his kidnapping, or the LLM. The men in that SUV were after me. Plain and simple. And now, I know why.

I hustle down the long corridor to the other side of the private residences and knock softly on Gran's door.

"Come in."

Her voice carries through the wood separating us, and I twist the knob and enter her suite. The familiar sweet smell of baking chocolate hits my nose, and my mouth instantly waters as I approach her in the kitchen.

"Gran, I could have been anyone. You need to check who's knocking. And why isn't your door locked? *Tebe nuzhno byt boleye ostorozhnym.*"

Valid questions considering the circumstances, but chastisement will get me nowhere. Gran does what she wants, when she wants, and she isn't about to change how she lives her life —even when there's a very *real* threat out there.

She waves a dismissive hand. "I'm too old to be worried about dying at this point, *dorogoy moy.*"

Given everything happening, it isn't a funny joke, but I still find myself chuckling along with her. It feels good to release a jovial sound, especially after my angry reaction to what she told me last night.

I lean in and kiss her cheek, glancing down at the pan of fresh brownies in her hands. "Who are those for?"

She sets the pan on the counter. "I thought Daphne might like some. When I was pregnant with your father, I had quite the sweet tooth."

Images of Daphne growing bigger with my child while I

feed her ice cream and anything else she wants flicker through my head. Anxiety tightens my chest, but it isn't the same feeling that hit me when she said she was pregnant.

So much has changed in only twenty-four hours. Now the thought of *losing* that because I've put them in danger makes me want to scream.

I lean against the counter, sliding my hands into my pockets, trying to appear casual when the possibility of seeing her makes my entire body tense up. "Oh, so she's here?"

Gran chuckles and pats my arm. "You don't have to act suave, Lev. She's not here."

Damn.

"She isn't? Do you know where she went?"

Casting a sideways glance at me, Gran cuts the brownies and sets the individual pieces on a cooling rack. I slide a hand around her and reach for one. She softly swats my hand away, but not before I claim a sweet treat.

"*Hvatit!* Those aren't for you!"

I bite into the warm chocolate and chew slowly. "Delicious."

She gives me the same chastising look she always gave me when I stole brownies as a child. "And to answer your question, I haven't seen Daphne today. Once you confirmed she was here and safe last night, I thought she'd need rest and didn't want to disturb her. I planned on heading to her suite later with these."

Shit.

"That's very thoughtful, Gran."

A smile twitches the corners of her lips. "She is carrying my great-grandchild. She needs to be taken care of."

The reproach makes me cringe and avert my gaze. Her disapproval of how I've handled things with Daphne still rings in my ears after our talk yesterday.

She grabs a dishtowel and wipes her hands. "Did you learn anything new about the attack?"

I look back at her and sigh, reticent to reveal what I discovered. "Yes, and you aren't going to like it."

Her entire body stiffens. "What is it?"

"We reviewed video surveillance from some cameras along the chase route, and I could see enough of the passenger to identify one of his tattoos."

Her fingers tighten on the towel, her knuckles whitening. "And?"

"It was the *Serp i Molot.*"

A gasp slips from Gran's lips, and she squeezes her eyes closed. "It's finally happening..."

"We don't know that, Gran. It could have nothing to do with...what you told me. It could be something that goes back to my time in Russia, what I did there."

Her head whips toward me, her usually warm eyes ice cold. "You have to protect yourself and that baby. Regardless of who is behind it, anyone connected to you is at risk. You must assume Daphne is in danger until you know differently."

I wrap my arm around her and draw her to my chest, hugging her close and feeling the frailty of her body. "I will protect her and that baby with my life. You know that, Gran."

She pulls back slightly. "See if Manuel knows where she is."

I pull out my phone and fire off a text to Manuel.

LEV

Do you know where Daphne is?

Almost immediately, my phone chimes with an incoming message.

MANUEL

I dropped her off at the airport twenty minutes ago. She said you knew.

The room spins around me, and I brace myself with a hand on the counter. "She left."

Daphne is gone...

Gran clings to me, reaching up to direct my face back to hers. "What do you mean, she left? Where did she go, Lev?"

"Manuel dropped her off at the airport. She's going back to America."

Fuck!

"*Idti!* You have to get her, Lev." She lightly slaps my cheek. "*Now, dorogoy moy!*"

It finally snaps me from my daze. "I'll get her back."

I kiss Gran's cheek and race toward the door, glancing back at the woman who has always been my rock.

She wrings her hands in front of her, shaking, a panic I've never seen before in her eyes. "Be careful, Lev. *Ya tebya lyublyu, dorogoy moy.*"

"*Ya tozhe tebya lyublyu*, Gran. It will be all right. I promise."

I turn the knob and rush out, locking it behind me because she won't. One of the most important women in my life is already in danger; I don't need the other to place herself in jeopardy.

18

LEV

THE PALACE HALLWAYS pass by in a blur. Shouts from guards and staff asking what's wrong go unanswered. My legs can't move fast enough. Every muscle burns as I sprint like my life depends on it—because it does.

Have to stop her.

This massive place seems to only get bigger until it feels like I'll never reach my destination, but I finally make it to the private garage and race past what's left of my Spider. Someone pulled in the bullet-ridden corpse at some point last night rather than leave it potentially visible on palace grounds.

That would raise too many questions no one can answer—especially since Manuel and I decided not to make an official statement until we have more information on the attackers.

I won't risk anything happening to Daphne, so I veer past the other "fun" cars and toward the bullet-proof SUV I use while on official Lovolian business. This monster will stop almost anything, which is good because I might not escape with a simple through-and-through next time. Not when it's apparent someone is targeting me, and managed to find me at the one place no one should be able to locate.

How the hell did they know about Elysium?

That question lingers as I slide in and fire up the engine. It roars to life, and I exit the garage and tear down the drive, through the gates the guards open for me, and onto the main road.

After my last experience behind the wheel, I keep my eyes peeled for anything out of place. Since whoever shot at me got away, despite Manuel calling for a lockdown of the ports and tightening security at the airport, anyone could be a potential threat.

At this point, we have to treat the attack as a threat to the crown and act accordingly—though the evidence suggests a different target altogether. The motivations of the attackers could run the gamut, and that means the Yates family could get sucked in even though I'm the one with a bullseye on my back.

I'd be hunting for them myself, but something far more important than my safety is at stake right now.

I floor the accelerator and weave through traffic, laying on the horn to get vehicles to move out of the way while maintaining a vigilant watch on everything around me.

Each mile might as well be a thousand—the small island suddenly seems vast and endless as I make my way across it. Blood rushes in my ears, my heart thundering in my chest. I can't risk Daphne getting on that plane.

I press the button on the steering wheel to activate the vehicle's phone system. "Call Lovolia Airport Authority."

Ringing sounds through the speakers, and after two, a familiar voice picks up. "LAA, this is Henry speaking."

"Henry, it's Lev Orlov. I need you to check a passenger name and ensure the plane hasn't left."

"Of course." Keys click on the other side of the line. "What's the name?"

"Daphne Jennings."

I lay on my horn and swerve around a vehicle that refuses to get out of the way, jerking back on the wheel to avoid a head-on collision. Waiting for Henry to locate the information, I take the final corner, and the airport comes into view a few blocks away.

"I see her, Mr. Orlov." He pauses for a moment, apparently reading his screen. "A flight to Rome—"

"Is the plane still there?"

"Yes, it just started boarding at Gate 3."

Thank God.

A tiny bit of pressure crushing my chest releases as I screech to a stop outside the airport in the no-parking zone, throw it into park, and practically jump from the SUV onto the sidewalk beside a stunned security guard. He opens his mouth to direct me to move, but I flash my identification and he backs away, inclining his head in understanding.

The same badge gets me easily through internal security, and I race past Gate 1 and Gate 2 toward the line at Gate 3 waiting to have their tickets scanned to enter the bridge down to the plane.

My eyes dart over every blond head, and my heart climbs up my throat when I don't see her.

Where the hell is she?

Already on the plane?

I'll physically drag her off it if I must, but I turn and scan the area around the gate before I barrel my way down to the plane.

Oh, thank fuck.

I take a massive breath, my heart finally returning to a normal beat as I take her in.

Daphne sits in a chair near the gate, a container of milk in one hand and a massive cookie in the other. I approach slowly, the way one does a wounded animal so I don't startle her or draw any attention to us.

I slowly lower myself into the chair beside her and wait for her to acknowledge me.

She glances my way, then does a double take, coughing and thumping her chest several times to dislodge some of the cookie. "Lev...what are you doing here?"

Isn't that obvious?

"I came to take you and the baby back to the palace."

Her lips dip into a frown, and she bites her cookie aggressively, casting me a look out of the corner of her eye that tells me all I need to know about how she's feeling about me. "Why would I go anywhere with you?"

Ouch.

If she intended to sting me with her words, she succeeded. But I deserve everything she has to say—and more.

I drove her here with my inaction and bloody-awful attitude, but I won't let her or our baby suffer because of my idiocy. "Because your safety is my highest priority, and if you leave Lovolia, my job becomes harder."

In hindsight, I never should have suggested she return to America. I never should have even given her that option. It never would have worked. I was a fool to believe it could. Sending her away could never be the answer.

"We wouldn't want that, now, would we?" Daphne rolls her eyes and sips her milk, her annoyance as prominent as her belly will be soon.

I have my work cut out for me.

She's pissed and won't be easily swayed by my opinion or my feelings about any of this—and I can't blame her for that. I've let my shock over the entire situation interfere with my ability to treat her in the way she deserves.

I give her my best smile, trying to inject a bit of humor into a tense situation. "Well, *I* wouldn't want that."

She bites her cookie again, unfazed by me, and chews like she has a personal vendetta against the sweet.

The bickering with her that once acted as the most potent foreplay now seems like a futile effort to stop a never-ending war. We don't have time for our personal issues with the threat looming over us, yet we've fallen right back into the way things were *before.*

I continue to scan our surroundings, checking for anything suspicious. People in line to board have turned to watch us, and a small crowd starts to gather nearby, leaning in and whispering to each other. I can't go unnoticed for too long in public. After thirty-plus years at Prince Fynix's side, I have some notoriety—for better or for worse.

Worse in this moment.

"You need to come back to the palace now, Yankee. I can't protect us when we're out in the open and so exposed." I lean in and brush my lips against her ear—both to ensure no one hears us and because of the undeniable need to feel the heat of her skin against mine. My fingers itch to brush over her belly, but I hold them back, along with all the other words I really need and want to say. "I need to keep the baby safe."

Her head snaps toward me, her brows winging up. "Safe? Keep the baby safe from what?"

I scrape my hand down my face at her loud question carrying through the terminal.

Bloody hell, Yankee.

"Quiet." I lean in again and wrap my hand around her bicep, pulling her toward me slightly. Her volume could alert everyone in the bloody airport that she's carrying my child. I'm not even sure she's capable of speaking at a normal level.

Something I'm not even sure she's capable of.

Her eyes widen, and she opens her mouth to snap back at me, but I press a finger over her lips. If she knew everything, she'd understand, but this isn't the time or place for that conversation.

I'm operating blind, and the longer we're exposed, the greater the chance the unknown enemy could strike.

"Yankee, please listen to me. I need you to quiet down." I scan the group around us again, hoping no one sees her unease and mistakes it for me being a threat to her. "Our situation must remain strictly between us. I can't have you shouting from the rooftops that you are carrying my child." I lock my eyes with hers and plead with her to see the sincerity of my words. "Please, Daphne, come with me, for the baby's sake."

Her perfect lips twist into a scowl. "We wouldn't want everyone to know that Mr. Lovolia went slumming with the American, would we?" She leans toward me, fury dancing in her eyes. "And don't you *dare* use this baby as an excuse to make demands of me. I won't allow it."

Shit.

That's exactly what this must feel like to her—me playing some fucking game with her and our child, trying to make a point about my role and power over her. Daphne's imagining all the ways I'll try to control her once he or she is born, and she's *scared.*

"That's not what I'm doing, Yankee. I am trying to stress how essential it is that you do not get on that plane. You must stay in Lovolia, so I can care for the baby. For once, can you not argue with me and just do what I am asking?"

It's likely too much to hope for after everything that's happened, but when it comes to their safety, I will not budge. If I do, the results could be catastrophic. Daphne cannot get on that plane, and if that means I have to ground it, I will.

Her jaw grinds, and her body vibrates with barely contained fury. Nothing but sheer willpower keeps her from lashing out and punching me in the junk—likely because of our growing audience.

"Fine." She bites it out through gritted teeth. "But I am *only* going because my best friend is the princess of this nation, and I don't want to cause a scene in this airport and end up on the news, tainting her image. This isn't how I want Bridget to learn that I didn't leave Lovolia and have been shacking up with you instead."

She glares daggers at me, but she rises to her feet and tosses the rest of the cookie into her mouth before reaching for her small bag on the floor. I beat her to it and sling it over my shoulder.

Her gaze immediately darts to it, then to mine. "I can carry my bag."

I press my palm against her lower back and lean in again. "Not while I'm around."

She grumbles, planting her feet like she intends to argue with me about something so petty, but I growl low and dig my fingers into her back. That edge I've been dancing along seems razor thin now, so much so that I barely trust myself not to do or say something I'll regret if she pushes me.

My gaze darts across the faces of every person near us, searching for a threat aside from the people snapping photos of us on their phones. As the crowd grows, so does that nagging feeling that makes the hair stand on the back of my neck.

"Time to fucking go."

Her body stiffens for a second before she relaxes slightly, the only sign I'm likely to get her to admit defeat.

I'll fucking take it.

It's all I can ask for after the mess I've created. Once she understands what's truly at stake, she'll see why I had to be so pushy about this.

And she'll probably continue to think I'm a controlling asshole.

I nudge her waist, and she steps forward, slowly making her way through the crowd. Dozens of sets of eyes follow us away from Gate 3, but we only make it a few steps before my phone rings.

Pulling it from my pocket, I glance at the screen while ushering her onward. Manuel can wait until we get out of the airport and can talk more privately. I send it to voicemail, slip it back in my pocket, and move Daphne past Gate 2 and Gate 1 toward where the vehicle waits.

It rings again, and I pull it out, frowning at Manuel's name popping up again. Whatever it is must be time-sensitive. My hackles rise again, and I scan around us for the millionth time.

"Manuel, hold on."

I slide my hand around her, tugging her to my side where she's better protected. Her skin against mine shoots an electric jolt straight through me. That crisp lemon and sunshine scent clings to her and fills each breath I take, but I ignore it along with the familiar unpleasant sound of her damn neon-green flip-flops slapping against the floor.

There's no time for distractions—especially ones as beautiful and frustrating as Daphne, not when I'm trying to keep her and our child safe.

DAPHNE

THE AUDACITY of this guy to show the hell up here at the airport and demand that I go with him.

Who the hell does he think he is?

Oh, yeah...

It only takes one second for me to remember exactly why he feels entitled to act like this—Lev has all the power in this country and this situation. He can have anything he wants, force anyone's hand.

What choice do I have but to go with him?

He could have grounded that plane had he wanted to, and there isn't a single thing I could do about it. Fynix and his family may wear the crowns, but everything I've seen over the last few years has convinced me Lev actually runs Lovolia behind the scenes.

The man knows everyone and controls everything—even more than Manuel, who is technically the head of the Royal Guard. He can command anyone he wants.

Including me at the moment.

I could call Bridget, and she'd put a stop to this macho, controlling shit, but then I'd have to tell her why I'm still in Lovolia and about the baby. It would ruin her honeymoon and shatter my best friend's heart because I've been keeping so much from her.

I'm not prepared to deal with that yet, so I'll play by his rules—for now—as assholish as they may be. But he better not get used to compliant Daphne. Once I learn Lev's reason for demanding I return to the palace, I can figure out how to leave Lovolia and get away from him. I had hoped the long plane ride and multiple connections would help me form a plan for when I landed on the other side of the world, but that will have to wait until I deal with this caveman.

Lev's phone rings a second time, and he pulls it from his pocket, frowning. "Manuel, hold on." He tugs me out of the flow of foot traffic heading toward the exit, constantly scanning the bustling airport like he's expecting something. "What is it?"

He listens for a second, keeping his arm wrapped around me protectively. His jaw tenses, and his entire body stiffens.

Oh, no.

Cold dread spreads like ice through my veins. I shiver against him despite the warmth of his body seeping into me, along with that damn leather and sea scent.

Something's very wrong.

His hand tightens around my waist. "How is she?"

I swing my head in his direction.

She?

He starts moving again and ushers me out the door to a black SUV parked at the curb in a red zone. Listening to whatever Manuel is saying, Lev opens my door and assists me in, then tosses the bag into the back seat and rounds the hood.

Goddammit.

My gaze eats up every gorgeous, tattooed inch of him as he moves so fluidly.

Bastard.

This would all be so much easier if I wasn't still attracted to the man, but even my anger can't overcome how my body responds to him.

Pure betrayal.

Shifting uncomfortably on my seat, I cross my arms over my chest as he opens the door and settles into the driver's side. He slams his door hard enough to shake the massive SUV, and I examine him and find his brows drawn low over his darkening eyes.

Whatever it is, it isn't good.

"Thanks, Manuel. I'll be there in a few minutes."

He ends the call and drops his phone into the center console before glancing at me. "Put on your seatbelt."

This isn't the time for a witty comeback or argument. Something serious has him rattled. I quickly click it into place, and he peels away from the curb like a bat out of Hell.

A heavy silence falls over us. Lev is usually quiet, but this is *different.* Like an untamed lion in the wild on the hunt— majestic and beautiful and deadly. Lev will eat you alive in a second before you even know he's there. He emanates the same warning—you better tread carefully because he is just as fucking dangerous, if not more so.

Despite knowing how volatile he can be, I still take the

chance to ask because I can't sit here, feeling like I'm in the dark about what's happening. "Is everything okay?"

His grip on the wheel tightens. "No."

Everything about this man warns me to leave him alone, to *run* whenever I get the chance, but that same thing that constantly gets me in trouble won't let me stop pushing. "What's wrong?"

He accelerates again, darting around several cars that lay on their horns and slam their brakes. I grip the door handle, clinging to it for dear life as I slide on the leather seat despite the seatbelt strapped across me.

For someone who insists he's trying to protect me, he sure seems intent on crashing this damn SUV.

"After I left to come to get you"—his eyes cut to me, and the pain there drives a stake straight through the heart I thought I had closed off to him—"Gran collapsed."

Oh, no!

"Is she okay?"

A muscle tics in his jaw, and he focuses on the road ahead. He doesn't answer, and dread settles in my stomach like a fucking rock.

"Lev...is she?"

This time, his gaze darts over to me for a brief second, long enough for me to see the shimmering unshed tears there. "According to the doc, it's not looking good."

"Shit, Lev." I swallow past the lump in my throat. "I'm sorry."

I ignore all the blaring warnings that scream *don't touch me* and rest my hand over his on the wheel. That same connection we've always shared sends little jolts through my body, a zap of heat that warms me to my core.

How does something that shouldn't be right feel so fucking good?

He glances at me. That shitty look he gave me mere seconds

ago has disappeared, replaced with something I'm not sure I've ever seen before.

A vulnerable Lev.

The *real* one he keeps hidden under a mask of bravado and stoic attitude. Like me, he's been mostly alone in this world without any family besides his grandmother, and now, he's on the verge of potentially losing her.

He turns his attention back to the road but twists his hand to entwine our fingers, resting them on the console between us. I squeeze gently, and we remain locked together the entire ride back to the palace.

For a brief moment, I can forget he's a giant jackass more often than not, who practically dragged me kicking and screaming from the airport. I can push aside our being at each other's throats because he needs a friend.

Maybe we *aren't* friends—perhaps we never will be—but if it came down to it, Lev would be there for me if I ever truly needed something.

How he's been acting since the wedding isn't who he is. Something eats away at him from the inside out, making him so volatile with me. He's loyal to a fault, and that loyalty extends to anyone his friends care about—including me. He needs to know he can count on me that way, too. He and I may be like oil and water, but Fynix is Bridget's happily ever after, which means taking Fyn's best friend as part of the package.

The gravity of the situation settles in as the palace gates open for us to pass through.

Please, God, let Mira be all right...

Lev will be lost without her. So will everyone else in the palace—including me. The kind woman who nannied for Fyn as a child has become a rock for everyone. Leaving today without seeing her, especially now that she knows I'm carrying her great-grandchild, broke my heart, but I knew she would have tried to stop me. If she doesn't make it, and I don't get a chance to say goodbye...

No.

I can't think like that.

Mira will be fine.

We pull into a garage near the private entrance, and my eyes immediately go to a red convertible riddled with bullet holes and shattered windows. My heart sinks like a pit in my stomach.

Shit.

I recognize it immediately, but compared to how it looked when Lev drove away from Elysium, it's hard to grasp what I'm staring at. "Is that your car?"

Lev releases my hand, and the loss of his warmth and touch instantly chills me. I turn away from the disaster and back to him.

"Yes."

He exits the SUV and slams the door.

Don't take it personally.

I unbuckle my seatbelt while Lev retrieves my bag from the backseat and opens my door like the gentleman Mira taught him to be. He offers me a hand, and I slide my palm across his, letting him assist me. But as soon as he closes the door, he drops my hand and shoves his through his unruly hair.

We hustle toward the palace, each step bringing us closer to the unknown. The guards outside the private entrance give us grim looks but remain silent. So does everyone we pass inside.

The eerie quiet follows us up the stairs and down the corridor toward Mira's suite, where the door stands open.

We enter to a flurry of activity—guards stand inside the door, women who look like nurses move between the open bedroom door and the living room area, and Manuel turns from where he stands near the kitchen counter.

He strides across the room to us, and I have a direct line of sight into the bedroom where Mira lies on the bed, Doctor Hatzis holding her hand.

Tears burn my eyes, but I blink them away, trying my best to stay strong for Lev. The foreboding looks everyone offers us and the sadness in Manuel's usually warm eyes warn of what's likely coming.

Mira isn't going to make it.

Manuel hasn't even said anything, but I can feel the truth deep in my bones.

"Lev..." Manuel stops in front of us, offering a tight smile. "She collapsed about an hour ago. I came to check on her as soon as I returned from dropping Ms. Jennings at the airport. I knocked, but she didn't answer and the door was locked. I heard her faintly calling for help, so I used my master key and found her in the kitchen, collapsed on the floor." He swallows thickly, running a shaking hand through salt and pepper hair. "Doctor Hatzis said she had a heart attack, but she refuses to go to the hospital or receive any treatment."

Oh, God...

All color drains from Lev's face, and he lowers my bag to the floor robotically. "Thank you, Manuel, for seeing that she was well cared for."

"Of course." He gives us a half-smile. "You know we all love Mira." He glances behind him toward the bedroom. "I haven't notified the king and queen yet, or Prince Fynix and Princess Bridget. Would you like me to call them?"

Lev shakes his head. "No, not yet. I need to see her first."

"She's been asking for both of you."

Both of us?

Lev glances toward me, his brow furrowed, then walks toward the bedroom, apparently expecting me to follow. Manuel places a hand on my shoulder and squeezes gently before I trail after Lev slowly.

I don't want to intrude on this moment with his grandmother, but if Mira asked for me, I won't refuse her anything. I never could. Not when she's done so much for me in the few short years I've known her.

How am I going to have this baby without her?

Lev kneels beside the bed, and I approach behind him, taking in how small and frail Mira appears. She has always been larger than life, a force of nature no one in the palace could deny. But now, it looks like she's given up and accepted her fate.

No.

Tears stream down my cheeks. It would be impossible to stop them even if I tried. I swipe them away, but more quickly replace them until I have to fight back sobs.

Lev takes her wrinkled hand in his and drops a kiss on her forehead, mumbling something in Russian. A single tear slips from his eye and drops to her pale skin.

He knows what's coming as surely as I do, and there's nothing I can do to ease his pain—even if he would let me.

19

LEV

I'VE DREADED this moment for years. Tried to pretend it would never come. Ignored the ticking of the clock and the advancement of time so I could convince myself Gran would be here forever. Yet, with every passing birthday, deep down, I knew my window of time with her was slowly closing. But I never prepared myself for this, for seeing her so frail instead of the vibrant woman who swatted at me when I stole a brownie only a short time ago.

Everything changed so fast, and it's all my fault.

If I hadn't fucked things up so badly with Daphne, this wouldn't have happened...

Daphne wouldn't have tried to leave, and Gran and I could have sat down with her and explained everything. She would have ensured Daphne understood her position. She would have helped me soften the blow. She would have had so much more time. She would have been able to meet her great-grandchild, watch him or her grow up. She could have been to my child what she was to me.

It's all my fault.

Doctor Hatzis settles a hand on my shoulder and squeezes. "She's in and out but with us right now. Just talk to her, Lev. She's been asking for you. You will bring her comfort."

The genuine emotion in his voice makes me choke back a sob. Everyone here loves her. She's surrounded by the people who care about her the most, the ones we consider our family. And it will destroy Fynix, Bridget, and the king and queen that they weren't here, too.

Fighting through the pain in my chest, I squeeze Gran's cold hand, trying not to think about why it feels that way. "Gran, *ya zdes*. It's Lev. Can you hear me?"

Her eyes flutter open, and she blinks and shifts her gaze unfocused for a moment before it finally lands on me. The same love and devotion the pale blue has always held still fills them, and I never want to tear my gaze away. Any second might be the last time I look into these eyes that have witnessed me grow from a boy to a man, witnessed my first steps, and watched over me as if she were my mother.

Everything good in my life is because of this woman. I am who I am because she loves me and committed her life to raising me after Mother and Father's deaths. She gave me my life, and at the end of hers, there aren't any words I can say that will express my love for her.

"*Dorogoy moy...*"

I adjust my grip on her smaller hand, the fondness in how she says my nickname the thing that will finally break me. "*Ya zdes.*"

My vision blurs, the tears flowing freely now.

She shakes her head slightly. "I'm sorry I didn't tell you everything sooner. I was trying to protect you. I thought we had more time, but now..." Gran manages to lift her other hand slightly and wave it. "*Eto konets, dorogoy moy.*"

I duck my head and press my lips to the top of her hand

gripped between mine. My tears drip onto her skin, salty and full of my anguish. "Don't say that, Gran. This isn't the end. There's a chance—"

"No, *dorogoy moy*. My time is limited, but I must speak to Daphne."

What?

I whip my head around and look up at Daphne, where she stands by my side. What she sees in my eyes must say a lot about how I feel sharing my final moments with Gran because Daphne takes a step back.

Gran raises her hand again. "Daphne, please come here."

Daphne's tear-soaked eyes meet mine, seeking permission that isn't mine to give. I want to savor every second I have left with Gran, tell her all the things I always wished I had, but it isn't my choice to make.

Who am I to deny Gran a single bloody thing?

I incline my head, and Daphne walks around to the other side of the bed and sits on the edge, taking Gran's other hand.

"I'm here, Mira." Daphne swipes a tear from her eye. "I'm not going anywhere."

Her words tighten that vise already wrapped around my chest.

Not going anywhere today. Or not going anywhere ever?

Gran swallows thickly. "I need to tell you the truth."

I squeeze her hand again. "Gran, I don't think that's a good idea." It will only upset her to reveal this story again. She barely made it through telling me last night. Her anguish and tears made me want to destroy everyone associated with our family secret, and the stress of reliving this will only hurt her more. "I will tell her, Gran. I promise."

It's the least Daphne deserves. She needs to understand the dangers she and our child will now face. But Gran doesn't need to spend what little time she has left revealing the tragic story.

Her old eyes meet mine. "Lev, *molchi*. Let me speak with Daphne."

A chuckle slips from my lips despite my world crumbling in front of me. Even now, Gran still commands the room —and me.

"Daphne, honey. I want to tell you how our family came to live here in the beautiful country of Lovolia."

Daphne offers her a sad smile. "I love your stories."

Our baby will never hear them from her...

I bite back a sob, squeezing my eyes closed. Having the mother of my child here with me for the final moments of Gran's life tears at something deep inside me the same way the truth did when I learned it.

But Gran and Daphne need this moment. Gran is right. Daphne needs to hear it from her, not me. It isn't my story to tell.

Even as weak as she is, Gran grips my hand. "Our family has a long, tragic history with Russia, but as much as we are Russian and love that country, we could never return. My ancestors suffered the unthinkable, and now, I need to tell you the truth because you carry the heir."

Gran coughs, and I release my grip on her hand to grab a glass of water from the nightstand.

"Here, Gran."

I help support her as she takes a delicate sip, and Daphne's confused gaze meets mine across the bed. She mouths *heir* at me, her brow furrowed. Daphne has every reason to be confused. As was I, last night, when Gran revealed the secret kept for over a hundred years.

Gran settles against the pillow, squeezing Daphne's hand. "The Orlovs, my family, are the heirs to the Russian Empire."

I hold my breath for Daphne's response. Gran was never one to mince words, and even after hearing the complete history only hours ago, it still hasn't sunk in—the truth of who we are. Who I am.

"What?" Daphne shakes her head, her gaze darting between us. "The Romanovs?"

Gran nods slowly.

Daphne's jaw falls open. "But...how is that possible? I just watched a documentary about how DNA testing confirmed there were no survivors of the family assassination."

I shared Daphne's confusion when Gran came clean. It's warranted, given everything presented to the public regarding that horrible night. What really happened has been a closely guarded secret for so long that the truth is almost unbelievable. I nod once, assuring Daphne that this is the truth.

My truth.

She focuses back in on Gran. "The documentary said everyone has been accounted for, and even the Anastasia rumors have been laid to rest with the DNA testing."

Gran nods. "Yes, those things are all true. Except there *was* an heir who escaped the massacre that day. Empress Alexandra was with child when they were prisoners, during the Bolshevik Revolution. It was never made public. They hid it from their captors and everyone else—save one trusted servant. When they were shot, no one knew about the unborn child."

Daphne places her free hand protectively on her stomach, and I can only imagine the thoughts racing through her mind. I'm still trying to process the horrors of it all myself, and I don't have another person growing inside me.

"The nanny to Emperor Nicholas and Empress Alexandra's children was left unharmed as she proclaimed she supported the revolution and was a secret sympathizer with the uprising. After the shooting, before the revolutionists claimed their bodies, she returned to the basement where they had been shot, to say goodbye to her friends. But she discovered something unexpected—the Empress was still breathing, though barely, despite a gunshot to her head. While there was no way to save the Empress, she knew there may be a chance to save the baby, and she performed a crude c-section, cutting it from Empress Alexandra's body before she died."

"Mira, no." Daphne shakes her head, pressing her hand over her mouth as tears flow down her face. "This can't be true. Lev, is this true?"

I nod. "It is."

"That baby, the sixth Romanov child, had to be protected. After the execution, the Bolsheviks celebrated the mass murder with vodka, and the nanny crept off into the night with the stolen heir."

Daphne opens and closes her mouth a few times, trying to process the story and what it ultimately means. "This is insane! Are you telling me—"

Gran coughs again, struggling to continue with the story.

I clear the emotion from my throat. "It's true, Daphne. My great-grandfather was that baby. The nanny, Ola, escaped the country with the help of a network of other tsarists, including one of the guards who had been assigned to the Romanovs and had refused to participate in the execution. To ensure the c-section would remain hidden from the Bolsheviks, that guard agreed to desecrate my family's bodies in order to conceal that there was another child."

Locking eyes with her, I choke back the fury that telling this story sends rushing through my blood.

"He survived because of her bravery. We owe Ola a debt that can never be repaid. She saved our bloodline and committed her life to hiding the heir. She took the last name Orlov because Orlov means eagle, which is on the Romanov crest, as a nod to her son's true parentage. It's why Grandmother kept the Orlov surname even after marrying Grandfather, because she is the Tsarina, and she wanted her children to keep the name and carry its meaning."

"But"—Daphne's gaze darts between Gran and me—"how did Ola end up here?"

Everything Gran told me last night comes out in a mad rush. "Fynix's great-great-grandfather, the King of Lovolia at the time, was very close with the King of England, who was the cousin to Tsar Nicholas. King George V had tried to save the Romanovs, but he was unable to rescue them in time. When he learned there was an heir, he knew how essential it was to keep him safe. They decided Lovolia was the perfect place to hide the one true heir to the throne, Alexander Orlov. They even lied to me and everyone else about when and how my family came to Lovolia to hide when they truly arrived and avoid suspicion." I rub my jaw, considering the family history I now know was a lie. "I always believed it was my great-grandmother, Irina, who came here and began working for the family. In actuality, she came from Russia to marry Alexander, my great-grandfather, who had been hidden here since Ola arrived over twenty years earlier, when he was a mere baby."

Gran coughs again, then clears her throat. "Alexander was my father."

Daphne's free hand goes to her stomach again. "So that means..."

She can't even say the words, and her chastisement over my inability to say *baby* last night rushes back.

"Yes." I answer for Gran. "You carry the heir to the kingdom of Russia, a Romanov. That baby and I are the only two direct descendants of Tsar Nicholas and Tsarina Alexandra."

♕

DAPHNE

THE ROOM AROUND ME SPINS, and my vision blurs. If I weren't sitting on the bed, my legs would surely give out under me.

They shake uncontrollably along with the rest of my body. A mixture of adrenaline and pure confusion make it impossible to think clearly.

I try to process what Lev and Mira just told me, but the words won't coalesce into anything I can wrap my head around. None of it makes sense. It's like floating in some mad dream, where everything I thought I knew got flipped on its head—Alice going through the looking glass and tumbling into a world she can't understand.

It can't be true.

Their story is too insane, too far-fetched to be real life. It sounds like some plot from one of the cheesy movies I watch alone at night back in Denver.

Murder.

Betrayal.

A hidden heir.

The things of fiction. Not reality. At least, not any reality I've ever been part of. Yet, Mira and Lev seem so certain it's true. Under any other circumstances, I wouldn't question their veracity. They've never given me any reason not to believe them about anything in the past, but this...this is too much to accept.

How could this stay a secret for over a century?

Mira lightly squeezes my hand, her usually strong grip faltering. "I know this is a lot to process, dear. But it's important you hear and understand it all because I fear those who would see the Romanov line destroyed have discovered Lev's true identity. Which puts all three of you in danger."

Danger?

"But...why?" I would never claim to be an expert on Russian history or politics. Everything I know comes from documentaries I've binged or what I learned in basic history class in high school, so I don't understand why anyone would be after Lev now. That was a hundred years ago. The world is so different now. No one could possibly care about a descendent of a long-defunct royal family. *Can they?* "Why is he in danger?"

Lev shifts slightly across from me, his body tensing. "Because things are changing. They have been for a while. The democratic government there has become a farce. There are talks of a coup. Of overthrowing those who control the country. There are still people who see anyone with Romanov blood as a threat to the current political leaders because we would have a claim to the ancient throne."

Jesus...

It doesn't matter that they tried to abolish the monarchy and moved to a new system of government all those years ago. His *blood* makes him the Tsar in the eyes of supporters of the old crown—and apparently, those who want to keep the current status quo, too. To them, he's a *threat*. This *baby* is a threat.

Gran nods, the motion making her wince. "Several of our allies, the very few who know an heir exists, have been rounded up over the last few weeks. Questioned. Imprisoned. One was even killed. Though none of them know Lev's identity, we have to assume those events are connected to yesterday's attempt on Lev's life. Someone has made the connection."

Oh, my God.

I had assumed the men who chased and shot at Lev were LLM, or maybe family members of those he killed during the uprising, perhaps even someone coming after Fynix, trying to use Lev to get to him.

This is so much worse.

Lev moves from his knees to sit on the edge of the bed. "One of the men in the SUV who shot at me bore a *Serp i Molot* tattoo—the sickle and hammer. It brings the attack right back to Russia. We're still hunting for them, trying to confirm their identities and bring them in to be questioned, but the threat is very real."

"Couldn't it have been someone connected to the bratva?" Everything Lev told me back at Elysium races through my head. "Revenge for what happened when you were there?"

Mira nods again. "Possibly. It was one of the reasons I was so vehemently against him going—the potential of someone somehow discovering who he is or that he might do something to draw unwanted attention to himself. But if anyone connected to the bratva knew who he was and where to find him, they would have acted long before now. This feels like something else. Another purpose."

Lev locks eyes with me. "If it is someone after the Romanov line and they know who I am, I have a literal target on my back." His gaze drifts down to my stomach. "Me...and our baby."

The baby.

The heir to the Russian throne.

How is this possible?

I want to believe it isn't real, that this is all some fucked-up nightmare born of my lack of sleep, stress, and all the damn vomiting this pregnancy has caused. But looking into Mira's eyes, I can see the sincerity there. The truth of what she's telling me and her genuine concern over what the future holds.

A future she won't be here for.

This *baby* is important. It explains why Lev rushed to stop me at the airport. His panic at me almost leaving. His *insistence* that I return to the palace with him.

He has to protect the heir.

Any thoughts that maybe there something more brewing between us fall away with that realization. From the moment he knew about his heritage, this baby was all he cared about—his sole focus and priority. Protecting the heir...

I glance out the bedroom door at the guards near the entrance to Mira's suite.

Are they here for Lev now?

For the baby?

Would they stop me if I tried to leave again?

Acid churns in my stomach, the anti-nausea meds unable to compete with the anxiety. I look back at Lev and then Mira. "Does anyone here know?"

Mira shakes her head, a slight panic flashing in her eyes. "Only the king and queen. Not even Fynix is aware of Lev's true lineage. As far as anyone knows, the attack yesterday had nothing to do with any of this. Until we know more about how someone might have identified Lev and who we can trust, we must keep everyone in the dark. Let them believe it was related to the LLM or Lev's work in Russia years ago."

Until we know who we can trust.

The ominous nature of those words settles over me like black fog, darkening the edges of my vision and turning my stomach. I squeeze my eyes closed, trying to clear it away, so I can fully process everything this means.

This secret has lasted for generations, and Mira has borne the burden of keeping it alone, save for the king and queen, since Lev's grandfather and parents died.

How could she look at Lev every day, knowing the truth, and keep him in the dark?

The pain must have been excruciating for her. Always watching over her shoulder. Wondering who might want to harm the boy she raised. Praying no one discovered his true identity. Protecting her grandson. The same way Lev is trying to protect the baby...

Lev won't let his child leave Lovolia.

I thought I had a chance to go back to Colorado and perhaps figure out a life there away from a father who didn't want this child, away from the trappings of palace life and the stresses that would bring. But that's off the table now.

The determination and anger simmering below the surface of Lev's dark gaze now make goosebumps spread over my skin.

This is Lev, the guard for the crown. This is Lev, the lethal right hand of Lovolia, and I know what he's capable of. What he *will* do to ensure I stay with his baby.

A soft knock sounds at the open door, and Manuel steps in. "Lev, I'm sorry to interrupt, but I have some information you'll want to hear."

Lev kisses Mira's hand and rises from the bed. "I'll be right back."

Mira watches her grandson leave the room, then turns to me with a weak smile. "Daphne, the top drawer of my bedside table...there's a journal. Can you hand it to me?"

She returns her attention to Lev and Manuel talking with their heads together outside the room.

What is so important that she insists on seeing this journal?

I open the drawer, pull out the bound leather book, and hand it to Mira.

"Thank you, dear."

She lifts a pale, shaking hand, opens it, and slowly flips through it, stopping after a few pages. Something about watching her do this feels like a massive intrusion, so I turn away slightly, focusing on the heated conversation between Manuel and Lev to give her a bit of privacy to do whatever she needs to with the journal.

A rattling cough drags my attention away from what's happening in the other room and back to her. "Do you need water, Mira?"

"No, darling." She holds out the journal. "Please put this back in the drawer."

Her words are barely audible. Any energy she had left when we first arrived has been zapped by the physical and emotional toll of relaying that story.

I slip the journal back into the nightstand, and she grabs my wrist, tightening her bony fingers almost painfully.

"Take this number." She shoves a piece of paper into my

hand. "Once I'm gone, ensure Lev calls." Another rattling cough slips from her mouth. "It's essential." She inhales a ragged breath. "Daphne, please watch over Lev. I know he is doing everything he can to run you off, to push you away, but he will need you, and he's a good man under that rough exterior. Take care of him...and my great-grandbaby."

Fighting back a sob, I clutch the paper in one hand and squeeze hers with the other. "I will, Mira."

Maybe I shouldn't be making that promise, not when I'm unsure I have the power to keep it—at least where Lev is concerned. I will do anything to protect this baby, to ensure he or she is always safe and loved. But when it comes to Lev, there is no certainty.

There can't be.

He walks back in, his concerned gaze bouncing between us before he retakes his spot on the bed and pulls his grandmother's other hand into his. The love in his eyes as he stares at her makes me feel like an intruder, but when I try to pull my hand away and leave them alone, Mira manages to find the strength to tighten her grip on me.

Lev brushes his lips over her cheek reverently, then drops his head to her ear and whispers something private that causes a tear to leak from her eye and roll down to her pillow.

She whispers something back and raises her hand to her necklace. "Take it. *Ti dolzhn*. It's yours..."

Lev offers a stiff nod and reaches to the back of her neck to undo the clasp. He slips it off and clutches it tightly in his hand. "*Do svidaniya, Babushka*."

Almost as if she's been waiting for those final words, Mira's lips turn up into a small smile, she releases a final breath, and the Tsarina slips away from us.

20

LEV

STANDING in the solitude of the garden and looking up at the stars, the overwhelming sense that I'm truly alone in my life settles over me. The insignificance of my life pales in comparison to the endlessness of what stretches above. Even the familiar scent of the ocean filling the air can't calm the tempest raging inside me—a violent mix of rage, confusion, frustration, and utter helplessness.

Gran is gone.

Kak ty mogla ostavit' menya?

The only true family I had left. My ever-present rock. She left me to face this terrifying new reality alone.

I swipe a tear from the corner of my eye, exhale a deliberate breath, and slip my hand into my pocket to grasp the single item that can confirm the truth that has flipped my world on its axis over the last twenty-four hours.

One of the Romanov sapphires...

The setting digs into my palm, but I ignore the bite of pain.

It's the first thing that's made me feel alive since Gran took her last breath a few hours ago.

I pull out the necklace and hold it up in the moonlight to watch the light filter through the magnificent facets, just as Empress Alexandra might have every time she looked at this beautiful piece of proof that I am a Romanov. The jewelry Ola took from the Empress' body as proof of the lineage of the child she rescued fits easily in my palm, yet the weight of this tiny piece might as well be a thousand pounds crushing down on me.

That reality, coupled with the loss of the most important woman in my life, means that the only way I can think to cope tonight is by drowning myself in alcohol.

Because that's always led to me making brilliant choices.

I raise the half-full glass to my lips and take a long sip of the same harsh liquid that landed me in the Reading Room with Daphne after the wedding. A light fuzziness fills my head, but it's nowhere near enough to dull my agony. Or my guilt.

It claws at me relentlessly. Tearing me apart from the inside. Vicious and unyielding.

I was so *angry* with Gran when she told me the truth last night. Furious that she had kept this from me my entire life and that I had been living a lie. I had insisted she should have come clean earlier, that I deserved to know everything as soon I reached the age where I was able to comprehend the monstrous reality of what runs through my veins.

My words were harsh. A way I had never spoken to her before. And even though I apologized before I left her last night and she acted no different with me today, I can't help but regret what I said to her. Because the longer I've had to sit with the life-altering information, the more I understand why she waited to tell me.

How different would my life have been had I realized who I really am?

I would have lived every day looking over my shoulder, expecting the worst. My world would have been different, tainted by the bloodshed that led to us being in Lovolia in the first place.

By guarding the truth, Gran gave me the gift of freedom from a family legacy of tragedy. I got to be Lev, a real kid with a real life. I didn't have to hide anything. I got to be carefree, growing up as Fynix's best friend and racing around the palace without any concerns.

Just as Father had been before she revealed the truth to *him*.

Only for him, it was far worse. Not only did she dump his lineage upon him, but she had to break the news that his chance meeting with Mother wasn't so chance after all.

A set up...

They were all set up...

That was the most disturbing part of Gran's confession— that every marriage since Ola brought Alexander here was by design. Each potential suitor for the heir were plants brought over from Russia, born of loyal Tsarist families. Families with power. Families who would be useful should the time ever come to reveal ourselves.

Fucking set-ups.

Great-Grandfather Alexander and Great-Grandmother Irina...

Grandmother with Grandfather...

Father with Mother...

All arranged to ensure the legitimacy of the family claim to the throne.

Did they ever truly love each other?

The question hasn't stopped rattling around in my head since last night. Despite Grandmother's assurances that their relationships grew naturally and there was love there, it's impossible not to question it. And the fact that they would have tried to set me up, too, still stings like acid on an open wound.

One of many reasons I haven't slept at all since the revelations.

What a bloody fucking mess.

Nothing like a million truths and a substantial life-altering
loss to fuck you up in the head—as if I wasn't already there
with my failure to protect Fynix and the situation with Daphne.

Blyat!

Fyn...

He and Bridget don't have the slightest clue what's
happening here. The decision to keep them in the dark about
the attack until we knew more now feels wrong. If we had told
them, they could have returned home, been here to say
goodbye to Gran.

Now I've taken that opportunity from them—another
failure on my part.

I toss back the remaining contents of the glass—Gran's
favorite vodka from Grandfather's hometown in Russia.

How ironic...

This very drink led to that baby growing inside Daphne's
belly.

My baby.

"Lev?"

Daphne's uncertain voice floats through the night air and
hits me like a sledgehammer, breaking through the wall of pain
I've surrounded myself with.

She's been so strong through all this, sitting beside Gran as
she took her final breath. I saw a different side of her tonight.
The side Gran always saw—her kindness, her willingness to
stay true to herself, her strength in even the worst of situations.

It's no wonder they became friends. They shared so much
in common. Undoubtedly, Gran was just like Daphne in her
younger years. I never noticed it because I never wanted to see
it. I never wanted to give Daphne a chance.

A modicum of peace settles over me, knowing Gran at least

knew about her great-grandchild before she passed. My child will never be able to fathom how much Mira sacrificed for the family, but they will know what an amazing, loving woman she was—Daphne and I will ensure that.

I turn toward her slowly, slipping the necklace back into my pocket, not wanting to say or do anything that might return any of the tension from earlier at the airport. Another confrontation, especially with her, would break me completely. "Hi."

The moonlight glows off her blond locks and highlights her beautiful features. I've always appreciated what a stunning woman Daphne is, but tonight proved something I can no longer overlook—her beauty isn't only external.

There's a very real, rare beauty to this woman.

Her heart.

All her cheeky comebacks and lashing out are nothing but a defense mechanism she created after having to raise herself. She never had a chance to grow up in a loving home with someone to nurture her and ensure she got what she needed.

And because of how I've been acting, she carries an unease around me now, twisting her hands in front of her. "Can we talk?"

After everything we just went through, the least I can do is give her a few moments of my self-imposed solitude. Considering what a shock this all was to me, I can't imagine what it must be like for her or what the stress might be doing to her or the baby.

"Of course."

She closes the distance between us and extends a small piece of paper toward me. "When Manuel came in to speak with you, Mira gave me something she said to give you. She said that you need to call this number now. No delays."

My world might be shattered, but the final command from Gran brings a twitch to my lips. "Sounds like her. Bossing me around from the beyond."

Daphne offers me a sad smile. "I think she gave it to me instead of you directly because she knew I'd make you do it."

I bark out a laugh and take the paper from her. Whatever it is, it must be important. Gran wouldn't have made it her dying request if it weren't.

For such a small piece of paper, it feels heavy in my hand, like it holds some secrets even Gran didn't tell me. I open it and immediately recognize the Russian country code and the sequence for St. Petersburg.

"Whose number is this?"

I flip the paper over.

No name.

Just a number.

Daphne offers a shrug. "I don't know, Lev. I'm sorry. All she said was to give it to you and make sure you called right away."

I move toward the outdoor table and chairs across the garden, Daphne following closely behind.

She watches me expectantly, pulling her bottom lip between her teeth. "Are you going to call?"

I lower myself into one of the chairs, set my empty glass on the table, and pull out my phone. My fingers hover over the numbers, my hand shaking before I can even dial.

What the hell could this be about?

Another secret the old woman held.

I hold my breath and force myself to dial the number. Daphne turns away, but I reach out and catch her arm before she can move a step.

"Stay." It comes out like another command, but I soften my request. "Please."

Whatever this is…it affects her life now, too. We'll be bound together forever by this baby, whether she likes it or not. She deserves to know everything I do.

She turns back to me slowly and gives me a tight smile. "Okay."

No more secrets.

I press the speakerphone button and wait. One ring. Two. Three. The line finally connects, and Daphne and I lock gazes as a brief moment of silence hangs in the air.

"*Alloh.*"

The heavily-accented voice makes me stiffen, my hackles immediately rising. I clear my throat. "I was told to call this number."

There's a rustling on the other end of the phone, like the man is on the move. A squeaky door shuts, and a lock clicks into place.

"*U vas, dolzhno byt' voprosy—*"

My gaze darts to Daphne. It would be easy to slip into Russian, but I don't want her to miss a word of this. "English, please."

"Of course. I know you have questions, and I will answer those, but first, is Mira all right?"

His question slices at my heart and steals my breath. Daphne steps forward and lays her hand on my shoulder, offering me what little comfort she can.

I inhale deeply and blow it out, summoning the strength to say it. "She passed away peacefully a few hours ago"—I lock my gaze with Daphne—"surrounded by family."

She needs to know how much her being there meant to me and how she is now, and forever, my family. No matter how things might be between the two of us, how much we may bicker or go at each other, I will ensure she and our baby are safe and cared for in every way possible.

"My condolences. My cousin was always the best among us."

"Cousin?"

Given Gran's mention of "distant relatives" in Russia when we spoke back when I was at Elysium, it shouldn't be a surprise, but after living my entire life believing we had no other family, hearing the word from a total stranger rattles my already grief-fogged brain.

"Yes. Mira was my third cousin, so I suppose you are my fourth. Though, distance doesn't matter. Blood matters. Family matters. And you need family and answers."

"Mira told me who I am...*what* I am."

"I'm glad you were able to hear it from her before she passed. I know it weighed heavily on her to keep it from you."

That pang of guilt over my initial reaction to the revelation returns, and I absently rub at the ache in the center of my ribcage. She wanted to say more, I could see it in her eyes, but I was so lost in my anger that I didn't let her.

"I felt there was more she didn't tell me, like she was holding something back..."

"Undoubtedly, she believed she would have more time to tell you everything you needed to hear. There's so much to discuss."

I release a sardonic laugh. "I'm not sure how many more surprises I can stand."

The baby...

Being a Romanov...

Being the *heir*...

Losing Gran...

I've always prided myself on my strength and ability to remain unfazed by anything thrown at me—personally or professionally. But too much has come too fast. It's as if everything is changing at warp speed, and I'm trying to play catch up.

And failing miserably.

DAPHNE

THE COLOR DRAINS from Lev's face as he reaches the same realization I just came to—there's even more Mira never told him, either because she was intentionally holding back or never got the chance.

More secrets.

More painful truths.

How could it get much worse?

As if everything we already know isn't enough to crush the soul of anyone hearing it. Lev might be the strongest person I know, yet he's on the verge of losing his ability to maintain his self-control. And absolutely no one could blame him for it if he did.

But the stranger on the other end of the line pushes right past Lev's comment, urgency in his accented voice. "It's important you listen. Your future and that of an entire country depend on it."

A shiver rolls through me at those ominous words.

Why does it sound like a threat?

Maybe because someone *shot* Lev and tried to end his life. The mangled hunk of metal that was once his car flashes through my head, and I shudder and wrap my arms around myself, rubbing my hands over my exposed skin to try to heat it.

Until Lev and I became...whatever we were at Elysium, I never considered how dangerous his job really is, how often he has to face life-threatening situations in order to protect Fynix. But now the threat is directed straight at him, putting *him* in the crosshairs of a determined enemy we can't find.

Lev takes my hand, pulling it toward him and softly rubbing his thumb across the top. The soft brush of the calloused pad along my sensitive skin starts to calm me instantly, but his tense shoulders prove he's just as unnerved by the statement as I am.

He glares at the phone, as if his cousin can see his anger.

"Don't place that on my shoulders. I'm not *who...what* you think I am."

"You're exactly who and what I think you are. The Bolsheviks ensured no other claims to the throne would be made by dissolving the monarchy and killing anyone who opposed their position. No one dared come forward to fight them, even those with legitimate claims through more distant lines of succession. They resigned themselves to living in the shadows. Most fled Russia. The ones who stayed were forced to blend in, to ensure it appeared they posed no threat. But they had supporters. Like your grandfather's and mother's families."

Lev reaches into his pocket and pulls out the necklace, letting the blue stone dangle and catch the moonlight. "Gran told me her meeting my grandfather was arranged. The same between my mother and father."

What?

I turn toward Lev with a raised brow. This wasn't anything Mira told us this evening, which means there's more I don't know.

The man sighs, as if acknowledging it is irrelevant to the entire story. "That's true. It was done to solidify the Romanov position within the highest echelon, so support would be in the right places when the time came."

What time?

None of what I'm hearing makes any sense. It's as if this man knows something we don't.

Lev tenses and meets my gaze with a question in his, but he lets his cousin continue.

"Our family received word shortly after the massacre, a coded message that a Romanov child had survived. We created the rumor that it was Anastasia, even knowing she hadn't made it, to mask their ability to find the one true heir because they'd be looking for the wrong person."

Oh, my God...

Lev squeezes my hand. "It was all a ruse?"

"A good one that kept the entire world occupied for a hundred years until DNA finally confirmed she was in the grave. Time we spent guarding the secret with our lives. Our hope was the rightful heir would someday return and claim the throne."

They've been waiting for a century...

"Your birth, right when the Soviet Union fell, was like a sign, an opening for what once was to be again, and we began working on plans to bring the Romanovs back to power. Sadly, your father's life was cut short before we could see him on the throne."

Lev's brow furrows. "See him on the throne?"

"Once Mira explained everything, she and your father were prepared to take their rightful places, but his death ended any prospect of that happening."

A faraway look reaches Lev's eyes, and he returns the necklace to his pocket and runs his hand through his hair. "I was only eight..."

"Far too young to be told the truth of who you were or what we suspected."

He freezes. "What you *suspected*?"

"That the *accident* that killed your parents might not have been an accident at all."

What?

I crush Lev's hand, and his head whips up until his confused gaze meets mine. Bridget told me Lev's parents were killed in a car accident when he was a child, but I never heard anything that might suggest it was anything but a random tragedy.

Lev shakes his head. "No. Gran always said it was a car accident. Even when she told me who I am, she didn't say anything about—"

"Because we don't have any solid evidence, just suspicion.

Enough to convince us that the threat was still too real, the time perhaps not right. Especially because you were so young. Your grandmother had just lost her only child, and she wouldn't risk your life by coming forward with her claim. So, we waited and watched, trying to uncover who might have been behind your parents' deaths. We waited for you to grow, believing Mira would know when to reveal the truth to you."

"She told me last night...after I was attacked, driving back to the palace."

He doesn't offer anything else, like the fact that my pregnancy, as much as the attack, was likely what spurred Mira into action. I rest my free hand on my stomach as if to protect the baby from the man on the other end of the phone.

What would he say if he knew there was another heir?

Visions of this baby being ripped from my arms the moment I give birth sear my brain, and tears slip down my cheeks. I quickly swipe them away before Lev sees.

"We feel this is the time to come forward, Lev. Every moment you've spent in Lovolia has led you to this."

Lev offers a humorless laugh. "I must be misunderstanding this. Do people actually think I should *claim* the throne?"

"That's precisely what your supporters believe."

Lev scoffs, and a low, rumbled growl escapes him. "*My* supporters? You can't be serious."

They can't be.

None of this makes any sense. These people...supporters... want Lev to rule a country that's been democratic for thirty years. Given what happened here in Lovolia, moving from a pure monarchy to a constitutional one and the unrest the call for democracy caused, suggesting Lev step into the role is true madness. It would cause a *war*, something the Russian people cannot afford to suffer through.

He's been blindsided by everything thrown at him the last few days. We both have, and neither of us has had the time to digest the loss of Mira, let alone something of this magnitude. And this man is dumping this in his lap, expecting him to take it up and accept it so easily.

Lev hates being told what to do, even more when he isn't the one in control, and I can see his anger boiling just below the surface, ready to blow.

Suddenly, I feel like a true intruder in this conversation. The other man doesn't know who I am or that I'm even here listening in on what is clearly meant to be for Lev's ears only. I try to pull my hand free from Lev's, but he tightens his grip, keeping me beside him.

"We think the time is right. The current government has crossed too many lines and upset too many people. Russia wants change. *You* are that change. *Everything* in your life has led to this moment."

Lev shakes his head, scrubbing a hand across his beard. "How can you even suggest this? I don't know the first thing about leading a country."

"Don't you?" His cousin issues a light chuckle, like there's something amusing about this conversation. "Why do you think your great-grandfather was brought to Lovolia and given such direct access to the royal family? It was by design, Lev, and it was a century's worth of planning and waiting."

Holy shit!

The pieces start to click into place in my head, and by the glazed-over look in Lev's eyes, it's the same for him.

"You've experienced firsthand what it takes to run a country. You witnessed a revolution of sorts there in Lovolia. You learned how to handle conflict and unrest. You trained in the art of warfare. You spent countless hours with the young prince as he has learned to be king. You were given unfettered access to everything *you* needed to learn to be what *you* were *born* to be, what lives in your blood."

Lev finally pushes from his seat and releases my hand to

pace in front of the table where the phone sits. "All the physical training, the hours spent by Prince Fynix's side as he watched his father...they were merely ways to train me on how to rule a country?"

"You were living there to remain hidden and to *learn* from them."

The lost look that settles on Lev's face is like a knife twisting in my gut, and I place a protective hand there.

These people went to extraordinary lengths to control the life of each heir since Alexander Orlov was saved. They've pulled the strings as if they were marionettes, not real people. That's no way to live.

Lev's gaze lowers to my hand. He moves toward me and slides his over mine, lacing our fingers across where our baby grows. His eyes darken to the almost black that terrifies me, but I know what it's directed at. What he fears now. The same thing I do—what this baby's future holds.

"This is the time to reclaim your birthright."

It might be easy to fall into his cousin's rhetoric, to believe that his blood gives him the *right* to something people have fought over for centuries, but that isn't the Lev I know. It isn't the one Mira raised.

"You're fucking mad if you think I'll agree to this!" Lev slips away from me and continues to pace like a caged tiger, his aggravation and concern making him downright feral, his body wound so tightly it appears he might snap.

At least he's concerned with the safety of our baby, even if he doesn't give two shits about me.

Scuffling sounds in the background come through the phone line before the man who has yet to give us his name returns. "I understand your reticence. There's much more to discuss. There are plans in place. We have resources. Many on our side we can rely on. But I must go now. Can I call you back on this line?"

Lev freezes and hesitates a moment, looking at me before replying. "I suppose so."

He ends the call and shoves his hands through his hair, dropping his head back to face the vast blanket of stars above us.

"Fuck!"

His curse echoes through the garden, but there's no one else out here to hear the anguish in it. No one to witness his cool and calm demeanor evaporating in a single moment of weakness.

Lev paces for a few moments, his hands fisting and opening at his sides, muttering to himself in Russian—words I can't possibly understand, but I can guess their meaning.

"Lev?"

He freezes at the sound of his name, his back to me. For a brief second, I hold out the hope this might be the moment we've needed to finally open the door to talking about this baby, but instead, he casts me a half-glance over his shoulder.

"I need to think, blow off some steam. I'm going to take a walk in the maze. We'll talk tomorrow."

Before I can utter a response, he grabs his phone from the table, tucks it into his pocket, and stalks off toward the entrance to the maze. I don't bother trying to stop him.

The only life he's ever known has been a lie. All of it. A meticulous fallacy designed to use him as a pawn in some political chess game.

Only they've vastly underestimated him.

He isn't a pawn.

He isn't weak and powerless.

Lev is the *king*.

21

LEV

No matter how long I stare at my phone screen, I can't seem to bring myself to connect the call. Every time I hover my finger over the *send* button, bile rises in my throat, tears sting my eyes, and I have to fight back both and try to regain control of myself.

Which seems utterly impossible at the moment.

Any semblance of control over my life flew out the window yesterday and can never return. Even wandering the maze, letting myself disappear between the high hedges, hasn't helped.

And not just because of the call with my mysterious cousin, but because I know I have to make this one.

How the hell do I tell Fyn that Gran is gone?

I swallow thickly and pinch at the bridge of my nose, trying to alleviate the headache growing there since I ended the call earlier and walked away from Daphne.

Another dick move.

I can't seem to get it right when it comes to her, but any conversation we might have had would have been tainted by my anger and frustration over what my cousin said and my misery over losing Gran.

When we *do* finally talk, I need to have a clear head.

Manuel will notify the king and queen, but I should be the one to tell Fyn. *I* have to do it. She was as much his grandmother as she was mine, and he's going to be devastated he didn't get to say goodbye, which is completely my fault. So, I have to tell him, no matter how painful it might be or how clouded my head is by all the bullshit that's happened in the last two days.

Dovay sdelay.

I finally jam my thumb against the *send* button and bring the phone to my ear as I walk along the pebble path toward the far corner of the maze. Moonlight illuminates my way, and a vivid memory of Gran chasing Fyn and me along this exact route assaults me. The pain is so intense, I stagger to one of the benches set throughout the maze and clench my eyes closed, waiting for the call to connect.

This late, he'll know it's bad news. No one calls in the middle of the night with anything good. He'll know something's wrong, especially with how we left things after our last call.

He answers on the second ring. "Lev, what's wrong?"

Fucking everything.

The word "wrong" doesn't even seem sufficient to describe my life or the world I'm living in.

"I have some bad news..."

"What happened?"

There's so much to tell him, so much I want to unload and confess that I can't at the moment. Not when the most important thing is allowing him to grieve for the woman who helped raise him.

I inhale a deep breath filled with the scent of the wisteria covering the gazebo in the center of the maze. "Gran is gone."

"What?"

He heard me, but I understand the disbelief in his voice. I watched her slip away, yet my heart still doesn't register that she's truly gone.

"I'm so sorry, mate. She had a heart attack. There was nothing they could do."

Fyn sucks in a sharp, pained breath. "When did this happen?"

"A few hours ago. There wouldn't have been any time for you to get back. I was with her when she passed."

"Bloody hell, Lev." He's silent for a moment, and all I can hear is my heart beating in my ears. "I'm so sorry."

"I'm sorry I'm ruining your honeymoon with this news."

"Christ, Lev. My honeymoon is the last thing you need to be worrying about right now. You just lost your grandmother."

Hearing him say those words clogs my throat, and I force down the sob that threatens to come up.

"Do my mother and father know?"

"Manuel was going to notify them. I don't know if he's made the call yet."

We both needed a few minutes to process everything before doing it. Considering how closely Manuel and Gran worked together for decades, this is incredibly difficult for him, too.

"I assume I would have heard from them if they knew..."

I lean back and drop my head against the hedge behind the bench, ignoring the slight prickle of the leaves and branches against my scalp. "Probably. We haven't made the arrangements yet. I thought you would want to know immediately."

Fyn releases a heavy sigh, full of the burden I share, the heavy weight in my heart. "She was a wonderful woman."

"She was, and she loved you fiercely."

"I don't even know..." His voice trembles, something I've rarely, if ever, heard from Fyn. Even as children, he was never emotional. Always tried to stay cool, calm, and collected even when he fell and skinned his knee.

Gran's death has rocked him as much as it has me, right in the middle of what should be the best time of his life.

He lets out a long breath. "We'll make arrangements to come home in the morning—"

"There's no rush."

She isn't going anywhere, and the funeral will take several days to plan. We won't bury her before Fyn and Bridget are scheduled to return anyway.

"Yes, there is."

"You shouldn't cut your honeymoon short."

"I loved your grandmother like she was my own. And you're hurting. I'm going to be there with you and with my parents, if I can. Bridget will want to be there, too."

Fucking hell. Bridget...

Maybe I should be the one to tell her about Gran. "Would you like me to tell her?"

"No. She's in the other room, talking to Daphne. Let her enjoy that call..."

Fuck.

What the hell is Daphne telling her?

We haven't discussed the baby or the tremendous life-shattering information we've received. I'm not prepared to discuss any of that with Fyn if Daphne is finally coming clean to Bridget.

"You should have her inform Daphne." The lie feels like acid leaving my mouth. "She would want to know."

Fyn releases another sigh. "I'll make sure she does. And Lev?"

"What?"

"I'm sorry about what happened the last time we spoke. I know things have been difficult for you since the uprising. And I had hoped your holiday would help you work through everything. Gran's death can't have made it any easier. I'm sorry I haven't been there with you to help you through all this."

"I'm a big boy, Fyn. I don't need you to hold my hand."

He chuckles lightly, the sound a welcome change from the darkness surrounding me. "Maybe not, but we could at least share a bloody pint in her honor."

I grin. "*That* I could definitely use."

"I'll make arrangements in the morning. Mother and Father have the jet with them in France. They'll likely fly home as soon as Manuel informs them, and then we can have them send the plane for us."

"I'll see you in a few days then, mate."

"See you soon."

He ends the call, and I release a heavy breath. I thought I'd be relieved once I relayed the news, but I've been lying to him for weeks about Daphne, and the truth of who I really am will rock him.

The fact that his parents knew and hid it. That Gran hid it. Not to mention that Daphne's pregnant...

Fucking hell.

I push off the bench and continue to make my way toward the one spot I might find some solace. The smell of the wisteria increases the closer I move to the center of the maze. Familiar and comforting, it brings with it a flood of happy memories.

Playing with Fyn between these hedges. Picnic lunches at the gazebo. Hiding from the guards in the maze because we knew it better than anyone. Gran chastising us for giving them a hard time and making their jobs more difficult.

What am I going to do without her?

Especially now, with this new future ahead of me, I need her companionship and sage advice. I need her to tell me what to *do.*

The man on the other end of that call didn't even give me a

name, yet I'm supposed to jump into whatever the hell this is head-first and try to retake control of a country that isn't mine...

Absurd.

But Gran insisted I call him.

Does that mean this is what she wants for me?

I take the final corner, and the gazebo appears, lit by the hundreds of twinkling lights strung through the wisteria blooms. This has always been the place where I can think and escape reality, but tonight, I feel as trapped here as I do in my own life.

The maze was meant to be the ultimate game, and this gazebo was the prize when you solved it. That's what this all is, one massive maze with dangers and dead ends. And I've lost my only guide.

👑

DAPHNE

"I'M SO GLAD YOU CALLED!"

Bridget's answering declaration immediately puts a lump in the middle of my throat. I slap my hand over my mouth to prevent myself from instantly unloading everything I've been dying to tell her for weeks.

"Daphne, are you there?"

Shit.

I swallow and walk to the cracked-open window, hoping some fresh night air might make this call easier. But deep down, I know nothing can.

How do I tell my best friend that she's lost one of the most important people in her life?

From the day Fyn brought Bridget back to this palace to start her royal adventure, she and Mira easily fell into a relationship Bridget so badly needed. After her parents died, she was always searching for someone to give her advice, a shoulder to cry on. Lev's grandmother has been that for her through all her struggles here at the palace—her sometimes turbulent relationship with Fyn, trying to fit into a mold she knew nothing about, during the kidnapping and wedding. And Bridget didn't even get to say goodbye.

I rest my hand on the windowsill and stare out at the maze. "I'm here."

"Oh, good. I thought we had a bad connection."

"I'm not interrupting anything. Am I?"

Images of Fyn and Bridget going at it on a boat or inside his grandmother's villa flutter through my head, and I cringe. It *is* their honeymoon, so it isn't out of the question. Though, I'd like to believe Bridget wouldn't answer the phone *while* that was going on.

She laughs lightly. "God, no. We were just having a bottle of wine and sitting by the fire. You didn't interrupt anything. I promise. You can call anytime time."

"It's your honeymoon..."

"That doesn't matter. You're my best friend...and I've worried about you since our last call."

She should be.

I'm a fucking wreck. One of those massive, mangled ten-car pile-up wrecks that you can't look away from on the highway. I peek down at the still-healing wound on my arm. No better evidence of exactly why I can't be trusted with anything. Even myself.

Yet, you're going to be bringing a baby into this world.

A fucked-up, overly complicated, far too dangerous one I can't even discuss with my best friend.

Shit.

It's best to lay the reason for my call out there. "There's something I have to tell you."

"Why do you sound so serious?"

I let out a long, slow breath. "Because I don't want to have to say it."

"Jesus, Daphne, you're scaring me here." Bridget's voice cracks. "Are you okay?"

"I'm..."—I try to think of the word—"...a little lost right now."

A lot lost.

Like I'm stuck deep in a dark wood on a moonless night, surrounded by predators circling me and waiting to make their kill.

Is Lev one of the predators, or is he the hero coming to your rescue?

"Why, Daph? What's happening?"

"So goddamn much."

But I can't tell her I'm pregnant over the phone, and it isn't my place to unleash Lev's secret when Fyn doesn't even know it.

Tell her what you can. Tell her why you called. Tell her the lie.

I tighten my grip on the sill, digging my nails into the painted wood. "I just received a call from the palace."

She hesitates a moment when I don't continue. "Okay..."

"Mira, she's..."

I can't bring myself to say the words. That somehow makes it real.

"Oh, God, no."

"She's gone." A sob slips from my lips. "I-I'm so sorry, Bridget. I know how much she meant to you."

"But...this has to be a mistake." The same disbelief I've felt since Mira slipped away hangs in her words. "Who did you talk to?"

Dammit.

I hadn't thought my lie ahead far enough. "Lev."

"Lev called you before he told Fyn?"

Shit.

"No, sorry. I'm just a little scatterbrained. It was Manuel. Lev *told* him to call me."

I freeze and wait for her to respond, to call me out on the lie because I *suck* at lying, especially to her.

She sucks in a sharp breath. "When?"

"Earlier tonight."

I try to block out the images of Mira lying in that bed, how frail she looked, and the rushed, whispered words she clung to life long enough to say.

"What happened? Was Lev there?"

"Apparently, she had a heart attack. And yes, he was there with her..."

So was I, holding her hand, learning the secrets she kept her entire life.

For the millionth time since I read that little plus sign on the test, I rest my hand over my stomach.

Bridget and Fyn will be coming back, and they're going to find a whole different world than the one they left. I just hope I don't lose Bridget when the truth comes out and she discovers how much I've betrayed her trust.

Her soft sobs float through the line and unleash my own. She sniffles. "You'll come back to Lovolia, right?"

Fucking hell.

Of course, she would ask that.

Mira meant a lot to me, too, and she knew I would want to say goodbye. Now would be the time to tell her I'm still here, that I was there with her in her final moments. But I can't bring myself to do it.

"You know how much I loved Mira. Of course, I'll return to Lovolia to be there with you."

Or *stay.*

Another lie.

So many now I can't even keep track of them.

A door opens wherever Bridget is, and the phone jostles.

"Fyn just walked in. Given the look on his face, he knows." She talks with him in the background for a minute and comes back. "He called his parents. They're still in France and will leave first thing in the morning. Then they'll send the plane for us to come back. It might be a day or two, depending on the weather conditions. There's a storm brewing that may ground us."

"Okay."

Two more days to figure out how to explain my actions... that's it. Forty-eight hours to get on the same page with Lev.

She sniffles again and blows her nose. "Start looking at flights. Get to Lovolia as quickly as you can."

"I will." It isn't a quick trip with all the necessary connections. They won't be expecting me until well after they arrive.

"Hey, Daph?"

"What?"

She pauses for a moment, like she's debating whether to say what's on her mind. "Are we okay?"

"What do you mean?"

"I could tell something was off when you landed the week before the wedding. You seemed...distracted. Not completely yourself. And how you've been talking when we've spoken over the last few weeks. I just...I feel like things have changed, and not in a good way."

Because deep down, you know *I've been lying to you.*

"I'm sorry." I swipe away an errant tear. "I've been in my head about some things."

"Is this...about me marrying Fynix?"

"What? God, no. I love Fyn. You know that, and I'm so happy for you two."

"Then why do I feel like every time we talk, we grow further apart?"

Because I've been keeping so much from you. Because I'm a shitty fucking liar.

I clench my eyes closed. "We can talk when I see you in Lovolia."

"Okay..." She sighs softly. "I love your face. You know that."

A smile pulls at my lips. "I love your butt."

She chuckles softly. "I know you do. I'll see you in a few days, right?"

"Right."

"I can't wait to squish you."

"Me, too."

I end the call and rest my forehead against the window, letting the coolness of the glass seep into my skin as I examine how the moonlight casts long shadows from the side of the maze closest to the palace.

Movement at the entrance to the high hedges catches my eye, and Lev steps out—his broad shoulders, disheveled dark hair, and fierce presence unmistakable, even from this distance.

He turns his head and looks up at the window, but with the lights off, there's no way he could know I'm here.

Then why does your entire body tingle the way it always does when he looks at you?

Because despite all the animosity and *many* unresolved issues, I can't deny the way I feel around that man. And we can't keep dancing around each other or the uncomfortable position we've gotten ourselves into.

He and I need to talk—*really* talk. After how he continues to walk away from me, it seems the only way that's going to happen is if I force it. But Lev isn't the type of man who takes too kindly to anyone telling him what to do.

I don't want to argue with him, knowing the pressure he's under right now, but it isn't just about me anymore. This little one is in for a very complicated future, one we need to figure out, hopefully before Fyn and Bridget get back.

22

DAPHNE

ANOTHER SLEEPLESS NIGHT has done nothing to relieve any of the disquiet that has ruled me for days. Even my walk this morning through the gardens, enjoying the ocean scent mingling with the blooming flowers and the magnificent splendor of colors the gardeners have managed to create, couldn't help.

Only one thing will.

My conviction to force the issue with Lev today holds strong. I thought the peaceful silence would help me figure out another way to approach it or allow me to step back and give him more space. But we don't have time for that.

Bridget and Fyn will be home soon, and after Mira's death and what his cousin asked of him last night, Lev will surely tell them everything. We need to be prepared for the questions that will come.

Which is why I wander the palace halls, trying to find wherever he's hiding out.

Why does this place have to be so massive?

My flip-flops slap against the marble floors, something I never would have noticed before Lev so aggressively noted it.

He has a point.

It is kind of annoying.

I'll never admit that to him, though. He just found out he's royalty, so he doesn't need anything else coming at him that might destroy his vision of reality—like me backing down on something.

A grin pulls at my lips, thinking about what that might do to him.

It's impossible to deny how the push and pull between us affects me. That *thing* between us has always been there. Sometimes mouthy and ugly. Sometimes sexy and undeniable. Hot and cold. Back and forth. All of it...it's...intoxicating.

Lev and what he does to me has become my drug of choice, my way of escaping the things I don't want to face. Mother had alcohol; I have the gruff, sadistic, complicated Romanov heir.

Who seems to be hiding from me this morning...

I descend the main staircase and take a right toward the direction of the gym. It's the only place I can think of to look that I haven't already. Given how incredible Lev looks naked, he must spend an awful lot of time in here.

Images of his rippling muscles, hard abs, perfect dips and valleys in all the right places, all covered by vibrant ink, fill my head, and my body heats instantly. With everything going on, the last thing I should be thinking about is getting hot and heavy with Lev, but my pregnancy hormones seem to be pushing me toward a full-on fantasy moment.

Down girl.

You're looking for him to talk. *Not* fuck.

I open the gym door and slowly weave through the empty room full of various equipment toward the row of smaller rooms along the back that serve different functions.

A loud male grunt stops me in my tracks.

I'd know that sound anywhere.

And it doesn't help push my earlier vision of Lev out of my mind because the man makes the same damn sound when he's plowing into me.

Good God, get a grip, Daphne.

I tiptoe as silently as my flip-flops allow, inching toward the open door and peeking around the corner.

Sweat glistens on the massive tattoo covering Lev's back, and beads trickle down his narrow waist to his perfect ass encased in gray sweatpants.

Sweet baby Jesus...

He throws another punch at the leather bag hanging in front of him, sending it rocketing back on the metal loop with a heavy creaking sound. It swings back toward him, and he slams his fist into it again, apparently unbothered by the wound in his arm despite blood seeping through the bandage.

Again and again.

Every muscle in his body bunches and flexes. The tendons in his neck strain. He unleashes a brutal assault on the bag as if he can somehow destroy all the things weighing on him by taking out the inanimate object.

Who does he see when he lands a punch?

Each one a deadly blow.

He isn't just trying to inflict damage; he's trying to kill.

Those hands he uses now as deadly weapons have brought me so much pleasure, and as much as I might try to deny it, I don't want it to end. Over the past few weeks, my feelings for Lev have somehow morphed from bare tolerance to an addiction.

"Are you going to just stand there and watch, Yankee?"

Shit. Busted.

Heat creeps over my neck and cheeks, my pale skin giving me away when he finally stops his relentless assault and turns toward me. His dark eyes travel over me, from my feet slowly up, pausing at my still-flat stomach, until they meet mine again.

"If you want to sneak up on someone, you need to lose those." He points toward my flip-flops with a smirk. "Or at least take them off and carry them until you've finished stalking your prey."

"My *prey?*"

He advances on me, one small step at a time, flexing his wrapped hands. "You're looking at me the same way you did in the Reading Room."

Hell.

I wish I could blame the pregnancy hormones, but I wanted Lev long before he knocked me up. And the more time we've spent together, the more I've gotten to see who he really is at his core. His attitude and behavior are a result of how he was raised—to be detached, analyze everything with a keen and skeptical eye, and keep people at arm's length. Which we now know had a completely different intent.

Lev is a good man trained to keep people out so he stayed protected, and it's forced him to push me away every chance he gets, likely when he doesn't even realize he's doing it.

But he's not going to do it now. It's time to lay my heart on the table and hope he doesn't shatter it to pieces.

"If I'm looking at you like you're *prey*, it's only because you've been running from me."

He remains standing a few feet from me, clenching and unfurling his fists at his sides.

I push off the doorjamb and take a single step toward him. "I'm trying to figure out how, after everything that happened yesterday, you could walk away from me. Didn't you think there was anything we needed to discuss?"

His jaw tightens, and his eyes narrow on me, but he doesn't offer a response. That wall he always keeps up blocks a path to him, and he has no intention of letting it down unless I *break* it.

"Our baby isn't the only one affected by your decisions and what's happening in your life, Lev." I bite back the angry words I *want* to say to relay the tangle of emotions in a way that won't make him run even harder from me. "You walked off and left me standing there, like you've done every single fucking time we've needed to talk." A small sob slips from my lips, and a tear leaks from the corner of my eye. "As if...as if I'm *no one*. It's like I'm *nothing* to you."

Saying the words should relieve a ton of weight I've been carrying, but the burden only feels heavier, knowing it's all out there now. I've said it all, laid everything I've kept so close to my chest out in the open. Somehow, through all this, I actually *want* to be with Lev and want him to want me, too.

There's nothing left to do but *wait* for this man to respond.

And Lev isn't exactly known for his ability to communicate —especially with me.

We stare each other down, and I wrap my arms around myself, suddenly needing the meager protection it provides.

He uses his forearm to wipe the sweat off his brow and steps toward me, his tongue darting across his lips.

This conversation would be much easier if I didn't have to stare at the man shirtless and sweaty, knowing what it feels like to have all that passion and power he used on the heavy bag directed at me.

And as much as I hate to admit it, I don't want to lose it. I don't want to lose *him* and whatever *this* is between us. Despite all the warnings that I should guard my heart where he's concerned, it's irrelevant. Because this man is a thief. He stole it the night of the wedding, and I just didn't know it.

I didn't want to see it. I didn't want to admit what was happening between us. I was too wrapped up in my drama back home and worrying about lying to Bridget to see what Lev and I were doing over the time we spent together at Elysium.

It wasn't just sex. It *never* was. No matter how much we

might have tried to convince ourselves otherwise. Every time we kissed, each heated caress, the intimate moments we tried to write off as merely fulfilling animalistic needs, they all brought us to something neither of us could have expected.

Something I *know* he feels too.

Yet, he stands silently in front of me.

"Is that what I am, Lev? *Nothing?*"

The word hangs in the air between us as I wait for *any* response from him, any acknowledgment that he's *hearing* me. But it feels like waiting for something he has no intention of ever giving me, maybe because he's incapable.

LEV

DAPHNE'S QUESTION might as well be a bullet slamming into my chest. It knocks me back a step, and I dig my fingers into the wrappings on my hands, fighting the urge to turn around and lash out at the bag with the anger her words bring.

Nothing.

I've somehow managed to convince the mother of my child that she means *nothing* to me.

You fucking wanker...

Every chance I've had, I've blown it. Royally fucked up everything with this woman since the night of the wedding. I've said and done all the wrong things. Acted like a selfish prick and treated her like a plaything, merely there to entertain my cock while I tried to work through my shit.

This may be my last chance with her before she walks away and leaves me for good. And I couldn't bloody blame her if she did.

My chest still heaves, my lungs struggling to get back to normal breathing after my workout. The wound on my arm feels like someone is twisting a knife in it, but I welcome the pain I deserve. It's why I kept driving myself, kept hitting when my body begged me to stop. I needed that punishment.

And now, I need to be straight with her; I need to unleash everything I've been holding back.

I start unwrapping my hands, slowly unwinding the material and letting it fall to the floor. "You want to talk about it, Yankee? Let's talk about it." I try to keep my anger out of my words because none of it is directed at the beautiful woman standing in front of me, but it's there all the same, weighing down each syllable. "My grandmother is gone. The only person on this Earth I shared blood with. My only true *family*. And if that's not bad enough, she left me with this massive secret, this responsibility I am in *no way* prepared for." I take another step toward her. "And to top it off, I got you pregnant—"

She flinches as if I've struck her and tries to look away, but I close the distance between us and take her face in palm, forcing her to meet my gaze.

Her bottom lip quivers slightly. "That's all you care about. The baby. Your *heir*. This baby is the only reason you came to the airport to stop me from leaving."

I tighten my grip on her. Daphne has never had anyone in her corner, no real family besides Bridget. Her piece-of-shit mother never gave her a warm welcoming home where she felt loved and wanted. So, I understand why she thinks that. Coupled with my behavior, it's a logical deduction. But she couldn't be more wrong.

"As usual, Yankee, you didn't let me finish." I lightly drag my fingers over a tear stuck under her left eye. "I got you pregnant, and I've been acting like an absolute wanker since you told me."

Her eyes widen slightly, and her lips part. I press my thumb over them, silencing whatever retort she has waiting for me.

Because I am nowhere near finished, and if she interrupts me, it could devolve into another argument.

"I may not have acted like it, but I'm bloody thrilled that you're carrying my child." The warmth blooming in my chest confirms the words I knew I needed to say. "I was shocked at first, overwhelmed at the thought of being responsible for a life when I couldn't even get control of my own. I failed Fyn, and now I was going to fail you and a baby. I was terrified of what it meant for *you*. Because you've been hiding something that's been weighing on you since you got here, whatever kept you here in Lovolia, and I didn't know that you'd even *want* this baby." I drag my thumb over her lips, feeling them tremble beneath my touch. "But I see that you do, even with all the complications that come with it, like being tied to me for life."

Certainly not anything I'd wish on anyone, *even before learning about my lineage.*

I hold her tear-soaked gaze and splay my free hand over her belly. "I love that I'll get to watch your belly grow with our baby. I love that I'll get to spoil you, care for you, give you everything you could ever need during this pregnancy..." I lean in closer, resting my forehead on hers and inhaling that lemon and sunshine scent that always makes my cock twitch. "But I'm scared to fucking death that I have no way to protect you, no way to keep you and the baby, our baby, safe, apart from locking you up within the walls of this palace surrounded by guards and never letting you out of my sight again." I inhale a shaking breath, but now that the words are flowing, I can't stop. "Knowing what you do now, I understand why you hate me."

Another tear slips down her cheek. She pulls her head away from mine and stares at me with so much confusion. "I don't hate you, Lev. Far from it. That's the problem."

"No." I shake my head. "The problem is *me*. That I've been such a bloody mess and have allowed it to make you think something that couldn't be further from the truth." I despise the uncertainty with which she looks at me, that I made her feel this way because I couldn't get a grip on my own emotions. "Yankee, you're not nothing; you're *every*thing to me."

Which is why knowing I can't protect her from everything that's happening shatters me so completely. It's the one single fucking thing I should be able to provide—safety. But I failed at keeping Fynix safe. I failed at keeping Daphne safe from *me*. And now, because of the blood flowing through my veins and those of the tiny baby growing inside her, I've put their lives at risk with no obvious way out.

Her silence seizes my heart, and I grasp her hand and place it over the spot that aches for her, right at the center of my chest.

"My heart is yours and will always belong to you, Yankee. If you want it. If you can ever forgive me for being such a bloody wanker."

Tears slide down her cheeks freely now, but she still hasn't uttered a word. Her silence is so unlike her that one question slams into my head.

Did I completely misread this?

I slide my hand from her cheek to grasp her at the nape, digging my fingers in the same way I have so many times in the past few weeks. "Say something, Yankee, or I'll start to feel like a real fucking idiot—"

Her lips twitch before they break into a genuine smile. "You *are* an idiot, *Yanky*. And you have been a real *bloody wanker,* but you're *my* idiot."

Bloody hell.

I never thought I wanted to hear those words from a woman's mouth so badly, let alone from *this* woman. But the moment they leave her lips, my heart starts beating under her hand again, finally feeling full for the first time.

All I want is to touch her, taste her, and let her know my words are true.

"Let me show you how fucking much you mean to me." I crash my lips to hers, dragging her fully against me so I can feel all of her. "Christ, Yankee...I need this. I need you."

Every soft curve.

Every little moan.

Every finger scoring my bare skin.

All of it belongs to me.

I glide my tongue along hers, the taste I've missed so much fully hardening my cock between us.

How did I ever resist this woman?

It seems impossible now. I was a fool to think once with her would satiate this desire. No matter how many times I touch her, kiss her, and feel her moving under and over me, it will *never* be enough.

I shift my hand from her stomach and clutch the front of her throat, palming it lightly.

"Lev..." My name falls from her kiss-swollen lips like a plea, and I drag my head back and find her blue eyes burning with a hunger I share.

I apply slight pressure, gently walking her backward until she's pressed against the door frame. "I need to be inside you." I kiss across her pink cheek to that spot just behind her ear. "Please, Yankee..."

Daphne issues a mewl, clinging to me tightly, and seeks my mouth with hers. I release my grip on her throat, but she captures my wrist.

"No, don't stop." She moves my hand back to her neck and directs my fingers around it. "Don't. Stop."

The vibration of her request against my palm is like kerosene thrown on an already raging fire.

My free hand drops to her waistband, and she reaches to help me shove down her leggings and knickers. I take her mouth again, a punishing, bruising kiss that matches my need for her, only pulling away long enough to help her kick off her damn flip-flops and tug her leggings free.

I let them fall to the floor beside us and trace my fingers down over her abdomen, pausing to acknowledge what we did. We may not have intended it. We may not be ready for it. We may be a complete wreck. But we created a life.

Our baby.

I lay my forehead against hers, our heavy breaths mingling. "So fucking perfect."

She returns her hand to my chest and digs her nails into my skin, silently pleading with me to continue. I squeeze her throat and drop my hand to swipe my fingers through her wet pussy.

"Oh, God…" Her head falls back against the doorjamb, her eyes rolling up and her mouth falling open. "Please…"

She's never looked more beautiful, so at peace. Everything that held us back has fled with recent confessions, and I can't deny what's really happening here.

I'm falling in love with the Yankee.

I push two fingers inside her tight heat. "So fucking wet for me, Yankee. Always so ready for my cock."

Another throaty mewl falls from her lips, and she clenches her cunt around my fingers. My cock jumps in response, eager to be embedded deep inside her again.

I pull my fingers free, earning a sharp gasp of surprise from the woman who absolutely destroys me without even trying.

Her open lips are too tempting to pass up.

I slip my wet fingers between them. "Suck."

23

DAPHNE

I SWIRL my tongue around his fingers, the flavor of my arousal making my pussy clench, desperate to be filled by the only thing that will satisfy the burning need that's only grown for this man since he said the words I've been longing to hear.

You're everything to me.

It felt like it would never come, that Lev would never admit he felt anything for me but lust and annoyance, but now that it's out there, there's no putting it back.

We can never go back to the way things were, and I wouldn't want to.

I suction around his fingers hard, sucking them the same way I did his cock a few nights ago. Lev's eyes darken to almost black. He pulls his hand from my neck and shoves his sweatpants down, freeing his cock between us. He jerks his fingers from my mouth and slams his lips to mine as he lifts me to his waist.

His hard length presses against my core, and I slip a hand

between us to align him so he can slide home with one drive of his hips.

I drop my head back. "Oh, *fuck!*"

My body strains to accommodate his size, stretching and clutching at him as he plunges in to the hilt. No matter how many times we're together like this, it always feels new. An exhilarating rollercoaster of pleasure and pain. A crazy addiction I can never quell.

I score my nails along his bare shoulders, grasping for purchase, and Lev drags his hips back and thrusts into me again, slamming me against the unyielding doorframe at my back.

Hard and rough.

Just like it always is with Lev.

But it's what I need.

What we both need.

Slow and sweet won't cut it after what we've been through the last few days. And it may never be like that between us. Our entire relationship is based on our aggression toward each other. Why would it be any different with sex?

He pounds into me relentlessly, like he's trying to drive the truth of his confession into me, as if the only thing that matters in this world is us in this moment in time. And I give into him, allowing him to own my body, my soul.

Because this man would never hurt me. He would give his life for me and this baby. He would do *anything* to ensure our happiness. Only his fear that he'll fail has held him back.

Until now.

I've unleashed something primal and feral in him. Some animalistic need to take what's his and mark me permanently.

"Fuck, Yankee..." His low growl at my ear as he drives into me again sends a shudder through my entire body. "I love how you take my cock."

I grasp the hair at his nape with one hand and cling to his

shoulder with the other, altering the angle of my hips so the head of his erection hits my G-spot. He grips my hips, digging his fingers into the soft flesh, and pistons into me ruthlessly.

God, this man can fuck.

All the passion and turmoil boil inside him, and he unleashes all of it on me mercilessly.

My orgasm slams into me as violently and unexpectedly as my feelings for Lev, and I spasm around him, my pussy clasping and clenching his cock. Tingling heat spreads through my limbs, my brain filling with the blissful fog that blocks out other thoughts.

He doesn't relent, fucking me through my orgasm without slowing, each slap of his hips against mine another statement of his claim on my soul. "Christ, Daphne, look at you, coming all over my cock right here in the gym where anyone could walk in and see how much you belong to me."

Oh, hell...

His slamming hips draw out a second orgasm I wasn't aware I was capable of, and he slips his hand between us and glides his finger over my clit, dragging it out almost painfully. Just when it starts to be too much, he trails his fingers through the wetness where we connect and shifts them back to my ass.

"What about here?" He swirls the digits around the tight opening. "Are you ready for me here, Yankee?"

"God...yes."

"I can't wait to fuck you here, Daphne, but for now, this will have to do."

He works two fingers into my ass. The foreign stretch makes my mouth fall open in a silent gasp. His hips drive forward, forcing his cock into me while he plays somewhere no one has been before.

Every nerve ending in my body fires simultaneously, and his pace increases, the muscles of his neck straining as he fights his release.

The slow burn of another orgasm starts, this one threatening to drown me. "Oh, God!"

Lev freezes, stopping himself deep inside me. "What? Are you all right?" His glazed-over eyes morph to concern. "Shit, the baby! Did I hurt the baby?" He starts to draw out of me. "Fuck! I was too rough! I'm so sorry!"

I can't stop the peal of laughter that falls from my lips before I press them to his. "No, Lev. I'm fine, and you can't hurt the baby by fucking me senseless."

His cock slips free, and he sets my feet back onto the floor. My body instantly mourns the loss of the connection, but Lev's worried brow draws a grin across my lips.

"You're certain? The baby is all right?"

I smile and step up to him, pressing my mouth to his, languidly stroking his tongue with mine as I take his wet cock in my hand. "Yes, Lev. The baby is fine and will be fine any time we do this"—I motion between us—"throughout my pregnancy."

He pulls back, and his mouth twitches as he fights a smile. "That's good to know because I don't imagine I'll be able to keep my hands off you for long."

Then why the hell did you just leave us hanging?

His still-hard cock juts out between his legs, my fingers wrapped tightly around it, and my clit throbs, overstimulated yet craving another release.

He grasps my wrist and pulls me free of his erection, then toes off his shoes and shoves down his pants to kick them free. With a grin, he grabs our clothes from the floor and takes my hand. "Come with me."

I thought that's what we were doing...

But I let him lead me through the gym and down a hallway to the side I've never ventured down.

"Lev, I don't have any pants on."

He tosses a lecherous grin over his shoulder. "I'm aware, Yankee."

How can he be so cavalier about this?

"What if other people show up?"

"They won't." He laughs like he knows something I don't and pulls me around the corner, through a vast shower room, and to a closed door tucked behind it. "In here, Yankee."

He releases my hand and opens the door to a small massage room, urging me forward with his palm against my bare ass. I step inside, and he follows hot on my heels, closing the door behind him before he spins me around and pushes me toward the massage table.

"Hop up, Yankee." Lev wraps his hands around my waist, lifts me easily to sit on the white sheet, then steps between my spread legs, putting his cock at exactly the right height to slip back inside me. But he holds back, toying with me, dragging the head of his cock through my soaked pussy and against my clit. "You're fucking beautiful, Daphne."

I wrap my legs around his hips, pulling him closer, forcing the tip of his dick inside me. But he stops me from moving him any farther, not giving me what I really want.

He smiles down at me and takes my face between his palms. "I need to hear you say it, Yankee."

In my lust-induced haze, I can't seem to grasp what he wants. "Say what?"

"That we're putting the past behind us." He presses a chaste kiss to my lips. "That we'll be all right." Another. "That you're *mine*."

He crushes his mouth against mine this time. Not just a kiss. A declaration. An agreement that we *are* together. And when he slides his hard length fully inside me, there isn't any question what my answer will be.

There can't be, not when this is exactly what I've been waiting for. I didn't even know I needed Lev until my world crumbled. He gave me a safe place to land, warm arms to secure me, and passion that ignited something dead inside me.

I finally understand how Bridget fell so hard, so fast for Fynix. If it's anything like how I feel about this enigmatic, complicated, dangerous man, it isn't something anyone could ever deny.

And why would anyone want to?

Nothing can compare to this rush, this high, this absolute ecstasy being with Lev creates—and I never want to let it go.

♔

LEV

DAPHNE RELEASES A LOW MOAN, her pussy instantly clenching around me, drawing me in deeper until it feels like I've been completely consumed by her. "I'm yours, Lev." She pants between thrusts. "God, I am *so* yours."

Those words ignite a light somewhere in the part of me that's always been clouded by a heavy darkness, a spark of life to my soul I never knew it needed to feel alive.

I've spent thirty years believing I knew who and what I was. I did my job. Protected my best friend. Watched him grow into his role and handle it with a grace I couldn't comprehend. But it always felt like something was missing. I just couldn't ever place what it was or see beyond the present to what my future could be.

Daphne and this baby *are* my future.

Whatever else might be requested or expected of me, *they* are what matters.

Their happiness.

Their safety.

Their love.

"Fuck. Yes. You. Are." I punctuate each word with a hard

thrust, then deepen our kiss and pick up my pace, determined to prove to her that I won't make the same mistakes I have recently, to make her feel everything I can't seem to voice. Because I've never experienced it before. I've never believed it existed. Even after I saw Fyn and Bridget, I couldn't let myself hope it would ever be possible for me.

And we've only just begun.

But the moment she forced me to look her in the eye and called me out, forced me to *see*, it hit me harder than any bullet.

I would kill for her.

I would *die* for her.

My loyalty to her trumps that of my country and my king.

All the things I thought I hated about Daphne are precisely what drew me to her and make it impossible to walk away. Her fiery spirit. Her smart mouth. Her ability to get under my skin with a simple look or word. Daphne Jennings doesn't back down from me, and that's precisely the type of woman I need by my side. Someone who will constantly challenge me and keep me on my toes. Someone who demands more from me.

I thrust harder and dig my fingers into her fleshy hips. She falls back onto the table, reaching above her to grasp the far edge to keep herself from sliding across it. From this angle, I can watch my soaked cock slip in and out of her tight cunt like my own personal porno.

Bloody hell, that's hot.

She clenches down on me with every retreat, and I shift my thumb to her clit.

"You're going to come on my cock again." I roll the rough pad across her tiny nub, lifting her hip with the other hand to alter the angle slightly. "Fuck you feel good."

I grit my teeth to keep from coming before she does and redouble my efforts, rolling my hips to meet hers, driving myself as hard as possible. She pants, shaking her head side to side, her tight grip on the edge of the table making it creak.

"Oh, fuck!" Her cunt grips my cock tightly, and her body convulses, bowing up toward me as she finds her release. "Lev!"

My name falls from her lips like a prayer—or maybe a curse —and she hangs in the air for a moment, her entire being suspended in that spot between Heaven and Earth.

She sags back to the table, panting heavily, and I slide my hand across her belly, palming her delicate, perfect flesh. Her eyes flutter open, and she rests her hand over mine.

I take a moment to appreciate the perfection of this moment. "Look at you laid out on this table for me. So fucking beautiful, Yankee. *Velikolepnyy.*"

Daphne pulls her hand from mine and sits, shifting toward me with my cock still buried deep inside her.

A grin plays on her lips. "You aren't so hard on the eyes yourself..."

In one quick motion, she plants her hands on my bare chest and pushes me back a step. My dick slips out of her wet heat, and I release a disgruntled groan.

"What the bloody hell are you doing, Yankee?"

It's taken all my willpower to keep from blowing my load while I got her off, and I'm right at the precipice, dangling over the ledge and barely clinging on. If she thinks she's playing games with me today, she's severely underestimated my need to fully claim her.

I grasp her thighs, keeping her on the table, and raise a brow. "Well, Yankee?"

Daphne offers me a slow smirk and nudges me out of the way. "Don't worry. I won't leave you hanging."

Growling low, I take my cock in my hand, stroking it slowly. "Yes, you would..."

She chuckles and grabs a white towel from a stack beside the massage table, dropping it onto the tile floor at my feet.

Bloody hell.

I feather my lips over hers and drag her up against me. "I think I know where this is headed...and I'm on board."

She scores her nails over my chest and down my abs, sliding to her knees before me.

"Fuck, Yankee." I slip my hand under her chin to tilt it up. "Look at you on your knees for me. So bloody sexy."

Sudden visions of people bowing, people on their knees before me for another reason, flash through my head, the reality I've tried to ignore pounding against my skull, trying to ruin this moment with Daphne.

But I won't let that happen.

I push away all those worries. The doubts. The uncertainty. So I can concentrate on the one sure thing in my life right now.

She takes my cock in her hand and stares up at me from under long lashes. Whatever I used to see there when we argued has disappeared completely, replaced with an affection that makes my heart skip a beat.

Is this what it could have been like all the time if I'd given her a chance?

A pang of guilt over how we've acted for so long hits me, and I grip her chin to ensure she meets my gaze. "We aren't ever going back to the way things were, Yankee. Everything else may be a clusterfuck of epic proportions, but I can promise you that."

Unshed tears shine in her eyes, and she leans forward and rubs the tip of my cock across her pouty mouth. My entire body stiffens at the simple contact, and when she opens for me and takes me to the back of her throat, I have to fight the urge to come on the spot.

She gives a little hum of approval. That slight vibration makes my balls tighten, and a low tingle starts at the base of my spine.

"I'm going to come in two fucking seconds if you keep that up."

The warning only seems to spur her on, and she pulls off my length to the tip and twirls her tongue on the spot on the underside that sets me off. My hips buck forward, and she swallows me again, taking me so far back that when she swallows, every nerve in the head of my cock gets a fucking massage.

"Fuck, Daphne. Fuck." I tangle my fingers in her hair, gripping the strands tightly as she works me over with her incredible mouth and those soft hands.

I can't hold back any longer. Watching her come again and again on my cock has ripped away any potential for me to contain the primal need. I piston myself in and out of her mouth, and like the strong, determined woman she's always been, she takes it over and over, deep into her throat, humming her approval.

The saucy wench knows exactly what that does to me. "Ah, fuck."

My hips jerk as I come down her throat, her blue eyes locked with mine the whole time. She swallows each spurt, taking it down like she needs it to live, but I'm the one who can't imagine life without her.

In a matter of weeks, Daphne has gone from Bridget's annoying best friend to my entire world.

I don't deserve her.

Not after the way I've acted.

Not when she's getting dragged into a deadly quagmire because of her involvement with me.

Not when our child's life may be at risk simply because I'm his or her father.

Almost as if she can sense the shift in my mood, she releases my cock from her mouth and pulls her hand from between her legs, her eyes flashing with concern.

Fucking hell. She was touching herself while she sucked me off.

"That's the sexiest thing I've ever seen, Yankee."

I swipe my thumb over her plump bottom lip, catching the

bead of cum there, and push it into her mouth. This time, I don't have to command her. Daphne grins around it and sucks it off, gliding her tongue around my finger the same way she did my cock.

A future that looked so uncertain even twenty-four hours ago has now solidified.

No matter what else happens.

No matter what decisions I make.

No matter where life takes me.

I won't go anywhere or do anything without this woman by my side.

24

LEV

A MASSIVE BOULDER of dread sits in my stomach as I make my way through the palace halls toward the king's private office. But I can't delay this conversation any longer, no matter how badly I wanted to stay in bed wrapped around Daphne for the rest of my damn life.

Bloody hell...so much has changed in the last few days.

I have a beautiful woman. We're having a baby...and I'm the bloody Romanov heir.

Too bad I still have no fucking idea what to do about any of it.

But I meant what I said to Daphne last night. No matter what happens, she and our baby are the top priority. They have to be. Which means this conversation with the king and queen could get very uncomfortable.

There's no telling what they expect of me, what they're waiting to tell me.

My hand shakes as I raise it to knock on the king's private office door. Part of me wishes Fynix were here for this meeting, so he could interject his thoughts and give me some backup with his parents, but this can't wait for him to return.

"Enter."

I'd rather turn around, bury myself in Daphne again, and pretend none of this is happening.

I pause with my hand on the knob, inhale a deep breath, and push it open to find the king sitting behind his desk and the queen in one of the armchairs facing him. They both bear the same redness around their eyes that Daphne and I do— along with everyone else I've seen around the palace. Losing Gran has hit all of us hard, and no one is bothering to hide it.

"Lev, dear, come in." The queen motions for me to enter. "Take a seat."

I close the door behind me and bow to them. "Your Majesties."

She waves a dismissive hand at me, giving me the soft smile she reserves for family. "No need for any of those formalities when it's just us. You know that, Lev."

I clear my throat and shift on my feet, avoiding looking at the two people who have been so central to my life, suddenly uncomfortable in the room for the first time. The new knowledge I have and the new role I'm expected to take changes everything. Something they've known about my entire life and helped Gran keep hidden from me.

And I'm expected to process all this and just fall into this role I don't even want.

The king motions toward the empty chair. "Please take a seat. I imagine you have a myriad of questions."

I manage a half smile and take a seat. "That would be an understatement, Your Majesty."

The queen reaches out and pats my arm. "How are you doing, dear? Are you eating? Sleeping all right?" She sucks in a deep breath, tears shimmering in the blue eyes she shares with

Fynix. "I'm so sorry about Mira. You know how important she was to all of us."

I rest my hand over the queen's, a move that would never be acceptable were we in public, and release a heavy sigh. "I'm sorry you two weren't here and didn't get to say goodbye."

The king shifts uneasily, glancing away and blinking rapidly. He doesn't want me to see him cry. "I am too, son, but you were with her, and that's what matters."

"You're right. Family is all that matters."

The king and queen exchange a look, and the queen pulls her hand away and smooths out her skirt. "I imagine you want to ask us some questions."

I chuckle at the absurdity of the statement. "A few."

She glances between her husband and me. "I think we should get Fynix on the line."

Hell.

I would've had to tell him as soon as he got back, but the thought of doing it over the phone instead of in person feels wrong. "Maybe we should wait until he and Bridget return."

The king leans forward, resting his forearms on his desk, his heavy brow furrowing. "I don't think that's wise. They're going to be traveling and need to be aware of this potential threat. I understand why you and Manuel withheld it from them when they were at the villa and safe, because you didn't want to disrupt the honeymoon, but anything could happened once they leave that compound."

Dammit.

"You're right, as usual, Your Majesty."

He offers me a half grin, grabs his phone, and dials, putting it on speakerphone.

Fyn answers on the third ring. "Father, please tell me this isn't more bad news."

The king offers me a tight smile. "I wouldn't call it bad, but it's something that can't wait until you return. You're still on schedule to get back tomorrow?"

"It appears that way. This weather system should clear by morning."

"Excellent." The king's gaze darts between his wife and me. "Just so you're aware, I have your mother and Lev here with me in my office."

"That can't be good." Fyn knows the tone of his father's voice all too well. "What's going on?"

The king leans back in his chair. "I'm going to let Lev take over since this affects him the most."

Shit.

I rub at the wound on my arm, wishing I had spent a minute considering how to tell Fyn any of this. Leaning forward, I rest my elbows on my knees. "Before Gran passed, she revealed something." I look between the king and queen. "A secret your family has helped her keep for a very long time."

"A secret?" The phone jostles slightly and the line crackles. "What the hell are you talking about?"

The queen purses her lips. "Language, Fynix."

"My apologies, Mother."

I push out of the chair and pace, suddenly feeling like a caged animal, trapped with the truth. "There's no easy way to say this, but...I'm the Romanov heir."

"Excuse me?" The disbelief and confusion in Fyn's voice matches mine.

"I'm the Romanov heir."

"Surely you're joking." He issues a strained laugh, his disbelief evident. "How is that possible?"

Pinching the back of my neck, I shake my head at the absurdity of the entire situation. "I asked the same question when Grandmother dropped this on me after I was chased and shot."

"Chased and shot? What the bloody hell has been going on there since I've been gone?"

"Fynix." The queen snaps and slams her palm against the desk. "You will watch your language."

Her husband offers her a stern look. "A little flowery language might be warranted in this situation, dear."

She leans back, giving him an *I can't believe you questioned me* glare before returning her focus to me to wait for me to continue.

"I was leaving Elysium to meet with Gran, and an SUV chased me. They shot, and I returned fire. I was struck in the arm, but I'm fine. When I got back to the palace, Gran revealed the grand lie that my life has been."

Fyn scoffs. "You'll need to start from the beginning here because I'm still not following."

I look to the king to jump in, because he's known about this giant secret far longer than I have.

He clears his throat and shifts forward slightly, closer to the phone. "Lev's great-grandfather, Alexander Orlov, was the child of Tsar Nicholas and Tsarina Alexandra."

"What?"

"I understand this is hard to follow, son, and I'm doing my best to explain it as simply as possible. When they executed the Romanovs, their nanny, Ola, was aware that the Tsarina was concealing a pregnancy and was quite close to delivering. Once the Bolsheviks abandoned the bodies in the basement where they had carried out the executions, she sneaked down and found Alexandra with a bullet wound to the head but still breathing. She realized there could be a chance to save the child, so she took action."

"Bloody hell, that's insane..."

Right there with you, mate.

The king grabs his pen and flips it between his fingers, apparently as affected by telling the story as I am. "With the assistance of other supporters, they concealed that she had performed a C-section and smuggled the baby out of Russia.

Tsar Nicholas' cousin, the King of England at the time, was also the cousin of your great-great-grandmother and believed that Lovolia would be a safe place for them to hide. The nanny took the last name Orlov and raised Alexander as her own child here at the palace." He looks up at me. "This was over a century ago, and we've managed to conceal the identity of the heir since then—Lev's great-grandfather, grandmother, and his father, and now...Lev."

Fyn releases an incredulous snort. "Then what the hell happened? Why was Lev attacked?"

I absently rub at the bandage on my arm. "We're not entirely sure. Grandmother said some of the Tsarists in Russia were being rounded up and questioned. When we reviewed the surveillance footage of the car chase, we saw a distinct tattoo on one of the gunmen. It's either connected to me being the Romanov heir or to what I did when I went undercover with the bratva. Grandmother believed it was the former."

"Good God." Fyn mutters something under his breath he doesn't dare say to his mother. "I can't believe you didn't tell me any of this."

Just wait...

If this is his reaction to me withholding the information about the shooting, I can't image how he'll feel when I reveal what's happened with Daphne.

Still, I can understand his anger. If he kept things from me, I would feel the same way. "I only learned it two nights ago myself, and I wasn't in any mental state to be unloading this on you after Gran's death."

"I meant the shooting and the car chase. You were *shot,* and no one told me."

"You were safe at your grandmother's villa. We doubled security without you knowing. It was safer for you to stay there. Manuel and I agreed."

"Jesus—"

"But now you'll be traveling home, you need to be aware of the risks. If someone is after me, they may also come after you, so your security has been alerted to a potential threat and you need to watch your back."

"That's your job, Lev."

At least, it was, before he forbade me from going with them.

"I know, but you wouldn't let me come with you, Fyn."

He barks out a laugh, bringing some much-needed levity to the tense conversation. "I guess maybe I should have."

For the first time since he sent me on the forced holiday, I'm glad he didn't. If I had gone with him, none of this with Daphne would've happened. She would've discovered she was pregnant alone—either at Elysium or back in the States—and we would've continued with the animosity and bullshit between us, potentially forever.

Fyn releases a heavy sigh. "Well, it seems we have a lot to discuss when I get back."

He has no idea.

The queen offers me a half-smile. "Keep us updated on your travel plans should they change. Be careful, son. Keep that beautiful wife of yours safe."

"You know I will, Mother."

The king ends the call and leans back in his chair. "Now the real question, Lev...what do you intend to do about your birthright? If this is about that, if you are being targeted because you're a Romanov, it may be impossible for you to stay hidden any longer."

I groan and drop back into the seat, running my hands through my hair. "Grandmother had me call one of her cousins back home, and he said my supporters believe this is the time for me to step forward. With the country in political turmoil and the questioning of the current leadership, they feel this might be the only chance for the Romanovs to regain control."

The king purses his lips and steeples his fingers in front of his mouth. "And what do *you* think?"

As if that's an easy question to answer.

I still don't have one, but I have to give him something. "I think my entire life has been scripted. That all this"—I wave my hand around his office—"was some big game designed to maneuver me around for other people's plans."

The queen rests her hand on my arm again. "I'm sorry you feel that way, Lev." She sighs. "I won't lie. We all knew what we were doing, Mira, the king, and I. We understood how important it was for you to be exposed to palace life, the intricate workings behind the scenes, and the types of decisions that need to be made every day, in case the time ever came. But I'll be honest with you; I didn't think it would. It's been one hundred years, and after your father's suspicious death, we truly believed this would be a secret that would never touch you during your lifetime. I'm sorry you feel like your life isn't yours anymore."

How could I not feel that way?

Decisions have been made about my life and future, since before I was born. But there are two lights shining bright in the darkness now, waiting for me out in the garden.

The king finally sets down his pen and levels his all too assessing gaze on me. "I need to know where you're at with this decision, Lev. As you know, this will greatly affect many tenuous political situations for Lovolia."

Talk about bloody pressure.

"I don't have an answer, Your Majesty. But please understand, Lovolia is my home, and I will always be loyal to you and the crown, whoever wears it."

A rare smile graces his lips. "I never doubted that for a second."

He rises, and I do the same, accepting his handshake across the desk. "Please keep us informed of any additional information or if you'd like to discuss your future plans further."

"I'm sure I will, but right now, I have a date."

♛

DAPHNE

FOR THE FIRST time in what felt like forever, I woke up content, grounded, centered. It had everything to do with Lev's arms wrapped around me, his lips on my heated skin, and the way he slid between my legs and gave me the best reason to stay in bed longer with his tongue...and then the rest of him.

My body heats at the memory as much as from the brilliant Mediterranean sun shining down on me from the cloudless sky above. The picture-perfect weather and beautiful scenery in Lovolia would make anyone want to stay forever. It's no wonder Bridget fell in love with this place as much as she did with Fynix.

But whether I can stay still feels like a massive uncertainty —because of what's been asked of Lev and what may force me back to Denver.

Could this really be my home?

Is that even possible?

The pleasant feeling hanging over me since I woke and came out to the gardens dissipates as the reason Lev is meeting with the king and queen hangs overhead like a dark cloud.

They're discussing his future—a future that now includes me and this baby. Maybe I should have accepted his invitation to join them, but that would mean revealing that I'm pregnant, and neither of us is ready to let that cat out of the bag yet. No one even knows I was at Elysium with him except for the doctor, Manuel, and the two guards who arrived with him to bring me back to the palace.

It's better no one knows or asks questions—at least until Lev has made his decision. And I don't think Elander and Elizabeth Yates will force his hand in that regard. Fynix's parents are Lev's family, whether he sees it like that or not. They look at him with the same tender love they look upon their son, and they'll protect him any way they can. Lev hasn't allowed himself to see that because he's been so closed off for so long to the idea of love—in any form. Maybe now, he'll see the truth of that relationship and the love the royal family has for him.

It's the only way he'll be able to make his decision with a clear head—if he has the support of everyone around him, those who truly want what's best for him.

And he will need to make a decision—sooner rather than later.

This is the time to reclaim your birthright.

The powerful statement continues to ring in my ears as I stroll along the pebble walkway through the garden. I stop to pick a few roses from a row of bushes lining either side of the trail, mindful of the thorns so I don't ruin my yellow sundress by bleeding all over it.

That would be just like me.

Or tripping in my flip-flops and ending up face-first in the gravel.

Again.

I still can't believe I climbed over the fence at Elysium...and broke the window...and that it all led to *this.* Waiting in the garden with a picnic basket and blanket for the man I never thought I could be in the same room without it devolving into violence or harsh words.

Or sex.

My cheeks heat, and I pluck a few more flowers and continue toward the small patch of grass nestled inside the maze, where I can spread out the blanket and wait for Lev.

The tall hedges behind me that make up the maze wall

provide privacy, yet I can still see the castle from here and watch for Lev when he comes out. And here, we can pretend nothing else exists, at least for a short while.

A peaceful, quiet spot in the center of a massive hurricane of uncertainty.

Something we both need because we're not going to have very much of it anytime soon. Bridget and Fyn will be home tomorrow, with Mira's funeral the day after. And we still have no clear idea who was behind the attack on Lev or exactly, though we have our suspicions.

I release a cleansing breath, trying to concentrate on our picnic rather than all the complications, and settle down onto the blanket, unloading the various items I snagged from the kitchen. My first effort to win over Lev with food ended with him caving and allowing me to stay at Elysium. Hopefully, this endeavor goes equally well and will help him find some peace for a few hours.

Like he gave me last night.

Cocooned in his arms, I could let my lies to Bridget go. I could forget the *mess* I left in Colorado. I could just *be* and feel. That's all I want for him, too.

If there were any way to help him with this decision, to offer him guidance on what he should do, I would offer it in a heartbeat. But though this affects me, it isn't my place to try to sway him. He'll have to decide for himself, and I'll have to do my best to support him, no matter what that means.

What his cousin suggested will be a massive undertaking—one I can't even comprehend.

How does one stage a coup, anyway?

It's the last question I thought I'd ever be asking. Yet here I am, hooking up with the Tsar by birthright, with a tiny prince or princess growing inside me.

Will Lev truly be able to keep us safe?

Whether we stay here or he accepts his role and returns to

Russia, it feels like stepping into a hornet's nest of problems neither of us needs.

Don't think about it today.

It will wait for tomorrow. On this perfect day, I want to enjoy being here with him for what little time we'll have before the proverbial shit hits the fan.

Perhaps Fyn will be able to offer Lev some much-needed insight. After all, he is the future king. He's been groomed to take his father's throne from the day he was born, and he is damn good at it. Just like I'm sure Lev will be.

Confident.

Strong.

Loyal.

Unyielding.

The man never wavers on his mission, whether that be to get me off or protect the crown. But what about when he's the one wearing it...

He swore this baby and I were the most important things to him—his *family*—but he can't simply turn his back on his blood.

Can he?

Birds scatter over the hedge behind me, making me jerk toward the noise. I press my hand over my racing heart, sucking in a deep breath.

Christ...

I'm too jumpy with everything that's happened. Despite doing my best to try to relax for my health and the baby's, every little noise seems to have me on edge.

Perhaps rightfully so, as the danger to Lev seems very real. But not here. The palace is the most secure place in Lovolia, and these gardens are the closest we can come to privacy.

My gaze drifts toward the palace, where I can barely see the private entrance Lev should be exiting from soon. The guard who usually stands near it must be blocked by the hedge, but from this vantage point, Lev should be able to see me easily as soon as he steps out.

The longer I sit waiting, the more time I have to think about the very things I don't *want* to. Lev's conversation with the king and queen has gone on for a while, hopefully because he's found the answer he's looking for.

If anyone knows what it takes to step into the role he's been asked to, it's them, and all I want is the burden he's carrying to be lifted—for all our sakes.

Is that so much to ask? To look into his russet eyes and not see them darkening with pain?

A sense of foreboding settles over me, and my hair stands on end. Lev steps from the palace, and I release all the tension I've been holding. He scans the grounds for me, his shoulders tight, jaw locked. His hard eyes land on me, and instantly, he relaxes slightly, a smile playing on his lips.

My heart races as he approaches, his dark-charcoal chino pants hanging perfectly off his hips, the colorful tattoos on his arms exposed beneath his rolled-up sleeves.

It really is unfair for him to be so damn handsome. Or for him to look at me this way, like he's ready to devour me instead of the spread I have laid out on the blanket.

Not fair to mess with a horny pregnant woman.

He eats up the distance between us, but halfway to the maze entrance, his smile falters, and he stops in his tracks. Something crunches on the pea gravel to my left, and Lev reaches around his back.

What the hell?

Strong arms band around me before I can turn toward the sound. Someone yanks me to my feet and against a hard chest, pressing a forearm into my neck and making my vision blur. A scream bubbles up my throat, but something cold and round presses into my temple, silencing me.

Is that a gun?

"Screaming would be unwise." The low, vaguely familiar voice vibrates with rage. "Shut the fuck up, or I will kill you right here, right now, in front of the last Romanov before I kill him, too."

The last Romanov?

The words and their meaning register slowly.

Every fear Mira voiced has come true—the attack was targeted at Lev because of who he is, which put me directly in the line of fire. And they've infiltrated the palace grounds.

They're going to kill both of us.

A tear leaks down my cheek, and I place my hands over our baby.

This can't be it.

This can't be the end.

Not when it's only just begun.

No. Lev wouldn't let that happen.

Blinking rapidly to clear my eyes, I finally focus my vision. Lev approaches across the grass with his gun pointed directly toward us. His black eyes lock on my captor, then briefly dart to meet mine.

That Lev is back.

It happened in a split second. He went from the kind, loving man he proved he was last night to the one he was *trained* to be. Capable of *anything* to complete his mission, and the mission right now is to protect our child and me.

A tiny piece of that terror seizing my chest releases because, if I know anything, it's that Lev won't be stopped. My confidence in his abilities trumps my fear of the man holding the gun to my head.

Crossing Lev Orlov is a death sentence, and whoever is daring to make this move either has no idea who he's up against or has greatly underestimated the father of my baby.

My captor pushes his forearm harder to my neck the closer Lev inches toward us. The smell of his sweat fills my nose, and the rancid scent makes my stomach roil. I fight the urge to gag, and he drags me back a step.

Lev follows, his hand holding the gun steady. "Release her."

The dark laugh at my ear sends a chill over my skin. "There's only one way this ends, Lev. With you dead. Lower your weapon, or I will kill her."

It takes a second for the voice to finally click in my head.

Greggory?

Lev snarls, his lips twisting viciously. "Greggory. Let. Her. Go."

It is him...

That a member of the Lovolian Royal Guard would get involved in all this, would betray the Yates and Lev, would betray *me* makes rage burn through my veins.

Greggory releases another chuckle. "You should be *thanking* me."

Lev sneers. "Thanking you?"

"They wanted you dead by any means, even if it meant harming Prince Fynix. I convinced them to wait until you were alone, to prevent a full-blown war with Lovolia. But they tried and failed, even though I told them precisely where to find you and when you'd be on the road. I saved the prince's life. So, yes, you *should* be thanking me."

He's insane.

Even if he does manage to kill Lev or me, Lovolia *will* burn down the world to ensure those responsible are caught.

War is precisely what they're bringing on themselves.

"Surrender, Lev, and I'll let her go unharmed. I never meant to get Daphne involved in any of this. I had intended to get you coming out of the palace, but then she showed up." He shifts his hold on me slightly, his gun flush with my temple. "I'll make it quick and painless for you. Just drop your gun."

Lev keeps his eyes locked with mine, assessing the situation and giving me the strength to keep breathing through this. A sense of calm settles over me. The knowledge that everything will be okay.

Something flashes deep in his russet gaze.

Without a single word, I know exactly what he wants me to do.

He slowly tilts the barrel of his gun up, dangling it from his trigger finger, and holds up both hands. His head tips slightly to the left. "Don't hurt her. Just do what you came here to do. Kill me."

Greggory cackles again, and I kick off my flip-flop and stomp down on his foot as hard as I can. His grip on my neck loosens slightly, and I lunge to the left.

Gunshots shatter the quiet garden air, piercing my ears before I slam into the ground, and everything fades to black.

25

LEV

Everything moves in agonizingly slow motion.

I flip my gun...

Daphne kicks off her flip-flop and stomps down on Greggory's foot...

He flinches...

I spin my gun and fire...

Daphne lurches to the side...

My bullets slam into Greggory's chest...

The agony of my ears ringing finally breaks through the absolute focus on my mission...

"Daphne!"

My scream cuts through the air. Tears blur my vision, and I stumble toward her. She slams into the pebble path, her head hitting the ground with a sickening *thud*, blood sprayed across her. Greggory crumples beside her, his gun tumbling to the grass.

Each moment we've spent together over the last almost two

years roars through my head like a tsunami crashing against the shore.

The arguments. Snide comebacks. Dirty glares. Annoyed huffs...

Hungry kisses. Heated touches. Longing looks...

All the things I love so damn much.

I fall to my knees beside her, dropping my weapon to pull her small, limp body into my arms, cradling her to my chest. Shouts and heavy footsteps move closer, and members of the guard spill into the garden and maze around us.

Manuel skids to a halt in the gravel next to me. "Lev, is she hit?"

I push to my feet, wobbling slightly, my vision fading in and out. The remaining flip-flop on her foot slides free and falls into the crimson puddle forming to the side of us. "No, but...I had to shoot. It's Greggory's blood—"

"Greggory?" His head whips toward the prone body on the ground. "What the hell is going on?"

His question barely registers as I stare at Daphne's closed eyes. Soft breaths slip past her slightly parted lips, but her steady breathing doesn't quell the fury or concern for her. "He had a gun to her head...I don't know..." And I couldn't give a single fuck. The only things that matter are in my arms. "Call Doc. Have him meet me at my suite."

Manuel pulls out his phone and dials as he ushers us toward the palace, past dozens of guards spreading across the grounds. Each man we pass draws a suspicious look from Manuel, but I can't concentrate on anything happening around me.

Not when Daphne remains unconscious.

Please wake up, Yankee.

If anything happens to her or the baby...

Bile climbs my throat, but I swallow it to rush up the stairs and down the corridor to where Doctor Hatzis waits for us.

Manuel uses his master key to unlock the door, and Doc follows me in and to the bedroom.

He sets his bag on the nightstand. "What happened?"

My worst bloody nightmare.

"She hit her head."

I lay her on the bed gently, resting her head on the pillow. She looks so small, so helpless, so unlike Daphne, who's always so full of life and attitude. For the second time in only a matter of days, I've put her in a situation where her life was at risk, where she ended up like *this*.

Bright-red blood contrasts against her pale skin, and I lift my hand to push her hair back from her face.

"She hasn't woken up." I glance at Doc, tightening my hand into a fist. "I'm worried about her and the baby."

Doc nods and digs in his bag. "She's probably gone into shock and may have a concussion if she struck her head. Go wash up while I examine her."

I hear him, but I can't make my feet move. My entire body feels numb.

He turns back to me again. "Lev, *go!*"

His clipped order finally snaps me into action, and I stumble to the bathroom to wash the blood from my hands. They tremble as the scalding-hot water flows over them. Red swirls in the sink, like countless times before, but I can't move on from it this time.

I can't stop my entire body from shaking.

Years of training and combat experience...

Dozens of missions that required me to take lives...

More blood on my hands than most people could fathom...

Yet seeing Daphne like this, the possibility she or the baby may have been harmed, finally pushes me to breaking point.

So help me, God, I will hunt down every last one of the bastards involved in this and put a bullet between their fucking eyes.

I shut off the water and dry my hands. Fisting them to stop

GWYN MCNAMEE & CHRISTY ANDERSON

the shaking, I return to the bedroom and pace alongside the bed while Doc works on Daphne.

Please be all right. Please be all right. Please, God, let them be all right.

Her head hitting the ground replays on a slow-motion loop in my mind. Each time, the sickening thud sound echoes louder in my still-ringing ears.

"Lev?" Daphne's voice cuts through the nightmare. "Lev?"

"Daphne..." I choke back a sob and rush to the bed, taking her hand in mine. "I'm here."

She turns unfocused eyes toward me, trying to blink away whatever fog envelops her. Her hand moves over her stomach. "The baby?"

I turn to Doc, where he stands on the other side of the bed, holding my breath waiting for the answer.

If anything happened to the baby,...

Nyet.

I can't even let myself think that.

Doc offers us a sympathetic look. "The baby appears to be fine." He looks at Daphne. "You're not experiencing any abdominal pain?"

"No..." She shakes her head gently, wincing slightly at the movement. "But my head..."

Fucking bastard.

This is all his fault. The fact that Greggory, someone we *trusted*, someone I was *friends* with, could betray us like this sends rage boiling through my veins.

Doc nods slowly. "You may have a mild concussion from striking your head against the ground." He shines a bright light into her eyes. "There may be some headaches or blurred vision over the next week, but you should be fine. I'm quite confident Lev will take great care of you." He claps me on the shoulder. "You know how to reach me should anything change."

He grabs his bag and slips out of the suite. The latch clicks into place behind him, and I squeeze Daphne's hand. All I want is to drag her into my arms and crush her against me, but I don't dare after what she just went through.

Her eyes dart to where we're connected, zeroing in on the blood still covering her. She tries to sit up, but I gently grasp her shoulder and keep her prone.

"Stay. I'll be right back."

Reluctantly, I pull my hand from hers and return to the bathroom for a wet, soapy washcloth. Her eyes follow me as I return and settle on the edge of the bed. "I'm going to clean your face."

If I have to stare at the blood marring her perfect skin any longer, I'm liable to say something to scare her even more. After seeing me like that, watching me kill Greggory, there's no way Daphne won't run for the hills.

I never wanted her to witness that side of me, to experience what I'm capable of, let alone to have to wear the result. Swallowing back the fury threatening to choke me, I gently swipe at the dried blood.

Daphne wraps her slender fingers around my wrist, stalling the movement. "You shot him."

I release a heavy breath, holding her gaze, willing to accept any anger or fear it might hold. "I did..."

She releases my wrist and cups my cheek. "Thank you for protecting us..."

"You're not...upset?"

"Not even a little bit." Tears trickle from her eyes, and she takes a moment before she sucks in a deep breath. "I mean, I'm still reeling from everything that happened, but I'm okay. And I am definitely not upset with you. Why would you think that?"

I swipe at her face again, but the blood refuses to wash away easily. "Because you saw me like *that*. In that mode. I thought..." I pull my hand back. "After you witnessed that, I thought it would give you every reason to want to get yourself and our baby as far away from me as possible. I brought that danger to you and then—"

She sits forward, taking my face between her palms. "That wasn't your fault, Lev. None of this is your fault. You didn't *choose* this. And you did what you had to."

The sincerity of her words melts away any lingering trepidation over taking Greggory's life to save her in the garden.

Daphne understands more than I give her credit for. She isn't some fragile flower who wilts at the first sign of conflict. One of the very things that always caused so much tension between us is what makes her so bloody strong. And exactly what I need.

So damn much.

I press my lips gently to hers, then slip my hand around her wrist and pull it from my face. "Come on, Yankee. Let's get you cleaned up."

She lets me lift her into my arms, and I carry her easily into the bathroom. I keep her back to the mirror so she won't see the carnage sprayed against the side of her face. Setting her on her feet next to the shower, I crank on the water.

The beautiful yellow sundress that fits her body and personality so perfectly now bears the ghastly evidence of what I had to do to protect her. I slip the straps off her shoulders, and the fabric slides down and pools at her feet. She steps out of it, bracing her hands on my shoulders, and as steam starts to fill the bathroom, I remove her bra and panties and strip off my destroyed clothes.

I want to obliterate any reminder of the terror she felt today, to convince her that I can keep her safe and prevent anything like this from happening again.

But can I?

This proved that we're at risk anywhere, anytime. Even here, the place that has always been my home. If I were to do what my cousin wants, what it appears *Gran* wanted, if I publicly announce who I am and make a physical move for control of a country already in turmoil, the dangers will only grow—for all of us.

That reality rests heavily on my shoulders as I guide Daphne under the spray. She releases a tiny sigh, turning her face up to it. The pelting water instantly begins breaking up the dried blood, and I slide in behind her and press my chest to her back.

She leans into me, and I grab the soap and gently wash away the remnants of the day, refusing to watch them spin down the drain. Instead, I concentrate on the woman in my arms, how right it feels, and how I refuse to let her slip away from me again.

For a few moments, we stand wrapped together, her heart beating against my hand pressed over it, the other laid over her stomach reverently.

She tilts her head back against my shoulder to look up at me. The fear that has returned to her gaze makes me tighten my grip on her. "This won't be the end of it, Lev."

The truth hangs heavy in her words—the same one I've known since Gran told me who I was.

"I know."

But for now, in this moment, all that matters is the three of us.

Everything else can wait.

DAPHNE

LEV WATCHES ME CAREFULLY, his dark eyes heavy with concern —just as he has every single minute since yesterday's incident. Like he's waiting for me to break. Watching for any crack that could lead to a total meltdown.

And I know the question is coming before he asks, since it's the twentieth time he's voiced it in the last hour. "Are you *sure* you want to go out to the garden?"

Before, I would have lashed out at him with some snide comeback. I would have started an argument and done my best to irritate him the way the repeated question does me.

But that was *before.*

Before I saw who he really was.

Before I knew what he was willing to do for me.

Before I fell in love with him.

I won't do that anymore. Especially now that I know he only worries because he *cares.* It isn't meant as a dig at my strength; he simply wants to protect me from everything.

How can I blame him for that?

He almost lost the baby and me less than twenty-four hours ago, and now, I want to return to the scene of the crime. I understand his reticence, but I won't let what happened ruin my favorite place on the palace grounds.

I push my chair from the breakfast table and round it to his side. He shifts back, giving me room to slide onto his lap, and wraps his hands around my hips. I settle across his thighs, loop my arms around his neck, and play with the hair at his nape.

Lev leans forward and brushes his lips over mine. "Are you sure?"

A little sigh slips out before I can bite back the annoyance in it. "Yes, I need to move on from that, and this is part of how I ensure that happens."

Face it head-on.

It's what I should have done with what happened in Colorado instead of hiding out here. I'll have to sooner rather than later, but one thing at a time...

Manuel assured us any evidence of what happened has been cleansed from the grounds. Once they knew Greggory was involved, they used his phone to track down his cohorts at an abandoned nightclub near the resort side of the island.

While I'm sure Lev would rather be personally interrogating those responsible for the attempt on his life and mine with the other members of the guard and Captain Nichols of the police force, he's done a good job of pretending to be one hundred percent present with me this morning.

I slide off his lap and tug his hand. "Come on."

He narrows his dark eyes at me. "If you're positive?"

I huff in answer and keep tugging him until he stands. He gives me a wary look as I lead him toward the hallway that will take us out the back entrance of the palace to the gardens and maze.

The halls feel different somehow.

More tense.

Everyone on edge.

How could they not be?

One of their own betrayed Lev, the king and queen, and the vows he took when he became a member of the Lovolian Royal Guard.

And for what?

Apparently, some mis-held belief that Lev stepping up as the Romanov heir would threaten Lovolia. The absurdity of it all could overwhelm me easily if I let it, but until Lev makes a final decision, I refuse to dwell on the thousand complications.

I lead Lev out the door and down the path toward the garden, forcing myself to look at what was to be our perfect picnic spot only yesterday. Though all that remains is pristine grass and pebbled paths, images still flash through my head, threatening to intrude on my plans for the day.

Lev will continue to dwell on the incident, on the tremendous decision he has to make, unless I can find a way to divert him with something far more enjoyable.

He always said the gazebo was his safe place growing up,

where he would come when he needed to be alone to think or when he and Fyn were hiding from Gran or the guards. But I want to give him another memory of it. Something that will be the ultimate distraction from the storm of uncertainty surrounding us.

We make our way through the maze, but a solid wall of hedges ahead stops me in my tracks. Lev sidles up behind me and wraps his arms around my waist, tugging me back to him.

"You lost, Yankee?"

Dammit.

"Hell. Apparently so." I release a sigh and allow myself to sag against his solid chest. "I was trying to get to the gazebo."

His low, deep chuckle rumbles against my back, a welcome sound I wasn't sure I'd ever hear again. "Then you are most definitely lost, Yankee."

He presses his warm lips to that spot behind my ear, and a little shiver rolls down my spine. "Come this way." His arms slide away, and he grabs my hand, tugging me back the way we came. He glances over his shoulder. "Try to remember how to get out so I don't need to send a search party for you next time."

I scowl at him. "Ha, ha."

A grin plays at his lips, the first one I've seen in what feels like forever. It gives me hope that there's a way out of this that doesn't end in disaster for him.

He leads me through the maze easily and to the center, where the gazebo stands surrounded by wisteria. The heavenly sweet scent fills my lungs, and I issue a little moan.

"God, it smells so good in here."

Lev stops next to the steps leading up the structure and pulls me into his arms. "One of my favorite smells in the world." He dips his head to nuzzle my neck. "After that damn lemon sunshine scent you carry with you." He nips at my ear. "And your cunt."

Holy hell.

My body flames to life, and heat pools between my thighs. I drag my head back and push up to my tiptoes in my flip-flops. "Kiss me."

He palms my ass and presses his lips to mine, moving them languidly, like he wants to savor every second before he tilts my head back. "You're all right?"

Staring into his eyes, seeing all the passion burning there, I can't keep lying to him. I hadn't intended to reveal this today. I wanted to wait until things were more settled, but I can't keep this up. Not after yesterday. "I'm okay, but there's something I have to tell you..."

His brows draw low, concern immediately overtaking the lust there only a moment ago. "What's wrong?"

Shit. This is so much harder than I thought it would be.

"I have to tell you why I stayed in Lovolia."

Lev's entire body stiffens, his arms tightening around me. "You don't have to tell me if—"

"I do...have to tell you..." I swallow thickly. "Because it could affect our future."

Way to ruin a moment with the cold, hard truth.

"Just lay it on me, Yankee." His words come out clipped and low. "I can't take any more secrets."

Fucking hell.

I try to pull out of his hold and put some distance between us while I make this confession, but he tightens his grip, ensuring I'm not moving an inch.

"Now, Yankee."

"Shit." I look away from him for a moment to the wisteria swaying in the ocean breeze. "Okay, so you know I work as an office manager for a doctor's office, right?"

He nods slowly. "Yes, I've heard you and Bridget discussing...what do you call him...*Doctor Douchebag?*"

I grin at those words coming from his mouth despite the tension of the situation. "Yeah, well, Doctor Douchebag has always been just that. He's arrogant, self-centered—a real prick. He's an orthopedic surgeon. Some of his clients are athletes who are just as bad. But he pays well, and the rest of the office staff is really great to work with. We all kind of just accepted his pompous attitude as part of the workplace and dealt with it."

Lev's gaze hardens, almost as if he can anticipate what's coming. "But..."

My skin crawls at the memory, and I shudder slightly. "But the day before I flew to Lovolia..." I swallow through my suddenly dry throat. "Doctor Douchebag cornered me in the employee breakroom right as I was about to leave and lock up. He was at a golf event with some of his patients all afternoon. He'd been drinking..."

He clenches his jaw. "Oh, hell no—"

I press my hand to his chest. "He said he knew I 'wanted the same thing he did.' It was clear what he meant."

"Did that fucking bastard touch you?" His grip on me tightens possessively. "So help me God, if he laid a fucking finger on you, I'll—"

"Stop, Lev. He didn't..." I release heavy sigh. "I'm sure he would have tried, but as soon as he said that, I laughed in his face, and said, '*What? A boss who isn't such a drunk asshole?*'" The pure rage that flashed in his beady eyes comes barreling back at me. "He lunged at me, but I grabbed the glass coffee pot and smashed it against his fucking head."

Lev's eyes widen. "You what?"

I cringe and drop my forehead to his chest. "I didn't know what else to do. I antagonized him with my comment. Then I assaulted him. I should have kept my fucking mouth shut and gotten out of there—"

"No." Lev grips my chin firmly and forces my gaze up to meet his. "It wasn't your fault. You didn't do anything wrong."

Tears burn in my eyes. "Yes, I did. I should have kept my smartass comment to myself. I—"

Lev pushes his thumb across my lips. "I love this smartass mouth, and everything else about you, Yankee. And you did *nothing* wrong. That bloody wanker deserved what you did to him."

"Lev..." I want to concentrate on what he just said, on the "L" word that popped out of his mouth so easily. But my rising panic at the mess I left in Denver overcomes my shock. "I could go to jail. Prison even. I assaulted him. As I ran out of the office, he was bleeding. He was hurt, and he screamed that he was going to call the police. That he was going to make me pay."

He squeezes my chin tightly, pushing his face closer to mine, until we're sharing the same breath. "The only one who will pay is him, with his fucking life. No one will ever touch you again, Yankee. Not another man. Not the fucking American police. You are mine, and I'll protect you from all of it. You *and* our baby."

The tears finally leak down my cheeks, and I rest my forehead on his. "You can't promise that. You don't have any power over the judicial system in Colorado, Lev."

His sardonic laugh fills the space between us, and he softly presses his lips to mine. "I think you've forgotten who you're talking to, Yankee." He buries his fingers in my hair and tugs my head back, forcing me to look at him. "That man would have *hurt* you, Daphne. You defended yourself—"

"And then fled the damn country. Do you have any idea how guilty that makes me look?"

He shakes his head. "It doesn't matter. Do you think anyone here is going to extradite you, even if they charged you with anything? Do you think the state of Colorado would want to try a pregnant woman who hit her attacker?" A sigh slips from his lips. "I wish you'd told me all this when you got here, Yankee."

"I didn't tell anyone, not even Bridget."

"Bloody hell." He smirks. "I'd be more worried about her

reaction to you hiding things from her than anything going on back in Denver."

I smack his chest lightly, fighting back more tears. "That's not funny."

"Yes, it is, Yankee." He kisses me softly again and dries my cheeks with his thumb. "Now stop worrying about it. I'll handle it."

Handle it.

He doesn't explain what *handling it* means, and when I open my mouth to ask, he presses his thumb across it, silencing me immediately.

"Trust me to take care of you, Yankee."

26

LEV

THE WOMAN who has become my entire world stares up at me, her tear-soaked eyes searching mine for something. "I do trust you, Lev. Even when we were at each other's throats, I knew you would never let anything happen to me."

"Shit, Yankee, I'd die before I allowed anyone to hurt you again."

Even me.

I slam my mouth to hers, releasing all the emotion her confession built inside me, pouring all my love and promises into the single action. She moans and clings to me, her fingers tightening in my shirt, like her legs might give out under her if she weren't clutching the material.

My cock swells against her, and she rubs her hips to mine greedily, seeking some sort of friction. Groaning, her hands slide down to my waistband and tug my shirt free. Frantic fingers fumble at my belt while I back her toward the gazebo steps.

Her feet bump against them, and I shift my grip to her arse

to lift her as I continue to devour her mouth.

"What the bloody hell is going on?"

Blyat!

I jerk my head away from Daphne and turn to find Fynix and Bridget standing under the arch leading into the gazebo area, their mouths hanging open.

"Shit."

Bridget's gaze darts from Daphne to me, then back to her best friend. "I thought you were still in Denver...and that you hated Lev..."

Daphne slides down from my waist until her flip-flops hit the ground. She smooths her dress and offers Bridget an awkward smile. "Um..."

Bloody hell.

Fynix's eyes narrow on me as he approaches and pulls me in for a hug. "It seems as though we've missed a lot..."

"You have no idea, mate."

Daphne glances my way, then rushes to Bridget and throws her arms around her. "I'm so fucking happy to see you."

Bridget embraces her friend, casting a confused look at Fyn and me. "I missed you too, Daph. Now, do you want to tell me what the hell is going on?"

That won't be a quick conversation, nor will the one I need to have with Fyn.

I rub the back of my neck and motion toward the maze. "Why don't you two take a walk while I talk with Fyn?"

It will give each of us some much-needed time to explain everything that's happened over the last few weeks, even if I'm still trying to get a handle on it myself.

Daphne links her arm through Bridget's and leads her out to the maze—hopefully remembering how we got to the gazebo, so we don't have to go rescue the girls later.

I turn back to Fyn to find him with one blond brow raised.

"You have a lot of explaining to do, mate."

"That's a bloody understatement." I climb the steps to the gazebo and drop onto one of the benches, scrubbing my hands over my beard. "So much has happened since you left..."

He drops onto the seat beside me. "Why don't you start with why your tongue was down Daphne's throat?"

I grin at him. "That was...unexpected. I'm sure Bridget will fill you in later, but Daphne didn't return to Denver after you left. She showed up at Elysium."

His eyes widen. "Bloody hell. Why didn't you tell me any of this when we spoke?"

Groaning, I drop my face into my hands. "Because she asked me not to. She said she didn't want to ruin your honeymoon by telling Bridget why she couldn't go back to Denver."

"What do you mean she couldn't go back to Denver?"

I lean back, the rage over what happened with her boss and the fact that she didn't tell anyone rushing back instantly. "She had a confrontation with her boss when he tried to attack her. Apparently, she smashed him good with a coffeepot and fled, but he said he was going to call the police. She thought she would get arrested if she returned home."

He glowers at me.

I hold my hands up defensively. "I didn't know. She told me she needed time to think, and I agreed to let her stay with me at Elysium to work through whatever it was. She didn't tell me about the incident with her boss until today, just before you arrived."

Fyn leans forward, resting his elbows on his knees. "And her staying at Elysium ended up with you two sleeping together?"

I wince. "That happened at the wedding first."

He jerks upright, his eyes wide. "I bloody knew it! In the Reading Room...you two scrambling out of there, looking like you'd just gone at it, but I assumed it was another *verbal* confrontation."

"Believe me, we did that, too, and shagging her was the last thing I expected to happen. Or for it to happen again at Elysium."

A playful grin pulls at his lips. "It doesn't surprise me in the least. You two always argued like you should be fucking it out."

I scowl at him. "Well..." I gulp. "There's more. She's pregnant."

"Jesus, Lev! You don't do anything by halves, do you, mate?"

My chuckle fills the afternoon air, and I pinch my nape and sigh. "Apparently not."

He sobers immediately, pressing his lips together. "Did Mira know?"

The way his voice cracks, saying her name has a lump forming in my throat. I try to swallow past it, but it takes a few tries. "Yes. That's what prompted Gran to reveal this whole Romanov thing to me in the first place. Well, that and things were getting more tenuous for her contacts back in Russia."

Fyn levels his hard gaze on me. "Manuel filled us in on what happened with Greggory on the way here from the airport."

The same fury that washed over me when I saw Greggory grab Daphne consumes me again, and I tighten my hands into fists on my knees. "I've never been more terrified in my entire life."

"You love her."

I slowly turn my head toward him and nod. "I know it sounds bloody impossible, considering that we were at each other's throats only a few weeks ago, but...yeah, mate, I do. And I want this baby, even though my life is a giant bloody mess right now."

He claps me on my shoulder and squeezes. "That's the way love works, mate. It shows up when and where you least expect it. Do you think I expected to stumble upon a beautiful American trespassing on my beach when I ditched royal duties to surf at Crown Point?"

I chuckle, remembering how livid I was when he sneaked out the window that day. "Definitely not."

"Nope." He grins. "And I never expected her to come back after my idiocy bungled it so badly with her, either. But we got our second chance, and look what we have now."

"I'm happy for you. I'm sorry if it hasn't seemed like it."

Fyn rises to his feet and moves to stand in front of me. "You've been my best friend since we were born, Lev. You don't need to apologize to me for anything. I knew you would beat yourself up over what happened with the LLM, and I knew you would see me forcing a holiday on you as a slap in the face. But I also knew you well enough to know you *needed* it." He smirks and offers a shrug. "And if I hadn't..."

I nod slowly. "If you hadn't...I might not have ended up where I am with Daphne."

"I'll call the consulate in the States and ensure there aren't any legal issues for her there."

"No." I push to my feet. "I appreciate it, mate, but I'll take care of it."

He gives me a wary look and runs a hand through his hair. "As the private guard of Fynix Yates, Crown Prince of Lovolia, or as Lev Romanov, heir to the crown of the Russian Empire."

Way to cut right to the chase on that bloody question.

"That isn't such an easy answer."

Fyn nods and paces the gazebo, arms crossed behind his back. "After we all spoke yesterday, I had a private conversation with my parents."

My hackles immediately rise, and I tense, waiting for him to continue. Anything I decide affects more than me—it impacts Daphne, the baby, Fynix and his parents, and all of Lovolia, not to mention the millions of people living under the current government in Russia.

Coming forward to claim a throne dissolved over a hundred years ago won't be an easy feat. Blood *will* be shed. No matter how much support the movement might have, or how disenchanted citizens may be with those in power now, it would be asking them to step back to a form of government that disappeared for a reason.

Maybe a good one.

Even here in Lovolia, with a royal family who bends over backward to do what's right for their people, a change was necessary.

Could a true monarchy exist without dissent?

"My father indicated you were uncertain how you wanted to proceed. He wanted me to emphasize that we will support you, no matter your decision. The Yates family *and* Lovolia." He locks his gaze with mine. "And that's true, Lev. Even without an order from the king, *I* will support whatever you choose to do." He smirks and offers a half-bow. "Your Imperial Majesty."

"Bloody hell, don't start with that shit, Fyn."

He chuckles and leans against the center post of the gazebo. "You'll have to get used to it. It's yours, by blood."

I start to pace the small space. "That doesn't mean I fucking want it, mate."

Did Gran really think I wanted this?

That I was ready for it?

Or was her hand forced by what happened to the Romanov supporters in Russia and by Daphne's pregnancy?

The click of my shoes against the wooden floor reverberates through the domed ceiling. Time ticks as I pace back and forth, but Fyn doesn't interrupt, just watches me carefully.

"I'd give anything to have Gran here."

He nods, his unruly blond locks falling over his forehead. "I know."

"She would know what I should do."

His eyebrow wings up. "Is it *her* decision to make or yours?" He holds up a hand when I open my mouth to answer. "I'm serious, Lev. I loved your grandmother as if she were my own.

She was a very wise woman, who apparently had a lot of secrets. But she also knew you and knew you would make your *own* decision."

"But she gave me the number to her cousin, in Russia, one who is tied in with the group supporting the Romanov claim."

He offers a half-shrug. "She wanted you to have all the available information. To have someone to ask questions. She didn't want to leave you alone with this decision, which is why my parents and their parents before them were clued in on the importance of the Orlov family. So you'd have a sounding board. But I don't believe for one moment that your grand-mother would have ever *told* you what to do."

I bark out a sardonic laugh. "Why not? She did with every-thing else."

Fyn sobers, offering a sympathetic look. "Because this is your entire *life*. That woman was a lot of things, but she was not cruel. It would be *cruel* to *force* anyone to take on the role being asked of you, to start a civil war for something ripped away from your ancestors so violently. It must only be done willingly. On that, I believe Mira and I are on the same page."

Tears sting my eyes. I wipe them and stare down at my hands. "When did you get so wise?"

He chuckles and walks over to squeeze my shoulder. "Maybe marriage has forced me to grow up."

I snort and shake my head, glancing up at him. "Bridget is good for you."

"She is." He nods, a knowing grin on his lips. "And I have no doubt Daphne will be good for you."

My chest aches, and I rub it absently. "She is. She makes me...feel like I have a family."

His eyes narrow. "I should be offended by that because you know we consider you part of *our* family, but I understand what you mean. Whatever you decide will change her life forever."

"It already has..."

He nods slowly, and the corner of his mouth quirks up. "And I think you've already made your decision. You just haven't said it out loud yet."

⚚

DAPHNE

THE MOMENT we leave the center of the maze and Fynix and Lev behind us, Bridget tightens her grip on my arm almost painfully, and the tension between us grows along with the silence.

I knew this was going to be hard, but I never imagined it would be *this* hard.

Christ, it feels like I'm about to confess to murder.

Maybe because, in a way, I am. When she finds out *everything* I've been keeping from her, it may kill my only real friendship. These aren't the things you keep from your best friend, from anyone who cares about you, no matter if your intentions are good.

My good intentions won't stop her anger—perhaps rightfully so.

My stomach roils, and I peek at her out of the corner of my eye. Bridget stares at me expectantly, waiting for me to vomit the truth I've held back from her.

I suck in a deep breath of the floral ocean air. "Before I say anything or *you* say anything, I just want you to know how sorry I am that I didn't tell you."

She purses her lips but stays silent, letting me continue.

"I didn't want to disrupt your honeymoon with my personal bullshit."

Bridget scoffs. "You know it wouldn't have been a disruption, Daphne. Something pretty major happened for you to be here and with Lev like that."

370

God, she's going to flip out when I tell her about the baby.

But I have to do this one step at a time. Start at the beginning. When things truly started to go to hell. I never thought I'd be able to get out the words, but after telling Lev, a bit of the panic I've had since my showdown with Doctor Douchebag has ebbed.

"Something happened before I left Denver. Something that made me not go back."

Her eyes widen. "You've been here the *whole* time?"

I wince and nod. "After you left on your honeymoon, I had Manuel drop me at the airport, then I snuck away in a cab and went to Elysium."

"You *what*?" Her screech fills the air. Hopefully, none of the extra guards milling about hear her and think we're in trouble. She drags me to a stop, her mouth gaping. "Daphne, what the hell?"

"I know. I know." I shake my head and clench her hand tighter, like I can keep her from bringing the Royal Guard down on us by squeezing her with all my strength. "I should have told you I wanted to stay. But then you would have asked questions about why and how I could be away from work and—"

She glowers at me, her annoyance rising the longer it takes me to get to the point. "Yeah, all the questions I have right now."

Rip off the Band-Aid, Daphne. Tell her.

If she were still in Denver, she would have been the first person I went to after fleeing from Doctor Douchebag. I would have pounded on her door, sobbing, and relayed the whole thing. Bridget would have immediately snapped into her public relations-superstar mode and figured out what we needed to do to protect me from any potential fallout. But Bridget *wasn't* there, and I had absolutely no one to go to for help—which got me to where I am today.

"I'm pretty sure I don't have a job anymore, and even if I did,

I can't go back to it."

Bridget's green gaze softens. "What happened?"

I sigh and tug her to keep her moving. Standing still with the high hedge walls on either side of us starts to feel like a prison the longer we're in here. "Dr. Douchebag was, well, a douchebag. He tried to..." I roll my hand in front of me, unable to say the words.

Her eyes widen. "Oh, God. Did he—"

I shake my head. "No. But he was drunk and forceful and cornered me in the office. I made the mistake of offering him one of my witty comebacks at his advances, and he came at me aggressively. So...I smashed him over the head with a glass coffeepot."

Bridget slaps her hand over her mouth and drags me to a stop again. "Oh, my God. Daphne..."

She tugs me into her arms and holds me so tightly I can barely breathe, but I don't fight it. Being back with her feels like finally being *home* after being lost for the last month. I've needed *this*, needed *her*. Finally being able to tell her everything releases Mount Everest from my shoulders.

"Anyway..." I pull back. "This was the night before I flew out to Lovolia. He threatened to call the police. I ran out, grabbed my bags from my apartment, and went straight to the airport. I slept there to avoid being at home in case the police showed up."

"Oh, God, Daphne." Her eyes shimmer with tears, and she rubs my back. "This is why you were acting so weird the whole time you were here. I should have known something was wrong."

"You did. You kept asking me, and I kept denying it because I didn't want to disrupt your wedding or the honeymoon with something that happened because I made a stupid fucking comeback to the guy. If I had just de-escalated the situation, I could have walked away."

"No, you couldn't have. Men like Dr. Douchebag don't take no for an answer. It was going to come down to this one way or another." She shakes her head. "I can't believe you went to Elysium."

We keep walking, and I rest my head on her shoulder.

"It was a surprise for Lev, too."

She chuckles. "Oh, I bet." Her eyes dart to my arm. "What happened to your arm?"

"Um...I kind of broke a window to get in and cut it on the glass."

"Daphne!"

Wincing, I lift my head and shake it. "I know, I know. It was stupid, but Lev stitched it up for me."

"And that's how you two ended up..." She waggles her eyebrows. "You know."

I chuckle. "Um, actually...the night of the wedding."

She jerks her head back and opens her jaw. "I *knew* it. Fyn and I both said something had happened. But you two wouldn't admit it."

"Again, I didn't feel like letting my personal shit interfere with your life. Me fucking your husband's best friend during a drunken run-in in the Reading Room didn't warrant a conversation right away." I sigh and stare at the blue sky as we wander farther into the maze. "But Lev and I battled again at Elysium. That led to...you know. Then all the stuff with his gran and this Romanov crap came up."

"Um, yeah." She offers a sympathetic look. "How insane is that?"

"I know, right? And there's more."

She pauses next to one of the benches. "I feel like this may be something I need to sit down for."

"You probably should."

Everything I've told her is nothing compared to this revelation. It's something we've discussed a thousand times—both of us eventually want to be mothers, to have families. It had been her dream until Barry betrayed her before their wedding, then when she found Fynix, it felt like at least one of us had a chance at that happy ending. But now, I'm the one having a baby.

I stand in front of her, twisting a strand of hair around my finger, trying to figure out how to say this.

Bridget taps her foot on the pea gravel. "Well, spit it out, Daphne."

"You're going to be an aunt."

She narrows her eyes. "What do you mean I'm going to be—"

I place a hand over my stomach, and her jaw hits the ground.

"Oh, my God." She jumps to her feet. "Oh, my God. You and Lev?"

I nod.

"Holy shit, Daphne." She drags me into her arms, and her warm tears hit my skin. "How long have you known?"

"A few days."

She pulls back, holding me at arm's length. "And you didn't tell me?"

"Well, given all the aforementioned lying, I couldn't call you and tell you I was pregnant by the man whose guts I hated the last time you saw me."

"And are you two, like, together now or..." One of her dark brows rises slowly.

"We're very much together now." I can't fight the smile. "I love him, as crazy as that sounds."

A slow grin brightens her face. "It doesn't sound crazy at all. The way you two were always going at it, you were either going to fall in love or kill each other. I'm glad it was the former and not the latter."

We burst out laughing.

Christ, it feels so good to laugh with her.

"Me, too. Only now we have this Romanov stuff hanging over our heads."

Bridget sobers instantly, her lips pressing into a firm line. "Manuel told us what happened with Greggory. I still can't believe it. He was always so nice."

"I know."

It's still hard to imagine how his mind became so tainted by what he thought was loyalty to the Lovolian crown.

"What do you think Lev is going to do?"

I sigh and usher her to take a seat on the bench. "He's going to do the right thing, whatever he thinks that is. Lev always does the right thing."

"What if the right thing for Lev isn't the right thing for you and the baby?"

It's the same question I've been asking myself throughout this entire ordeal.

I take her hand in mine and squeeze it. "I guess we deal with that when the time comes, but I have faith that the decisions will hopefully be the same.

"Christ." She shakes her head. "So much has changed. I feel like I've been gone for three years instead of what? Not even three weeks?"

I laugh and drop my head back. "I know, and again, I'm so sorry I didn't tell you all of this while it was happening. I felt like a fucking asshole. But—"

"But you thought you were keeping your best friend's honeymoon from getting ruined. So, I get it."

"You're not mad, or worse, hurt?"

She glares. "I'm both. But I'll get over it." A slow grin plays on her lips. "You might have to kiss my royal ass for the rest of our lives to get my forgiveness." She nudges me. "Then again, if you and Lev marry, you would be an empress, right? That would make you higher ranking than me until Fynix is king."

I grin at her. "So, that means I get to lord over you for a while?"

She chuckles. "That depends. Are you going to marry Lev?"

Hell.

With everything else going on, we haven't even broached the subject, nor would I expect to this early in any relationship.

I shrug. "He hasn't asked, and I think we have bigger things to worry about right now, like the fate of an entire country resting in his hands."

"True." She elbows me playfully again. "Still, he's pretty easy on the eyes. Looking at him for the rest of your life wouldn't be bad."

"No, it certainly wouldn't."

And a man like Lev doesn't do anything halfway. If we get married, it will be because it's the real deal. Because all the emotions we're feeling now aren't just caused by adrenaline, uncertainty, and lust.

I want to believe they aren't. That this is *it* because it certainly feels like it to me. But with nothing to compare it to and no role model relationships growing up, there's always the slim chance I've misjudged the entire situation.

"Don't."

Bridget's command drags me from my thoughts.

"Don't what?"

She narrows her green eyes at me. "Don't think whatever you were just thinking. I know that look, and it means you're questioning things you shouldn't be." Her hand finds mine, and she squeezes. "I saw the way Lev looked at you back there. I've watched you dance around each other and eye-fuck for years. It's real, Daph. It's the really real that Fynix and I have."

"I hope you're right."

"I am." She smirks. "And Lev always does what's right. He will by you, too."

27

LEV

DAPHNE'S FLIP-FLOPS smack against the marble as she paces.

Thwack. Thwack. Thwack.

The sound that once annoyed me so much instead draws a grin. Fynix smirks at me across the room, where he stands with Bridget and his parents. He inclines his head toward Daphne, indicating I should do something about her nerves.

I move from my spot near the door to the Reading Room and step in front of her, blocking her path to stop her nervous movement.

She jerks her head up and locks her annoyed gaze with me. "What?"

I rest my hands on her shoulders. "You have to stop, Yankee."

Her brow furrows, her lips pouting out. "Stop what?"

"This incessant pacing." I lean in closer, placing my lips near her ear. "You're going to make me nervous. The only way I'll be able to shake it is by shoving my cock into you...and we don't have time for that."

Daphne's hands move to my chest, and she digs her fingers into my shirt, her nails biting into my skin even through the crisp fabric. "I know what you're doing, Lev."

I flutter my lips against her cheek. "What am I doing?"

She releases a little huff, her annoyance doing nothing for the semi pressing between us that I've sported since the moment she walked into the room in this dress. "Trying to distract me."

"Is it working?"

Because all it's doing is making me want to postpone this press conference and drag her to the nearest empty room to do what I just threatened.

Twice.

Daphne pulls back slightly, until she can look me in the eye, and that familiar fire blazing there makes my heart skip a beat. It's still hard to believe I ever saw it as anything but love.

She pushes up on her tiptoes, her hand slipping down surreptitiously to cradle my growing erection. "It is, but I'm more worried about it distracting you from what you're about to go out there and do." One of her brows rises. "Should we duck into the closet quickly to take care of this before you go talk to the world?"

I tug her closer and brush my lips over hers. "Don't tempt me, Yankee."

"*Ahem...*" Manuel stands off the side, arms crossed in front of him, eyeing us with an amused smile. "We're ready for you."

Leaning down, I press my mouth to hers again. "Raincheck."

Fynix approaches and slaps me on the back. "You two are going to have to learn to be more discreet in the future."

Daphne snorts and pulls out of my arms, placing her hands on her hips. "Oh, yeah, that's rich, coming from you." She inclines her head toward him and Bridget as she approaches. "I've seen you two sneak away from dozens of events and come back rumpled, flushed, and looking very proud of yourselves." I lean in so Manuel won't hear me. "And let's not forget what you did to Bridget during that breakfast with your parents when she came to the palace for the first time."

Fyn gapes at Bridget. "You *told* her about that?"

A flush spreads over Bridget's cheeks. She locks her arm through her husband's and elbows him in the ribs. "I tell her everything."

"Bloody hell, love. You could have warned me nothing we do stays private."

She offers an unapologetic look and shrugs. "If you stopped trying to do me in every room in the palace, I wouldn't have anything *to* tell."

He grins at her and waggles his eyebrows. "Touché, love. Touché."

"*Ahem!*" Manuel clears his throat again. "Lev...the king and queen are waiting for you at the door to the Reading Room."

Shit.

He's stepped right into Gran's shoes to chastise me when I need it. I nod toward him to let him know I've been appropriately reprimanded and plant a final kiss on Daphne's forehead.

"You look stunning in this dress, Yankee. I can't wait to get you out of it later."

I step away from her because if I stay one more second, either Manuel will drag me away kicking and screaming, or I'm liable to bend her over the damn table and rail her with a full royal audience.

But I force those thoughts away and concentrate on what today is really about.

After burying Gran yesterday, I couldn't wait any longer to make this announcement. Too much is at stake to leave any uncertainty, and any delay would have only resulted in this information getting out another way.

Manuel confirmed the group Greggory was tied to intended

to leak my lineage to other groups they knew would join them in their efforts to eliminate the Romanov heir. It would have resulted in me dead or, at the very least, exposed.

It's now or never.

Either I take control of my life, or others will continue to do it for me. After talking with my mysterious cousin again, my decision was made, and I rushed to schedule this press conference as soon as possible.

I'd much rather be on my board at Crown Point, or better yet, alone with Daphne, but some things can't wait.

I pause outside the Reading Room, inhaling a deep breath to steady myself before I go out there. A familiar chocolatey scent hits me so strongly I almost stagger back.

Gran's brownies.

I'd know that smell anywhere. My mouth waters remembering the last time I ate one, and I smile at the memory of her swatting away my hand.

She's here with me.

Always.

With that knowledge, I step inside. Cameras flash, and a slow murmur ripples through the gathered reporters as I walk toward the podium set up for the press conference, the royal crest of Lovolia hanging from its front edge.

I would have chosen another location to make this statement, but the king insisted the Reading Room set the right tone. He has no idea I can't be in this room without remembering what it felt like to be inside Daphne on the table to my right.

Clearing my throat, I scan the familiar faces of the reporters who attend every press conference where the king, queen, or Fynix take center stage. Manuel now occupies my usual spot to the side of the small stage, his ever-vigilant gaze scanning those gathered, even though we locked this place down tight and did thorough searches of everyone allowed in the palace.

We can't be too careful with everything that's happened, but I hope today's announcement will end any future violence or threats. If it doesn't, buying a remote island and secluding myself there with Daphne, Fynix, and Bridget seems like a real possibility.

I clear my throat and glance at the notes left on the podium for me. "Good afternoon, and thank you for joining me today. This press conference has been called, first and foremost, to protect my family." I glance toward the back of the small stage, where Daphne stands flanked by Bridget and Fyn. "And my friends."

Fyn tips his head toward me. It's all the encouragement I need that this is the right decision. But I let my gaze drift to his right, where the king and queen stand, offering me kind smiles.

Turning back to the podium, I grip the wood tightly. "I also wanted to get ahead of this situation and let it be known where I stand, as I had good reason to believe this news would break before I could voice my opinion on the matter publicly."

Here goes nothing.

That same chocolate scent invades my nose, and I square my shoulders, feeling her small hand on my shoulder.

"My name is Lev Orlov. The Orlovs have worked here at the palace for the Yates family for generations. You likely know me as the personal guard to Crown Prince Fynix Yates. But I have recently learned more about my family history. A bloody, brutal, and tragic one." I steel myself for the response I'll receive to the next words. "I am the only living direct descendant of Tsar Nikolai Aleksandrovich Romanov and his wife Tsarina Alexandra Romanov."

Finally saying those words out loud lifts a massive weight from my chest as a chorus of gasps and whispers grows. The camera flashes blind me, and I glance at the podium to clear the white spots from my vision and swipe a hand down the length of my tie.

How the hell does Fynix handle these all the bloody time?

I wait for the conversation to die down before I continue. "My family lineage has been a well-guarded secret for over a century, but recently, a group of individuals who see a Romanov as a threat to the current government has made an attempt on my life. I've come here to let it be known who I really am and where I stand."

Emotion I wasn't expecting starts to clog my throat. I grab the glass of water on the podium and take a quick swallow, glancing behind me at Daphne.

She smiles softly and gives me a thumbs-up that makes me chuckle to myself.

Who gives a damn thumbs-up at a royal press conference?

Daphne—that's who.

My brash Yankee has zero qualms about violating every rule of decorum this palace has in place.

I turn my attention back to the crowd. "I have been the personal bodyguard for Crown Prince, Fynix Yates, since I was eighteen. But even before that, my entire existence has been devoted to protecting the future King of Lovolia, by any means necessary. I will gladly lay down my life for that cause because that is who I am and who I choose to continue to be. I am a son of Lovolia, and guarding the heir to the crown is my purpose."

And I won't fail at it again.

My life is that woman, our baby, and the family who have brought me into their home and taken me under their wing my entire life. We may not share blood, but sometimes, family is who you choose.

Doing this protects them as much as it does Daphne, the baby, and me.

"This will be the only time I address this issue, and I speak for myself, my family, and the Crown of Lovolia. I hereby denounce any present or future claim to the now dismantled throne of Russia, and I request the respect of the media and the public in allowing me to do my job without interruption in the future." The words rush out of me so fast I barely even hear them. Cameras flash again, and another rumble of excited chatter flows through the crowd. "Thank you."

Shouted questions fill the air, but I turn away from them and focus on the most important thing in my life.

Daphne offers me a knowing smile and tightens her grip on Bridget's hand beside her, fighting the urge to lay her hand over her stomach. The last thing we want is for the media to get wind of her pregnancy and turn it into an even bigger story.

It will happen eventually, but we'll bide our time for as long as we can and enjoy what will hopefully be a brief respite from the constant microscope they put us under.

I may have renounced my crown and everything that comes with it, but I will always have my queen.

Daphne *is* my kingdom.

♕

DAPHNE

LEV CONTROLS THE PODIUM, completely in command of the room, like he is in every situation. The reporters hang on his every word, enraptured by what he's saying and his presence.

Like I am every single time I'm in the same room with him.

It's impossible not to be sucked in by his strength, energy, and the "give no fucks what anyone thinks" attitude rolling off him like the waves surrounding Lovolia.

Every word he speaks leaves no room for debate or question.

Decisive.

Determined.

Stubborn and unyielding.

Sexy as hell.

Dressed in his Lovolia Royal Guard uniform, his tone stern and unwavering, wide shoulders squared, one thing is abundantly clear now if it weren't before—Lev was born to be a king.

Yet he stands here today, rejecting that role for the one he *wants.*

To protect his best friend. To defend the Yates legacy. To safeguard the entire Lovolian nation. Because this *is* his home and always will be, regardless of whose blood flows through his veins.

And though he struggled to make it to this point, let the weight of the decision drag him down since the moment Mira told him the truth, he always knew what he would do. It was probably the easiest decision Lev has ever made in his entire life, especially after what happened with Greggory.

Protecting what he loves takes precedence over what others want from him, what others demand simply because of who they think he should be.

I know *him.*

The massive heart in that strong, tattooed chest beats for this place and *these* people.

For this baby and me.

Almost as if he can sense my thoughts, he glances over his shoulder at me. Instinctively, I move to rest my hand over my stomach, but Bridget squeezes my other one to stop me. The last thing we need is the media getting wind of me carrying his baby. It would only add fuel to the fiery shitstorm that is sure to ignite because of this revelation being made public.

Everyone will want a piece of him.

His cousin in Russia has already indicated he won't give up on trying to convince him to reconsider his position, despite this intended announcement. This will never go away. The Romanov blood flowing through his veins—and those of our child—will always bring complications and unwanted attention. We'll have to live with it, but he's doing what he can to mitigate it for all of us.

"Thank you."

At his final words, I release the breath I've been holding, and Bridget squeezes my hand again, always my fiercest supporter.

Lev turns back to face us, and the look he gives me makes my insides flip flop. Pure fire radiates from his gaze, as if he's barely containing a conflagration.

His earlier threat makes me squeeze my legs together against the throb there.

Holy shit.

Bridget leans in and brushes her lips to my ear. "Good God, it looks like he wants to devour you."

I lean toward her, never breaking eye contact with the man who has managed to completely change my life in a matter of weeks. "He probably does."

She smirks. "Lucky girl."

I elbow her playfully, careful to do it in a way that the cameras and media won't notice, since it's frowned up on to assault a royal—even one by marriage. "Like anything is lacking in that regard where your husband is concerned."

She grins, her cheeks reddening. "True."

Lev reaches us and inclines his head toward the door that will take us out of the Reading Room.

Of all the damn places in the palace to have a formal press conference, the king had *to suggest here...*

The austere space will always hold memories that will equally heat my blood and haunt me. We were so different then. Me lost. Him angry. Both searching for some way to connect with the world and another human being.

Has it only been three weeks?

Did I really think I hated Lev such a short time ago?

Bridget is right; so much has changed. So much that can

never go back, and I wouldn't want it to. When I left Denver to assist Bridget prepare for her wedding, I was lost, alone, and scared. All I wanted to do was hide from the world.

Despite all the animosity between us, Lev gave me a place to do that. However reluctant he was to have me invading his personal space, he still took care of me and gave me the time to regroup while he ravaged my body in the best ways possible.

He gave me something to think about besides all the ways I had messed up and all the reasons I had not to go back. He gave me a reason to *stay* and feel like *this* is home.

And now we're surrounded by the people we both consider family, and with this statement made, maybe we can finally have some peace. Especially now we're certain there are no outstanding warrants for me back in Denver.

I have no doubt Lev will take a personal trip to see Doctor Douchebag soon, but knowing the asshole was too chicken or drunk to call the police and report what happened is enough to put that incident to rest.

And saves me from having nightmares about delivering this baby in a prison infirmary.

Lev places his large hand on my lower back and ushers me forward, following the king, queen, Fynix, and Bridget from the room into the hallway.

He leans toward Fyn. "We'll catch up with you later."

Fyn gives him a knowing look and tugs Bridget to his side, but the king reaches out and stops Lev with a hand on his arm.

Lev immediately stiffens. "Yes, Your Majesty?"

King Elander's eyes soften, and he squeezes Lev's arm. "You did well, son."

Hearing him call Lev *son* makes tears pool in my eyes. Lev shifts, slightly uncomfortable with everything and the words from the man who has been his father figure since his parents were killed over twenty years ago.

The queen steps forward, her eyes wet. "I know how hard

that was for you, especially without Mira here, but it went as well as can be expected."

Lev sighs and rubs the back of his neck with his free hand. "They're not going to leave me alone, are they?"

The king offers him a sad half-smile. "Probably not. All you can do is continue to live your life on your own terms and avoid falling into the trap of caring what they say."

Like that's so simple.

Lev nods and slides his hand from my back to my waist, tugging me into his side.

The queen smiles softly and inclines her head toward me. "And keep this one safe."

Lev glances at me and grins. "Always."

And he means it.

That's what Lev does—he protects. Fyn, Lovolia, the king and queen. He will not stop until every threat disappears, including those against me and our baby.

"Now if you'll excuse me." He offers a slight bow and urges me forward. "I have something to take care of and will meet up with you later."

We make our way down the corridor, and I glance back at a raised brow from Bridget. But I don't have a clue what's going on.

"Lev, where are we going?"

Leaning down as we walk, he feathers his lips against my ear. "You and I have plans."

"We do?"

He smirks and nods. "We do."

I don't remember any plans other than the dinner we're supposed to be at...and we're currently heading in the wrong direction.

"What plans are those?"

He grins, tightening his hold on my hip. "You know what I was thinking about the entire time I was up there?"

I turn my head slightly to narrow my eyes on him. "No."

We turn down another hallway, and he leads me into the conservatory. The scent of all the plants and flowers fills my nose instantly, calming what was left of my nervousness from the press conference.

He immediately turns and pushes me against the wall, caging me in with his strong body. "I was thinking about how if I ever lost you or this baby, I wouldn't be able to go on."

I press my hands to his chest, his heart beating a rapid tattoo against my palm with his fear. "Oh, Lev. You'll never lose us."

"You're right. I won't allow it. I won't miss one second of this baby's life or time with you." He drops his forehead to mine, releasing a sigh. "I was a fool and wasted the last two years bickering with you when we could have spent our time like this."

He grinds his hard cock against my thigh, and I issue a low moan at the pleasure fluttering through my body at the simple movement.

"I could have loved you this whole time. Taken care of you. Ensured you were happy and safe. You wouldn't have suffered what you did back in Denver. You wouldn't have been lonely—"

I press my finger to his lips to silence him because his rambled confession only makes my chest ache for the guilt he carries. "But it's okay, Lev, because everything that happened brought us here, right?"

It takes him a moment to answer, as if he isn't quite ready to admit that maybe all of this was *supposed* to happen this way for a reason. "Right. I just..." He shakes his head. "I just want all this"—he motions toward the press conference—"to be over. I want to go back to how things were, where I protected Fyn and no one noticed me."

I laugh, pulling my head back from his. "Oh, trust me, Lev. People noticed you."

He smirks. "You know what I mean. I prefer to blend into

the shadows. To be part of the background. To let Fynix and his parents have the limelight."

"I know. But that may never be possible. You may have renounced your claim, but you're still a Romanov, no matter what your last name says."

His jaw tightens. "I know, Yankee, and I'm terrified of what that means for us."

I place my hands on his cheeks. "I'm scared, too, Lev. I would be lying if I said I'm not worried about what this means for us, for this baby. But something helps alleviate that fear each time it flares up."

He kisses the inside of my wrist. "What's that?"

"*You.* Knowing *who* you are, *what* you are, and what you're capable of when protecting something you love. I know you'll do everything in your power to ensure we're safe."

His eyes shimmer with tears, and he brushes his lips against mine. "I'll protect you with my life, just like I do Fyn."

He's said the words to me so many times and made the same promise over the last few days since our worlds were turned upside down, but today, I truly feel them deep in my gut.

This man is deadly, and he will be for me.

Whatever it takes—nothing is off the table for Lev.

I press my lips to his gently, but he quickly changes the angle and tenor of the kiss, devouring my mouth and gliding his tongue along mine with a desperation I share.

Every. Single. Time.

It still feels like this, like something new, something exciting, something both of us need, and neither of us is willing to give up.

When I'm in the arms of *my* king, all the problems seem to fade away, because loving Lev will never be complicated.

EPILOGUE

FOUR YEARS LATER

DAPHNE

Sᴡᴇᴀᴛ ʙᴇᴀᴅs on my skin from the hot sun beating down on me, but the almost-constant ocean breeze picks up off the water and offers some respite from the heat.

The salty sea air fills every breath, and the smell I associate with Lev allows me to relax onto my towel for the first time in weeks.

A very real paradise on this tiny island I call home.

I'd love to stay on the beach all day, but the reality of our situation never allows this to last more than a few hours.

I turn my head toward Bridget, who sits next to me, watching Elander and Mira work on a sandcastle near the water's edge. "How long do you think we can stay here before Manuel comes looking for us?"

She laughs and tilts her head to look at me over the top of her sunglasses. "Fyn told him we'd be gone all afternoon, so unless there's a dire emergency, hopefully, we'll be unin-terrupted."

Uninterrupted.

As if that's even possible with as busy as we always are.

The words barely leave her mouth before an excited squeal fills the air. I push myself up on my elbows as Elander races toward us across the sand and launches himself at his mother.

"Mama."

Bridget catches him. "What, baby?"

Mini-Fyn twists his lips and motions toward the ocean. "I want to surf."

She gives me a look and pushes her glasses back up as she settles him onto her lap and points out to the water where Lev and Fyn wait for the next set.

"Your father and Uncle Lev are having a good time, just the two of them right now, but I'm sure he'll take you back out again later."

Mira pushes to her feet from the sand and pouts, popping her hands on her hips. "I want to go, too, Mommy."

Of course, she does.

Anything Elander does, Mira also has to. Those two are like peas in a pod—a pod filled with mischief and attitude only three-year-olds have.

I pull off my sunglasses and meet her intense stare. "If Fyn takes Elander out, I'm sure Daddy will take you."

Her bottom lip pouts out even more, and she stomps her foot in the sand. "But I want to go now!"

Here we go.

Leaning toward Bridget, I lower my voice even though the kids won't have any idea what I'm talking about. "They weren't kidding about the threenager thing..."

She chuckles and hugs Elander to her closely. "I have no idea what you're talking about. He's a total angel."

I drop my head back and laugh. "Yeah, okay, *right*...that's why his father couldn't wait to get out on the water alone with Lev."

Bridget smirks. "They needed a break—from the kids and life. Can you blame them?"

"Not at all." I shake my head. "We could all use one."

Especially after the last few crazy months. It never ends. As soon as we think things are starting to settle down, something else pops up that occupies both men to the point of exhaustion, and these two little ones running around and demanding their attention doesn't help.

It's been so long since Lev and I got to spend more than an hour or two alone together that I'm starting to consider kidnapping him and dragging him to Elysium for a few days and leaving Mira with Aunt Bridget so we can relax for a while.

I lean back on my elbows on my towel and watch the next set of waves roll in. Lev and Fyn start paddling, then pop up on their boards as the giant wall of water starts to move over them.

Even after watching Lev do this hundreds of times, my core still clenches, watching his muscles bunch and flex with each movement. The way he casually rides the wave would terrify most people. But he belongs in it. Just like he belongs in Lovolia. And we've never once questioned that we made the right choice, even if it's been nothing but royally complicated since then.

Elander scrambles from Bridget's lap and rushes over to the castle, kicking loose sand at it.

"Eli, knock it off." Mira shoves him, knocking him onto the sand and starting a typical three-year-old squabble.

"Their birthday party should be fun this year." Bridget laughs and gives me an exasperated sigh. "I have to say, giving birth within a week of each other does make it a lot easier to plan."

I laugh and cringe. "Oh, God. Could you imagine having to plan *two* parties?"

No one ever tells you it's possible to get sick of all the opulence, but the sheer number of social events we have to attend is enough to make me want to build a shack and live on this beach—especially if it means watching this all day.

Our husbands ride out the wave and tumble under the water, shooting back up and shaking their heads. Lev turns and looks back at us. Even from here, with almost a hundred yards separating us, the heat of his gaze lingering over me immediately makes me flush and my body heat in a way that even the sun couldn't.

Bridget releases a sigh. "You know that man will probably keep you pregnant for the rest of your life."

I scowl at her and place my hand over my growing belly. "Oh, no, I've already told him two is my limit. I'm getting that man snipped."

She lets out a peal of laughter and shakes her head. "I'd love to see you try. There's no fucking way."

"Well, that's the only way I'm going to keep from ending up like this all the time."

She elbows me playfully and rests her hand on her flat stomach. "I know what you mean."

Her words take a minute to register, and my jaw drops. "Are you pregnant again?"

A smile spreads across her lips, and she nods. "Doc confirmed it with a blood test yesterday."

I smack her shoulder. "And you waited until today to tell me?"

Bridget scoffs. "Um, considering the way I found out about your first pregnancy, I don't think you have any room to complain, Daphne."

Sitting, I hold up my hands in surrender. "Fair enough." I pull her into my arms and squeeze her tightly, the smell of the coconut sunscreen filling my nose. "I'm so happy for you guys. Do the king and queen know?"

She shakes her head. "Not yet. We'll tell them when they get back from Italy."

"Let them enjoy their little holiday while you and Fyn handle all the crises here."

Because it seems like they just keep coming.

Bridget pulls off her sunglasses and rolls her eyes, wiping at sweat under them. "It isn't exactly a crisis, *per se*. Just something else we have to handle."

The fact that criminal groups trying to move into the hotels and casinos on the island isn't considered a crisis compared to what we usually deal with is the clearest sign that life has truly changed for us.

In only a handful of years, Bridget went from being engaged to a boring, disloyal asshole like Barry to married to a prince, and I managed to find a man who loves my smartass mouth as much as he does my actual ass.

All the stressors that come with being married to those men out on the water are well worth it, considering the joy they bring to our lives.

"I guess not. I know Fyn, Lev, Manuel, and Captain Nichols have it handled, but still, it would be nice if we could do this all the time, wouldn't it?"

She slides her shades back into place and watches the guys, while I double-check that the kids haven't killed each other, but they're patiently rebuilding the sandcastle.

"We are pretty lucky."

I follow her gaze to where Lev and Fyn sit on their boards, laughing. They both look so carefree it makes my heart clench. "I know. Things could have ended a completely different way. I never imagined any of this could have happened when we came here for your non-honeymoon."

She smirks. "If you hadn't correctly told me I was dating the wrong men, I never would've stormed off with that bottle of tequila and ended up on this beach."

"And you never would've met Fyn. And you never would've been miserable without him for a year. And you never would've come back and ended up marrying a goddamn prince."

She elbows me again. "And you never would've married a tsar."

I scowl at her. "You know he hates when you call him that."

Shrugging, she grins. "I know, but he is."

We knew it wouldn't be easy to escape his Romanov heritage and people would make demands of him. We knew there would be expectations he might not be able to live up to, but nothing could have prepared us for the last few years.

The media circus after Lev's announcement grew beyond what anyone could have anticipated—refusing interviews and dodging reporters only fanned the flames of the firestorm. But he's handled it with a grace and dignity that only makes me love him more.

He may be a Romanov, but when it comes to reigning over a kingdom, the only one he needs is in my heart.

"No, he isn't. He's just Lev, and he's all he ever needs to be."

♔

LEV

FYN and I float on our boards, watching the Mediterranean. The afternoon sun glints off the perfect water as we wait for the next set.

Daphne lets out a squeal, and Fyn glances over his shoulder. I follow his gaze and find the girls embracing while the kids work on building a sandcastle near the water's edge.

"What the bloody hell is that about?"

He smirks and turns back to face the water. "I think she just told Daphne."

"Told Daphne what?"

"She's pregnant."

"What? Bloody hell, mate. Congrats." I slap him on the back. "I didn't know you two were trying."

He chuckles and runs his hand through his wet hair. "I mean, aren't we always trying without *trying*?"

Considering the number of times I've stumbled upon them trying to get a little "alone" time around the palace, they're not doing anything to actively prevent it. Not that we were, either. In fact, if I could see Daphne like this the rest of our lives, I'd be thrilled. Being a father and raising Mira with her has been the greatest joy of my life.

I grin at him. "True."

"We found out yesterday."

"I'm so happy for you. Truly."

"Thanks, mate. We're thrilled. Elander could definitely use someone else to harass besides Mira."

I glance over my shoulder in time to catch Mira pushing Elander over in the sand to get to his bucket. She steps over him, snags it, and returns to her spot, a satisfied grin on her beautiful face. "She holds her own."

Fyn laughs, running his hand over the scruff growing on his cheeks that he'll have to shave off before his meetings tomorrow. "She certainly does. She gets that from her parents."

I chuckle. "You mean her mother?"

Fyn shakes his head. "No, both of you. Everything you've gone through in the last few years, you two are quite the pair."

He isn't wrong about that. I'm not sure I would've survived the fallout of learning about my Romanov blood without Daphne because I was right—that press conference didn't quell any of the drama I hoped it would.

Constant media inquiries, calls from distant relatives, people coming out of the woodwork to make demands of me simply because of who I'm related to. All of it continues even four years later, and all I can do is ride it out the same way I do these waves, trying not to let it touch my family.

"You're doing fine, Lev."

I turn back to him. "What?"

Fyn sobers. "You have that look in your eye you always do when you're thinking too hard." He inclines his head toward the beach. "My guess is it's about that new baby coming and whether you're being a good husband and father."

I run my hand across my beard. "Force of habit."

He nods. "I get it. I overthink everything, too. Especially now that Mother and Father are getting older."

"You're worried about stepping up. What will happen when they're gone..."

Something I don't even want to consider...

Fynix nods slowly, dragging his hands through the water absently. "More worried about what it will mean for Elander and the new baby than me." He shrugs. "I've always known I'd be king. Granted, it was in a much different role before the uprising. With the prime minister and all the representatives making the decisions for the people, it takes a lot of weight off my shoulders, but I'm still the face of the country and the one they look to for leadership."

"And you're doing a bloody good job, mate. I couldn't do it. I wouldn't want to. That's why I've fought so hard against doing anything related to the Romanovs."

"I know, and you're doing everything you can to keep Daphne and the baby safe, by staying as far away as you can. But just know if anything ever changes, I'll support you no matter what."

I bark out a laugh. "Trust me, nothing's going to change. I'm perfectly happy here in Lovolia, watching your back and surfing and going home to that beautiful woman at night."

"Good."

The next set comes in, and Fyn and I start paddling. We jump up on our boards and ride the wave. The tremendous force and power of the ocean cocoons us in a perfect spiral until the water crashes over us, dragging us toward the bottom.

We come up, sucking in deep breaths, and I incline my head toward the beach.

"I don't think we can leave them alone with the kids for too much longer without facing consequences later."

He chuckles and shakes his head to remove the water from his hair. "You're right, mate."

We swim for the shore, dragging our boards with us, and Elander and Mira race toward us.

Mira stops at my feet and points toward her creation. "Daddy, Daddy, did you see my sandcastle?"

I scoop her up and settle her on my hip. "I did, love. It's fantastic."

"I made it look like the palace."

I make my way over to it and examine the mounds, along with something she drew in the sand with her finger. "And what's this?"

She struggles out of my hold, walks over to it, and points. "Duh, Daddy. It's the maze."

So much of her mother in her...

Slishkom mnogo.

And that attitude will only grow as she ages. We are in so much trouble when she hits her teens.

I squat to look at it, narrowing my eyes at the bends and crooks. While Fyn talks with Elander about something, Daphne pushes to her feet and heads our way, standing next to me and placing her hand on my shoulder.

"What are you looking at?"

Rubbing my hand over my beard, I sigh. "She drew the maze."

Daphne lowers herself to her knees in the sand next to me and examines it. "Damn."

I turn my head to look at her, and she pushes her

sunglasses up on her head. The blue eyes I love to stare into look back at me with love and trepidation.

She narrows her gaze back on the sand drawing. "Is it just me, or does that look perfectly accurate?"

"It is." I grin at her. "She's already memorized the maze."

And we're screwed.

Daphne sighs, probably imagining the same thing I am— Mira causing as many problems as Fyn and I did for the guards and for us. "We're in for a lot of trouble with this one."

I shake my head. "You're telling me."

"She was ready to take Elander down by force a few minutes ago."

Chuckling, I pull her into my arms, pressing my hand against her belly. "She's going to terrorize her brother or sister."

Daphne wraps her arms around my neck and presses her lips to mine. "I know she will. Same way you and Fyn go at each other. But you're still best friends and always will be, just like I'm sure she will be with whoever shows up."

"I'm the luckiest man on the planet, Yankee."

She twirls her fingers in the hair at my nape. "Why is that?"

I grin at her. "Because I have a beautiful wife and daughter and everything I've ever wanted. Everything I could ever possibly need."

"I can think of one more thing."

"Oh, yeah?" I raise a brow. "What's that?"

She leans in and brushes her lips over my ear. "Remember the threat you made at the wedding?"

My cock twitches between us, and I growl in her ear. "You better watch yourself, Yankee. The kids are here."

Pulling back, Daphne offers a smug grin, knowing exactly what she's doing to me. "We can always head back to the palace early."

"Daddy, Daddy!" Mira tugs on my arm. "I want to go surfing."

Fyn motions toward the water with Elander at his side. "He wants to go, too."

I turn back to Daphne. "Rain check." I dip my head to her ear again. "When we get back to the palace, meet me in the Reading Room, lights off, and wear that dress."

She chuckles in my ear and presses a kiss to my cheek. "I won't fit into the wedding dress like this."

I squeeze her belly. "Then wear nothing."

A shudder rolls through her at my words. I grin, kiss her quickly, and push to my feet to take Mira's hand. "All right, let's go, *printsessa*."

She rushes toward my board, dragging me with her. Elander does the same with Fyn, as Bridget holds out a hand to Daphne and helps her to her feet.

Standing at the water's edge with the waves gently lapping at my ankles, a true sense of peace settles over me. What I said to Daphne is true. I have everything I could ever want or need, all because of the woman with the smart fucking mouth who challenges me every day.

I once told her it was complicated, and it always will be. Duty. Honor. Family. Legacy. They always are. But Daphne will never let me forget what's important.

Her. This. Us.

That will never be complicated.

♕

We hope you enjoyed *Russian and Royally Complicated.* If you missed book one in the series, *Royally Complicated,* grab Prince Fynix and Bridget's story now:
Books2read.com/RoyallyComplicated

For more co-writes from Gwyn and Christy, check out The

Small-town Spicy Bites Series and the Warren Family Holidays Series, available at all retailers.

To stay up to date on new releases, sales, and other news from Gwyn and Christy, sign up for Gwyn's newsletter here: www.gwynmcnamee.com/newsletter

ABOUT THE AUTHOR - GWYN MCNAMEE

Gwyn McNamee is an attorney, writer, wife, and mother (to one human baby and two fur babies). Originally from the Midwest, Gwyn relocated to her husband's home town of Las Vegas in 2015 and is enjoying her respite from the cold and snow. Gwyn has been writing down her crazy stories and ideas for years and finally decided to share them with the world. She loves to write stories with a bit of suspense and action mingled with romance and heat.

When she isn't either writing or voraciously devouring any books she can get her hands on, Gwyn is busy adding to her tattoo collection, golfing, and stirring up trouble with her perfect mix of sweetness and sarcasm (usually while wearing heels).

Gwyn loves to hear from her readers.
Here is where you can find her:

Facebook:
https://www.facebook.com/AuthorGwynMcNamee/
FB Reader Group:
https://www.facebook.com/groups/1667380963540655/
Website:
https://www.gwynmcnamee.com
Tiktok:
https://www.tiktok.com/@authorgwynmcnamee
Twitter:

https://twitter.com/GwynMcNamee

Instagram:

https://www.instagram.com/gwynmcnamee

Bookbub:

https://www.bookbub.com/authors/gwyn-mcnamee

ABOUT THE AUTHOR - CHRISTY ANDERSON

Writing with a whole lot of sarcasm and humor, mixed with a bit of Southern charm, Christy Anderson ain't no sweet tea kinda storyteller.

As an author of romance, Christy believes it doesn't always have to be hearts and flowers; sometimes, it is dark and twisted, but romance nonetheless. She mixes terror, revenge, and a sliver of love and hope into stories about family, friends, struggles, blurred lines, and happily-ever-afters.

Christy lives in the beautiful mountains of Eastern Tennessee with her husband and 152 cats (not really, but close), where she enjoys writing one twist at a time.

Website: https://www.christyandersonauthor.com
Facebook: www.facebook.com/Christy-Anderson-Author
Facebook Reader Group: https://www.facebook.com/groups/
461018120762644
Goodreads: www.goodreads.com/christy_anderson
Instagram: Christy_Anderson_Author

www.ingramcontent.com/pod-product-compliance
Lightning Source LLC
Chambersburg PA
CBHW072259020726
47501CB00002B/316